THE BUI
OF WA

BOOK I OF THE CHRONICLES OF THE ANDERVOLD THRONES

BY E.M. THOMAS

Also by E.M. Thomas

Fortress of the Sun (A Novel of Ancient Greece)

The Bulls of War

Map by E.M. Thomas
Cover designed by E.M. Thomas

www.emthomas.com

Table of Contents

Map

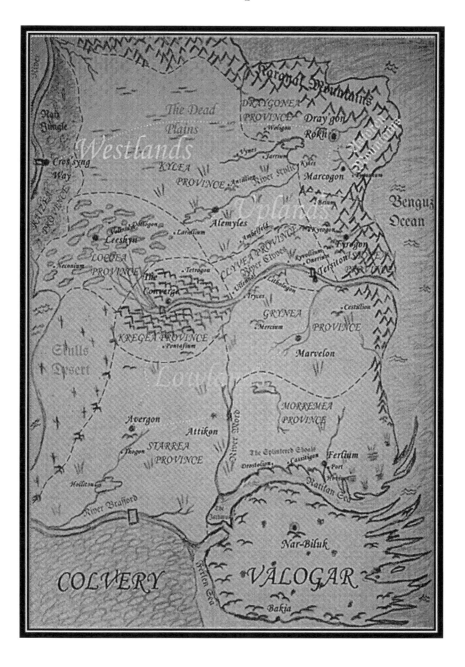

And so Stygus shunned the mighty stallion and choseth instead a bull of
four horns to be his mount;
And upon this bull did he cry havoc and conquereth the kingdom of the
gods;
And with this conquest did he thus join their pantheon and riseth Stygus,
god of war.

"Birth of the War God", Rokhish Fable

PART I

Chapter I

"So much wasted on the land of Valogar. Countless men. Chests of gold. And for what?

For a land of poor soil, few coffers, and a savage people.

It's a blemish on a map, best scorned and forgotten. It's nothing, this Valogar.

Yet – it is everything."

Last Speech of Lorrion Vallius to the Rokhish Imperial Council, Y. 363 P.C.

Central Valogar, 5ᵗʰ Day of the Tenth Month, Y. 371 Post-Cataclysm (P.C.)

Ten years, two months and this morning, Kyrus thought, blinking away drops of sweat. *Yet still… still it's not any easier.*

For the thousandth time, his hand slid to a blade's hilt, body braced against a gust ripping through the sweltering berry thicket. Wide eyes scanned the crush of steamy greenery all around him, ears hearing only his own short breaths and a heart that pounded like a drum. Even as the wind petered out, his anxiety held firm, held him frozen in place.

Ten bloody years of this… a wonder I've any wits left about me at all. He grunted. *Or do I have any?*

He'd grayed since then, since his first days in Valogar. Wrinkled too. Bones ached from the constant marching, mind frayed from the perpetual fear of knowing *they* were out there, somewhere, always itching to add another Rokhish scalp to their belts…

It's never going to be easy, he chided himself with a shake of his head and a swat of a branch, hum of cicadas returning. *Never was, you knew that from the start. That's the dream of the weak, the naïve… dreams have no place in this hell.*

The gray column of bearded Rokhs he led into the brush had come to a halt with him, taken by their leader's concern. They knew that forage missions in this foreign land were about survival as much as they were finding food for their camp. Gauntlets to be run, the soldiers called them.

In truth, Kyrus hated the patches themselves as much as any Natives within them. Hated their denseness, hated their thorns that poked every bare piece of flesh, hated everything about them. "A lifetime of training for what?" he grumbled. "To go and fight where it's too tight to swing a damn sword? Barely room to even piss." He lowered into an observant crouch with a grimace. "You bastards out there today? Hm? Bet you're not… bet you don't have the –"

A blackbird landed on a branch above him, jarring him from his thoughts, his paranoia, his false bravado. With a frustrated sigh, he rose and returned to the line's midpoint, hoping he was right – hoping that the Native danger was imagined yet again, that it was yet another false alarm.

"Alright, carry on, then, dammit," he barked, annoyed and embarrassed to have stopped for nothing. "Carry on!"

As the line relaxed, he found his teenage son at his side, dark braided hair cascading down his back, blue eyes full of guilt and indignation. It was his alarm that brought the column to a halt, his word to his father that he'd seen something in the brush. The problem was that lately he was *always* seeing something in the brush; three times during this march alone, in fact, and the Elder was at his wits' end with it. In that moment, he saw no blood of his, no beloved son, no new Academy graduate, only an undisciplined young man – no, an undisciplined young *soldier*, and one who was quickly turning the rest of the troops ornerier with every delay.

"That's the last time, aye?" he quietly burned through gritted teeth. "No more of this nonsense or you get the lash."

"I-I'm sorry, *pari*, I thought –"

"*No more*. And it's not *pari* on the march, it's 'General', I've told you that too many times!"

"Aye, I said I'm sorry, but I –"

"I don't want 'sorries', I want *obedience* – now *obey!* You *cannot* keep squealing every time you see a leaf move! So why do you keep making me repeat myself? Why embarrass me, embarrass our name? You see me watching for 'em! We're all watching for 'em, aye? All worried about them!"

"But I think –"

The Elder's face flushed a furious red. "You either *know* or you keep it to yourself 'til ya' do, it's that simple!" he growled, finally quieting the boy. "Now do you *know* you saw something?" The Younger looked back towards the spot where he'd been so certain of a threat, but offered no response. "Next time's the lash," his father snorted and looked to his eldest at the front. "Alright Bulls, final push now! Be drinkin' and eating soon enough!"

Rhythmic marching had resumed, men stripping branches clean of red berries along the way. In the lead was Kyrus's oldest son, Kylius, who did nothing to hide his annoyance with his little brother's interruptions. At only two years removed from the Academy himself, Kylius's spot at the column's head was hardly one of honor more than it was a deadly rite reserved for newer recruits - a rite that paid no mind to the family he was born to. Indeed, 'the younger the blood, the younger they bleed' was a maxim beyond challenge among the legions.

He shot a look towards the opposite end of the column, finding his veteran Tygustus and his three-man rear guard maintaining a steady, unflinching air. While the rest of the column had swords and coats of mail covering torsos but leaving arms bare, the rear guard bore sleeves of steel ringlets and teardrop black shields emblazoned with the four-horned Bull of Stygus – indeed, they were there solely to fight, should the need arise. With a look that belied his many years and battles, Tygustus nodded under Kyrus's gaze.

Why can't they all be like him? Strong, ferocious, never bothers his commander with a speck of nonsense. Just takes orders and sees them through. Alas...

Kyrus shook his head in lament, hands wringing sweat from the silvery black hair matted against his skull. *Always something on these bloody runs. Always something and today it's my own blessed flesh and blood.* He sighed. *Then again, we always seem to make it back in one piece, don't we? No reason to think otherwise today, so think right and it'll be so.* He wanted nothing more than to be done for the day like the rest of them, roasting meats back in camp, downing the aged grog they'd carted with them from the Provinces, burying the terror of daily life in a sea of spirits. *Gods above, do I want that drink!* The inklings of a grin appeared, but a bird's piercing screech quickly sent it back into a scowl; within seconds, he could barely think at all, the bush suddenly alive with dozens of the shrieking bastards.

He tried to distract himself from the noise by letting his eyes fall on his youngest again, the lad's sleeveless mail and tunic hanging loosely off a skinny frame. Seeing through the Younger's mask of defiance, his father marveled at how far he'd come since he was – despite the Elder's strict discipline – a stubborn, spoiled little eight-year-old being sent off to the War Academy in Avergon, a school that only his highborn blood and lauded family name gained him entry into. True to form, he took orders as insults and loathed anyone that criticized his technique, a spite that carried him through the eight brutal years as a cadet. Nevertheless, his petulance changed after graduation and a few months in the Valogarian countryside, hundreds of miles from the hearth and home of Imperial lands north and west. Fear crept in here, where allies and enemies looked the same; where not a night went by without an alarm horn blown or a Rokhish life taken. It was hard to blame him for letting the shrieks and the crush of the patches get to him, for seeing enemies everywhere.

He's a good boy, a strong boy, but he's scared still, Kyrus thought, pondering how much harsher he could have been, what things he could have said to quell his son's fears, his unbecoming cries of alarm. But then he frowned. *No, he* should *be scared still... gods above,* I'm –

Shadows molded into one as the sky darkened above them, ceasing the birds' screeching in an instant. Just like that, his pulse quickened again, thoughts of comfort and grog and family vanishing into the steamy air.

"God of light," he quickly whispered to himself, prayers always on the tip of his tongue on the march. His ears rang as the column again grinded to a halt, this time on their own accord. *"Don't you leave me now... just give me a few more minutes... just a few, so I can get on through these patches."*

No one stirred as a deafening silence took hold.

"Son?" he called out quietly into the darkness, eyes squinting, searching. "Son, you thought you saw something back there, aye?"

"I don't *know* that I did," the Younger offered coldly.

The Elder's temper overtook his fear for a moment, but he caught himself. "I don't like havin' to scold ya' like I did, you know that."

His son grunted. "Well, I'm telling the truth, I don't *know* –"

"I'm not asking what you know anymore – I'm asking you to tell me again what you *think* you saw, because I saw nothing. So be a man now, be a soldier."

"I *am.*"

The father's hand latched on his son's neck, feeling a sweaty lather underneath. "Tell me *now*."

With a wince, his son's façade finally cracked, turning pale blue eyes on the commander. "It was a m-man, I think, I saw —"

A lone shriek returned as the Elder's eyes widened.

He leaned in closer. "A man? *Them?* You're cert-"

The shrieks multiplied. Louder this time, though less high-pitched. More guttural.

"Aye! I mean, I think so... looked blended into the brush. I swear they were—"

"*They?* Natives?"

"I-I-I saw –"

"Kyrus, bloody tell –"

"*Ambush!*"

* * *

"*Whoooooooooo!*"

Spears flew everywhere. Grayshirts dropped where they stood.

"Damn it all, double lines! Double lines! Back to back soldiers! Brace up! Brace for charge!"

War cries and Rokhish screams drowned out swords unsheathing.

"*Whoooooooooo!*"

The crouching Elder suddenly became lost in his surroundings, recognizing nothing, seeing just a dark green mass, overbearing and hostile. From his awkward squat, he whispered again for divine mercy. *"Great Stygus, god of war, give me the strength! Give me the strength, I beg you –"*

The man on his left crashed into him, green-tipped spear protruding from his chest. It was only a moment before the poison set in and the gurgling ended, the man's face frozen in horror. It was a ghastly expression, but one that snapped the Elder back to awareness.

With head kept low, he pivoted to see Tygustus at the rear kneeling with shield held high, rejecting javelins with ease. For a brief moment, however, their eyes met, the sergeant's expression that of a man reliving a nightmare, of someone not far from earthly deliverance.

The war cries ceased.

The assault paused.

Bushes lightened as clouds parted way, a tresswork of shadows cast upon the Rokhs. Kyrus found the column riddled with dead and wounded, soldiers everywhere keeled over on a floor of dead leaves slickened by squashed berry pouches. Dying moans provided a somber serenade as all gasped for breath in the cauldron.

"A quarter down, at least? Dammit! Maybe a third? *Dammit!*" he

7

muttered.

The Elder wet his lips through quickening breaths, head darting back and forth, when he saw the Younger staring stoically ahead with blade at the ready, tears spilling from his eyes. His father leaned over to him, thoughts moving faster than he could say them.

"Son... Kyrus... you need to listen to me, now more than ever."

The Younger's lip quivered uncontrollably.

"Son, you stay next to me, you *do what it takes* to bloody stay next to me, aye? Nod at me, Kyrus!"

The boy gave a rapid nod.

"Good... good... now, whatever comes outta this bush, no matter *what*, you stay here until I tell you. On my word, you make a run back out the way we came, but listen – you run too soon, they'll cut you down; too late, they'll seal the path, so you *must* run when I say you should, aye? Once you make it out, don't ever, *ever* look back in this direction until you've reached camp. Am I understood?"

The Younger bit his top lip 'til blood trickled out, but nodded once.

"Now son... if I should fall..."

"Stop it, pari!" the Younger choked out, tears gushing.

"Listen to me! If I should fall, you don't forget this! Any of this! You carry on, you carry my name and you do it with pride!"

"I'm not leaving!" the Younger protested, swordhand shaking violently.

A shout came from the rear guard. "Bolster the flanks, men! Compress the line!"

The Elder rose to find Tygustus scrambling to rally the shaken men.

"I can see them! Attack on the rear flank coming!" Tygustus yelled. "Compress the damn line!"

The column shortened as Kyrus tried desperately to make out a foe so perfectly blended into the foliage.

"*Whoooooooo!*"

The bellows repeated every few seconds. Branches shook uncontrollably, as if the very bush frothed for battle. A terrifying effect.

"*Demons in these woods,*" Kyrus breathed, humidity choking him as restless clouds once again blotted the sun. *This is it. This is really it, I can feel it.*

"Alright men, brace yourselves!" he finally shouted, rush of the moment seizing him. "You are men of the Empire, you are the Bulls of Stygus, the *Bulls of War!* You're meant to die for a better cause than this, I promise you!"

The enemy grew louder.

Closer.

"So brace yourselves! Brace for charge, dammit! *Brace for charge!*"

The Imperials found their nerve and let out their own war cries.

"*For the Glory of Man and Empire! For the Glory of Man and Empire!*"

"Whoooooooooo!"

"Brace for charge!"

The charge came.

Scores of wild-eyed warriors exploded out of the bush, swarming the column like wolves. Painted green and white, Native blades swung at any bearded man within reach. There were three for every Rokh, doubly so against the rear and front ranks. On a path barely fit for four, cramped soldiers fought off rushes on all sides, sheer force crushing man against man.

It was hell.

It was Valogar.

Two emerged on the Elder's left, one with a cleaver, the other a war hammer; he jammed his sword into the former's throat, but the latter smashed his free arm. Kyrus furiously headbutted that one – twice, three times, the Valogarian's white facepaint smearing over his forehead. Blood gushed from the Native's nose until Kyrus gutted him from the side.

He glanced up and down the line. At the rear, Tygustus had the flank attack at a standstill despite the odds, but the column's opposite end appeared obliterated. With only swords and little battle experience, Kylius and —

Kylius!

With horror, Kyrus recalled his eldest in the lead and desperately craned to find him over the carnage of spears and blades and limbs. *Where are you, son? Where are you my-*

A hand clutched his throat like a vise; Kyrus looked down to see the man's scythe clip his calf. With an anguished cry, he stabbed at the choker's belly, spilling him open without breaking his grip.

"Drop... you filth..." Kyrus wheezed.

As both men fell to their knees, his vision yellowed, lungs screaming for air. Releasing his sword, he shot fists into his enemy's blood-red eye, but the blows steadily weakened. Consciousness giving out, he fell backwards with the man on top.

Fight, the Elder thought plaintively as he felt himself slipping into the blackness. *Fight... fight -*

A sword's hilt caved in his attacker's head; blood showered Kyrus's face.

Prying free of the lifeless hand, his sight cleared to see his namesake standing over him, whirling to impale another charging Native. With so many on both sides having fallen, the Younger had room to swing his sword the way it was meant to be – and swing it he did.

Five down...

Six down...

Seven, eight...

The Elder watched in slack-jawed wonder as his son struck down nine before his eyes, an image of Stygus himself but for tears streaming down dirty cheeks and a body that teetered in sudden exhaustion.

A groan shook the Rokhish line; Kyrus turned to see the crushing news – mighty Tygustus brought down at last, two killers grinning ear to ear over his broken body. He glanced around for Rokhs to avenge the great man's death, for someone to punish the Natives' hubris, when reality struck -

There was no one left.

No soldiers. No Kylius. No Tygustus.

No, the only men left were a father, his youngest, and two cursed Natives, closing fast. A twisted sneer of the Fate gods if there ever was one.

Gods above, don't let this be it, he pleaded, waves of fear reverberating through his defenseless body as he tried righting himself on his one good leg. He'd always hoped to die well, but now that it was here…

Don't let me die in these filthy patches… don't let my son, my last blessed son…

"Now, tob'!" he screeched through crushed throat. "Bloody run now!"

The Younger's head wobbled wearily towards his gasping father.

"Get *out!* Through the bush, go! Don't forget this—"

A pike burst through the Elder's chest from his back, silencing him. He looked down at the protruding weapon in confusion, until his killer kicked him off face first to the ground.

His breaths grew slower but louder as his sight faded to dark, pain so intense it turned euphoric. *This is it? This is it… this is…*

I'm sorry, my boys… I'm sorry, my wife, my beautiful…

* * *

"Pari!" Kyrus the Younger screamed as his father fell before him. *"Pari!"*

He crawled helplessly towards the Elder's lifeless body, desperate for one last moment with his hero, the man he adored. Crawled over the dead, the dying, feeling more akin to them at that moment than to anyone living – until his vacant eyes locked on his father's murderer, he and his comrade nothing but silhouettes against the thicket's opening.

"No… no! You… *no! C-curse you!*" he roared unintelligibly, breaths growing heavier, hands grasping for weapons on the path's floor as he stood. One enemy limped badly while the other'd lost an eye, but it was the latter's bloody pike that Kyrus fixated on.

The contemptuous pikeman kicked his father's head as he passed, pasting it with a ball of spit. *"Lahama helila onahi, anafa?"* he said, appearing to chide the Younger. *"Soatu."*

Kyrus watched the bloody phlegm drip down the Elder's hair as the Valogary words rolled in his head. He didn't know much of the vile language, but he knew '*soatu*' – 'coward.' He gripped his cleaver and sword tighter as spittle dripped from an open mouth, silently advancing.

The Native's smile disappeared.

"*Asi, naza…*"

Still no response.

"*Diamy! Dia—*" the pikeman's face was split down the middle by the cleaver whirling end over end, collapsing him. The man at his side halted, eyes widening at the scrawny specimen standing before him.

"*Ayr hazi atam…*" the man quivered, pointing to Kyrus's father then pointing to his own chest, then skywards. "*Ayr!*"

Ayr… 'father'. Kyrus frowned but said nothing, heart afire.

The Valogarian pointed at the sky again. "*Ayr hazi tinamandra!* Onahi hazi tinamandra nafitana! H-h-hazi v-vakanai!*"

'*Vakanai*'… '*family.*'

"*That* was my family," he finally growled in broken voice, pointing at his father's corpse. "*Vakanai* you – you – you –"

Kyrus's tears welled up, bladehand shaking again.

The Valogarian took one tentative step back, and in a flash Kyrus's blade was deep in his chest.

"*Vakanai!*" he screamed, yanking the sword back to give one final hack at the Native's neck. Kyrus watched him fall, watched the blood mix with green paint to form a grotesque brown.

And then it was over.

He was alone.

Alone in a horrible, overwhelming silence that would certainly never end.

Kyrus dropped his crimson weapon and sank to his knees at his father's feet, letting emotion overtake his quaking body.

"Pari, no," Kyrus said through sobs. "Pari… pari, I'll never forget… I won't, I can't, I promise you…"

The clouds parted way to cast a red glaze over the thicket.

"*Never.*"

Chapter II

"The gods' paradox:
That those within the dirt should cast longer shadows than those upon it."

Quote from Tome Three of Nidax's <u>Musings</u>

Clyvea Province, South of Dray'gon Rokh, 12th Day of Ninth Month, Y. 383 P.C.

My Dear Family,

I should start with an apology, shouldn't I? I should write you more, I simply haven't. I'm embarrassed to say that I don't even recall the last time I did – was it two, maybe three years ago? Tyghus says it's been at least five, but I pray that's not true.

I've been away from the Upper Rokhlands long enough to forget its beauty this time of year, with its reddening groves atop rolling amber hills, its rivers and runs snaking through fields of green and golden; it all makes Starrea and the rest of the Lowlands seem so flat and boring by comparison. Of course, that beauty means the winds will be growing strong and cold as summer's warmth gives way to autumn's chill. It means the harvest is in full swing, whose yield this year is especially good I'm told, more than enough to last us through the winter snows. The seers say it's Nacuvia's blessing, a reward for the people's piety this year. I'm inclined to believe them.

Seeing the harvest, smelling the crispening air, it all reminds me of my youth, of all the days spent playing soldier in wheaten fields, of pari sharing spirits with Ruhls and commoners alike at the great Harvest Festival in the town square, of mari putting fresh honeybread out to cool. Wasn't that just yesterday? Wasn't it just yesterday that you were seeing me off to the Academy, just yesterday that instructors were chiding my swordwork, my shieldwork, my posture, my bite, and everything in between?

"Mind your form, mind your parries", they'd say, remember? Gods above, they'd say it til I wanted to bury my head in the dirt. They'd preach about "form" as if it were a god, yet for all my battles with the Valogarians since then, "form" has rarely carried the day. Battle's not about form, never has been. No, it's about managing your darkest fears, "reconciling with your mortality" you told me once, pari, something the instructors never said. And since the gods saw fit to let me realize my darkest fears early on, it's always come naturally to me. How many times have I charged into Native hordes, only to walk away unscathed? A dozen? Two? And every time, my men couldn't believe their eyes. "Form" – it's a trite concern.

Maybe it's the savages' fault for my delay in writing. Khorokh Rynsyus demands countless written assessments of Valogar, ever since He "promoted" me to command the Sixth Dyron in Avergon. Who'd have known I was actually being demoted to a scribe? If you'd ask Him, it's all in the name of His plan to keep peace with the Natives, creatures that they are, a peace he looks to seal by marrying off a Ruhl maiden to the Valogarian King Andran – Tyghus's sister playing the part of the maiden, in fact! This, He says, will create an independent kingdom, yet one that pays homage to the Rokhs – a decree He makes all the way from the Capital I must note, a tidy thousand miles north. A decree he makes without ever having shaken the hand of the man he means to rule by marriage.

What a "peace" it is. We quit Valogar, that's the truth of it. A land barely a third the Empire's size, a land with almost no iron, few stone walls, and we quit it. We launch no more campaigns there, hold no more outposts; nearest one's the garrison at the Rokhish Gates. The mighty Sixth Dyron, the Bulls of Stygus, withdrawn from the place

13

where it earned its fame, and I, a general without a war, is there any darker irony? Would you ever have believed this, pari? Of course you wouldn't. You'd have liked to vomit about it as much as I do.

I shouldn't be surprised with Him at this point, I suppose. His actions show He's an idealistic man, one who's all but forsaken war now. Rynsyus says that letting the war perpetuate in Valogar would only result in more bloodshed with little to show for it, and perhaps he'll be proven right. But is it better now? Tensions simmer throughout the region, despite a "truce" going on two years. We don't trust the Valogarians, the Valogarians don't trust us, and everyone knows their "Pureblood" sect swears undying war against the Rokhs, regardless of what the leaders dream up. They're few, but their bite outstrips their bark. How can this peace ever last?

Perhaps it's wrong to sully the man who honors me so soon, and in turn honors you. In fact, I write to you at this stop en route to the Arxun of Dray'gon Rokh – your youngest son in the Capital's Royal District, can you imagine? The journey north from the Lower Rokhlands has been long and rough, its roads a world apart from the Uplands'. As for the Capital, I don't believe I've been back since I watched pari's honors bestowed as a boy. Fifteen, twenty harvests ago?

Tyghus rides with me, on leave from the Sixth Dyron and Avergon himself. He seeks business – or maybe distractions - of his own in the Capital, as he carries a broken heart with him from the Lowlands. He's learned that women are not as predictable as life in the barracks, and even if he won't admit it, it's shaken him to his core, all twenty-four years of him. Not sure of his plans when we reach Dray'gon Rokh; not sure he knows either, but at the Tersic Pass, he heard of some mercenary mission setting out from the Capital, something about the Westlands' Dead Plains. Maybe it'll help heal what ails him.

It strikes me to see him now, as it would you, no doubt. The man I took as a little brother all those years ago has become a respected sergeant in his own right, and that should have brought us closer, but... something's amiss between us. One moment, it feels like it did when we were younger, back when I helped mold him into a man after the savages took his father; during those times, I feel there's no more trustworthy person in the world than Tyghus. But other times… it feels different, like he's pulling away – or pulled away.

I think the soldiers he surrounds himself with in Avergon have had something to do with it. They've tried to push me out I'm sure, make him feel like he no longer needs me. Like those twins. Those twins from Fyrogon feed him lies about me… well, I think they do, but… sometimes it just feels like Tyghus is one step away from betraying me, just like so many others have done; just like they've all done, really. Sometimes it feels inevitable, even though I beg the gods not to let that be true, and if it is, then I beg them to turn him back, to strike down those lying influences around him. Will you watch out for me, too? I know you will, I needn't ask. Forgive me.

It's time for us to take to the road again. I pray that you all are well and that I will see you soon... and pari, mari, tell Kylius to keep his hand steady and his head low when he must march through the brush.

Your Eternal Son and Brother.

* * *

A red-cloaked man sealed the letter with wax before leaping off the back of a horse-drawn wagon idled in a grove. A man in black soon followed.

"Don't be long. Need to be at least within eyeshot of the road by nightfall," said the second man. Bracing against a chilly gust, he watched his hooded friend work his way through the undergrowth to a stone obelisk some twenty feet high. The structure itself was simple yet striking, its point piercing through the trees' low canopy such that the tip shined under a fading light.

"Won't be but a minute."

The sun hung low in the sky, the light filtering through the trees to cast an orange glow across the men and caravan. Shadows crawled as branches shifted in the wind.

The man in red knelt before the statue, brushing dead leaves and moss from its base. Beneath the lichens was the swirling Imperial emblem, though the writing atop it was so caked in dirt that it was unintelligible. With his hands as shovels, he set about deepening the dirt crevasse in front of the base until finally, he sighed and closed his eyes.

From a distance, the second man watched the first with somber detachment. Although his heart was preoccupied by more immediate sorrow than their fathers' long ago passings, he empathized with his friend, still obviously so grief-stricken after all these years. The man in red's words only underscored his anguish.

"I hope I do our House proud in Dray'gon Rokh," he started, the last word catching in his throat before he dropped the letter into the groove he dug. "I have this letter for you, full of news. I hope it brings you happiness and peace. Know that I love you and know that not a day goes by that I don't think of you. That I don't beg the gods to bring you back." He exhaled deeply. "I'll write again soon, I promise."

Turning finally, he headed back towards the caravan, rolling icy blue eyes at his patient friend. "I don't know what I pay the villagers for... the grave looks worse every time I visit."

"Five years is a long time between visits... looks nice to me, considering."

The red man grunted. "Couldn't possibly have been five years..."

"As you say, Kyrus," the black-cloaked man replied with a smile, patting his friend on the shoulder. "You're a good man for looking after it, all the same. And you *are* gonna do your family proud, I know it."

"Aye... thank you, Tyghus."

After one last look at the obelisk, Kyrus turned away, disappearing into the caravan so it could rumble back out the way they came.

It was getting dark earlier by the day, and the Capital awaited.

Chapter III

"Take heed, for the ashes of thine despair are a fertile mulch, from which a tree will surely rise. Choose to be the tree, my son – lest you become the rot that grows upon it."

Quote from the <u>Tribulations of Kaliaktus</u> by Bithyinus

Draygonea Province, Nearing Dray'gon Rokh, 15ᵗʰ Day of Ninth Month, Y. 383 P.C.

"Kyrus the bloody Lorrion," Tyghus said over the din of caravan wheels traveling the Tersian *Som*. "The gods *must* have a sense of humor."

Kyrus had said little in the days since they left the grove. He'd spent the ride instead wrapped in his crimson cloak over an army gray tunic, peering at the poplar-lined road through a slit in the wagon's siding. At last, however, he turned towards Tyghus, pushing long dark hair from his eyes over a narrow face covered in beard stubble.

"Oh?"

"Aye."

"And why's that?"

"Why?" his friend echoed, trying to maintain a straight face. "Because look at you. You're a bloody jester, that's why. Surely, the Khorokh's just looking for a new fool. A juggler, perhaps? A 'man-of-the-night', even? *Surely*, he's not calling on *you* to join the *Lorrio*."

"I don't juggle," Kyrus said, allowing a small grin. "He'd have been better off choosing you, I assume?"

"Couldn't have done much worse."

Still smiling, Kyrus looked away. "No telling why I've been called."

Tyghus arched a brow. "You don't seriously still believe that," he said, before looking at the wagon's canvass roof. "Gods above, tell me he doesn't."

"You of all men calling to the gods, now that's humor."

"Only the divine can explain this," Tyghus said. "I figured four weeks rattling along in this wagon would've softened up that head of yours by now, but how wrong I was."

"Aye, say what you want, but we *don't* why I've been called. Could be nothing."

"Mm-hm… so a Dray'gon Rokh courier travels a thousand miles south to Avergon," he said, counting items off on his fingers. "He tells you Lorrion Onzero's leaving the Council, he *orders* you to report to the Capital on the fifteenth day of the Ninth Month for a 'ceremony', and it's nothing to you?"

"It *could* be nothing…"

"And it *could* be why I call you a fool."

"Well, let's think on it – Lorrions advise the Khorokh, aye?" Kyrus said with a shrug. "How's that a general's job, let alone one who hasn't seen the Capital in almost two decades? I know battlefields, I know soldiers, I know what blade cuts what, what formations work – what the hell do I know of politics?"

"More than you realize, apparently!" Tyghus chided.

"Aye, well you, *you're* the real fool here, letting yourself get torn up over that Attikon lass like you did."

It was a stinging jab, but Tyghus knew he'd earned it. "You're a bastard," he said with an embarrassed smile.

Kyrus gave a weak laugh, but then sighed and looked back towards the slit.

"Stay light now, won't you?" Tyghus said for what had to be the tenth time, frustrated as he watched him sinking back into a somber mood. "You need --"

"I know, you don't have to say it again," Kyrus interrupted, raising a hand. "Just hard to get that image of the grove out of my thoughts. Soon, it'll be twelve years since my father's..." He trailed off shaking his head.

"Aye, I know that too, I just think it'd serve you well not to dwell on it. Not today."

"Twelve years he's had stolen from him," the older man muttered as if he didn't even hear his friend. "Twelve years and counting. Would have been in his fifty-third year by now."

"Well, you've done well by him, that's all you can do, aye?" Tyghus demanded, somewhat irritably. "Commanding the Empire's most lauded Dyron, joining the privy council of the most powerful man within a thousand miles? That's more than a life's work for most men, you should be proud of that."

"Maybe so... but I'm missing something. I don't know what it is, but I am."

"He was married with two lads by your age, so how about a family of your own? A good woman? She'd *have* to be good to put up with you."

"Perhaps," Kyrus replied dismissively. "But it's something more."

Tyghus rolled his eyes. "Well, this moping's unbecoming. 'Live today, for we die tomorrow', is that not what you've always preached to me?"

"'You could lose all tomorrow, so give all today,' that's what I told you."

"Aye, near enough. So? What of it?"

It was remarkable how vastly their roles had reversed over the years. With Tyghus five years Kyrus's junior, the latter took the former under his wing early on, and the two spent their summers off from the Academy together in Attikon, a town just a short ride east of Avergon where soldiers' families lived. After their fathers perished in the Valogarian bush, Kyrus acted as a brother and father to him, constantly checking on his progress at the Academy to make sure he was following the honorable, respectful path. It was a role Kyrus certainly wasn't obligated to assume, given his fame as the massacre's sole survivor and his rising star in the eyes of the military. But given how far away Tyghus's remaining relatives in Tygonium were from Avergon, he was forever grateful for it.

Gratitude notwithstanding, that mentorship began revealing darker quirks of his friend, quirks that became more pronounced as Tyghus neared his own graduation. More than once, Kyrus's explosive temper appeared without warning, violent outbursts that spared no one their wrath, from dyron "greenies" to respected veterans. He grew steadily more paranoid of those around him – and those around Tyghus – such that even Kyrus's long-time colleagues would suddenly find themselves on the outs with their volatile general. While no one questioned Kyrus's impeccable record on the battlefield, his instant distrust towards those he suspected of slighting him alienated many of the men beneath him – grumblings that Tyghus did his best to assuage. At times, Tyghus wasn't sure Kyrus trusted even him, despite the fact he was the only one the general still talked to on a regular basis.

"You know, that was actually your father's quote," Kyrus said after a pause. "Something he told my whole cadet class, fresh from the Academy. Had to be the first or second day of my Run in Valogar. It stuck with me."

It was appropriate advice was for soldiers on their "Runs". Fresh Academy graduates served in their assigned war zone continuously, without home contact, for five years in order to hone their skills as quickly as possible and cement their ties to the Empire and their fellow soldiers. Veterans liked to joke that it was five years running for their lives, hence its nickname, the "Five Year Run".

"Well, if you won't listen to me, then listen to him," Tyghus said as he pulled long brown hair behind his head.

"I'd consider that," Kyrus said less somberly. "Wonder where 'Ol' Tygustus' would be now, had he lived?"

"You'd know better than I; with the dyrons still, probably. He'd be the first one to tell me to me to love them like family, just as he did. Follow orders, trust them without question. 'Wrap yourself in the cloak of honor, tobbie'," he said, smiling softly at the thought. "He was right."

"Your father was a fine man, and honor's all well and good, but *you* haven't had to lead yet," Kyrus replied with a surprising sharpness. "Not always so easy to say what's right when you have to make the decisions others have to live and die with."

Tyghus glared at him. "I lead a *kord*."

"A thousand men isn't the same. I'm talking about standing for –"

"I stand for plenty. Maybe not with thirteen thousand like you, but I am where I am today by standing for things. By standing by my father's creeds. That's all I was bloody saying."

"So be it, then," Kyrus said in a conciliatory tone. "I just simplify what he said – all I ask for is honesty."

Tyghus shook his head. "Aye, you and your demand for honesty. It'd drive the gods mad."

"It'd have made your father's list."

Tyghus smirked. "Aye, maybe."

He thought back on the scant memories he had of his father, before frowning. "I often wonder what he'd think of this peace. Whether he would think it could last; he never really told me his thoughts on such things."

"Your father?"

Tyghus nodded.

Kyrus grunted. "Probably be as doubtful about it as me."

"He couldn't be *that* bleak. Probably tell you to give it enough time and you'll see it hold."

"Aye?" Kyrus asked with a disbelieving snort.

"Aye. Deepest wounds heal if you give 'em time."

"Sometimes," Kyrus offered before scowling at his friend. "Or sometimes the wound festers."

Tyghus only smiled back. "Guess all we can do is wait then, see if it heals proper. The Lowland Provinces support the peace, so that's a start, I suppose," he sighed. "Not sure what the tone's like up here."

Kyrus scoffed. "Ugh, you don't have to remind me that the Sudos support the peace. Proventor Serriax talked my ears bloody with their complaints ever since I became Dyrator; about warring with Natives they'd rather trade with. The ones along the Brafford's banks and the Morremean coast may as well have been Valogarians themselves the way they talked about them."

"That's –"

"As for the Uplanders, I'm sure they still want war, same as they ever did. And why wouldn't they? Maybe the Khorokh fancies himself a sorcerer, but you don't get rid of four centuries of hatred with the wave of a pen in Dray'gon Rokh."

Though he was more optimistic, Tyghus knew his friend was right to an extent. The enmity with Valogar dated to the Empire's founding, when the Rokhs were fighting for their existence against the Clannic invaders sweeping through Andervold. Instead of joining the fight to support their northern neighbors, the Valogarians chose to hide behind the seas surrounding their peninsula while allying with the Colverians of the Forests below the River Brafford. They'd hoped to deter the Clans from venturing farther south than the Lower Rokhlands and to that end, they succeeded; nevertheless, the Rokhs never forgot the tens of thousands of deaths they suffered while Valogarians watched.

But even when the Rokhs shocked the known world by defeating the Clans at the hallowed Last Stand of Dray'gon Rokh, Cataclysm as it was thereafter known, it was two hundred years later before they had the strength to seek vengeance on a powerful Valogarian realm still backed by allies in Colvery. A bloody war ended with Rokhish banners flying from the ramparts of Nar-Biluk, Valogar's capital, after which Rokhs were encouraged to flood the annexed land. They did so in abundance, trading and even marrying with the Native peoples – but that only sowed the seeds of the modern conflict.

A devout core of "untainted" and "pure-blooded" Valogarians known as *Chibin* rose in rebellion, fierce opponents of any intermingling with the "occupying" Rokhs. By 347 P.C., Rokhish troops had crushed the decade-long rebellion and appointed a new *Lij*, as Valogarians call their kings, named Andran; the Chibin, however, were bowed but unbroken, sparking the Second Uprising when they slaughtered General Torrus and his two thousand in 360. A guerrilla war ensued that eventually drove Rynsyus to announce Imperial withdrawal from Valogar, albeit on condition that the Lij wed a *Ruhl* – a member of the Rokhish nobility. Even with this compromise, rumors abounded that few Imperials of importance were happy with the arrangement.

"Doesn't much matter, I suppose - not from the Rokhish side," Kyrus scoffed. "It's the Valogarians that'll never keep the peace. Fifty years of rebellion, now we think they'll just concede? Melt away and bow to a false-king and his Rokhish bride? All due respect to your sister…"

Tyghus bristled at her mention. "For her sake, I hope so."

"The Khorokh's most vital pawn. You know I wept for your family when I heard she'd agreed to wed the barbarian."

"She's not a pawn for going willingly when the Emperor's envoys called on her – no more than you are now."

"A beautiful Upland Ruhl known to sympathize with the plight of the Natives; a perfect fit for Rynsyus's purposes – a pawn."

"She doesn't 'sympathize' with them, she just bloody wants peace," Tyghus shot back annoyedly. "Peace for Rokhs, peace for them."

"Well, a lovely union for the savage King, in any event."

"Sounds to me like you're jealous of the 'savage King'."

"She's a philosophical heathen as far as I'm concerned, but I'm not ignorant to her – charms."

"Aye?" Tyghus warned jokingly.

"So I'll just pray he doesn't feed her to his fellow savages."

"A gentleman's tongue, as always," he said with a shake of his head. "You speak of the Lij like you know him."

"I'd say the same to you. You talk like you trust him, but why? Give me a single reason."

Tyghus laughed in exasperation. "I'd give you a reason to trust anyone if I could with the way you see snakes in the grass everywhere! Look at Nironus, for gods' sake."

Kyrus looked away in disgust. "Ah, to hell with Nironus."

"Aye, more or less. Poor bastard still doesn't know why he was expelled from the Sixth after five years of faithful service."

"Hardly faithful! I'm not a mad man, dammit, he lied to me!"

"See? Liars everywhere. You're going to thrive in Dray'gon's politics," Tyghus said, laughing off a glare before his mind turned contemplative again. "I don't know what'll happen, brother, I just hope the peace holds. Pattern seemed to be that when we killed one Native, five more took his place anyway, ready to fight on."

Kyrus looked back at him, pale eyes illuminated from stray rays of sunlight sneaking their way into the caravan. "If you kill one, then aye."

Tyghus stared back blankly. "Kill the whole lot, would you?" he said, then as monotonous as could be, added, "the 'Savage King's' going to be delighted having you on the Lorrio."

"You jest, but it'd work!" Kyrus said, finally laughing again. "You've said yourself they won't submit otherwise."

"Aye, so I did," Tyghus conceded.

Kyrus sighed before slamming his head back against the caravan cover. "Ugh, the thought of politics. Every time I block out the thought, it comes right back... the lies, the bribery, the – "

"Oh, you'll master it in no time, I keep telling you. And how much grain *will* you give the peasantry this year? What new monuments will you build? Will you push for stronger terms with the Stolxian oligarchs in lieu of their agg –"

Kyrus waved his hands as if shooing a fly. "Quiet, you bastard!"

They both shared a hearty laugh, but just as it faded, the land outside came alive with sounds of other wagon wheels creaking along the smooth stone road. Traders could soon be heard advertising their wares to passersby.

"My lords, we approach!" called the voice guiding the friends' train.

Tyghus poked his head through the slit he had used earlier – and gasped at the sight.

Sheer white city walls climbed higher into the air than he could crane his neck to look. Atop the western and southern walls, black and red pennants bearing the insignia of the god Bregnomen billowed under the fading light. A colossal conical tower formed at the junction of the two walls, while the opposite ends raced into the mountains. The castle was truly apart of those mountains, its "eastern wall" the Astorens, its "northern wall" the Karanaks, all to protect the million souls dwelling within.

More astounding was the diamond-shaped tower known as the *Khorian Brex* – the Fortress of the Emperor – that rose triumphantly in the distance at the northeast point where the mountain ranges met. From each of the tower's corners hung gently rippling banners, criss-crossed in black and red and almost as tall as the structure itself. The image was all the more magnificent as the sun burned the walls and tower a fiery red as it sank towards the horizon.

The road straightened towards the southern face's massive drawbridge, an auburn monstrosity that spanned a moat surrounding both walls. As they drew closer, tiny points dotted the top of the walls, barely visible behind its block-toothed ramparts, with Tyghus only belatedly realizing the "points" were soldiers drawn up in full battle regalia. Even at a distance, their sleeveless crimson tunics stuck out against shimmering shirts of chain mail underneath, their left arms masked by red-striped black shields, their right hands enveloped by their swords' hilts. Their appearance was ghost-like, tiny slits for eyes the only windows to their faces, all else about the head ensconced in steel.

"Gods above," Tyghus gasped. "When you've been away from the Capital so long, you forget its majesty."

Kyrus too had arched his head out of the wagon. "Avergon's battlements look juvenile compared to this," he said, before chuckling. "Looks like the *Rubitio* waiting for us atop the walls – you'd think they were daring us to scale them."

"Who else but the Emperor's guard to oversee the rise of great Kyrus?" Tyghus asked with a smile. "And oh, look at your constituents up ahead."

The volume of wheels and beasts increased the nearer they drew to the drawbridge, as rudimentary feeder roads from the villages orbiting the Capital joined the Tersian Som. Crowds of curious villagers packed themselves in between the Som's seventy-foot poplars, restrained only by the risk of being trampled beneath the wagons' iron wheels or the mammoth steeds that pulled them. The wide green and blue eyes of folks in long brown tunics pored over the vehicle, excitement turning to restlessness among those that speculated who the caravan might carry:

"Avenge m'brother's death in Valogar!"

"Lower the prices of necessities, I beg ya'!"

"Help us fight da' plague in da' foothill towns! M'family's dying!"

The commotion eventually grew so loud that they could no longer hear individual pleas, and the crowds crammed in so tightly that Kyrus and Tyghus withdrew themselves back inside the safety of the wagon's interior.

"Smells like shit out there," Kyrus muttered, the odors of hundreds still lingering in the air.

With a thump, the friends felt the wheels transition from the stone road to the bridge's wooden planks. A roar went up from the crowd they departed as massive iron gates creakily opened the fortress to their guests, only to rumble the earth as it slammed shut behind them.

A wave of sensations hit the two travelers within the walls – music blared from horns and lyres; smells of sizzling meats, both familiar and exotic, so permeated the air that Tyghus could nearly taste them; teeming mobs of men and women danced in all manners of style and color, either to entertain others or merely themselves. Pathways lined with iron torchlights spiderwebbed off the main thoroughfare they travelled, every one jammed with shops and alehouses, to say nothing of their thousands of patrons. No one seemed interested in anything other than sharing the city's revelry. The city felt alive, as if it possessed a heart that beat along with the people's.

Tyghus smiled and rapped Kyrus's shoulder with his hand. "So it begins, my friend."

* * *

The *Khorian Soelum*'s walls climbed forever, Kyrus thought. Ten, maybe fifteen men high?

Built of painstakingly refined rock, the Dining Hall of the Khorokh's walls were so perfectly polished that they practically shimmered like silver. Massive windows carved into their sides let daylight pour over the room in the Living Hours. Now, of course, the sun had long since faded, the room instead kept alight by candle-laden chandeliers descending from above. Between the windows, red and black banners cascaded down from the ceiling like swaths of paint, settling above a floor inlaid with white and gray mosaics.

The Hall was rectangular in shape with the narrow sides a hundred steps across. Kyrus stood inconspicuously near the main doorway at one of those sides, opened now to reveal a red carpet criss-crossed with gold thread, running all the way to a raised ceremonial altar at the opposite end. To either side of the carpet lay banquet tables parallel to the room's long walls, overflowing with the bounty from harvests across the Empire; from the common figs and cheeses of nearby estates to the exotic meats and fruits of the Raizan Jungle, the displays were interrupted only by the tables' candles. One table, however, sat perpendicular to all others, facing the altar directly, with two chairs awaiting guests – clearly a table of honor.

The floor itself was awash with mingling men and women of Ruhl stock, clad in the finest blue and green threads that the city's artisans had to offer. Men enjoyed long, lavish cloaks wrapped around their bodies and pinned over one shoulder, their faces bearing beards if they were able and formally braided hair that fell deep down their backs. Women, meanwhile, adorned strapless dresses with light, sheer coverings draped over their shoulders and chest, their hair pulled back tightly into buns and beautified with golden tinsel. Interspersed among the Ruhls were busy servants in white, darting to finish preparing the tables for the great ceremonial feast.

Be they Ruhl or servant, however, frequent glances shot towards the altar, betraying a sense of anxiety. Doing nothing to diminish that tension were the Rubitio that lined the hall's perimeter, the brilliance of their red regalia even more apparent against the pale walls. They moved not a muscle, their ghostly helmets revealing not the slightest sign of a heartbeat. They simply stood, shields held as if braced for charge, swordhands dangerously poised.

Kyrus looked down at his own attire, suddenly feeling out of place in his battlefield gear – a shirt of chain mail covered by a sleeveless ashen gray tunic that dropped to his knees and tied off at the waist by a sword-bearing belt. He forewent his mail stockings at least, opting for simple – likely too simple for this crowd – black trousers that fell over his boots. His hand ran over an unkempt beard, and his hair was certainly not braided; no, it –

"Kyrus."

The voice startled the man's survey of the room. He turned to see a smiling gray-bearded man with long, silvery hair pulled back into a short ponytail. A bright red tunic covered a shirt of silver mail with a sword dangling from a black belt about the waist. He looked middle-aged judging by his wrinkled grin, but gray eyes suggested a more youthful spirit. His outstretched hand awaited Kyrus's.

"Yes?" Kyrus replied, cautiously clenching forearms.

"Apologies, my lord, didn't mean to startle you. And apologies again for taking so long to find you... but seeing that I have, I thought it was best that we find you to your seat."

Kyrus glanced from the man's shirt to his eyes again. "You play chauffeur to the dining hall as well as its guardian?"

The man glowered at the suggestion. "Not quite, my lord. We seat you out of an abundance of caution... and you look rather lost."

Kyrus grimaced. "Caution against what?"

The Red chuckled. "I'm not trying to rile our honored guest. Your nerves tighten quite enough today I would guess."

"Then what dangers are you concerned with?" said Kyrus, a slight annoyance rising within.

The man started to answer but then just looked at Kyrus, nearly incredulous. "Have you really been told so little of the atmosphere in the Arxun as of late? Of its ministers' and Council's reception to your appointment that –" He shook his head. "Forgive my questions. In any event, nothing that need trouble you tonight, my lord. Let's find your seat."

Kyrus's eyes darted around him, suddenly seeing everyone in the crowd with suspicion. "Are you mad? I was summoned here by the Emperor, who'd resent me for that!"

"Ha! You'd be surprised. Please –"

"Give me some bloody answers!"

"You're my responsibility my lord, please come," he said, casually turning and starting down the carpet.

"Responsibility? Face me, damn it! Who the hell are you?"

26

The grizzled man stopped, returning briskly to within a few paces of Kyrus. A creeping smile overtook his face. "My name's Jarax, sire," he uttered, before ticking his head towards the guards lining the walls. "And the Reds? They're mine."

The guest flicked his gaze over the same. "Yours?" he asked rhetorically, answered by a nod. The realization sank in. "You're the *Rubator.*"

Jarax stepped in even closer, barely a breath's distance away. Voice lowered to almost a growl, he said, "Yes. They're *all* mine. And if something were to happen to you – the honored guest, the... Candidate –" his gray eyes bored into Kyrus's, teeth clenched. "It would be *my ass.*"

He stepped back. "So I beg you, most humbly and kindly and eager for your most gracious consent... will you *please* allow me to show you to your seat?"

"And what if I say no?"

Jarax laughed, looking to his feet briefly before meeting Kyrus's eyes again. "Stubborn bastard, aren't you?" he said with startling candor. "Let's just pretend that's not an option, hm?"

Kyrus glared at the man, face feeling flush. *You don't even know this man, Kyrus... you don't know these people. You can walk right now. Just walk and never come back...*

With every instinct telling him to leave, Jarax simply watched him with a confused smile.

"You know you're about to be made one of the most powerful men in Andervold, don't you?"

Kyrus sighed. "I don't know what the hell I'm doing here."

With a shake of his head, Jarax turned to lead the way. "Sorry to ruin the surprise then. Just follow along, my lord."

After a pause, Kyrus finally conceded, following on the Rubator's heels. In doing so, he sensed thousands of eyes drawn to him as the room fell to a hush. He knew that although the majority of the audience must have heard rumors of his exploits, whether real or embellished, slandered or lauded, the vast majority were seeing the tall, dark-haired man for the first time. He could feel them absorbing every detail about him, down to the subtle limp in his stride towards the Honored Table. Whispers abounded.

"Look at that ratty garb..."

"Was it one hundred he killed? More?"

"This is the Khorokh's pick?"

"Your seat, my lord," Jarax said as they finally arrived at the table.

Kyrus eyed the fine dark wood of the table with unease. "Now what?"

"Now you wait."

"For *what*, by the gods?"

Jarax smiled. "You'll know," he said, before departing into the crowd.

Kyrus's watched him for a bit, taken aback by the guard's haste to leave. His searching eyes met a hundred other gazes, however, so he quickly faced forward.

The pounding of drums suddenly crackled across the room, the noise amplified by its echoes in the vast structure. The crowd came alive again, loud mutterings spreading throughout as a corpulent man, clad in a black robe with a red sash from shoulder to hip draped overtop, strode out from behind the altar to take position at the lectern perched at its forefront. Even beneath the billowing robes his massive girth was evident, a full beard doing little to disguise fleshy chins writhing below his mouth.

Out of the corners of his eyes, Kyrus noticed the entire assembly but him had taken their seats. He stood awkwardly at a loss, and with his head rattling from the pounding drums, he hardly had an opportunity to gather himself.

A wave of the fat man's hand silenced the beatings, but his booming voice reverberated almost to the extent of the instruments.

"*Esteemed guests of Khorokh Rynsyus!*" he bellowed to the crowd with a slow, deliberate prose. His arms spread wide as if to encircle the whole room. "*I* am Oratus, Nineteenth Speaker for the Realm. On behalf of the Khorokh of the Unified Rokhs, he who is Warden of Raizea, Protector of the Mesas, First and Only Lord of Loccea, Chief General of all the Dyrons, all the ships – I welcome you! May the gods watch over this great gathering, and bless the evening's festivities."

The Speaker's eyes drifted down to the table of honor, locking on its lone attendant. With a slow nod, he continued. "For three hundred and eighty three years the Empire has fought, shed blood, *conquered*. In the name of Bregnomen and his pantheon, she's *taken* lands that were meant to be hers, granted clemency to those who deserved it. Rokhs have never sought nor received such clemency from others, of course, for the greater man's kingdom becomes, so too does his list of enemies, rife with jealousy. We need only look to the swirling crimson and black of our glorious coat of arms for this maxim – *black*," he gestured towards a black banner, "to remind us of the blood *spilled* for the Empire through the centuries; *crimson*," he waved towards a red banner, "to remind us that *fresh* blood must always be ready to protect what is ours."

Oratus's furious animations turned his face a bright red, his hands pointedly underlining every statement made. "*One element* has always defined the greatness of the Rokhish Empire, and that is present in this very room tonight. It's what no other nation across this land can understand, which few could even try," he said, pausing ever so slightly to punctuate his next words.

"*Ruhl blood.* The very blood that ran through the veins of the victors o'er the barbarian hordes, the bringers of Cataclysm, the vile Clans of the faroff wastelands – that blood runs through all of us. Every man and woman in this room can trace their heritage back to a hero of the Last Stand three hundred and eighty-three years ago. To *know* that your ancestors fought with nothing but audacious hope and ferocious gall… that is what it means to be Ruhl.

"Tonight, we celebrate the elevation of another Ruhl to take his place upon a most prestigious Imperial seat. Tonight, we bear witness to the rise of the One Hundred and Second Lorrio of the Empire in this thirty-fifth year of our great and merciful Khorokh Rynsyus. As the legendary Cassyus of Kyles realized in those first years following Cataclysm, it was a union of all the Empire's Ruhls, be they north of the Clyves or south, that bound together to defeat the hitherto invincible Clans. Ergo, only a council of their representatives could do justice to their bravery, to en*sure* that every Province of the Empire was ruled with an even hand. So it was, then, three years after the great battle that the First Lorrio was convened; it was a shadow of an ideal, but the experiment has endured through the centuries. Unless otherwise volunteered, every five years the longest tenured Lorrion *must* be supplanted with a hand-picked replacement, thus infusing the Lorrio with fresh vigor to complement its sage wisdom.

"Tonight, we have such a volunteer," Oratus said dramatically, hands clasping loudly together. "Tonight, the wise and lauded Onzero stands down as Lorrion for Clyvea Province after thirty-five years of faithful service. Onzero! Please rise!"

Instinctively, Kyrus turned to see a hunched-over man rise from one of the tables to the right of the carpet. A thin, whispy white beard framed his face beneath sunken blue eyes, his bluish-purple shouldercloak alone a testament to his high standing. He never looked at Kyrus, however, focusing solely on the altar's Speaker. His voice came out raspy but firm. "Oratus."

"Onzero, do you bring before the Lorrio's company a nominee to replace your seat?"

"I do, Oratus."

"Please step forward to the Honored Table if you see that nominee."

With a lurch, Onzero weaved his way past several tables to take his stance next to Kyrus, finally meeting his eyes but only for a moment. His face was far more aged up close, cracked like desert soil, wracked with twitches.

"Oratus, I n-nominate Kyrus the Younger of K-Kyrogon… s-son of Kyrus the Elder and m-mother Servia… brother of the late K-Kylius… the m-men warriors of the Imperial Sixth Dyron."

Murmurs spread throughout the crowd again as Kyrus shifted his eyes from Onzero to the Speaker.

"On what basis, good Lorrion?"

After a deep breath bordering on hesitation, his weathered eyes searched either side of the carpet, his tongue licking dry lips to summon the words that failed him. The murmurs increased until he finally stammered a reply. "He-he's clearly fit for it... goin' through what he did in the bush... he's a glorious heritage... forefathers fightin' f-for the Empire since its birth... aye, he's fit for it, in-indeed."

Oratus eyed the shaky old Lorrion as if expecting more, before glaring at the reception to squelch any lingering undertone. His voice once again poured forth like a cannonade.

"Very well. Will the remaining members of the Lorrio come forward? Stand behind your present and future peers!"

Instantly, three men and a woman to the left of the carpet, accompanied by the same to its right, arose and made their way to the altar area. All were clad in the same brilliant regalia as Onzero.

"Lorrio, Kyrus the Younger comes here before this gathering, prepared to swear the oath and commit himself to death before dishonoring his land, his Khorokh, or his Lorrian peers; he'll represent the interests of the same with every last breath of his being; do you accept this man into the Lorrio?"

The Lorrio, now in a line directly behind Kyrus and Onzero, exchanged brief looks before uttering in unanimity –

"We do."

With a sharp nod, the fat man fixed his glowering eyes upon Kyrus, who instantly felt smaller. "Kyrus the Younger, do you recognize the honor which this illustrious body seeks to cast upon you?"

"I do, Oratus," he replied with dry mouth, not knowing how else to respond. *What choice do I have?*

"Do you pledge to weather no ill word or action to be taken against his Majesty's name?"

"I do, Oratus."

"Do you pledge to govern with the dignity and grace befitting your office?"

"I do."

"Finally, do you pledge to *never forget* the sanctity and sacrifice upon which this very Lorrio was founded?"

Kyrus shuddered. He didn't know why, and it was only for a moment, but he did – and long enough to raise his questioner's eyebrows.

"Kyrus?"

"I do, Oratus," the candidate quickly recovered after a cough. "I do so pledge..."

A stare lingered between the two men, Kyrus steeling his spine in response. Finally, the Speaker uttered, "my fellow Ruhls, Lorrions, and attendants – please welcome the newest member of the Lorrio... Kyrus the Younger."

Drums blasted as a deafening roar erupted from the banquet room, though Kyrus was sure it wasn't unanimous acclaim. Like a whirlwind, however, members of the congregation from either side of the carpet suddenly swarmed about him, eager to meet the newest Imperial power-broker. He bewilderedly shook hands and took congratulations, a sea of eyes, smiles, and grimaces flooding his every vantage.

Get me out of here.

With his hand heartily embraced by a stately matron – *of the Plains region was she?* – Jarax appeared like a wraith at his back shoulder, breath reeking of grog.

"Enjoying yourself, Lorrion?" the Guard shouted with mocking cruelty.

Craning his head towards Jarax's, he replied, "not the kind of crowd I'm used to… or enjoy."

"Know all their names yet?"

"Not a single damn one of them!"

Jarax laughed. "Like I told you, just follow along and you'll be fine. Though you should at least know the name of that woman you were speaking with – she shits gold coins!"

Kyrus allowed a grin. "Seems most of the people here have that affliction, no?"

"Aye – a lot of golden troughs!"

Kyrus shifted uncomfortably under the people's suffocating weight. "So what now, Jarax?"

"Ah, your favorite question," Jarax chided, brows sunken. "This is it, that's what's now."

"Then what later? How long –"

"I'll drag your sotted ass to your new chambers in the *Lorrian Halum* at night's end, don't worry – at least it better be sotted. Then every night thereafter for the next couple weeks you'll repeat the same process, meeting one family you'll hate after the next." Kyrus's bloodless face must have betrayed his horror as Jarax let out a gritty laugh. "It'll be good preparation for meeting the man who's most excited to see you in the flesh."

"And who claims that honor?"

"Rynsyus, my lord. The Khorokh requests a personal audience."

Amidst the fete's din, Kyrus felt light-headed as the name rolled off Jarax's lips. He managed, "I see."

The older man rapped Kyrus on the shoulder. "Welcome to Dray'gon Rokh, General," he said with a devious grin, before falling back into the crowd's abyss.

Before he could even turn his head to track the Rubator, another man was at his side, smiling and clasping forearms like they'd known each other for decades.

Welcome,   *indeed.*

31

Chapter IV

"One-hundred ninetieth year Post-Cataclysm, Month 6, Week 3

"By the gods and mine Emperor, let me beg of thee one thing – that I never have to tread the Dead Plains alone.

Though I know the Clans that wiped the Early Kings from this land faded from our vistas more than a century ago, there is still a sense of dread here, as if the latter could return at any moment, as if their spirits haunt these barren fields. Worshippers of the Dark Gods have taken root in the Early ruins that dot the landscape, kidnap'n' ransomers run rampant upon the lonely traveler, and bandits come and go without the slightest fear of retribution.

Yea, traders that cross through here are a brave lot, for these are truly plains of the damned."

Letter to Khorokh Cassyus III from Tollivus,
leader of Western expeditionary force, Y. 190 P.C.

Draygonea Province, Dray'gon Rokh, 16th Day of the Ninth Month, Y. 383 P.C.

Sunlight poured over an eastern horizon jagged with mountain peaks. The crisp autumn air tasted dewy sweet as Tyghus trotted his horse towards the convoy waiting for him just across the Southern Wall's drawbridge. He longed for his war stallion Fidipodus back in Avergon, but putting the beast through the thousand-mile trek seemed a waste to him. The brown mare he'd taken from the fort instead seemed sturdy enough, although after one festive, spirits-filled night in the Capital, he would have proceeded on foot, if necessary – one night was a week too long.

Tyghus counted fifty men on horseback milling about the grounds, before a dismounted man strode towards him. He was slight and pale-skinned with a small face and large black eyes, his head topped with thin, stringy hair. Draped in a simple gray tunic over a black cuirass, a short sword hung at his side, round leather shield behind his back.

"Good morning, General," the man said. The exacting soldier in Tyghus admired the man's proper form, the crispness of his attire, the sword hilt without blemish; even still, he couldn't help being amused at seeing him already so stern and drawn up for battle. The direst estimates Tyghus had heard said they wouldn't be crossing hostile territory for more than four weeks into the journey west, well into Kylea Province.

At least his helmet's at his side, he thought.

"Morning, my good man. Name's Tyghus," Tyghus replied, dropping from his horse to exchange forearm grips.

"Whit Harrall, General."

"You can call me Tyghus, I don't mean to carry rank here. Just here to help."

"Of course, of course," he fired back in the rapid tongue native to the Jungle regions. "Though as the only Ruhl to join us, rank is yours by right."

Tyghus was indeed well aware of his status, and as a Kordette of the Sixth Dyron he was almost certainly the ranking officer among what appeared to be a motley crowd. He'd ventured north, however, to seek distractions from the army and the heartache it reminded him of, not to be saddled with any demands beyond peaceful reconnaissance on the Plains; alas, it appeared not to be, and he didn't want to argue with the fidgety man in any event. "As you wish, then, call me what you will."

There was a nervous energy about Whit, from his wide eyes to his fingers' constant picking. Coupled with his small frame, he fit the frantic caricature of the Jungle Rokhs that Tyghus had heard, rumored to stem from the nightly shrieks of the native Raizana – the "Beastmen" as they were nicknamed – living atop the trees.

After a sharp nod, a look of confusion overtook the man. "How *did* you come to join us?"

Tyghus sighed as he looked around. He was embarrassed enough to have taken this temporary leave of the Sixth in the first place, and he had no desire to bare his soul to anybody, let alone this squirrely chap. "Happenstance, really," he finally said. "I headed north to accompany my commander to the Capital, not much more of a plan than that. When we hit the crossing at the Clyves, I heard you were looking for riders for a scouting party out west. The timing worked and I'd always had a desire to see the Early King ruins on the Dead Plains, so here I am."

The man's eyes darted back and forth. "You just... decided to head north? Only a month or two before the snows?"

Tyghus tried not to glare at him and in truth, it wasn't a total lie – he always *had* wanted to see the ruins of those kingdoms that had ruled the lands before the terror of the Clans and the rise of the Rokhs. There'd been at least a dozen of them – the Kylics, the Clyvics, the Grynics, to name a few, all of whose history had been honored by the Rokhs through the names of their Provinces. On the few trips Tyghus took back to his ancestral hometown of Tygonium as a tob', his aunts and uncles and cousins would fill his head with tales of the ghostly temples and castles of those old realms, their abandoned blackstones covered now in moss and even trees – trees, growing right out of the rock! Many had been left standing just as the Clans discovered them, others bearing scars of Clannic or Rokhish torches. Like many Rokhs, Tyghus was fascinated by the Early histories, their fates – it's just that that fascination *might* not be why he was in the Uplands *this* time; it was perhaps an elusive, hazel-eyed young brunette in Attikon that was most to blame...

"On my general's behalf I headed north, aye," he said curtly, ignoring the man's disbelieving expression. "In any event, my friend gets celebrated as the great new man while I chase tumbleweeds on the Dead Plains; seemed like a fair trade to me."

Whit's beady eyes lingered on him still, so Tyghus tried again to change their conversation. "And yourself? Tell me about you, about your station."

"I'm the Quartermaster of the Cros'syng Way garrison. I came to the Capital on behalf of Bonilus, Dyrator of the Tenth Dyron."

Tyghus's brows peaked when he heard the man hailed from the Empire's westernmost city, nestled deep in the Raiz Jungle along the River Anonga, the increasingly tense border with the Stolxis. The Stolxians, for their part, were a race of huge men and women marked by shaven heads and eyes light as snow; they were easily as ancient as the Rokhs, though they'd organized into a realm far earlier, even prior to the Early Kingdoms. For at least a millennium, in fact, they'd dominated the iron-rich though nutrient-poor lands west of the Anonga, furiously warring with anyone who tread upon their territory. They never wanted for expansion until the Clannic onslaught engulfed their realm like the rest of Andervold, forever fracturing what had been a unified but isolationist throne into what was declared an oligarchy, but really a collection of princely fiefdoms.

Despite this disunity, the Stolxians were still rightly feared throughout the land, as much for their size – the smallest stood no less than seven feet tall – as for their stunning array of steel armor and axe weaponry. The Rokhs weren't immune to this fear when the two peoples pushed their borders to opposite sides of the Anonga around the same time in the early fourth century; indeed, had Valogarian issues not taken precedence, Rokhish officials everywhere were certain war was inevitable from proximity alone, regardless of the countries' burgeoning trade. Practicalities on both sides let cooler heads prevail, but tension remained.

More so than the Stolxians, however, Tyghus was piqued at the mention of the *eastern* side of the Anonga – particularly, the Raiz Jungle and its inhabitants. "You're at Cros'syng Way?" he asked curiously.

"I am," he said briskly.

"Never met someone from the 'Gateway', I'm sure you have stories to tell."

Harrall forced a quick nod and thin smile. "As do you, I'd think."

"So is it true what they say about the Beastmen of the Jungle? They wail all day and night?"

"They're a restless folk, aye. Loud… skittish… suspicious," Harrall replied, apparently without a hint of self-awareness. Then, with a thoughtful pause, he added, "but truth be told, it was hard coping with the silence of the Plains on my journey out here."

"Aye? Well, I hope half of what I've heard of them is exaggerated. Heard they'd just as soon trade their wares with a Rokh as they would eat him."

"Aye… aye, well, we've all heard such stories too."

"You've seen 'em?"

Whit's eyes danced as he began gnawing at his cheek. "Aye."

Tyghus smiled at the Rokh's quirks. "So what do they look –"

"They're half-man, half-beast as I'm sure you've heard, General," Whit said shortly. "With a straight back, they'd stand a bit over five feet but they walk with such a hunch that they appear well below. They're fantastically stout and strong, muscles bulging, especially about the torso. Gray faces. Yellow eyes that flush red when agitated; fangs for teeth, and a small, upturned nose. That's it. That's the long and the short of them – well that, and that they still *hate* the Stolxians for what they did."

Expansionist Stolxians weren't renowned for assimilation, so 'what they did' was eradicate the Raiz Jungle and its Beastmen that flourished west of the Anonga, though it took a grueling, years-long affair amidst the dense canopy to do so. The battle-scarred Raizanan survivors took root on the Rokhish side of the river, seeking sanctuary with their cousins already under

Imperial protection. The Stolxians, of course, spitefully made sure that not a single tree was left standing following their victory, lest their inhabitants seek cause to return.

Though Tyghus yearned to press the Quartermaster further, his fidgeting made clear the Raizana were not his topic of choice. "Forgive my questions, I'd just never spoken to a person who'd seen them in the flesh."

"They're hideous. Horrible creatures. Not pleasant memories."

"Maybe you can tell me more on the trail," Tyghus said before surveying the band of soldiers again. "Quite the mercenary party you've rounded up."

Following his eyes, Whit nodded. "Trade's been drying up for months – Stolxian merchants above all have been reporting increased raider attacks between the Gateway and Dray'gon Rokh, 'specially on the Plains," he said with a scowl.

"The Plains are Kylea Province's problem. The Proventor there wouldn't lend you an ear? Maybe send out the Second Dyron?"

"If Proventor Ankus had any say over where his dyron can be sent, I'd be kissin' his feet in Alemyles right now, not dawdling around bloody Dray'gon Rokh. Second's not going anywhere without the Capital's blessing."

Tyghus gave a respectful nod. "Hm, well you wouldn't know of any trade problems by the looks of the Capital last night."

"Aye, well... some say the Capital is the Capital's *only* concern," Whit replied with scorn. "Even they'll feel the pinch eventually, though. Just like the rest of us."

Tyghus was taken aback by the man's bite. "I'd mind yourself saying things like that. They wouldn't just turn their back on something that serious. Can't be much more than scattered bandits or they'd have paid it more –"

"Scattered bandits!" Whit irritatedly echoed. "Scattered bandits if the gods smile upon us..." His voice trailed off as he turned away from Tyghus.

"Why do you think otherwise, then?" Tyghus called after him, annoyed at the man's distrust.

The Quartermaster never broke stride toward his horse. "I don't, General. Not at all. But we should depart – the first caravans have already headed off."

Perplexed, Tyghus allowed a smile to creep across his face. "You know you're quite pleasant, Whit."

* * *

The night in the Capital had been a whirlwind for Tyghus, and for Kyrus's sake – and health – he hoped it wouldn't be symbolic of his friend's stay. Even amid Kyrus's own celebration, however, Tyghus still found himself acting as a sounding wall for the new Lorrion, who managed to drunkenly lob suspicions at the gathering in between being whisked away to meet one person or another. As with the ride north, Tyghus was baffled that Kyrus preferred condolences as to his new-found fame, rather than congratulations.

Apart from his talks with Kyrus, Tyghus's experience differed little in terms of the attention given to him. From the moment he joined Kyrus in the massive Soelum, supplicating ministers and wealthy Ruhl merchants jockeyed to establish favor with him, a veritable frenzy erupting once they realized he held a trusted position with the Lorrion. When he finally arrived at his inn to sleep in the Capital's West Gurums, coins, trinkets, and other such bequests already awaited him at the innkeeper's counter. Such were the politics of the day, and only a few hours of it made Tyghus long for the campaign trail; Kyrus felt likewise, but was bound to his fate for the time being.

The cavalry platoon he now found himself in bore little resemblance to the rigid formations of the campaign marches he was used to with the Sixth. The fifty horsemen traversed the gray stone of the immaculate Rokhish road at a fair distance from the trade convoy's rear, with no one asserting much command over any of them. As far as Tyghus could tell, their goal was to stay out of the eyeshot of anyone – or anything – that might be preying upon these caravans. The caravaners were loathe to be the "bait" in the scheme, but given that they had to make the trek back one way or another, they were better off having this bit of protection a few miles back.

The men Whit gathered from the city were mostly Rokhs of other Imperial dyrons who hailed from the western Kylean grasslands outside the Jungle, and were eager to see home again. Though the Rokhs rode Imperial horses as recompense for their services, Tyghus realized after a few conversations with them that they were hardly the trained cavalrymen Whit bargained for – they were foot soldiers atop horses. Given that Ruhls alone received cavalry training in the army, common Rokhs' familiarity with the equines stemmed from their use in transportation or ploughing croplands back home, not from frenzied battlefields.

Tyghus's "conversations" with the Rokhs, moreover, were curt and brusque. Their stature and edgy body language mirrored that of their kinsman Whit, with the exception of skin that had bronzed from being stationed beyond the jungle. But like Whit, they were reclusive towards him, preferring to trade stories with each other about families and happenings back home.

With this as his riding environment, the first couple weeks passed slowly and quietly. Mile after mile, the royal blue sky kissed the golden plains in a perfectly straight line, with hardly so much as a knoll or tree once they were a few days out from the city. Wind-blown fields of wild grain surrounded either side of the trail, reaching high as a horse's saddle at times. It was a beautiful monotony that by daylight kept his thoughts of her, his thoughts of Vara, at bay. But at night, the same questions came back to haunt him...

What did I do wrong? Always done things the 'right' way, followed the 'right' path at every turn, haven't spoken ill of others. I've trained and fought and lived exactly as a Rokh – as a Ruhl *– should. I courted her proper and her family name's as respected as mine. I did all that I could, by the gods, so why?* He'd stare into the blankness of the night waiting for the gods' answers only to grow frustrated when they never came. *Meanwhile, Kyrus spends his whole life cursing good fortune yet there he is awash in it,* he'd think bitterly.

Inevitably, he'd succumb to exhaustion against a serenade of howls from prairie wolves dotting the Plains, but it was a rare night that his pleas didn't follow him into his dreams:

Free me of these thoughts... show me my purpose.

* * *

On the fourteenth day of the trek, Tyghus awoke in the early morning hours to a motionless camp, lit as much by a fading moon as a rising sun. He filled his tin cup with water and spicegrass before setting it by his firepit for the teaish brew to steep. He squinted in the dawn's early light, watching the fire's smoke spiral into the air –

And mesh with a plume of dust rising on the southern horizon.

His eyes shot open, instinctually reaching for his warblade as he stumbled to his feet in his body length tunic.

"*Wild horse? Couldn't be a rider... middle of nowhere out here...*" he muttered under his breath.

The plume grew larger as it drew nearer – and there was no mistaking which direction it was headed.

No wild horse, he thought.

Tyghus kept low to the ground as he headed for a patch of tall grass just on the camp's edge. He hadn't a shred of armor on him, only his sword.

His heart quickened as the rider quickly closed, his hooded brown cloak fluttering from his speed. Tyghus was intent on baiting the approach, certain he was safely blurred amongst grassy stalks.

Ten yards. The heavy gallops were loud now. Blade in hand, he sprang to his feet –

"*General, no!*"

The horse bucked. Tyghus froze with sword held high in striking pose, his eyes locked with the stunned rider's.

"General!" Whit's voice came again from the rear. "He's with us!"

Still tense, neither rider nor Tyghus stirred. "Didn't know we had guests arriving... 'specially not at the break of dawn..."

"Apologies, General – I didn't expect him for days..."

A silence ensued.

"Treos," the rider finally said.

"Pardon?"

"Treos is m'name. Treos Lokner."

Tyghus eyed him curiously. "Mine's Tyghus. And forgive my greeting, but when a man riding with a party to hunt bandits sees a rogue horseman approach at full gallop –"

"Ya' fancy him a bandit?" A broad smile crossed the man's face. "Ya' needn't explain ya'self to me, lad. Lend me a hand?"

"I wasn't trying to explain my—ah, no matter," Tyghus said with annoyance. He planted his sword into the earth with a twinge of embarrassment, then approached Treos with forearm raised. The rider nimbly lept down with his aid.

"Brew?" Tyghus offered as the two men walked back towards the fire, horse in tow. Tyghus could see his cup piping off steam.

"Please," Treos replied with a nod. He removed the hood from his cloak to reveal a bald head with hair around the sides and back to form a long braided tail. His face was lined with creases about the mouth and eyes when he smiled, but appeared youthful otherwise. He was a tall, thin man, arms and legs built of wiry muscle, covered by an aged, sun-kissed skin – skin that had to be cold. The sleeveless sand-colored tunic under his cloak and worn sandals strapped to his feet were vastly out of place with the morning chill of the autumn Plains.

Tyghus jabbed his finger at Whit as he walked by, growling, "you *tell* me when someone's due – friend *or* foe."

"Good to see ya' again, Whit," Treos offered immediately after, the Quartermaster barely making eye contact. "And you – what's a Ruhl doin' all the way out here without his dyron?"

Tyghus rolled his eyes. "Let's just leave it that I'm here now."

Treos snuck a glance at him. "Okay, lad. Leave it at that, then."

It wasn't until they each had a cup of brew in hand that Tyghus recognized the emblem on Treos's tunic. It was faded, but the blood drop emblem of the Empire was unmistakedly stamped across his chest.

"You a soldier, Treos?" he asked, secretly hopeful.

The guest's brown eyes were fixed on the western horizon, away from Tyghus. A calm, wistful expression blanketed his face as he spoke in relaxed tones. "I was, lad."

"No longer?"

"No longer. Served my twenty years and no more."

"So what's your trade now?"

A deeper smile returned to the older man's face. "Not much of anything, I s'pose. I'm a bit of a wanderer."

"Where'd your day's journey begin, then, answer me that. I mean no offense, but you're ill-fitted for the Plains."

"South of here. Far south, by the Lakes. Grew up there, actually; raised on the water 'til it was 'bout the time I was eighteen, nineteen years– gods, has it been twenty-five years? Well, either way, Dray'gers started showing up around then to get us to go fight their battles in Jungle, given how bad it was becomin'."

"The Raizana revolts?"

He nodded, then pointed at Whit. "Ran into him while I was stationed at Cros'syng Way."

"He's an odd one."

"A bit," Treos said wryly. "But most of the Rokhs living in the Jungle are the same way – the Raizana just don't let ya' sleep. When they weren't screaming at night then packs of them would roam the trees, snatch ya' if you ventured outside the fort's battlements. Maybe eat ya'."

"He hinted as much. Twenty-five years of that? Amazing you can sleep even now."

"Twenty," Treos quickly corrected, gaze ever westward. "Finished up several years ago. Married a Cros'syng Way lass but she was barren. Lost her to the Beastmen two weeks before I's to leave."

The blunt revelation caught Tyghus off-guard. "Sympathies, Treos."

"Such is life."

Tygus marveled at his placid face. "You're quite stoic about it."

"Ah, still hurts, lad. Every day there's an ache, a reminder of her, of something I should have done." He shrugged his shoulders. "But ya' must look forward," he offered. "And bein' back among the women of the Lakes helps," he added dryly.

Tyghus laughed. "Aye? Their reputation's well-earned, is it?"

"Aye. Hopefully ya'll have cause to 'protect' the Lakes someday."

They sipped their spicegrass in silence for a bit, Tyghus watching their fellow soldiers packing up camp for the day's ride ahead. "So what brings you here, then?"

Treos was slow to answer, but eventually offered one word –

"Rom."

"Rom?"

Treos trained his sunken brown eyes squarely on Tyghus. "Rom Blakkus."

"Who is that?"

The Lakeman shook his head. "Whit really didn't say much, did he?"

He whisked the last of his brew down his throat and tossed the mug onto Tyghus's kit. "Come, lad. Let's ride and we'll talk."

* * *

"'Bout ten, twenty years before they dropped me in the Jungle, some Rokhs began choppin' down its eastern fringe, pushing the 'Zana farther west. The wood trade was booming, everyone was rich 'cause *everybody* wants the Raizan wood. But the Beastmen – they're enraged. They protest by slaughtering, eating, maiming – everything their version of diplomacy permits. Dray'gon Rokh steps in, tries to settle things. They send in my men to keep the peace."

He nodded sharply, countenance full of painful remembrance. "But it continued. So a year ago – maybe two – Rynsyus announces renewed protection for the Beastmen and their homes. Penalties put in place like fines and dungeon lock-ups. The plan worked great on parchment but not in the woods. Not only were the woodcutters now angry, but they're going ahead with their deeds anyway."

The Lakeman sighed. "Then Rom showed up."

"To what end?" Tyghus asked.

Treos laughed. "To what end? I'm not sure he even knows."

"Well, who is he?"

"He started poking around the Jungle when the Beastmen were in full rage. Not sure he knew a thing about the woods, but he was there all the same and got caught up in a scrap with the Beastmen, lost a crop of his men. So he goes and rounds up a group of old soldiers retired near the Jungle to go get him some revenge; another big scrum, one he apparently got the better of even if he lost a fair bit."

"Not much of the businessman, it doesn't sound like."

Treos nodded leisurely, "No, and that's the problem – he realized he didn't need to be. Rumor has it he's been mad since those 'battles', if ya' want to call 'em that. Asked for help from the Cros'syng Way garrison, but didn't get it–"

"He's a bloody agitator!" Whit quickly interjected. "Got the whole region on edge!"

"Easy there, lad," Treos said calmly. "Anyway, he knows how to whip people into a fury, ya' give him that much. He's been trolling the countryside, fixing to form an even bigger mob... then all of a sudden these caravans start disappearing..."

"Blakkus? A bloody woodcutter is behind this?"

"I'd wager a crown or two. Not many say no to him – ya' don't die well, if ya' do. So when I received a visit from his cohorts at the lake a few days ago... I knew it was time to 'wander' on again..."

Tyghus jerked the reins of his steed abruptly and eyed Treos with alarm. Without breaking stride, the Lakeman said, "I'm no assassin for Rom, lad,

41

but believe me – if I'd agreed to help him, ya'd already be dead."

"Of course not!   He'd never think of it!"   Whit quickly offered in support.

"Perhaps so, perhaps not.   Perhaps he leads us to ambush – to Blakkus."

Treos still didn't break pace. "I'm telling ya', I don't lead ya' to ambush. But I *can* tell ya' that if he sought me out, he's not far away, and if he's not far away, he's…"

"He's what, Treos?"

"Well,   I   hope   ya'   kept   ya'r   blade   sharp."

Chapter V

"7th mo., 360 P.C.
Nar-Biluk, Capital of Rokhish Valogar

Most Honorable Rynsyus, Khorokh of the Unified Rokhs,

This letter I pen to you bears news I can hardly bring myself to believe, let alone relay. I'm not one with prose, so I'll simply say the facts as I know them:

General Torrus is dead. Aye, the Dyrator of the Imperial Sixth Dyron. To make the tragedy worse, he lost two kords of the Sixth's finest. Two thousand Bulls we'll never get back.

I know little about the circumstances. One of the kordettes that survived the slaughter — Tygustus if memory serves? - tells me they were patrolling deep into Valogar's southeast when it happened. Entered a shadowy grove, rainstorms erupted, and in a flash, they'd been surrounded by Puries.

Aye, Purebloods, my Khorokh. They're still here. Thousands of them, and it seems like they've only grown stronger in the interim if this is true. The base is on edge… I'm on edge…

I shall write you further as the information comes."

Report to Khorokh Rynsyus I from Bokrus,
Quartermaster of the Rokhish Garrison in Nar-Biluk, Y.
360 P.C.

Dray'gon Rokh, Khorian Brex, 1ˢᵗ Day of the Tenth Month, Y. 383 P.C.

The two men climbed the winding staircase for what felt like hours. The cylinder of stairs enclosed within the Tower's diamond walls gave way to doors every twenty steps, candles nestled into alcoves all the way. It was quickly apparent, however, that the Khorokh awaited him far beyond the lower floors.

"His Majesty travels these steps often, Jarax?" Kyrus asked through labored pants. "He's an old man, by the gods…"

Without breaking stride, Jarax replied, "he only uses the Brex for his most important meetings; ones that demand privacy."

"What could he possibly want with me that's so important at this point? I don't even know –"

"I wouldn't let it vex you, my lord. You'll get your answers shortly – probably."

"Astounding candor, as usual."

The staircase ended abruptly at the foot of two massive doors, parting at the middle with torches on either side. Before them were two Rubitian Guards standing like golems, hands crossed in front of them to rest on downturned swords. Kyrus could hardly see the soldiers' eyes through their silver helmets' slits, distracted by the flames reflecting off their polish.

"Your audience awaits, Lorrion."

Kyrus, fatigued from the climb, managed a look at his escort. "Leaving again?"

"He didn't beckon for *me*, my lord."

Desperate to resist the wave of tension gripping his every muscle, he extended his arm to the Rubator. "Very well… farewell for the moment, then."

Jarax clasped Kyrus's forearm with a smile. "Best of luck in there… he's usually pleasant."

With a turn, he disappeared back down the spiraling stairs, echoing footsteps fading with each second. Soon it was silent, with Kyrus standing alone between the two statuesque Guards.

"I'm Kyrus – Lorrion Kyrus… the Khorokh summoned me," he said quietly, hardly believing his own words.

Silence persisted, until finally, from the depths of one's helmet came, "proceed."

Nodding to the speaker, Kyrus hesitantly eyed the doors before pushing them open, rusty hinges groaning as they gave way. The square room within was barely aglow with the flicker of a dying fire along the wall to his left. Eyes straining, Kyrus saw a large table in the middle of the cramped room, covered with scrolls and chalices. Above the fireplace was a sprawling map as tall as he and thrice as wide; he walked towards it –

jumping as the twin doors crashed shut behind him – and saw the expanse of the Empire etched into the worn-out paper. Waning embers warmed his legs as his gaze instinctively fell upon Valogar's peninsula south of the Lowlands, protruding east from the Isthmus like an egg on its side. Its capital of Nar-Biluk was nearer to the northern Ratikan Sea than the southern Ferlen, while tendrils from its eastern shore reached deep into the dark expanses of the Benguz Ocean, and –

"Out here, my son."

Startled from his studies, Kyrus whirled around to see a hooded man's silhouette disappear onto a balcony outcrop opposite the firewall.

"Majesty?"

No reply.

He followed the voice onto a balcony barely large enough for a handful of people. At the balcony's edge stood the silhouette, framed now in beaming moonlight, hunched over as if only his arms kept him upright. Kyrus cautiously approached the edge himself.

The stunning view beyond showed a kingdom bathed in the moon's white, eerily silent at such heights yet alive with the fires of thousands of homes throughout the city. Kyrus could see all sectors of the great Capital, from the royal Arxun District immediately below to the commoner *Gurums* to the south, east and west. The massive oval façade of the *Stylian* Arena in the northeastern Gurums looked positively quaint from his vantage.

"Highness – Highness, I… it's an honor to meet you."

His counterpart didn't stir nor utter a word. Confused, Kyrus searched the folds of the man's hood for a well-hidden face. "Highness, I came from Avergon almost two weeks ago now. Jarax told me you –"

"I know you came from Avergon – now tell me who you are."

The Khorokh's head swiveled towards his guest. His eyes, barely open more than a slit, offered only exhaustion, while thin white hair spilled down onto his shoulders. Wrinkles looked like canyons in the moonlight, at least those that weren't covered by a full beard. The furry cloak covering his body billowed in the breeze, revealing one hand on the railing, the other gripping a goblet.

"Forgive me, Majesty but… what about me?"

Taking a long sip of his cup, the raspy voice continued. "Kyrus, you were born into a family famous for sacrificing sons for the Empire. You've trained and fought and seen war for most of the years of your young life, only to train again; only to suffer the most hideous losses a lad could suffer. Yet despite *all* that, you promoted peace in Valogar when I asked you to; me, a gray old man you'd never even met. So now I ask you why."

Perplexed, Kyrus offered, "Majesty, I… follow the orders that I'm given. That's it. When I was told to give battle, I gave battle. But when you chose to make peace –"

"Should I have?"

"Highness?"

"The peace with Valogar – was that the right decision?"

"I –"

"I think it was," the Emperor answered with a shake of his head. "Truth be told, Kyrus, I'd much prefer to focus on our Western frontier, maybe Loccea too. I'd like to send sailors into the Benguz, explore her depths beyond the Astorens like we've talked about for years, but is that right?"

The back of Kyrus's neck began to burn, even in the night's chill. "I'm not sure how to answer you, Highness. I've – I've never seen myself as anything more than a… than a sword in your hand. I've never pretended to be one to comment on policy… *your* policy, anyway."

The Emperor's eyes sprang open as they fixated on Kyrus. "But now you *must*. Now, you are a *maker* of policy."

The younger man's mouth suddenly smacked dry. "Am I, though? I'm a Lorrion… as I understand it, aren't I here just to put in place whatever it is that you –"

Rynsyus interrupted him with a dismissive wave. "Your naivete's refreshing – at least I hope its naivete. But in any event, you go too far – you don't realize yet just how much power is vested within the ranks of the Lorrio. Khorokhs that ignore their Councils aren't long for their positions – some say we're meant to be *servants* to the Lorrio – but regardless, it's only through my work with the Lorrions that I've cobbled together that Valogarian peace accord… though with Onzy's departure, that accord teeters in the balance, I'm afraid."

"Was Onzero so influential that –"

"Quite the opposite – he abstained. He withheld his support on Valogarian matters. So while the Sudos behind Lorrion Castus advocated peace, the Nortics behind Antinax war, my proposals could run through the Lorrio unobstructed. When the Lorrio's deadlocked, the Khorokh's word is deemed unchallenged. You understand what I'm saying?"

"The deadlock prevented either side from claiming victory…"

"Indeed, indeed it did."

"But it's peace, the Sudos don't see this as a victory? They weren't pleased?"

"No, they were not," Rynsyus said with a hint of scorn. "Either the peace didn't move fast enough for them or I didn't make enough amends with the Valogarians or they frowned upon my insisting the Lij marry a Ruhl." The Emperor broke gaze at last, peering into the distance with a derisive chuckle. "You see, most Lorrions and ministers of the Court will be loved by all the Arxun until they reveal their politics, then once they do, they'll be hated by half. Only the Khorokh gets to be hated by all – well, not *only* the Khorokh anymore, I suppose."

"Who else takes that honor?"

Rynsyus sighed. "You."

Kyrus stared blankly at the old man. "What?"

"You, I said."

"I heard you, but why –"

"You're a man with Clyvean Ruhl blood, like me, Kyrus, so Sudo ministers suspect you; yet you spent your entire waking life in the Lowlands and Valogar – thus, Nortics wonder if you sympathize with the Natives, especially after you've preached peace as I've asked. You've a unique mix – a hated mix like I."

"That's how I'm seen here?" Kyrus blurted out, his suspicious instinct in the two weeks since the Soelum feeling completely validated.

"Unfortunately so…"

Kyrus's initial anxiety descended into distress. "Highness, with due respect, I – I," he stuttered, trying to gather himself.

Rynsyus looked to him again. "What, my son?"

"It's just… I mean this whole process has been… it's been…"

"Confusing, lad?"

Dishonest, he thought bitterly, trying to remain civil. "Well, I was summoned to Dray'gon Rokh with virtually no reason given, I was never told I'd be some sort of reviled figure within the Arxun, I was never even told about the ceremony I was called to attend – not even the bloody attire! And Onzero – I'd never even met him before –"

"I didn't want you to meet him. I didn't want you to meet *any* of them."

Well, dammit all, I did! he thought with an incredulous look, desperately fighting a rising anger. "That may well be, but… but…"

It's bloody dishonest, no other word for it!

"Kyrus –"

"It's just that honesty, it's something I hold most –"

"*Kyrus, you need to listen to me!*" the old man suddenly snarled, followed by a rash of hacking coughs.

Kyrus's chest heaved with frustrated breaths. "I'm listening, Highness."

"I want you to trust me, I truly and sincerely do, but in the end, I don't give a damn about your demand for honesty."

The Lorrion blanched.

"Not one bit. I give a damn, I give my *all*, about the Realm and the Realm alone."

Kyrus couldn't have removed the shock from his face if he wanted to. He'd rarely been spoken to like this by anybody, let alone a complete stranger to him… even if he *is* a royal stranger.

"The point is, you knew as much as I wanted you to know, and nothing more!" Rynsyus continued as he gathered himself and looked down at the castle grounds below. "Forgive my tone," he resumed in lower voice, hinting of jest. "And though I can assure you the Arxun's hatred is worth the people's love, I *am* sorry for your confusion – but it was necessary. It was all necessary." After a pause, the Khorokh chuckled again. "Otherwise, you might not have come when I beckoned for you in Avergon."

"The Khorokh tells you to come, you come," Kyrus said curtly, despite calming a bit.

But the Emperor shook his head. "You might not have come."

Kyrus didn't persist and looked out over the grounds himself. "So then what's the end of all this? You wish me to abstain as Onzero did?"

"It's the only way. With the factions at odds with one another the way they are, abstention's the only means to let them salvage their pride. Onzy recognized that. A decisive vote on Valogar for either side would tear the Arxun apart, with the Provinces following suit. So yes... yes, the stalemate must continue."

The Khorokh sighed and a long silence followed. Kyrus searched for something to say but felt too overwhelmed or angry or confused or all of those things to say a word.

"You enter these chambers at a time of great strife, my son, but also one of great potential," Rynsyus finally said reflectively. "The troops are gone from the Peninsula and a historic marriage of Rokhish and Valogarian blood is only months away. You – *we* – have an opportunity to guide the Empire towards an era of peace not seen in nearly a century. Do you understand that number? Peace unseen in at least a half dozen generations." He shook his head. "So now it's on you to help see us through to that peace. You have to learn to carry favor where you can, use your heritage to sway Nortics and Sudos alike. With hope... perhaps the pot doesn't *have* to boil over."

Rynsyus bowed his head and turned away from the edge at last, heading inside. "It's a poison, that Valogar. Vallius was right. A bloody poison," he muttered.

Kyrus looked back to see the Emperor briefly stoke the fire with an iron rod, sparks fluttering into the air. His head tilted to survey the Imperial map, hands clasping behind his back. "Come and sit. You'll deal with the Lorrio's schemes the rest of your days. Now, I want to know about you."

Kyrus left the windy perch to take a seat at the table, though given what the old man had told him already, he was hardly in a mood for pleasantries. Instead, he sat silently watching Rynsyus trace a finger along the map, his anxiety nearly paralyzing him.

"So?" the Khorokh finally asked without turning.

Kyrus shook his head. "There's nothing much to know, Highness."

Rynsyus snorted. "So you'll be known as the 'Modest Lorrion'.

Wouldn't be the worst addition to my Council."

"Well, there isn't, really."

His host snuck a glance at him with a frown before his eyes returned to the map. "You've enjoyed your stay in the Capital these weeks?"

Dark thoughts clouded his ability to fib. "No."

"No?"

"No. With due respect, it's been dreadful. I've met Ruhls of one house after another around the Arxun and it seems that every one of them tries to out-slander the next. Every one of them deals in gossip like they traded sacks of gold. Nortic houses feuding with Sudo; Sudos sparring with fellow Sudos. It's unbecoming of Ruhl houses to be –"

"That's the beating heart of Dray'gon Rokh you describe. The beating heart of the *Empire*."

Kyrus's eyes narrowed in disbelief. "Well, it's rather vile to watch," he said. "And the reality is that my province is on the battlefield, and now I'm – now I'm – now I'm wandering Dray'gon Rokh's streets to listen to a hundred strangers tell me how to act as a Lorrion. I don't understand how you –"

"Processes, Kyrus!" the old man suddenly exclaimed, head turning sharply at his guest.

"What –"

"*You* are focused on the wrong thing – you're focused on the *process!* You must focus on the *product*. The *product* is often beautiful, but the *process* is often not." Rynsyus let a poignant pause linger before continuing. "Now you'll admit that the Empire, its size, its breadth, its power – it's beautiful, is it not?"

Kyrus avoided the Emperor's gaze for a moment. "Aye."

Rynsyus nodded. "Then don't let the process detract from that."

Despite his resistance, the young Lorrion had to admit that he saw the Emperor's logic. Even still…

"I don't understand though, if balance is so important to you, why would you let Onzero step down at all? Why leave his selection to chance – if it was chance?"

"You're wise to assume Onzy received my 'advice' on a replacement," Rynsyus answered with a chuckle. "But the answer's rather simple – he's mortal. And at his age – much as I must do at some point – we could not leave his successor to chance; should he perish before annointing a replacement, his nearest family would receive the honor by law. Much like my sons, those family members aren't nearly as passive as he's become."

"He's not always been so eager to please you?"

Rynsyus smiled. "Certainly not. He joined the Lorrio to fill my vacancy when I took the throne. He was brought to power on his reputation as one who reviled Valogarians and wouldn't think of the word 'peace'. He'd campaigned for years during the First Uprising with his seven sons at his side, and was eager to keep the Lorrio on a war tilt. He was a rallying figure for the Nortics, the only man I've ever seen Antinax defer to – gods above, even Sudos voted with him at times."

"But he changed…"

Rynsyus finally peeled away from the map, tapping it as he did, chalice still in hand. He slumped into a chair opposite Kyrus, gulping whatever still filled his cup. "After he was appointed to the Lorrio, Onzero's seven sons joined service under Torrus."

Kyrus's eyes bolted open. "They –"

"Every one of them perished at the Massacre in the bush. And for months –" he started, before swallowing deeply. "For months afterwards, the Natives would leave limbs of his boys at their family's abode in Attikon, or Onzy's estate in Clyvea; some rotten remains were even dropped off within the walls of Dray'gon Rokh if you can believe it. Quite remarkable, really, given how deep in the tribal lands the slaughter took place. But however they did it…"

Rynsysus shook his head. "As the months passed, Onzy's vigor in Dray'gon Rokh began to wane. Nortics could scarcely catch sight of him, let alone count on his support for the war. He never spoke out against it, of course, he just never spoke at all. He faded from public view, appearing only to cast his abstentions before retreating to his empty estate by the Clyves. He's the living dead."

The description fit the broken person Kyrus saw the night of his ceremony, but beyond that, he was overcome with the imagery of the Massacre and its gruesome packages. He suddenly felt seventeen again and surrounded by the sweltering patches; surrounded by Valogarians, Valogarians that stood over the impaled body of his father. He blinked the thoughts away before looking hard into the Emperor's eyes, whose head sat leisurely cradled by a hand.

"My friend's father was at Torrus's Massacre. He – he trained me in Avergon. He didn't talk of it much but said enough to warn me to never find myself along a similar path."

"The father of the young woman that's to marry the Valogarian Lij, I'm aware," the Emperor said with a smile and nod. "Yet – you did find yourself along such a path."

Kyrus could only nod back, startled by his eyes' sudden dampening.

"You've seen the horrors, Kyrus; the gods know you probably see them still," the Emperor said, pushing his chalice over to the grieving soldier, who graciously accepted. "The bleeding had to *stop*. That's why I pulled us out of that land. I know you weren't pleased to have your proud Dyron abandon posts that so much blood had won –"

Looking up sharply, Kyrus started, "Highness –"

"— which I understand, but *this* is the way towards healing the wounds which run so deep among the Onzeros and Kyruses of the Realm; it's the *only* way. In his heart, Onzy believed that, and we pleaded with the gods that another may exist to bring the land back from the brink... and gods willing, we believe that man is you. Your plight's widely known among the people even if you personally are not, but *I* know of your reputation as an able administrator and a peerless general of our most famous corps. So, you were chosen."

"Yet you said yourself I'm not trusted –"

"Trust is *not* respect," the Khorokh said firmly, before his lips upturned. "But ideally, they coincide."

The Lorrion inhaled deeply. "And so I'm here."

They listened to the fire crackle for a silent few minutes, Kyrus still reeling at the conversation. Only two months ago he was reviewing books and records in Avergon or overseeing the Sixth's training regimen. Then that fateful courier arrived, and in a blink he was shedding tears before Andervold's most powerful man, over a tragedy he'd rarely discussed even with Tyghus.

"Enough for tonight," the Khorokh said as he rose creakily to his feet. "This old man must retire to his chambers if he wants to fend off Death another day."

He offered his arm to Kyrus, who rose to accept with the Emperor's gaze searing into him. "Give me your word that won't forget what we discussed here," he said quietly before showing a mischievous smile. "But that you *will*."

Fire reflecting in his eyes, Kyrus replied, "I gave – I *give* my word to never forget. But I will."

"Accolades, Lorrion."

Kyrus bowed his head. "Majesty."

With that, the grasp was broken, Kyrus departing through the same weathered doors he'd entered.

This time, he scarcely flinched when they slammed shut behind him.

✳ ✳ ✳

The Emperor's stare lingered on the doors for a moment before he collapsed back into his chair, fighting a fit of coughs with both hands. Blood dripped from his palms.

His eyes closed.

"Gods   above...   let   him   be   the   one."

Chapter VI

"NOTICE AND ALERT FOR THE ARREST OF ONE "ROM
BLAKKUS"

Rokhish citizens, bewarned of this man:
Name of Rom, Name of Blakkus
Said to have Eye of Brown, Eye of Green, Hair of Black
Build of Average Rokh

HEREBY SOUGHT BY THE PROVINCIAL COURT OF
INQUISITION FOR:
Unlawful Killing and Looting of a Citizen
Unlawful Killing and Looting of Raizana
Unlawful Killing and Looting of Stolxian
Unlawful Harvesting of Imperial Timber
Offenders of Peace on Imperial Tradeways
Inciting Discord with Imperial Allies

REPORT SIGHTINGS OF THE DESCRIBED TO GUARDSMEN OF
RAIZEA PROVINCE"

- Notice posted in Cros'syng Way,
as issued by Folliux, Proventor of Raizea Province, Y. 382 P.C.

Kylea Province, The Dead Plains, Second Day of the Tenth Month, Y. 383 P.C.

"Ride, damn you!"

The horse strained from the heels of its rider as it sped towards smoke on the western horizon.

"Ride!"

"General, wait! Let us form ranks!"

"Treos stays with me, Whit! The five riding ahead are enough! Take the rest and circle the wagons! Do it!"

Screams carried eastward towards them.

"Shit! *Shit!*"

He took a split second to slip into his silver cuirass and helmet before kicking his ride back into full sprint. "It's too *soon!* They *can't* be this far east!"

"Don't be reckless, lad – they want this!" the Lakeman called out.

"Then keep pace, Treos!" Tyghus turned and further bellowed, "And I will *not* die here but know that if I do and you betrayed me, by the gods high and low I'll haunt you the rest of your days!"

"Two days ya' been eyein' me, even with Whit's backin' - for the last time, I'd have done so already if I –"

"Just remember! *Ride!*"

With one more crack of the reins, the past and present soldiers broke away.

✳ ✳ ✳

"Gods above…"

The Rokhs approached the lead carts on froth-mouthed horses, but found no signs of the advance cavalrymen, the raiders, or any other life. Strewn about the burning wagons were the motionless shells of merchants.

"Bloody hell," Tyghus muttered. "Stripped everything. Killed 'em all."

"Loosed the wagon-beasts, too. The hell are they?"

Though the choking smoke was thick and almost blinding, Tyghus soon saw a smaller column lofting into the pale blue sky about a dozen yards off. "You see that?"

A howl of laughter broke out, emanating from the smaller plume. The Rokhs exchanged wide-eyed glances, then without a word, Tyghus pointed two fingers in the laughter's direction, breaking into a trot. Though he hoped the laughter stemmed from his forward unit, intuition told him otherwise.

"Blades out, Treos. Eyes for ambush."

The Lakeman drew his blade. "Honored to have ya'r trust."

"You don't, believe me…"

Within eyeshot of the smaller firepit, the succulent smell of fire-roasted meats wafted towards him. Three figures bearing black shirts sat around the flames where meaty ribs on a spit seared, taking turns in carving off chunks of flesh to feast on. One figure had his back turned – the other two did not, and arose with a start as the two Rokhs approached. Tyghus quickly realized they weren't the Jungle Rokhs.

"Morning," the seated figure offered with hand raised; his head cocked to the right, revealing a green eye. Tyghus eyed the two standing men with alarm.

"You two, sit back down."

"You two can leave," the seated man ordered.

"Sit down *now*."

"Both of you – get outta here."

Tyghus scowled. "If either of you even flinches, you die. Treos, take position behind them."

"Treos? Treos Lokner?" the head turned to the left, eyeing the Rokhs with a brown eye. "It's a – it's a – it's a... oh, what's the word?" the man said as he returned back to the slab of meat. "Pity. Aye, that's it. It's a pity you turned us down, old friend."

Tyghus's eyes flitted to Treos.

"Not ya'r friend, Rom," the Lakeman replied in menacing tone.

"No? See, I thought you were," Rom replied with a chuckle. "Wouldn't have come to see ya' if I thought otherwise. Wouldn't have made much sense climbin' over those Loccean dunes of yours, notwithstandin' the tits on those women."

Treos shook his head as looked at Tyghus. "Don't even know ya', Rom. Don't wanna know ya', if this is ya'r work."

"Well, it's uh... aye, this is my work, as you put it. Not sure why that'd put you off though, old friends that we are."

Treos shook his head vigorously again at Tyghus. "Ya'r a mad man if you believe that."

The bandit nodded. "Aye? Mad how? Mad angry? Mad crazy? Been called worse either way, I s'pose. Just remember, though, I'm always willing to listen should you reconsider."

Tyghus watched the exchange with suspicion, but had finally heard enough. "Rom –"

"Rom Blakkus, aye."

"My name's Tyghus, Rom. And you're –"

"Ha! Just the one name? I'm to believe they found a Ruhl bored enough to waste his time out here? For what? For *me*?" Rom burst into cackles as Tyghus's face burned with a rising temper. "I tell you, Imperial – that almost takes the sting out of hearing my friend pretend not to know –"

"Enough nonsense!" Tyghus barked. "Get up and –"

"Did I not tell you two to *leave!*"

Rom's two associates suddenly dashed in opposite directions. Treos calmly kicked his horse into action and hammered the first man's head with the broad side of his sword, crumpling him, before about-facing to trample the other. He could hear ribs snapping, the man wheezing – but alive.

"More value breathin' at this point, Tyghus."

"Ah, they're useless," Rom inserted. "You see how well they take orders. Helped kill your guards, kill those big Stolxian bastards in the wagon, but…" he threw his hands up in disgust. He turned all the way around to observe Tyghus still mounted behind him.

"Please, sit. Take a meal. Plenty of meat."

The man's the lunatic I've heard him to be… Tyghus thought with heart pounding.

Before Treos's shocked eyes, however, the General obliged, taking a seat opposite from Rom. Silence ensued for several moments. The bandit's stretched, thin face was caked in dust even as he continued his voracious consumption, every bite revealing a gap on the right side of his mouth. His long, black braided hair was pulled back into a tail, revealing a scar running down the right side of his face from hairline to jaw.

"So you're a wanted man, Rom," Tyghus said, glare searing into the bandit. "And I have to confess, I wanted to sit down and look at the man who revels in slaughtering these people – women and children alike."

"Eh," Rom quickly waved the statement away. "Let me explain something to you –"

"You don't deny responsibility for this carnage?"

Rom looked back at the burning wagon. "Why would I deny it?" he asked with complete sincerity. "You think I looted this wagon train by accident?"

"You'd deny it to save your rotten life."

Rom laughed. "Okay, then I deny it. None of this is my work!" he said, spraying flecks of meat with every laugh.

Tyghus's hand slid to his hilt which the bandit apparently saw.

"Stop, stop," he said, still smiling but with hands outstretched. "Listen to me, Imperial, listen to me… let me explain something to you uh – your name again?"

"You don't need to know that."

"Right, right," he said, before throwing the meat down and pointing all around him, face suddenly cold as ice. "This – this is not your business here."

"Imperial trade is absolutely our business. These caravans carry merchants from all over Andvervold, most importantly from across the River Anonga –"

"The Stolxis? They're dolts. Big dolts, but dolts all the same."

"- and when they pass through *Imperial* lands, they do so under *Imperial* protection, so –"

Rom shrugged. "Okay, so protect them, then. I'm not stopping you. Surely, you knew I was out here!"

"- what you've done is far more than simply rob a few peasants! The Stolxian border's tense enough without animals like you preying upon their innocents!"

"Okay, okay, okay… listen, I don't gather we'll be agreeing on this," the bandit arose sharply. "So I'm just going to leave."

Tyghus watched incredulously as the lanky man walked towards a horse tied off nearby, his fury almost at a boiling point. "Rom, you're not going anywhere but with us! You're headed to Dray'gon Rokh where you'll be tried and executed before the people for these crimes – if you're lucky, it'll be quick!"

Rom cackled again as he began loading up the horse with sacks of jewels and other spoils. Tyghus rose from his seat as his temper flared. "Rom, unless you want to make the journey with one leg, this is your last warning!"

The raider, back turned to the general, froze in mid-load – then pointed east. "*You*, Nameless One, have much bigger issues on your hands!"

Tyghus followed his point – and saw a new column of smoke go up.

Impossible! he thought. *The wagons should be encircled, yes?*

"This is much bigger than you realize, my friend!"

Shit.

"Now I'm leaving."

Tyghus sprinted towards Rom, dropping him with a crushing tackle.

"Tyghus, don't kill him! He's not any use to us dead!"

He quickly mounted his chest and hammered the bandit's face with fists. "Oh, he's not dying, Treos. Not yet, he's not!"

He briskly fetched and unfurled a spool of rope from his horse. "I tried to treat you like a man rather than the animal you are. Tried to make reason with you. You don't respect that? You're not interested in that? So be it."

The General quickly tied the woozy bandit's ankles together, with the other end secured to his saddle. He knelt down to grip Rom's bloody cheeks. "*You* listen to *me*, Rom…" the mad man's bi-colored eyes barely cracked open. "Do *not* die on me."

Leaping into his saddle, he kipped the horse and sped east towards the latest plumes.

"*Ride!*"

* * *

This is madness.

Treos and Tyghus watched from the edge of a roiling mob surrounding the caravan's wagon laager.

"This is madness," Tyghus repeated, aloud this time.

The Lakeman sighed. "Aye… aye, it is."

"Hundred, you think?" Tyghus said, eyeing the scene.

"At least that much." Treos glanced at the General. "We doing this, lad? Should we try to find –"

"We're doing this. It's not right to leave them there while we take off trying to find help that may not even exist… it's not right and we don't have the time for it anyway."

"Aye," Treos replied uncertainly.

"You don't have to stay, Treos. Trust you or not, you didn't sign on for this."

"I told ya', dammit, I gave ya' my word. This point in m'life, I got nothin' much left but my honor," the Lakeman shook his head. "Not lettin' these thieves steal that too."

Tyghus smiled, even as his nerves began to tighten. "Aye."

"They're just men, don't forget… not uh… not soldiers. Just gotta get 'em to panic…"

"Aye, I'm telling myself that…" the Ruhl replied with a nod of his head. He glanced behind him at a bow and quiver slung over his beast's saddle. "You much of a bowman, you?"

"No."

"Me neither… but just gotta make them panic, like you said. How bout that ball and chain of yours? You can wield it?"

"Aye…"

"So you launch your links, I'll loose what I can of these bloody sticks, then…" he looked the Lakeman square in the eyes. Treos nodded.

"Then…" Treos smiled.

The two men clasped forearms for a moment before Tyghus looked scornfully behind him.

"And *you*, you stay alive! I've great plans for you!"

The General glared down at the bloody and torn figure of Rom, dragged across the plains all the way. No response came.

A figure suddenly tumbled off the top of the defenses; a roar went up from the mob.

Tyghus took a deep breath. "Gods have mercy… *ride!*"

They dug their heels in and flew into the fray.

* * *

Whit fought like a man possessed, in spite of the terror gripping his limbs. Every raider that climbed up he'd slice down, but they mounted the wall in surging numbers. He jabbed three of them through the waist, keeling them all and sending them off. A fourth, however, stumbled forward into him, knocking him onto his back.

No!

Then he saw it:

Like a knife through lard, a lane carved through the blackshirted mass. He couldn't move but he watched with elation as Tyghus and Treos aboard two tons of horse flattened and hacked their way to the wall. His comrades saw the same and let out a primal scream of their own, rallying their last ounces of strength.

As he'd seen before with these bandits, a panic rippled through them like drops on a pond; before long, those that had not mounted the laager broke and ran. Those hapless enough to remain atop it either flung themselves off or were finally taken down by the guards.

He sighed in relief. *Not today,* he thought, before shaking his head. *Not yet today, anyway.*

* * *

Tyghus finished walking a circle around the laager, having slain the injured bandits around its edge. He would have preferred keeping them as prisoners, but he knew he'd have few to keep watch over them – he barely had enough men to guard the walls against a renewed attack, even if the bandits ran for now. Almost as soon as he had begun his charge and saw the wall's resurgence therewith, the blackshirts melted away.

Tyghus, exhausted now, climbed atop the laager and confirmed his suspicions about his defenses. Barely a handful of the guards remained fit to fight, at least two dozen dead outright, and even some of the women in reserve had fallen. Civilians in the middle huddled in fear, breaking his heart. "I know what this must be like for you," he called down to them. "Believe me, no one expected this."

"*We* expected this!" a Rokhish merchant cried out. "*We've* known of these bastards on the trail for months!"

"Aye, I don't doubt that you have. And trust me when I say I'm going to personally bring this to the attention of the proper folks in the Capital when I return. For now, though, we have to worry about the issues at hand – first and foremost, getting this caravan moving back east. I don't imagine this bandit scum has ventured far and we just don't have the manpower to fight off many more of these attacks. Not an attack on this scale."

He surveyed the wounded. "Pile the dead for a burning. Bind up the wounded –"

"Burn them *here?*"

"Aye, here and now, we can grieve later. We have to lighten any loads in order to make distance from this place by nightfall."

The General slipped down into the center to seek out Whit as others set about unlashing the wagons. But soon, a voice called out from beyond the circle –

"General, what do you want to do with this bounded man?"

Tyghus' eyes burned at the question.

"I'll take care of him."

* * *

They made only a handful of miles before the rains began. The pristine morning sky that oversaw so much death morphed without warning into a menacing gray, the pace of the showers steadily increasing with each hour. The clouds brought nightfall earlier, forcing the group to make camp far sooner than originally planned. Laagered up once more, small firepits beneath wagon overhangs provided the makeshift camp's little light; the dimness fit the somber, quiet tone.

Tyghus stood in the center of the laager, head back with mouth agape, letting the fresh water slake his thirst. Dirt, blood and grime ran down his face and tunic, moreso with his hands' assistance. He was exhausted but couldn't sleep, and he knew it gave the people a small comfort seeing him stand watch. With a shake of his head and a rinse of his eyes, however, he prepared for other business.

He jostled Treos awake in the wagon where he'd been resting. "Treos, I need you to stand guard. I have to tend to something."

Groggily, the Lakeman nodded.

"Gather ya' wits before ya' go in there, Tyghus. Don't lower ya'self to his level…"

Tyghus cracked his knuckles in succession. "Aye."

* * *

"Wake up."

A lone candle sat atop a stool. Its faint light flickered across two faces in the wagon's darkness like wraiths in the night, rain pelting the roof above them.

"Wake up, scum."

Rom's head rolled towards the direction of the voice.

"You hear me?"

Even in the wagon gloom, the raider's face was clearly mauled.

"Untie… me." It was barely more than a whisper.

"No. We tried things your way, remember? You stay in the chair."

"I need… to leave, my friend."

"Not an option. Let me explain how this is going to work, though it's fairly simple."

The face across from Rom disappeared only to appear next to him moments later.

"I'm going to ask questions, you're going to give answers. Do we understand each other?"

"Give me a drink."

"No. Do you understand me?"

"No need for threats, I've nothing to hide. I should warn you, though..." a fit of coughs overcame him. "They'll be here soon."

"Well, we better start then. What's this venture of yours? What do you want?"

"Why assume... that I want anything?"

"What is it? Money? Is that all it is?"

"Why can't I just be passing the time?"

"Because you don't get that many people following you unless you're making them some pretty big promises, Rom."

The bandit snickered. "You'd be surprised how little men will fight for. Maybe at one point it was about money, but not now."

"So what is it now?"

"Nothing," Rom wheezed out with another laugh. "We just like to watch things burn."

Tyghus's exhaustion made it hard to keep his anger at bay. "Whatever your motivation is, what you're doing's forbidden by Imperial law."

"Ah, the life of the black and white soldier. Right is right, wrong is wrong, isn't it, Imperial?"

"You don't make it very difficult."

"You think you're a strong man for failing to see shades of gray. Nothing we do is any different than what the 'Empire' does under color of law. Not a thing. The difference my friend, is that they don't have to sit before me to justify their actions."

"How many are there? Help yourself, Rom, how many are with you?"

"Must be near a thousand by now. Perhaps more."

"A thousand. Inciting rebellion is high treason."

"Aye. But that mistakes our purpose."

"How's that?"

"We don't wish to fight – "

"No, you don't wish to fight those who can *fight back!*"

"We don't wish to fight anybody –"

"And all those assaults reported along the tradeway? Men, women, and children alike?"

The bandit was slow to answer. "Well... they resisted."

"I see."

"And now my question to you –"

"You don't get questions for me –"

"Oh, but I *do*, Nameless One, because they *will* be here tonight," the bandit said with a laugh and a grin, his stale breath permeating the close quarters. "And you have a camp full of injured with a whole lot of people *missing* from that first wagon…"

"Who's missing from the first wagon? Who lives?"

"Now, you *need* to kill me, but then you can't bargain with 'em."

"As if any of you've the nature to bargain."

"We do. They'll just want me back. So what'll *you* do?"

"You lie. Where do you operate from?"

"Southeast of the Jungle's edge. But that's irrelevant. Only thing that's relevant is what you choose tonight… so what'll it be?"

He strained at the waist to lower himself as close as he could to the candle flame.

"Kill me?"

The light danced off his eyes, his hair dangling in the flame.

"You kill me and they might charge… then again, you let me go, they might *still* charge. So tell me, what's 'right' and what's –"

A fist flew out of the shadows into Rom's jaw, rocking his body back into the chair.

"I've seen your friends 'fight'. They don't have the stomach for it."

The bandit wheezed. "Per – haps… but even they… know a wounded beast… when they see one."

Tyghus leaned close to Rom's ear. Then a whisper…

"Then I'll take solace in knowing those vultures will get you back in pieces."

The candle was pinched out, blanketing the wagon in darkness. Rom cackled against the drumbeat of the rain.

"These morals of yours are going to be the death of you, Nameless One. Don't fall asleep - we'll see each other soon! *You better kill me!*"

Rom's laugh reverberated far and wide through the camp.

* * *

"Sleep, Tyghus. Middle of the damned night, I'll stand watch."

"Can't."

The General was delirious with exhaustion, but his attempts to rest in a wagon for even a moment were fruitless. His stomach twisted like a vine, his pulse pounded, his hands shook uncontrollably – the same afflictions that always wracked his body in the hours after battle. He stared straight through the ceiling of his cart before finally giving up and joining the Lakeman atop the wagon wall. Both huddled in dark brown animal skins primed to resist the showers' soaking, drops pounding the wagon tops around them.

"You were right, you know."

"I'm sure I was," Treos replied with a sly smile. "About what, though?"

"Shouldn't have gone in there 'til I had a level head."

"Ya' hit 'im?"

Tyghus nodded.

Treos was slow to respond. "Well, ya'd already given him a roughin' up earlier..."

"Aye, but that was different. He was a threat to flee then; he wasn't any kind of threat in that wagon," he said, shaking his head in shameful frustration. "I shouldn't have let that happen."

"Hard to let my heart bleed for a man like Rom. And sometimes it pays to just do what feels good, not necessarily what *is* good."

Tyghus shook his head again. "No, not for a man of the Sixth. The Sixth's supposed to be better than that. The Sixth doesn't assault its prisoners – not without an order, anyway; it's in our oath."

"Mercy lad, then excuse ya'rself because ya'r not with the Sixth at the moment."

The General thought on the comment briefly then frowned in agreement. "That's the best I can do, I guess," he offered. He turned to look at his companion. "Treos, mate... I'm sorry I questioned your loyalties. The circumstances –"

"Worry not. It was understandable."

"It wasn't, though. I'd no *real* reason to suspect you and it was unfair to do so. Anyone that's fought under Rokhish banners for twenty years deserves better," Tyghus said, before letting out a long sigh. "Gods above, was it really just two days ago that we met?"

"Three now, maybe?" Treos asked with a wink.

"Aye... maybe so."

The two men fell quiet for a moment, staring off into the abyss of the steady rain.

"Ya' know ya' never told me why ya'r even out here, lad."

Tyghus smirked. "Told you I was out here to see the Plains, didn't I?"

"Aye, and that's why I just said ya' never told me why ya'r out here."

"Not a trusting man?"

"Not when I'm being fed bullshit."

The Ruhl laughed. "I –" he started, suddenly feeling embarassed. "No reason, I suppose."

"So I can charge at ya'r side, I can bleed with ya', but I can't know ya' secret?"

"The secret's ridiculous, you're better off with the bullshit."

"So –"

"So I don't know, Treos," he said, rather briskly now. "Why am I out here? Thought I'd find some purpose, I guess; thought I'd find *my* purpose, that is, or with any luck, maybe my purpose would find me."

"Ya'r purpose, eh?"

"Aye."

"Ya'r a man of faith, I take it?"

The question made him smile. "In truth, I am not."

The bald man's expression perked up. "Then whose bloody purpose ya' waitin' on?"

"I told you, I don't know," Tyghus said with a deep exhale. "Maybe my purpose is to die out in here in the rain, on these gods-forsaken plains of the damned."

"I hope that's not true."

"Nor I."

Treos grunted. "So being a soldier isn't enough purpose for ya', eh?"

"Aye, I thought I'd found it in the Sixth, found it in Avergon… thought I'd found it with the right person…"

"Ah," Treos said as he brought a hand to his mouth, stifling a laugh. "So that's what this is."

Tyghus arched a brow at him. "What?"

"The gods, lad," the Lakeman replied with a shake of his head. "Ya' have to laugh at their ways."

"In what sense?"

"In the sense that they'd craft a man brave enough to charge a horde of angry bandits with hardly a care in the world yet leave 'im so a single woman's words can bring 'im low."

"Aye, the power of a woman," the General replied, laughing a bit. "I told you it was silly, didn't I?"

"But much of life is, I've found. That's why ya' can't take it too seriously."

The men shared a chuckle as Treos ran a hand from his bald head down his face to clear away a cascade of rainwater. "Think they'll they come, lad?"

"Rom said they would."

Treos scoffed. "And what's that worth?"

"Rom's a mad man, no doubt. But I do think he's an honest one."

Their silence resumed. With time, Tyghus' head dropped to his chest, finally asleep as the rain beat down upon him.

* * *

"*Imperial!*"

The bellow shattered the night's calm.

"We want him back!"

Tyghus's head snapped up. *Dark still but what hour was it?* His eyes scanned the ground in front of him, but the rain left him blind beyond ten or fifteen yards.

"Treos, do you see them?"

The Lakeman shook his head.

"We want him, Imperial. Give him to us!"

Tyghus's heart raced uncontrollably. "Tell me why I'd even consider it!"

No response at first. Then, *"I'll let these folks tell ya'."*

Suddenly, wailing could be heard. Closer and closer, until figures appeared from the mist, lit by the camp's faint glow. The lead figure was a woman.

Didn't the lead cart bring only men? Tyghus thought hazily. *Did she flee another wagon?*

"In all the excitement earlier, you left your friends behind," screamed the voice once more. *"They can live or die, I leave it up to you!"*

Tyghus's temper flared anew. *"Do you realize who I bloody am?* Who you're trying to extort?"

"Aye. But we both know extortion's the least of our offenses. This is your last chance."

The wailing grew louder. By this point, the remaining able-bodied Rokh fighters had heard the commotion and climbed aboard the makeshift ramparts.

"Three."

How do I even know she's from the caravans? Does it matter?

"Two."

"Don't you touch her –"

"One."

"Don't –"

The crying suddenly stopped – the figure slumped forward. Tyghus' jaw slackened. *"You bloody cowards!"*

"How many more, Imperial?"

Another figure suddenly appeared in the lead. Closer this time. A large Stolxian man shorn of a shirt with hands bound behind him. Shivering but silent.

"Three... two..."

"Show yourselves!"

"One."

A gurgling gasp arose from the man – he fell forward.

"Vermin!"

"Tyghus, fetch him."

The General looked at Treos incredulously.

"Lad, there's a thin line between foolishness and courage..." the older man burned into the younger. "One can quickly become the other."

"*Three.*"

Tyghus slicked his soaked hair back with both hands. He looked to a Rokh at his right.

"Guard… fetch the prisoner."

"*Two.*"

"We're bloody fetching him!"

The counting stopped.

"Send the rest forward!"

"*Not until we see him.*"

After several tense moments, Rom appeared on the wagontop with Treos and Tyghus. The bandit locked eyes with Tyghus, grimacing with each limping step he took to the edge.

"You see him. Now send them forward."

A huddled collection of horrified Stolxians appeared out of the mist. Though an inhumanly stoic race, fear pervaded their faces. Tyghus looked back to Rom.

"Your freedom awaits."

"I see that, friend."

"I *will* be back for you."

The bandit broke into a broad, bloody smile.

"I know."

With a mocking salute, Rom gingerly climbed down the outside of the wagon wall. Passing through the mass of Stolxians, he turned and waved one last time before disappearing into the darkness.

"Help the hostages in, guards," Tyghus said finally. "Then brace for charge."

He sank to one knee and waited.

* * *

The attack never came.

Dawn broke within an hour of the last parlay with the bandits. But for the slain merchants outside the wagons, there wasn't a trace of the voice or anyone that may have accompanied it. Like the whole thing never happened. Tyghus ordered the convoy back on the move, east whence it came, but despite the trek remaining surprisingly attack-free, there was little discourse in the party.

Treos said he stayed with the group as an added blade but Tyghus could tell it was to mend the General's wounded pride and anger. Sure enough, he saw the twenty-four hour frenzy in his mind over and over, and on more than one occasion Treos had to talk him back from tracking the bandits on foot. By the time they arrived back at the Capital almost seven weeks later,

Tyghus had but one object on his mind:
    Revenge.

Chapter VII

Even when you've turned your gaze from Fortune,
Fortune hasn't turned its gaze from you.

Rokh Proverb

Dray'gon Rokh, Tanokhun, 19ᵗʰ Day of the Eleventh Month, Y. 383 P.C.

By the day's High Sun, thousands of frenzied Rokhs jammed the Tanokhun. Every vendor within a mile of the Capital's market square had their makeshift pavilions set up to peddle their wares, with no shortage of customers to oblige. Golden obelisks towered over the crowd at the market's four corners, which marked the formal end of the Rokhish tradeweays by listing distances to all the major establishments of the Empire; 1,320 miles to Nar-Biluk, 1,144 miles to Avergon, 792 miles to the Converge, 1,232 miles to Cros'syng Way, to name a few.

But Tyghus was in no mood to indulge in the bartering or learn distances. Adorning black trousers and an ashen long-sleeved tunic beneath a white shawl, he perched six-feet high on a marble wall surrounding the market's central monument. His eyes were fixed on the paveway sloping south towards the square from the Arxun, the rows of Gurum homes next to it dwarfed by the *Styliun*, the mighty arena looming in the city's northeast.

"I've never seen anything like this," Treos called to him from the ground below, shouting to be heard over the market's din. "This many people, this many buildings – this much stone – can't imagine living this way, lad."

Tyghus's face was blank. "Nor I."

He sensed the Lakeman taking in the scope of the massive statue behind Tyghus, thrice as tall as a man. Carved from the blue stone peaks of the Karanaks, the figure stood in a billowing robe up to and including the head. A bearded face peered out over the crowd, right hand steadying a sword pointed to his feet, left hand outstretched as if pardoning an enemy.

"Cassyus?"

"Pardon?"

"Cassyus of Kyles I presume?"

Focus broken, Tyghus glanced back to the Empire's founder and first Khorokh. "Aye, looks to be."

Treos's eyes probed him, clearly catching the General's curt tone.

"Ya' know lad, I warned ya' before about talking before your head's cooled –"

"Kyrus knows me, Treos."

"Aye, but do ya' know him now?"

Tyghus looked down at the man with annoyed incredulity. "What?"

"He's not Kyrus, ya' childhood friend anymore, is he? He's Kyrus, one of the *nine* Lorrions."

Tyghus's gaze returned to the paveway. "Well, in either case, I approach him on Rokh business, not personal. Gods above, the Empire's allies and citizens are being slaughtered by a bandit-king on one of our most vital trade routes! I consider it my *duty* to seek him out."

"Just remember who he works for now – he works for the Throne."

"We all work for the Throne."

"But he's gotta be careful 'bout who he shows himself with – everyone'll be watching him now."

The General clenched his jaw as he thought about it. "And here I thought you'd be loathe to politics."

The Lakeman smiled broadly. "Loathe to 'em, but not ignorant to 'em. The Gateway was a mini-kingdom in its own right, so I saw the schemes myself, day in, day out," he said before a shake of his head. "'A man of importance is a man watched', they used to say out there."

"So what's a friend of the important?"

"Suspicious," Treos laughed, his partner smiling despite efforts not to.

"A jester and a soldier."

"But anyway, ya' approach on Rokh affairs – nothin' personal..."

"That's right, and that looks to be him now."

A brilliant cascade of red paraded down the whitestone bricks of the Khorian Som, the Capital's main road running as far as the Gurums south of the Market and north through the Arxun. Patrons of the Tanokhun soon took notice, especially when they saw that the "red" formed a hollow square around a tall individual adorned in purple stripes draped across a gray tunic. A neatly trimmed beard framed his mouth with long hair braided down his back.

"There's the damn Lorrion," Tyghus allowed with guarded excitement. "Come on."

Tyghus leading the way, the pair snaked through the crowd to the point where the Som spawned two additional paveways – one westward towards the Merchant Gurums, which, in conjunction with the Som formed the market's northeast corner; another led eastwards towards the Metal Gurums. From the intersection, the General stared directly at the cadre while forming a fist over his heart.

As he drew closer, the Lorrion saw the salute and grinned. "Guard, let the men pass."

The square dutifully parted at the middle, allowing Tyghus and Treos to enter and give a hearty forearm exchange.

"Well damn it all, I'd heard you died reaping grain on the Plains."

"And you from boredom in Lorrio sessions?"

"Probably more than once. How are you, my friend?"

"I'm alive – and for that I owe a debt to my friend here, Treos Lokner. He's formerly with the Tenth at Cros'syng Way but was born to Loccea."

Kyrus's mouth tightened a bit. "A friend from the Lakes," Kyrus echoed as he eyed Treos and exchanged arm grips.

"A *man* from the Lakes, anyway," Treos replied with an easy smile.

The Lorrion didn't reciprocate. "Indeed."

Tyghus quickly saw that Kyrus didn't catch Treos's quip – or didn't want to – and moved to intervene. "After what we went through, he's a friend, believe me."

Kyrus glanced at Tyghus then back to the Lakeman. "Well then, pleased to meet you, Treos."

"Lorrion."

Tyghus looked at the Rubitian ghosts around him and smiled. "Some entourage you have here."

"A necessity of my office, I'm told," Kyrus said, before waving beyond the square to the gathering of Rokhish commoners nearby. "Though frankly it'd be impossible to venture beyond the Arxun's gates otherwise."

Tyghus surveyed the mob edging towards them. "Maybe we'd be better off talking within the gates then?"

Kyrus leaned in close to Tyghus's ear, whispering, *"that's not a place to speak freely."*

"I see… I just wanted to discuss –"

"Personal or Imperial matters?"

The General considered the question for a moment. "Both." *May as well be honest.*

Kyrus pulled back, silently nodding. He turned to a Red at one of his square's "corners".

"You – take half and keep the crowd from following. The rest, head east with us."

He turned back to his two guests. "We'll fetch a groghouse in the Gurums east of here."

"There's grog there? Thought the East Gurums were just metalshops."

The Lorrion gave no response but continued gesturing towards his guards. Soon they were split as instructed, and the group headed east. Tyghus and Treos exchanged glances as they adjusted to the quick-step of the unit, Kyrus a few steps in front of them.

"They're crime-ridden at best, no?" Tyghus called to him. "Are they any safer for us than here?"

His friend turned sharply and drew in close again, whispering harshly, *"in the absence of a unit of Reds? No, but state deals are resolved in those backwaters, away from the ears and whispers of the Arxun and Tanokhun."*

The dash eastwards then continued in silence. The frenzy of the market crowd faded as the winding road took them deep into the desolate rundown borough, ringing with the sporadic sounds of hammers striking anvils. The manicured stone of the Khorian Som was left behind in favor of the worn, cracked rock of the Gurums. Smoke from the district's countless metalworking shops flooded the area, casting a gray pall over their movement. The sun was nothing but a dull orb.

Wedged in between workshops were huts of sloppily stacked stones and straw beneath red-tiled roofs. Through any windows, the homes were black as night.

"By the gods, where is everybody?" Tyghus managed between gags.

"Asleep. The City forbids them from forging in the daylight hours. The westward winds would carry smoke and ash down over the rest of the Districts."

Tyghus grimaced. "This is the fog when the workers are asleep?"

"It is – most keep their furnaces smoldering through their 'night'."

Tyghus looked to the Lakeman trotting with him. "Far from the pristine Lakes, aren't we?"

Treos could only nod as he suppressed coughs with his fist.

"Stop. In here."

The party halted on Kyrus's command. At first, Tyghus saw no sign of tenancy – then to his left flickered a faint light inside a structure looking no different than any of the huts they'd passed. He looked to Kyrus, who only nodded without expression, then addressed the guards.

"Block the entrance."

The Reds immediately fanned out in a semi-circle around the entryway to the purported groghouse.

"Come, Tyghus," Kyrus motioned towards the General. Treos followed suit until Kyrus's hand immediately shot up. "No – not you."

The Lakeman's eyes flitted from Kyrus's icy blues to a surprised Tyghus. "Kyrus, he's a friend, I told –"

"Can't permit it. He waits here."

With a turn, Kyrus disappeared into the hut.

"Apologies, I wouldn't have wasted your time had I known."

Continuing to battle coughs, he simply stared back and offered, "understood."

* * *

The air was thick in the dank, musty bar. The floor carried not the slightest trappings of elegance, just dirt mixed with smashed stone. Beyond a few ancient wooden tables, there was no reason to believe the room was fit for humanity at all.

A grisled man hunched over a countertop, his blackish shirt masking layers of filth and grime. Long ebony hair matted his head and face, blending in with a nest of a beard. His eyes were open, though they appeared vacant in the dim light. He immediately served up drinks when his patrons entered, seemingly without any expectation of payment. To the farthest corner the friends took their grogs.

"The hell was that, Kyrus?" Tyghus immediately demanded, pointing to the door.

"I don't know know the slightest thing about that man. Frankly, how can you?"

"Almost two months on the Plains with him, I think I can vouch for him. What's your suspicion?"

"Suspicion? He's from the Lakes for one, that's not enough? Loccea Province's been rebelling for centuries."

"Gods above, Kyrus," Tyghus said with a roll of his eyes, even if Kyrus was right in at least one sense – the Province's reputation was well-earned, its history as turbulent as any in the Empire. Unlike the other Early Kingdoms taken over by the Rokhs, the Loccycs had rarely been ruled a single person, its natural state given more to a roiling pot of rival fiefdoms and strongholds. The region's unique geography was to blame, with its lush oases and crystal-clear lakes isolated from each other by stretches of arid desert. Warlords, under the guises of 'kings', each claimed a lake but rarely mustered the power to dethrone more than a few of their Loccean rivals, and certainly proved no match against the eventual Clannic tidal wave. When the Rokhs expelled the Clans from Loccea in the 90s, however, they found the natives just as hostile toward their 'liberators' as they'd been toward their conquerors. The last three hundred years, in fact, were marred by no less than five rebellions led by Loccean princes claiming descent from their Early days, notwithstanding the extensive Rokhish fortification and settlement in the Province since.

But all that being said, Kyrus was ultimately in the wrong here, Tyghus thought stubbornly. "Those of *Loccean descent* have been rebelling for centuries," he said. "Which Treos *isn't*. He's born of Rokhs who settled there."

Kyrus glanced away from the logic. "Aye, well I still find it interesting that he simply happened to join your party and the next thing I know I'm getting reports that your convoy was sacked by raiders."

"Maybe so, but he took his fair share of raider heads during that time. He bloody well saved my life and a whole slew of others out there."

"It's irrelevant anyway," the Lorrion said sharply. "No discussions of the state can be had with commoners, and with his two names I presume he's no Ruhl?"

"Okay, so leave it at that, then," Tyghus said, unconvinced. He recognized Kyrus's tell-tale signs of jealousy and insecurity from the moment he shook hands with Treos. "Don't sit there and call *my* judgment into question."

Kyrus looked to the table with hands spread deferentially towards his friend.

Tyghus shook his head, trying to keep their meeting from spoiling. "So why don't you just disguise yourself, anyway? Take the damn colors off for a moment? Trim that hideous beard."

"The colors are sacred I'm told," the Lorrion replied, refusing to lighten just yet. "When I adorned them, I adorned them for life."

Tyghus's eyes widened. "For life? Even when bedding a wom—"

"Aye…" the Lorrion groaned, suppressing a smile.

"I foresee some astounded women in your future."

"I was kidding, you boar-ass," Kyrus corrected as they finally shared a chuckle. "Beyond my chambers, I must wear them."

Tyghus took a drink before looking back at the door they entered through. "This is all necessary? You're really so watched?"

"We're just better off here. The moment I'm seen talking with someone within the gates, the rumors spread, and rumors are as good as facts here. I can't have it, at least not until I figure out who I can trust in the Arxun – though I don't think that person exists."

"Making friends, Kyrus?" Tyghus said. "But besides, I'd think the crown and Council would want to know what's happening out on the Plains, regardless of their affiliation."

"They already know, Tyghus."

"What do you mean, 'they know'?"

"They know about the turmoil, there's just only so much the Lorrio is willing to dedicate to the Westlands."

Tyghus felt his blood start to boil. "No, with all due respect, they don't have the slightest idea," he growled, smiling in annoyed disbelief. "There's practically an *insurrection* taking place on the Dead Plains, Kyrus. This man, this – Rom character, he brought what had to be hundreds to bear on my caravan train, alone. How's that right? How's that fair?"

Kyrus stared back blankly.

"That means nothing? What more's the Lorrio looking for before 'dedicating' their attention to it?"

"Tyghus, it's more than just simply 'right' or 'wrong' –"

"It's not! The rest of it is just –"

"All I can I say is that you don't know what goes on within the Arxun. Every man, from the lowest minister to the Khorokh himself, he wages his own campaign. And any suggestion that troops are sent anywhere causes suspicion if not an uproar."

Tyghus grimaced. "It's that fractured in there?"

Kyrus's eyes said it all, but his friend shook his head and persisted. "Kyrus, get me troops. A thousand. Even with five hundred I could bring these honorless bastards to justice and cleanse the Tradeway of their filth!"

"You're not even stationed in the Westlands, you're a kordette of the Sixth in Avergon! Now you want a *kord* of some other dyron's men? How would I even broach the topic to the Lorrio?"

"Well, if not me, then tell Kylea's Proventor to have the Second Dyron lining the roads; the Plains are in his bloody province, by the gods. I'll testify before the Lorrio myself and tell them what I saw, I'll leave you out of it. Let them tell me 'no' –"

"I'm barely two months in, Tyghus, and I'm telling you that the Lorrio rests on a pane of glass when it comes to the army. That the pane hasn't broken yet is a sign of the gods' good graces."

Tyghus's heart still raced as he bore down on his friend. "Valogar?"

"*Shh!*" Kyrus snapped, apprehension clearly growing. He dashed his head around to glimpse the barkeeper – who thankfully looked no less comatose than he did upon arrival. The Lorrion's fingers began to fidget. "Speaking of which, what about your sister? You're leaving for the union soon anyway; Nar-Biluk's at least several weeks' off, even if you beat the snows."

But Tyghus wouldn't be deterred by the banter. "I'm telling you, Kyrus, there's a pane cracking in Kylea Province as we speak, maybe even the West as a whole. Do you realize at least one of the Stolxian kings are threatening to arm their trade convoys if the chaos doesn't cease? Stolxian troops on Rokhish lands, and this latest debacle won't help!"

Kyrus scowled in disbelief. "They wouldn't – who said that?"

"Whit!"

"Who?"

"Whit Harrall, that impish fellow that organized the troops for the convoy in the first place. He's the Quartermaster of the Cros'syng Way garrison; tells me he gets threats almost daily from Stolxian diplomats; that they're waiting for the slightest pretext to cross the Anonga. And he doesn't need to say that if the Beastmen caught wind of Stolxians in their midst, the whole Jungle would erupt!"

Kyrus slugged his drink back, a good portion streaming down either side of his mouth, before slamming the mug down on the table. "I see."

"Does the Crown want to be remembered as the one who finally touched off the war with the Stolxians? Does the Lorrio?" Tyghus warned. "Trade issues aside, the shortest of them has to be seven, eight damn feet high – their battle axes even more so!" He pleaded with his eyes. "There's a *reason* you were stationed in the Arxun –"

"Indeed there is."

"—and it's to resolve matters like these!"

The Lorrion looked to the table for a moment before meeting the General's eyes. "I'll mention it, Tyghus, you have my word. But you stay in Starrea Province. You stay in Avergon."

Frustrated, Tyghus shot back, "Kyrus, they humiliated me. As a *man*, I'm begging you to let me –"

"Tyghus, I've recommended you for command of the Sixth."

The General froze like a sculpture. "What?"

Kyrus let out a smile. "I recommended – I *told* the Lorrio that you'll be taking over command in Avergon – assuming you accept."

Seeing Tyghus was speechless, the Lorrion continued. "I'd have done this in Avergon and given you the procession this honor warrants had I known the decision was mine to make. Unfortunately, the Emperor only informed me a few weeks ago, after you'd headed out."

"You've spoken with the Emperor?" Tyghus muttered.

Kyrus's eyes danced away from Tyghus's. "Through his channels, aye. A man named Oratus runs his affairs, and he told me the Emperor gave his blessing to my choice of Dyrator. So, in light of that..."

Kyrus reached his hands down the front of his tunic and pulled out a silver necklace, slipping it over his head. As he dropped it to the table, Tyghus could see a sizable brooch attached bearing the swirling Imperial blooddrop seal and a Stygan Bull emblem. With a flick of Kyrus's wrist, the necklace skitted across the table until it struck Tyghus's hand. "Take it. The Bulls of War are yours."

The younger man just stared at the brooch, speechless again.

"Moments ago you wanted to ride forth and re-conquer the West, now the Empire's most famous post is too much?"

"I just don't think I'm worthy of it."

"So keep proving you are. You know how to command, your battles in the Desert show you can throw your welfare to the wind when the time calls for it. Now, you just need to focus on this," Kyrus said, tapping his head.

"Well-taken, brother, I promise you," Tyghus said, eyes still transfixed on the brooch.

"I believe you," Kyrus said with sincerity, chuckling as he watched his fiery friend grasp what he was given. "Your sister's in for a shock at her wedding next month, isn't she?"

"Aye," Tyghus said, holding the necklace for the first time. "Thank you, Kyrus. Your name's going to be impossible to match."

With an approving nod in the General's direction, Kyrus turned toward the bar. "Two more –"

A Red stood silently in the doorway.

Kyrus eyed him with suspicion. "Aye?"

"You've been beckoned to a meeting, my lord," the Red's hollow voice boomed.

"I'm in a meeting right now, by whose orders?"

"Jarax, my lord."

"Jarax?"

"On behalf of His Highness. He convenes the Lorrio at the *Halum*."

Kyrus slowly turned back towards Tyghus, who met him with concerned eyes. "*Unusual?*" he whispered.

"*Very.*"

"My lord," the Red called sternly. "I'm told His Highness must not be kept waiting."

"I heard you, Rubitian, you think I didn't?" the Lorrion snapped. The helmeted Red stared back silently. "I guess this means farewell for now, my friend. I'll call on you again before you head out; we'll finish this."

Tyghus rose to exit with him, but after Kyrus passed the Red thrust an open palm into Tyghus's chest. "Wait here," the helmet bellowed. "Lorrion Kyrus returns alone."

Were it not for being startled at the man's bluntness, the General's fury might have returned. But restraint prevailed, and after a spell, the Red ceded his position at the door. Tyghus cautiously made his way out onto the blackened street, but found desolation broken only by Treos's silhouette against an adjacent building. In either direction he looked, there wasn't a trace of the party.

The only sound was a westward wind whistling through the narrow corridor.

Chapter VIII

"To carry on the rebuilding and rebirth of the blessed Rokh peoples, let my heir stem from the men of the learned Lorrio; for they have proven to me, through their tireless efforts and guidance, that there is no better sample of men."

Succession Proclamation of Khorokh Cassyus I,
to the People of Dray'gon Rokh, 30 P.C.

Dray'gon Rokh, Lorrian Halum, 19th Day of the Eleventh Month, Y. 383 P.C.

Footsteps echoed through the cavernous hall. Nine Lorrions sat entranced around an oval table blanketed in cool blue light from high-walled windows above. Tension infected all that were present – after all, the Khorokh rarely convened meetings with his Lorrio beyond the usual four dates per year, and certainly not without providing the issues beforehand.

Kyrus's position at one of the head seats split the table into rival halves. To his left sat Antinax of Kylea Province, the eldest and most prominent of the four Nortic Lorrions. His thinning mass of short, silver locks was pushed back to reveal a massive forehead punctured by deep brown eyes. His face wore a permanent grimace, cheeks and jowls sinking inexorably downward, and even when he talked, his face hardly moved. But as unassuming as the man's appearance may have been, his mind was sharp as a blade's edge and his guile was legendary among allies and foes alike in the Arxun.

To Kyrus's right was the Nortics' most hated antagonist. Though shorter tenured than his three fellow Lowland Lorrions sitting next to him, Castus of Morremea Province had quickly seized the mantle for representing Sudo interests. Keeping with the style of his homeland in the Splintered Shoals, his long hair flowed only from atop his head, leaving the sides completely knife-shaven. His circular, handsome face's blue eyes angled towards the steps, small creases of aging just beginning to appear at their sides.

A platter of chalices sat unfilled in front of Kyrus, with no one having the stomach to drink at the moment. That the two rival factions sat opposite each other without bickering spoke to their perceived gravity of the meeting. Indeed, even their breathing seemed to stop upon closer inspection of the man approaching them.

Khorokh Rynsyus I hobbled towards the gathering. A cloth in his right hand appeared soaked in blood as it stifled phlegmy coughs, while in his left, a staff of the finest wood propped up a famished, enfeebled body. Dark blankets covered the man from shoulders to feet, despite the room's warmth from nearby fires; even with his insulation, however, his pallor was unmistakable. Two servants followed close behind with a royal seat to be placed at the head of the table opposite Kyrus, which the ruler gratefully fell into. More booming hacks shook the hall, but after several wheezing breaths, his gravelly voice rolled across the table.

"For thirty-five years, I've held the title of Khorokh, Emperor of the Unified Rokhs and the Ten Provinces. For fifteen before that I served on the Lorrio as you do. Over those decades I've worked with this Lorrio towards the betterment of the Rokhish people, though whether I've met that goal is for the scribes to decide, I suppose. Whatever the outcome, I've done what I thought to be right; right in my heart, and right by the lowest commoner affected by my decisions."

More coughs.

"I'm dying, brethren."

The group remained motionless as Kyrus's stomach turned.

"The healers… they say I may've a day left in this world, maybe a month. I've beseeched the gods to let me live long enough to know the Valogar-Rokh union in Nar-Biluk came to pass, for I believe my legacy will be set by that marriage – I've seen it in my dreams, I swear it. It's the gods' will."

A servant offered the Emperor a cup of water, but he hardly consumed any before he had to dismiss it. He cleared his throat before laboring on.

"Thirty-five years ago, Emperor Terrius selected me from the Lorrio as heir apparent to his throne. Today, by Imperial law, I do the same."

Antinax and Castus's eyes immediately met. A hint of an upturn appeared on the Sudo's mouth.

Rynsyus's still lively eyes scanned the gathering for a moment before his eyebrows spiked. "But never… *never* did I anticipate having to choose from a pettier, more *selfish* gathering than what I see here today! Your consumption with your own interests, a drunkenness born of such *vanity* that I scarcely recognize you as my Council, it's held this realm hostage for the better part of my tenure. And part of that is my failing," the old man said, jabbing a finger into chest. "It's my greatest regret that I could not emulate the lauded Emperors of past generations; that I could not… *inspire* my Lorrio to the collaborative exploits that marked the greatest rulers before me. But still, it baffles me to think that *you* –" The ruler's hand flew out to his right towards Antinax. "—would rather vilify and scheme against those on my left, all in the name of your own bloodlust towards Valogar. And *you* –" his wobbly hand waved over Castus's side. "—what do you do for the sake of unity beyond oppose every breath they take or even spread rumors of Lowland secession? Threaten it, even! For shame, all of you!"

Stillness gripped the table as the Khorokh's last words finished echoing. "So in lieu of your deadlock, *I've* had to rule these lands without guidance or input from my own Council, the very body set up by our forefathers to do so. Where do you find such – such – such *gall* to elevate your own conceits over those of the Empire?"

"There's right, and there's wrong, Highness."

The table's eyes instantly shifted in Antinax's direction.

"How *dare* you speak against the Crown?" Castus demanded, incensed.

"He asked a question," the Nortic said calmly. "His Highness clearly wants our candor this day as he beats us about the brow with his fraudulent lamentations, so let's indulge him and speak plainly – Terrius thought he was giving his seat to a man who would *finish* off rebellious Valogarians, not one that would bow to them once his conscience began to weigh! Besides, you, young one, have spoken against the Crown as much by your actions as any words of mine."

"Meaning what, Antinax?"

Antinax glared at Castus. "You know precisely what I'm referring to."

"Then speak candidly, as you promised," the Sudo challenged. "Speak it before the Emperor if you're so confident!"

The Nortic let a silent stare linger between the two. "I'll leave the specifics of your indiscretions for another day," he growled in near whisper before a louder tone returned. "If rejecting the foolish idea that placating Valogarians will somehow coax them into a lasting peace means that I've 'elevated personal conceit' over that of the Realm's, then so be it. That 'peace' –"

"Are we *really* getting drawn into this, *today* of all times?" Castus groaned.

"*That peace* is simply allowing them and their Colverian allies to rearm and rebuild, and no marriage of Valogarian and Rokh can change that. We are peoples whose aims and cultures are fundamentally opposed to one another – *we* hold a mandate descended from the gods to rule the lands within our reach; *they* –"

"The Rokhish Empire, divine beyond the ability to compromise!"

"– do nothing but harbor and *encourage* those vile Purebloods to seek destruction of Imperial interests, north of the Clyves or south! So I'll say it again as I have so many times – there is right, and there is *wrong!*"

"Oh, we're all aware of your definition of right and wrong, Antinax," Castus snapped, rising to his feet. "It's right when you speak, wrong when anyone else. Though I'll say, your comments on Valogar ring most hollow of them all, given that you've never even shaken the hand of a Valogarian, let alone bartered with one."

"*Quiet!*" the Emperor bellowed.

"So I must shake hands with a heathen to know he's a heathen?"

"No, but it'd lend credibility to your boasts of speaking for the Empire – an Empire that includes Lowlanders elated with Valogarian peace. Even a peace that doesn't go far enough."

"*Quiet I say!*"

But the Emperor was drowned out by a table erupting, both sides jockeying to be heard.

With a sudden sweep of his arm, Kyrus sent the chalices crashing to the marble floor, shattering in tremendous cacophony.

"*Enough!* I pray that you're so disrespected as you give your dying declarations some day! Agree with him or not, he *is* the Khorokh!"

Silence ensued, Antinax sitting placidly with his scowl, Castus lowering down gently. Kyrus's chest heaved with disgust, having never borne witness to such dysfunction in the flesh. He was certainly no proponent of Rynsyus, but no leader of men deserved such insult, and the Lorrions' sadly typical behavior only further eroded his desire to reach out to any of them. "I mean, gods above!" he blurted out in an exasperated, scolding tone.

Only man one looked at him – the Khorokh himself. The old man's eyes were flushed with blood, and a trickle of the same fell from his lips. The blankets rose and fell with his heavy breaths.

"What's a ruler to do? What would Cassyus have done in his time? If I could ask the Founder but one question, just one – *that* would be mine." He sighed. "Alas, my decision springs from a more humble, less learned mind…"

Castus bowed his head toward the table, barely able to watch the words come from the Emperor's mouth.

"Kyrus the Younger will take the throne upon my demise. Whenever the gods so will it to be."

Gods, no.

He'd charged against ten to one odds. He'd seen his family taken from him before his very eyes. But nothing prepared Kyrus for the tremor that rippled through his body following the Khorokh's statement. His heart pounded, his vision tinted yellow. Tightness gripped his chest. Every ounce of anger he'd felt moments before turned to utter terror.

No one stirred but Castus, who reeled as if struck by an arrow. An uncontrollable "what?" escaped him.

"You cannot be serious," a blunt young Nortic named Volinex said.

Rynsyus glared at the Nortic. "Effective immediately, he will be stationed in the Brex under Rubitian supervision. He'll assume the Honor the moment I take my walk with Death."

Let this be a nightmare. Let me awake.

"This is a travesty," Antinax grumbled. "*This* is going to be your legacy, you know that? Not some marriage that will crumble before the bride's even been deflowered."

Rynsyus ignored the comments and let his eyes fall upon Kyrus. "I beg you all to unite under your new Khorokh, in a way you never seemed inclined to do under me. Kyrus, you have my congratulations. Jarax will see to it you are properly accounted for in your move from the *Norum*'s lodgings to the Brex."

Castus remained dumbfounded, his temperament betrayed by his face. "But – his Lorrionship? What of it?"

"As Anti' no doubt recalls from my selection, given his recitation of Rokhish history this evening, the void left on the Lorrio is to be filled by one selected and agreed upon by a majority vote of the remaining Lorrions. Until that agreement is reached, the Imperial Scribe and Speaker stands in the departed's stead."

"*Oratus?*" Castus exclaimed. "The man's no mind for Lorrian matters!"

"I disagree. As part of his lifetime appointment, he's charged with being learned in Rokhish history and affairs, and to dispose of that wisdom in assisting the Lorrio. Nevertheless, that is Rokhish law, something I'd expect a Lorrion to have known." The Emperor cast one last glare at the Sudo upstart, before looking to his rear. "Your assistance, my good men."

The two servants rushed to the dying man's side to hoist him up. With cane back in hand, he was able to turn and begin shuffling back whence he came. A pall gripped the room, its quietude broken once again by heavy feet. For a moment, however, the steps stopped.

"And Antinax —"

The scowling man looked to the Emperor, whose back faced him.

"— say what you will about why Terrius selected me; say it's because he thought me a warmonger. But it's not weakness that causes a man to see the error in his ways — it's his greatest strength."

Darkness shrouded the door the Emperor finally left by, but the moment he passed through it a torrent of bright red appeared, headed by Jarax's familiar face. The Rubator strode towards the table with eyes locked on one target, his platoon of guards forming a square around the gathering. Even in his stupor, Kyrus was familiar with Jarax's protocol, who reached out to the Lorrion with open palm. *"This is really happening,"* he muttered to himself.

"I believe we're to escort you to the Khorian Brex, my Lord?"

Kyrus's eyes flicked around him, still unmet by the Lorrio at large. "Aye," he finally offered.

"Very good."

Clasping forearms, he hoisted Kyrus to his feet. The sea of crimson flowed back towards the darkened exit like water to a drain. Kyrus hadn't even the time to glance back at the Lorrio he was leaving before the door slammed shut behind them.

* * *

Antinax's comrades were furious.

Upon gaining the composure to leave the Lorrian Halum in good order, the four Nortics retired to the lodgings of their youngest member, Volinex, who had ascended to the Lorrio representing Loccea Province only ten years prior. Lorrions had lavish abodes called Norums in the floors above the Halum, this suite in particular sprawling over six different rooms, all cut from light-gray marble and adorned with relics of Lorrions past. Man-sized statues of its former inhabitants stood solemnly in the main hall from which the rooms branched off, silent watchers over all who passed. Brownshaded spiraling mosaics were cut into the floors, while sprawling arches interrupted the columns that lined the walls. The party gathered where the hall ended, in a magnificent circular atrium, perhaps ten yards abreast. Pillars, wrapped in dying vines, soared upwards to prop up a concave glass ceiling. A serene pool of water formed the room's centerpiece, around which curved stone benches topped with plush, downy pillows were arranged.

Antinax sat silently on one of the benches while taking in two of his colleagues' histrionics. To his left reclined Wollia, a wealthy woman with ancient estates west of Dray'gon Rokh. Representing Draygonea Province, she'd served alongside him for thirty of his forty-three years on the Lorrio, though her lush auburn locks made her look someone half her age. Her chestnut eyes had reduced men to a babble through the years, and the creases which made their way onto her face managed to convey only refinement, not agedness. A deep blue robe of the finest thread flowed down the length of her body, accentuating the curves that had made her so desired. Since becoming a widow some ten years prior, she had been the object of many statesmen's pursuits; though she quite clearly enjoyed the attention, she appeared content to remain unattached. Her detached air hid an underlying intensity, and Anti' knew she must have been stifling a laugh watching Volinex's pacing.

"Two fucking months he's been on the Council. *Two.* How the hell could this have happened? I mean, two months!"

"Old man's lost himself, clearly," said Barannus, a squat, chubby man from Astorea Province with a penchant for erupting only behind the safety of closed doors. "That disease of his has taken his mind."

"Aye. And who even knew he was so ill? How did no one tell us this? What do we pay our spies for, their good humor?"

"But by the gods, *Kyrus.* Why not just pick Castus, at least he's an evil we *know* —"

Antinax soon had enough. "Because the Emperor treasures the chaos that has mooted the Lorrio over the last decade, you should know that by now!"

Barannus grimaced. "That's not —"

But Anti' had no time for the junior's offense. "*You should know that by now!* How else could he have done what he's done since?"

"Well —"

"After ten years on the Council, you still don't know his mind, Barannus? He knows if he assigns a Sudo to the throne then we'd just vote in a fifth Nortic and have majority again, just as the opposite is true. He knows that *we* know about the coin Castus and his friends have been channeling to Nar-Biluk all these years, and he *knows* we'd make that public should he ever gain power. Hell, Castus bloody well knows it, too."

Antinax sighed. "So it always had to be Kyrus, whether now or ten years from now," he said, before sardonically adding, "much as I think your talents go to waste here, Voli'."

Volinex hardly noticed the slight as he continued pacing, asking questions to no one in particular. "Who *is* Kyrus? Looks so morose all the time, I don't think I've spoken a word to him in weeks. What could *Rynsyus* really know of him?"

Barannus rubbed his bald sweaty head. "His Ceremony said all anyone seems to know, as far as I'm aware. Survived one of the bush massacres in the '70s; strong reputation in battle. Father was an ascendant figure at the time of his death. Native of Kyrogon."

Voli' waved his arms dismissively. "His estates may be in Kyrogon but his family raised him in the Lowlands if what little I've been told is correct. His father was stationed in Valogar, so probably spent his youth in Attikon with the rest of the army families."

"Aye, I've heard the same."

"So from Kyrogon... grew up in Attikon..." Volinex muttered, rubbing his chin thoughtfully as Antinax's hunched figure looked on. "Well, either way, he's an army grunt, not a man of politics. So who could he know up here? Or who *does* he know up here, should I say? Kyrid families haven't been relevant in the Capital in years."

"Only one he's been seen mingling around the city with is Tyghus of Tygonium, a soldier of his dyron. His old dyron that is – he's given command in Avergon over to Tyghus, so he clearly favors him." Barannus frowned. "Though I'm hearing Tyghus is just as wide-eyed about the Capital as Kyrus; no sign of an interest in political affairs, although it *is* his sister that weds the barbarian king next month."

"We'll have to account for him, then. But one man? There's no one else he's known to favor? No other soldiers? No woman?"

Wollia intervened with a whimsical indifference in her voice. "My son served with them both in the '70s; he mentioned Kyrus's affinity for Tyghus – but he told me far more interesting things than that," she said, her eyes fixed on her delicate folded fingers. "The only stories that made it north of the Clyves spoke of Kyrus's courage in the face of ghastly odds, no?" she paused and arched her brows. "But in camp, at day's end – my son would tell me – he could often be heard wailing long into the night, sometimes screaming, other times thrashing his quarters. And despite his troops' revering his feats on the battlefield, he apparently brooded to himself more often than not, confiding in no one beyond this Tyghus." She smiled. "So a little different version than what we typically hear."

Volinex looked to Barannus who wore a mirrored expression, before back to Wollia.

"You saying he's mad?" the younger one asked.

"Oh, I couldn't know…" the matron said, casually flicking dust off her priceless robe. "But rumors abound that he took a peculiar delight in the torture of Valogarian prisoners. He'd ask them questions of his family, it was said…"

"He's mad…"

Wollia lazily shrugged her eyelids with a whisper of a smile.

A spark grew in Voli's brown eyes – before they were drawn to the eldest man, who had hardly flinched at Wollia's revelation. "You knew of this?"

The elder nodded slightly.

"Then surely Rynsyus did too…"

"Rynsyus only knows what takes place under his nose; Castus's treachery, for example, but what's that prove? Castus has no shame and sends his coin to the Natives using Imperial couriers – a blind man would know of it. But Rynsyus hasn't a clue as to matters along the Lowland frontier – he hasn't ventured beyond the castle gates in years."

"Then why – why would he pick someone he hardly—"

Antinax finally rose from the bench with a vengeance, smashing a fist into his other palm, his voice a crescendo. "Gods above, open your eyes – Rynsyus is infatuated with the *idea* of Kyrus! The *idea* of an Upland Ruhl raised in the Lowlands, yet a veteran of the Valogarian Wars. The *idea* that Nortics and Sudos alike could rally around him as a result. He's as predictable as the day is long! Rynsyus made a fool's gamble on a boy whose wits are obviously in question; wagered an empire on nothing more than an ideal. That's why I say to you that this is the greatest gift we could have ever been offered."

"A gift?" Barannus' brow spiked.

"A gift. At worst, Kyrus is a shell of man; at best, he hates the ones that took everything from him. Either way, he's pliable… pliable to *us*."

Voli' shook his head. "No. No, Rynsyus must have known…"

"What he knew or didn't know is irrelevant now – he's made his choice!"

The young one still would not accept it, turning towards the doorway. "I hear what you're saying, Anti', I do. I just think you underestimate your old friend."

Antinax's face flushed red. His eyes darted to Wollia, but she just calmly shook her head.

"Doesn't matter. Whichever side his protégé falls, he'll reveal himself soon enough."

"Aye, and how's that?" Voli' asked, without turning from the window.

After a deep breath, Anti' lowered his head before continuing. "Couriers will speed south to Nar-Biluk spreading news of the succession." Voli's head flinched. "Or to be more precise – speeding news of *Kyrus's* succession – a warmongering general thirsting to avenge his father and brother's slaughter." Voli' turned completely from the window towards Antinax. "The Chibin, animals that they are, have dreamt nightmares of this for years; they've worried all along that this 'peace' was simply a breathing spell for Roklis to rest and rearm. When they catch word of this – and they *will* - then with Fortune's aid, it will be *they* who attack *us.*"

"But the Emperor's a day or a month –"

"They've already been sent, my boy. They awaited only my sign as we left the Hall that the meeting was indeed for succession." The elder looked to Wollia before the younger members again. "Apologies, but these were contingencies we felt best kept secret."

Volinex exchanged glances with Barannus before breaking out in wide smile. "You've really done this? You really think they'd take the bait?"

"They've lashed out for much less. But if not this lure then another… though I confess: our first chance is our best."

"But we've been through this – the Sudos won't stand for war. They'd sooner walk out before allowing retaliation for anything."

"The Sudos can leave the Lorrio at their leisure – but every loss gives us the majority we need to authorize war anyway. Castus will recognize that."

"And Oratus of course will vote as Kyrus tells him," Voli' announced, grinning further as he clapped Barannus's shoulder. "So the Sudos must stay and gamble on Oratus – or Kyrus – voting with them?"

Anti' nodded. "Just as we must."

Barannus frowned at this. "So this all hinges on a gamble of our own, then?"

"Any reliance on human nature is always a gamble, but as your colleague said, Oratus will follow the Emperor's command; know the Emperor's mind and you'll know Oratus's vote!" the elder said as he pounded his hand in emphasis. "Though it bears repeating, I am *not* a man that bets at the risk of losing," he said, glancing down to the stately woman reclined on the bench. "So Wollia and I will visit the young ruler at the appropriate time… so that we can 'know' his mind."

Wollia smiled, still pretending to find interest in her robe.

Antinax spread his hands out before him. "*This is it. This* can give us our war. More than a decade of humiliating retreat, a decade of concessions and kowtowing to a race of barbarians can all be undone and set right."

Voli' and Barannus only nodded, incredulous smiles on their faces.

"I've matters to attend to now; by his own words, Rynsyus may last a day, or perhaps a month."

Antinax turned to leave the atrium before Wollia's voice stopped him.

"Volinex, we need full watch on this Tyghus fellow going forward, and you're in charge of seeing to it. Couriers sent, visits to Kyrus or any other

Rokh of import, everything. No letters to or from the man get through without our having seen and permitted them first. This faith Kyrus puts in him has to be... dealt with."

"It has to be broken, let's be honest," Voli' replied.

Wollia frowned. "A lesson in discretion would serve you well, but yes, you're correct. This will take *subtlety*, do you understand?"

"Of course."

Though his companions couldn't see it, Antinax smiled to himself. "Leave nothing to chance."

Chapter IX

If love and respect form the bedrock of sound friendship,
doubt and suspicion are the blights that bring it low.

Rokh Proverb

Dray'gon Rokh, Tanokhun, Twenty-Sixth Day of the Eleventh Month, Y. 383 P.C.

The General stood alone in the empty market square, dusk quickly approaching. A stiff wind whipped his black cloak in every direction, the air smelling of impending snow. The plaza's denizens had long since departed, leaving only a few merchants remaining to pack up their wares. They eyed the visitor curiously but said nothing, used to his omnipresence over the last week. Every day they'd watched him take position by the Founder's statue to survey the Khorian Som. Waiting. Now and then he'd indulge in dried fruit or roasted fish, but he'd never stray far from his post.

A lanky man approached the lone figure on sandaled feet unprepared for the Uplands' late-autumn chill. A heavier shawl gave his torso more protection, though his bald head was raked by the cold breeze.

The General addressed him without need of turning about. "Poor Treos. Gods pity the Lakeman out of his element."

Were this not the recurrence that it was, Treos may have found humor in the quip. But his patience clearly wore thin. "How long ya' gonna do this, lad?"

"Your patience is noted."

"Tyghus, how long? We've been at this for a week. How much coin ya' wanna waste on dingy inns in this city? Doubt it's safe even bein' out here this time 'a night."

"It's not, but tell me what other options I have and I'll be happy to listen," Tyghus said, noticeable irritation in his voice. "You know the answer to your question anyway, so why even ask it? You know I'm leaving for Valogar soon, so you know my stay's not indefinite – nor is my supply of coin."

"Then ya' should depart, lad. This vigil hasn't brought ya' any more closure than ya' had last week."

"I'm told I've been appointed commander of the Sixth Dyron, I'm told he'll call on me before I'm to leave, that we'll settle things, then he disappears in a cloud of dust on the Khorokh's orders. Not a word from him since? Nothing from the Arxun at all? Not a correspondence, a letter, a messenger? There's been no sign of movement from North City in a week," the General complained. "It's just odd."

"Is it really so incredible that a Lorrion would be too busy to –"

"Seven days without reply?" he shook his head. "He knows I'm still here waiting, that I have to leave soon, or at least the half dozen letters I've sent by courier should have told him as much. And again, he *told* me he'd be reaching out to me. It's odd, Treos. What the hell's going on up there?"

Treos simply sighed and huddled up tighter in his overcoat. "Can ya' not just seek 'im out in the Arxun?"

"He warned against making even the slightest greetings to him or he'd be seen to give me favor, just like you predicted. I've only been trying to honor that."

"I think him making ya' Dyrator of the most celebrated unit in the Rokhish army speaks loudly enough who he favors, lad," Treos said bluntly. "Gods above, there's only ten Dyrators in the whole Empire, how much more favor could he show?"

The statement gave Tyghus pause, suddenly aware of the brooch resting beneath his tunic. "True."

"So go to his bloody abode in the Arxun and demand an audience and be done with it."

"You know people aren't allowed upon the Hill without royal invite," Tyghus noted, recalling the spiked ten-foot wall that surrounded the entire Royal District and the sole gateway allowing access. "Not even Ruhls. Reds patrol the grounds like ants, especially at the Arxun Gate."

"Tyghus, just –"

"But you're right," Tyghus concluded matter-of-factly. "And I do want answers."

Treos looked startled at the breakthrough. "Ya' go now?"

"I do."

The Lakeman shivered. "Well, with ya' blessing I'll retire to the inn until your return. We've still paid through the evening."

Tyghus finally looked at him with a bemused smile. "Seven days in the market and you buy nothing but fish and figs – perhaps boots wouldn't have tasted as sweet, but honestly, Treos…"

His companion replied with his infectious grin. "Don't get robbed on the way up there, General."

"I'll try."

The two left each other on divergent paths – a lanky man headed to the hearth of an inn a few blocks south of the Tanokhun; a general northbound to the Arxun. Wind gusts masked their steps.

* * *

With a violent kick, the inn door flew open.

Seated by the room's firepit, Treos turned to see his impetuous friend striding through, bringing drafts of chill and short-lived snowflakes along with him. Tyghus's face betrayed his agitation, even beneath a mat of wildly blown hair. He brusquely tossed a wadded piece of parchment to the fireplace's edge.

The Lakeman looked at him warily. "That was quick?"

The General went immediately to his belongings splayed out across his half of the room, vigorously shoving them into a carrying sack in silence.

"Something happen?"

The General snorted derisively. "Aye."

"So –"

"So I get to the Lorrian Halum's gate, only to be greeted by its keeper who refuses to let me in, refuses to even attempt fetching Kyrus. Says he's not only unavailable but that he hasn't any record of my letters or couriers, nor's he aware of Kyrus trying to reach me. Nothing!"

"Then –"

"And upon finally realizing who I am, the troll hands me that scroll of nonsense," Tyghus barked with a wave of his hand towards the wadded parchment. "*That's* my answer? That's what I've waited for?"

His face burning red, Tyghus abruptly stopped packing to take a seat on his cot's edge, peering back across at the fireside man. "So you want to go on another adventure with me, Treos?"

The Lakeman had no chance to respond before Tyghus continued.

"I know you've had plans to depart ever since you arrived here, and that's certainly still your option. But I'd like you to ride south with me."

"Lad, I'm too –"

"You said it yourself, you can't head back to the Lakes. Not with Rom prowling about – now more than ever."

"No, I can't return to the Lakes. But lad, I spent twenty years on the campaign trail – maybe not in Valogar, but fightin' nonetheless," Treos said gently. "That life's not for me anymore. In all honesty, I wouldn't have joined the lot of ya' on the Plains had I known it would erupt like it did."

"So then what do you plan to do? You're not cut out to be a market vendor or the gods know what else!" Tyghus snapped, worn by the day's frustrations. But he spoke again in a more measured tone. "Listen to me, forget campaigning. Ride as one of my advisors, see the Rokhish Lowlands and the Valogarian countryside that's caused so much grief through the years. More selfishly, just ride as a voice of reason for me, I obviously need it. Your advice has already proven its worth."

The Lakeman looked to the ground as his hands ran across his head. "I can't do campaigns, lad."

"Don't do them, then. I consider you a friend, Treos; I'm about to take control over a regiment of some thirteen-thousand men, many of whom are also my friends – and until last week, my co-equals. I can't imagine that won't raise some problems, so your counsel would mean a lot."

"I'm not lookin' to kill anymore."

Treos looked up with wet eyes, giving Tyghus pause.

"I promise you, on my word as a man and soldier of the Empire, your blade will not be called upon unless your life is at stake... if mine's at stake, I'll leave it up to you," Tyghus said, eliciting a chuckle. "Can I count on you, my friend?" the General continued, standing to extend a hand. "If so, I make but one demand."

The Lakeman rose to offer his own hand. "What's that?"

"You buy some blessed boots!"

The men shared a laugh before clasping forearms.

"Ya'r a tough dealer, lad."

"Pack up, we need to depart – I've a wedding a thousand miles south to attend. If we don't get beyond range of these mountain snows, our time'll be shot. Pushing it as it is."

"Aye – I think the innkeeper has some nightwomen waiting to come in, anyway."

Tyghus shook his head in disgust. "I won't miss this cell."

Within moments, the pair had gathered their belongings to leave. The light-traveling Treos finished first, hustling out into the cold. As Tyghus followed, his eyes caught the parchment wad at the firepit's fringe. Scoffing, he kicked it into the flames, its brief, cryptic words no less baffling as he recalled them again:

"*Tyghus, Safe travels to Valogar. Remember, change happens not in a single leap, but in thousands of imperceptible steps. Kyrus*"

Chapter X

"O'Valogar
Little iron do we have,
Little steel can we make,
But we shall not want it,
We shall not need it,
For pyhr we do take.
O'Valogar"

Valogarian song

Valogarian Coast, Northeast of Nar-Biluk, 14th Day of the Twelfth Month, Y. 383 P.C.

"You're certain of this?"

"As certain as the messenger was…"

Twelve men gathered around a fire, its flames bouncing light off terrified, long-bearded faces framed by black coils of hair dropping to their waists. Pocketed belts slung over bare chests, each pouch stuffed with berries, small knives, and warpaint. Waves of the Ratikan Sea crashed distantly behind them, droplets carrying over the men in the breeze.

"What were his words precisely?" a burly man inquired of the young newsbearer.

"It wasn't just one man, Lijan. Many're saying the same thing, the same message over and over… even if they say it just a little bit differently each time."

"Hajan, what were the words!" Lijan replied, flailing his three-fingered hand.

"The same that I said! The Rokhish king is dying of the Bloody Cough. He could live for a moon… or he could already be dead."

"But who? Who says this?"

"Fetran – he heard as much from Rokhish couriers in Nar-Biluk."

Lijan threw his hands to the air. "Ah! Old Fetran's a fool! He's not even Chibin!"

"Nor is our own Lij…" the man to his right grumbled.

"But Fetran supports us as if he were!"

Lijan groaned.

"He does! He may be part Rokh but he's fully Pure at heart! But again, it wasn't just him—"

"Aye, it wasn't just him, we heard you," Lijan interjected, black eyes rolling. "And what else did the old fool say?"

"He said the king's successor has also been named…"

"Very well… and?"

"He's a general from their fortress in Avergon—"

"A general?" Lijan exclaimed incredulously. "The great 'Peace King' of the Rokhs enlists a general to carry that banner of peace!"

"Silence!" an old man interjected, the only one of the group with a ponytail atop his head. His eyes fixed on Hajan. "What of the successor? Tell us everything."

Hajan swallowed deeply, his mouth suddenly sounding dry and hoarse. "Well, I'm told that the general suffered great losses at Chibin hands over the years. His father, brother. And now he promises to all those that will listen that he will avenge those losses, and those that suffered like him. He plans on shattering the 'Peace'… he plans to set the Peninsula on fire."

A pall fell over the circle. Hajan looked around him, but only wide dark eyes looked back, as if he kept something unsaid that might ease their shock. Finally, the older man broke his silence. "You see? This is the man our great Lij surrendered his pride and country to!"

"Could it really be true?" Hajan asked pleadingly.

"Well, you were the one that heard the messenger, so is it or isn't it?" Lijan asked annoyedly.

"I heard what he said, I *told* you what he said... but I can't believe it."

"Why?" Lijan asked. "That peace treaty wasn't worth the parchment it was written on, all of us knew that."

"But we've *proven* they can't win here, so what's changed? Why would the Rokhs bother now?"

The group murmured approvingly at the Great Struggle's mention. "Nothing's lasting with the Rokhs!" the older man's neighbor angrily shouted. "We tried to convince the Lij of this!"

Lijan nodded. "As Hajan said, the Lij is part Rokh, so of course he's open to their deceit. He sits and grows fat pretending he's a king, while he disgraces what's left of his people by marrying the Rokhish whore."

"That's a battle for another time. We've known since the Chibin's founding – we've *pledged* to it – that we are the only ones that truly guard Valogar's heart," the old man declared. "*We* are the true people of her breast, so *we* must continue taking up her defense."

The group affirmed with silent nods.

"And if that is so, then there's no peace to be broken because no such thing can exist between Rokhs and Valogarians, not while a Chibin heart beats. And if there's no peace then they are enemies that must be struck down! We must remind them of the horrors that a few years of tranquility have made them forget."

"What shall we do, *Illyasan?*" Lijan beseeched of the old man.

The Illyasan, or Chibin war chief, folded his hands under his chin and closed his eyes in contemplation. "*What shall we do?*" he whispered. "*You ask the only question that matters.*" The fire crackled as the party awaited his response, custom and respect dictating that the Illyasan lay the groundwork for any plan of war, upon which the rest may build. He let his mind wander.

He'd always reviled Lij Andran, the eighteenth member of the Andri lineage to hold the kingship. The Andri dynasty was said to have ties all the way back to the first Valogarian tribes from beyond the sea that settled the Ratikan Peninsula more than a thousand years prior. The "Valogar" name was symbolic of the tribe that came to dominate its brethren – a tribe led by the first of the Andri bloodlines. Thus, many within the land proudly declared themselves sons and daughters of that original tribe, whether they shared common blood or not.

Men of the Chibin's ilk were appalled then, when the current Andran's forefather not only sat on the throne when Valogar fell to the Rokhs in 203, but in fact married into Rokhish royalty lines. The resulting heirs ended what the Illyasan's people saw as millennia of Valogarian purity; even worse was that many Valogarians took the marriage to be an endorsement of the Rokhs settling and co-mingling among them on the Peninsula. Indeed, the sight of Rokhish Valogarians, or "Rokhals" as the Chibin derisively called them, was hardly shocking anymore, as many Natives chose the wealth and status that the immigrants brought over ties to heritage. Defiant men like the Illyasan were a waning breed, and he shook his head ruefully as he contemplated what might have been avoided had that earlier Lij been less cowardly, had men like the Chibin Awakened a century earlier.

What to do, indeed, he thought, thumbs kneading his chin.

He smiled often thinking about the Chibin's birth, his father Ihafan chief among its founders. They were a group of pure-blooded Valogarians with unsullied minds, unaffected by the sickness of greed, and their creed found ample converts in the Valogarian southlands that had been largely uncolonized by the Rokhs. Their murderous campaigns against Rokhals soon flourished across Rokhish areas of Valogar, with the Rokh-aligned Lij Andran XVII too petrified to intervene.

Then, of course, came the Great Ascension, and the Illyasan beamed further as he pictured his father Ihafan taking the Valogarian throne. Once a Chibin dagger found Andran XVII's throat in 337, Ihafan seized power, declared an end to Rokh sovereignty in Valogar, and issued a nationwide call for uprisings of the *mirami*, the Valogarian village militias. The memory wasn't diminished by the fact that Rokhish arms smashed the resistance and left Ihafan hanging by the neck from the *Tayshihan*, the massive stone spire protruding from Nar-Biluk's hill. No, the real insult was the appointment of Andran XVII's fourteen year-old son to the throne in his father's stead. The Illyasan grimaced and nodded his head with closed eyes, mumbling his thoughts as they came to him. "I see my father now at the Great Stone, spirit departed but eyes still wide. As if – as if, even in death, his eyes couldn't believe the sight before him. Rokhs taunting his body, desecrating the Tayshihan with their execution, careless to its almighty power…"

Murmurs spread around him.

"The Rokhs… they worship only long enough to acquire more lands and wealth," he muttered with contorted face, before his voice turned to a low whisper. *"So how does one desecrate such a people in turn?"*

His thoughts drifted towards their Second Resistance. Though a vile race, the Rokhs were no fools after his father's uprising failed, choosing to protect Andran XVIII in Nar-Biluk with their own troops and marching others across the land to stomp out a Chibin menace that had melted away into the countryside. The Illyasan recalled the times when they watched

96

Imperial troops from the hills, sometimes no more than a few dozen yards away. Stripped of the mirami or royal support they'd enjoyed during Father's reign, they'd sometimes spend days without food, rarely venturing out to resupply with Rokhs or traitorous Valogarian bounty-hunters lurking about. They simply bided their time, staying alive for those brief moments when they would take their vengeance.

It was so glorious whenever it came. Small packs of Chibin warriors took to slaughtering the isolated and unwary at every turn, preying especially upon Imperials foraging amongst the shrublands. Their horrified screams were deliciously addictive, enough to make Pure eyes weep. Yet despite their raids' successes over the next decade, the Illyasan was stunned when the Rokhish king suddenly declared peace through the false Lij and quit the fight – stunned and elated.

It was the perfect time to strike, he recalled with a wince. *The perfect time to rectify two hundred years of humiliation.*

After Andran "agreed" to the Peace, the Illyasan and his men begged the Lij to betray it and send out a call for a full mirami uprising. *The Rokhish columns are prone,* they told him. *They're ripe for attack. They chose to come here, so they're not deserving of an honorable retreat. They've admitted defeat!* Though the Rokhs were still many, they withdrew from the lands in thin, vulnerable lines that a wave of Valogarians could have swept aside had the order been given. Now was the time, they pleaded. Now was the time to rout them, and finally punish their hubris. With Chibin valor leading the way, Valogar could finally be rid of its bondage.

But of course it was not to be, the Illyasan lamented bitterly to himself. Instead, the False King turned his back to the Chibin messengers and reaffirmed his commitment to marry the Rokhish whore, just as his forefather had done so long ago. Imperial troops filtered out of the province unmolested as the Chibin sat seething, convinced it was a matter of time until they returned en masse.

"After ten years of 'peace' we stand at the precipice again, ready for the cycle to resume ..." the old chieftain said under his breath, before finally looking up and addressing his men. "For thirty-five years I've watched this bumbling Lij claim rule over our country. A rule never earned on the battlefield, never honored by his peers; no, it was a rule given by those without the slightest shred of authority to do so."

"*You* are Valogar's proper king, Illyasan," Lijan said with frantic eyes. "You've the blood of Pure kings running through your veins."

"This is not about me, Lijan. It must *involve* me, but it's not *about* me." The Chieftain sighed. "If the Rokhs are indeed on their way to our land once again, the Lij will not resist them. False King or not, the mirami are bound to rise to him if he'd only give them the order, but of course he won't. He'd sooner serve the Rokhs a banquet than fight them – he may *welcome* them back to stamp us out, since he's too afraid to do so himself."

Grumbles immediately broke out amongst the group.

"So now here we are. Heads that the False King could have taken a decade ago now come searching for ours – how much more obvious could the gods' indictment of him be? But let's not fool ourselves into believing the Rokhs will come here with chins down and shoulders slouched. Any animal that survives one fight will come back wiser if not stronger; they'll learn," Illyasan said, before scanning the group. "And so must we."

"*Uny,*" Lijan agreed as other heads nodded.

"We must *learn* from what worked before; we must *learn* from our failures. We know now that the Rokhs will stop at *no* desecration of Valogar, so that is all that they will respect in kind; we *know* that our few warriors humbled their mighty army, so we don't need the False King's help to do it again. We've cut the Rokhish beast, seen him bleed – we know he's a heart. We've seen him run, seen him forsake battle – so we know his mind." The chief suddenly rose to his feet. "Now we must take both! *Attack both the head and the heart!* Yes, if we take *both*, then the beast *will* fall!" he shouted, pounding his chest and head before a roaring audience.

"To attack his heart we must take his will, and his will comes from his ability to make war upon us; to attack his head, we must strike where but a few can sow fear among the many; where the smallest man appears a giant!"

"We can and we will Illyasan!" Lijan said, nearly frothing. "*Unleash us!*"

"We can roam freely until they arrive; we will use this time to prepare our strike."

"From the moment they cross the Isthmus we'll whittle them down! We won't give them a blade of its grass, a breath of its air!"

"You mistake me, brother," the chief quickly corrected, eyes piercing through his frenzied follower. "The enemy already fears us *here*," he continued, before pointing across the sea. "Now, we must make him fear us *there*."

The chief lingered for a moment and looked over his listeners, before nodding his head in finality.

"We'll attack them on their own grounds. An attack that our children will recount to their children, and their children to theirs. And we'll take their filthy head and heart in one fell swoop."

The group looked at him in stunned silence. The Illyasan smiled, knowing by their faces alone that he'd chosen the right path.

Lijan broke into wide smile. "Only in my dreams have I seen myself killing Rokhs on Rokhish lands," he said with burning fury, eyes misting over. "You'll give me this chance?"

"I will," the Illyasan said with a tight, vengeful sneer. "The *gods* will. And as guardians of this land, we must."

Lijan leapt to his feet in jubilation, dancing in place and sending a maniacal laughter adrift on the sea's winds. He broke into Chibin war cries, sounds which his comrades soon echoed. The Illyasan was happy to let them rejoice in the glory to come.

Watch over us, Father. Your people are soon to rise again.

Even over the crashing waves, their whooping screams rippled through the night.

Chapter XI

"This union of Rokhish and Valogarian Royalty will usher in an era of peace unparalleled in our time. What arms wrought apart, marriage will bind together."

Speech of Emperor Rynsyus I to the One Hundred and
First Imperial Lorrio,
Y. 382 P.C.

The Isthmus, 21st Day of the Twelfth Month (the "Winter's Ebb"), Y. 383 P.C

The horse bucked and whinnied as its hoof drove into a piece of wood protruding from the soil. Tyghus looked down to see the splintered remnants of an Imperial shield, the Ninth Dyron's three crocodile sigil still visible after centuries.

"The Isthmus," he muttered.

Peering off to his left he saw the choppy blue of the Ratikan Sea sprawl out before his eyes, a mirrored view of the Ferlen Sea to his right. At barely five hundred yards across, the narrow land span provided spectacular vantages of both seas' power as waves crashed into the bottom of three hundred foot cliffs. A thin earthy layer coated its surface, a trail of green that snaked off into a horizon appearing close from a dense fog. The air was only slightly cooler than the mild Lowlands, but its dampness caused a shivering chill.

His older friend scanned the blade shards, spear shafts, arrowpoints, and fractured shield chunks littering the ground in every direction. "Looks like they had it out just yesterday."

The General nodded. "It does. Amazing that it's been almost two hundred years since they fought here. I lost a forefather on this ridge fighting Valogar and Colvery." Tyghus chuckled. "May be his sword and shield we tread upon."

"As long he knows that ya'r the one doin' the tramplin'," Treos replied to more chuckles. "Stalemate here went what – nine, ten years?"

Tyghus shook his head. "Six years, two months, and a week. Ended with the scaling of the cliffsides on the fourth day of the sixth month, 203rd year after Cataclysm."

"Ya' know ya'r history, lad."

"The hell you think we did half the time at the Academy? Studied the scrolls 'til our eyes bled."

"Sounds worse than this bloody ridge."

The General smiled. "It's dull work but you learn a lot from those scrolls."

"Aye, probably true. Six years, though!" Treos said. "Can ya' imagine?"

"What's your take - appealing as twenty in the Jungle? At least we can cross this in a day."

"Agreed!" Treos laughed.

They trotted on in silence for a bit, serenaded by the waves' pounding and blanketed in salty air. Despite Tyghus being almost twenty years his partner's junior, he felt like the senior many times in their conversations. The Lakeman seemed to marvel at every step of the journey since crossing the Clyves into Grynea Province, then Morremea and Starrea after that. Tyghus enjoyed regaling him with his stories about the same, especially since he was the one usually peppering friends with questions.

"So humor me, lad, because ya' know more 'bout this feud with Valogar than me," Treos said at last. "But the Khorokh dies some day, aye?"

"He's mortal, aye."

"So this union we're goin' to watch – it survives him?"

Tyghus pursed his lips as he pondered his response. "A thousand seers could answer you a thousand different ways on that, my friend."

"And ya'?"

"I think it does. I think we've done right by the Valogarians even if some people don't like it. We've honored our word and they respect that, or at least they should. We've proven committed to peace and surely whoever takes the throne after Rynsyus will share his views. I can tell you that with my sister being queen of Valogar, it won't be the Valogarians breaching the peace; not a chance, not if she holds even an ounce of power."

"She's a good woman, ya'r sister?"

"The best, Treos."

"Ya'r sure the two of ya' share kin, then?"

Tyghus laughed. "My whole family believed that had she been born a man, she'd have been the fiercest warrior that ever lived. It's a shame *mari* and *pari* weren't alive to see the Emperor's envoys propose the marriage to her last year; they wouldn't have been surprised to see her so honored and eager to serve His wishes, even if it meant her husband being chosen for her."

Treos's brows arched as he snuck a glance at the General. "She never met the man?"

"Until three months ago when she left the Rokhlands for Nar-Biluk? She had not."

"Didn't concern her, eh?" Treos asked with notable perplexion. "What did she even know of him?"

"As much as I do – that he carries himself with immense pride, carries himself like a king – or a "Lij", as the Natives call it. You have to respect that, given how he's been propped up by Dray'gon Rokh for decades. A lot of people in Avergon thought he'd collapse without his Imperial protection, yet still he stands. He's finally getting his chance to prove he deserves the throne and he's not wasting it."

Treos shook his head in disbelief. "Ya'r sister's a brave one if nothing else. I hear it's dangerous enough bein' a common Rokh in these lands, let alone a royal one."

"Aye," Tyghus nodded. "The land north and west is safe to walk freely; it's the Purebloods to the south and east that honor no truce. Andran has a loyal enough guard in Nar-Biluk to protect her, and she'll keep her Rokhish kord there for as long as she wishes. But beyond the walls... well, she must tread lightly," he said, when his eyes were finally rewarded. "Ah, you'll soon see for yourself."

A broad wooden palisade began taking shape through the mist, no more than two men high, and Tyghus smiled as he recognized the Valogarian Gates. The simple structure, built precisely where the Bloody Neck met the Valogarian Peninsula, was a far cry from its stony Rokhish counterpart from which they'd set out that morning. There, a twenty-foot gatehouse had loomed with four massive stone towers punctuating the corners of the gatehouse square.

No, the Valogarian Gates were simpler, and beneath its wooden walkway, large doors criss-crossed with iron slabs had already parted ways at the middle, though not for the approaching Rokhs. Instead, a cluster of merchants and carts emerged heading westwards towards the Lowlands. The brown-cloaked cluster stationed four men ahead and the same behind each of the four carts, a common sight in Valogar since the Natives possessed few large draft beasts. The beds of the carts were loaded with bulging woven sacks, likely full of the Valogarian berries prized throughout Andervold. The merchants paid the outsiders no mind save for one man, who peered out from under his hood at the passing General. His deformed hand caught Tyghus's attention as he passed, and for a moment their eyes connected.

"My lord!"

Tyghus and Treos snapped their heads around to the top of the palisades, where a Valogarian waved down to them.

"We expect you, my lord!" Their broken Rokhish was evident after just a few words, though from their appearance they clearly had Rokhish blood in them. Their Valogarian faces were softly rounded, eyes relaxed ovals, with hair draped down to their chest in shiny black spirals, versus the squatter, boxier, and brown-haired heads typical of Rokhs. However, their color and build was pure Rokh, a broad-shouldered frame underneath a pinkish skin.

Tyghus greeted them back. "Good day, my friends."

More smiling Valogarians soon emerged at the gateway, gently taking the reins of the two men's horses to guide them through. All of them bore sleeveless shirts of wooden armor, made up of dozens of thin rows of hardened uniform rods. From their midsections to their knees each of them wore beige cloths, pinned at the middle with a large silver brooch. Circular shields two feet across were strapped to their forearms, complementing the seven-foot spears in their opposite hand. Wooden sandals ensconced the toes, heels, and balls of their feet, leaving gaps at the arches.

"We take to *Nahbilick*," onc man said, pointing eastward with his weapon. "Lij look forward to see you."

"Feeling's mutual. And your name?"

"Name?" the Valogarian replied with blank expression. "Ah, name. Name is Jihan. With Lij guard. You are 'Ty-gees'?"

"'*Tie-us*', aye," the General answered, though Jihan's smiling nod suggested the Valogarian had no idea what he had said wrong. "My friend is *Tre-os*, *Tre-os Lok-ner*. A fellow Rokh from far, far northwest of here," he said, gesturing beyond the sea.

"Trees... Locker..." the man said carefully. "Trees Locker."

Treos politely nodded back at him.

Meanwhile, their attire baffled Tyghus. "You don't find yourself cold, Jihan?" he inquired, simulating a chill with this hands.

The guard laughed. "No cold, Tygees. Cold is *here*," he said matter-of-factly, pointing to his head.

Tyghus smiled back. "Fair enough. A fine time for a wedding anyhow, isn't it?"

"A fine day," Jihan responded. "We go?"

"Lead the way."

Twenty Valogarians quickly mounted *lekeys*, small ponies native to their lands. They were barely half the size of the massive Imperial warhorses, and looked a bit spooked as they lined up on either side of their larger cousins.

Jihan personally held the reins of Tyghus's horse as they began the final leg of their trek to Nar-Biluk. After a few moments of silence along the well-worn dirt path, his proud face turned back to Tyghus.

"Today is great day for our peoples."

* * *

Tyghus had been away from Valogar for more than two years, but it was precisely as he remembered it: damp, green, and noisy with wildlife.

The journey from the Isthmus took him briskly past the stony hills that ringed the Peninsula's coastline to its low-lying "shrublands" – a misnomer given that the "shrubs" often grew as large as the giant oaks from back home. The party was treated to thousands of creatures' howls and songs along the way; for their part, the animals paid them no mind, evidenced by the herds of deer-like *bolahmy* nonchalantly crossing the road just ahead of the men while sleek feline predators known as *bamas* eyed them from nearby shrubs. The shrieks of long-tailed *tinama* monkeys already taking residence there made it known they were none too pleased.

It wasn't long before they came upon the typical Valogarian hamlets Rokhish soldiers referred to as "mushroom fields" after the houses' architecture. Each home consisted of a single fifteen-foot wooden pole upon which a canopy of inter-woven branches rested. Fluffy moss and grass were crammed into each canopy to keep out the elements, while thick woven blankets attached to the canopy's edges were pinned up during the day and dropped down at night. The "mushroom fields" tended to cluster roughly twenty or thirty of these simple "mushrooms", with cultivated berry bushes and livestock ringing the entirety of the hamlet.

But nothing Tyghus had seen or heard to that point could match the twilight image of the *Tayshihan*, or Great Stone, looming large on Nar-Biluk's hill as they approached the city's gates. He wasn't alone in his awe.

"Gods above, what is that?" Treos asked, pointing at the hundred-foot white protrusion sprouting from the ground like a wolf's tooth.

Tyghus smiled. "The Great Stone. It's the most sacred point in the whole country to the Natives. Everything here revolves around that chunk of rock – religion, calendar, Nar-Biluk itself. The city's nothing but a flattened hilltop all around the Stone so they could cram those mushroom-looking homes all the way to the walls."

"How many are there?"

Tyghus frowned in thought. "Maybe a hundred thousand commoners? Another wall surrounds the Stone itself; the priests and the Lij reside there if I recall, but it's been some time since I've seen it."

"Ya' station here?"

"No, I was out in the surrounding villages. Until Rynsyus's drawdown, we kept the Sixth's base right in the middle of the city though, so I was no stranger to it. You can't miss the old Imperial buildings – square stone blocks standing in the middle of all the wood around them. Mostly empty now, of course. Nothing but Tygha's kord."

"Well, damn it all, that Stone is beautiful," the Lakeman burbled. "Have ya' ever seen such a thing?"

"Perhaps the walls of Dray'gon Rokh... but not much else compares," Tyghus said as his eyes shifted to the lone trail sloping sixty yards down from the hilltop walls to a flattened, ten-foot wide path ringing the hill's mid-point. A circle of palisades bristled outwards at the ring's edges, interrupted only by a gateway spanning the trail's width. "And I might add that this is a damn strong fort."

"I don't doubt it."

Despite its formidability, the mid-point, then the hilltop gates, opened peacefully enough, albeit with Valogarian eyes poring over them all the way. Thousands fixated on Tyghus in his conspicuous silver armor beneath an ashen Imperial tunic, to say nothing of his beautiful brown mare. More curious Natives touched the greaves about his shins or stroked the huge horse's mane, and from smiling faces chatter ensued in a tongue which the General had never completely mastered.

Anxiety beginning to grow at the crush of people, Tyghus leaned forward on his saddle to Jihan. "So where do we head again, my friend?"

Jihan looked back, clearly proud of the honor and attention his guests, and in turn he, were receiving. "To Tayshihan," he replied, pointing at the Stone. "Andran is there. Sa—sees – seester is there, too."

Tygha's mention immediately replaced his worries with excitement. He admired his sister beyond words for her courage in coming "into the hornets' nest", as Kyrus derisively put it. Though he couldn't help but feel an urge to protect her, he also knew she'd be the first to tell him she didn't need it – before then telling him to protect himself. She was probably right. His time would be better spent focusing on living the virtuous life he was taught to live than worrying about the inordinately savvy Tygha.

The party slowly made its way through the throng to the city's center, the Stone growing more massive the closer they came to it. The torches surrounding it made it glow a magnificent orange, and its polish bounced the light onto the entire village, most especially the "mushrooms" dotting the inner ring. As the tall wooden trunks of the inner ring's gates creaked open for the visitors, Tyghus saw that the frantic townsfolk were replaced by equally frantic priests and priestesses. The pious men were dressed little differently than the party that escorted them, and without their elaborate headdresses there would have been no distinction at all. The priestesses, however, had the General immediately piqued. Not from their clothes, of course, which paralleled their male counterparts' except for triangular-cut shirts tying off at the apex around their necks, leaving them backless.

No, it was their striking beauty that intrigued him so.

Tyghus glanced at Treos who simply smiled back, saying enough with one look. The priestesses were more demure than their non-holy sisters, and in place of the latter's short crops of coiled black hair were long, straightened locks which spilled down either side of their faces, save for a tuft in the middle that was pinned back by a brooch. Around their heads they wore simple tiaras cut from the shrubs, their berries painted a brilliant gold. Their skin looked even more bronzed in the torchlight, and a closer look showed subtle stripes of blue paint lining their limbs and faces.

"Tyghus!"

With a shock, he recognized one of the "priestesses".

"My gods! Tygha!"

He leapt down from his horse, nearly tumbling onto one of his escorts. His sister quickly flew into his arms and he squeezed her tight, relishing his first sight of her in months.

"It is so good to see you!" she gushed, tears welling in the corners of her eyes.

"Likewise, my girl."

She stepped back for a moment to look her brother over. "You look good, how do you feel?"

"Like I just sat in a saddle for a thousand miles, to be honest," he said with a sly grin. "And you?"

"I truly could not feel better. I'm so excited for this; so honored to be part of whatever this will be; hopefully, the end of this horrible feud."

Tyghus nodded. "There's *no* more honorable thing than what you're doing. Your example's what every Rokh should strive for, I believe that."

"Well, let's not overstate it..."

"I'm not, not in the slightest. The Khorokh called upon you and you did what you were asked. You did the right thing."

Tygha smiled. "In twenty years' time, I hope that's what the scrolls will say," she said, before shaking her head as she studied him. "I can't believe you're here!"

"Nor I! Trek feels never-ending at times, especially after the Som ends in Marvelon."

"No, no, I mean I didn't even think you were still coming; I didn't think you even remembered about it, to be frank."

"Of course I did. I've thought about you and this day ever since I learned about it."

"Well, I just hadn't heard from you in months."

Tyghus's brow furrowed. "That's impossible, I sent swift-riding messengers from Dray'gon Rokh weeks ago... they should have easily beaten me here."

Tygha shrugged. "Haven't seen anything from you here. Maybe robbers took them?"

"Aye... maybe..." Tyghus said, still surprised. "I sent more than one, though."

"Sure you did, Tyghus," his sister said with a wink. "It's not important, you're here now. Will you stay with us long? Many would like to meet you, especially the nobles. Most of them have Rokhish blood."

"No, I can only stay the night, unfortunately."

The disappointment was evident in her face. "You timed it perfectly then, didn't you? Not a day to spare?"

Tyghus laughed. "Not an hour? I'm renowned for my planning."

"Where do you leave for so soon?"

"The Converge. Need to inspect the supply shipments to Avergon, figure out why they've been held up there for months. Shouldn't be more than a two or three week trip I wouldn't think; we'll split the Attikon-Avergon gap and ride in from the southeast."

"That's a pity. You'll stay longer another time."

"Another time, I promise," the General said, as he finally stepped back to take in the sight before him. "Gods above, Tygha," he said with a grin. She stood almost a foot shorter than her tall brother, her slight frame adorned in the same garb as the Valogarian priestesses, although her crown was a dyed in several colors instead of the one. Her wavy brown hair and fair skin, if not her angular face, betrayed her non-Native roots. "What a beautiful queen you'll make. And the way you bossed me around when I was a tob', I think the job'll suit you just fine."

"I warned you to be nicer to me all those years," she laughed, as Tyghus feigned shock.

"So you're really ready for this, then?"

"Of course."

"Be honest with me."

"Well, obviously I'm nervous!" she said as she whacked him on the arm. "Not made of stone like you."

"Ah, see? You should have invited Aunt Caia to liven things up a bit. Or maybe Uncle Tyghriox?"

She chuckled. "There's a reason he's still in Tygonium," she said, eyes drifting beyond her brother. "That's not him behind you, is it?"

Tyghus whirled towards Treos, embarassingly realizing Treos hadn't yet been introduced. "Ah, apologies, my friend – this is of course my sister Tygha, future tyrant of these lands. Tygha, this is Treos Lokner, a man of the Lakes. He was kind enough to ride with me from Dray'gon Rokh, I hope it's not a problem that he's here."

"Not at all! A friend of yours is always welcome. I *think* I can trust your judgment."

Treos dismounted to join them with an easy smile. "Pleasure to meet ya', my lady."

"Pleasure's mine. Welcome to Nar-Biluk," she said happily.

Tyghus laughed. "You're a natural ambass—"

He stopped as he felt a tap upon his shoulder.

"*Jiupan shengdin?*" a quiet voice asked. Tyghus heard the foreign question but as he turned to the priestess that asked it, his voice failed him, words stolen by her beauty. Like the other priestesses, her black hair spilled onto her chest, but in contrast to them, she flashed emerald green eyes more brilliant than Tyghus had ever seen. A creamy, silver make-up that covered her eyelids made their impression all the more striking, to say nothing of her berry-bush tiara laced with flower petals. Her delicate arm offered him a cup of purplish liquid.

Say something, you idiot.

"I – thank you –"

"This is Tyghus, my brother," Tygha intervened smoothly. "He's a Rokhish general, er, '*Mondid*' as you say, no?"

The girl smiled approvingly, eyes darting between the Tyghid siblings. "Rokh *Mondid*."

"Tyghus, this is Mikolo," his sister continued, then took the drink held out for her awestruck brother. "Close your mouth and take this – it's fermented berries, you'll love it. Quite strong if you've never had it, so mind yourself. Thank you, Mikolo."

"Welcome, *Manam* Tygha," the petite woman replied with slight bow before flicking eyes back upon her brother. "Mondid."

The priestess turned and offered a drink to Treos which he gratefully accepted, before disappearing into the masses.

Tygha broke out in a laughing fit, soon joined by Treos. "They really taught you nothing about women at the Academy, did they?"

"I –"

"We're still people, you brute! You have to at least say *something!*" she teased, before cackling again.

"I did say something!" Tyghus said as his face flushed. "Well dammit, you should have *told* me about these women—"

"*Priestesses*..." she corrected, still laughing.

"Priestesses? They're the *goddesses*, every one of them!"

Tygha's smile shrunk a bit. "They're beautiful to Rokhs, maybe, but most Valogarian men see them as dainty and weak – the worst qualities a woman can have here. That's why they remain unwed with their hair uncut. Now, they're committed to worship on this Hill for the rest of their days."

Tyghus's mouth gaped uncontrollably.

"That's the law for Valogarian women past their thirtieth year," Tygha continued.

"But that one—" Tyghus started, pointing in the direction the priestess left.

"Mikolo..."

"— was... where did her green eyes come from? They were greener than any Rokh's."

Tygha shook her head ruefully. "She's a tragic one. She's actually not Rokhish at all – she's Chibin."

"No!"

"It's true. Every so often, the Chibin give birth to a green-eyed child. Among them, it's considered a curse or mark of disgrace. No man dares to touch them unless they want to risk the Chibin's wrath."

The custom struck Tyghus almost as hard as Mikolo's beauty. "That's madness."

"Maybe it is, though they've said the same about many of our practices," she said, before noticing he still perused the crowds for the departed priestess. "Did you hear what I said, brother?"

Tyghus frowned. "What?"

"She's 'marked' *and* she's of the Hill now."

"So?"

"So stop looking for her... she's married to the Stone."

Tyghus's head floated back to his sister with a devious grin. "And *she's* happy with that groom?"

"Tyghus..." she cautioned, echoes of their mother.

"Alright then, *mari*," he muttered, downing a good bit of his drink.

"Proud a' ya', lad," Treos said, clapping the General on his back.

"I guess I should be happy that you've gotten past Vara, shouldn't I?" Though she clearly meant only a simple jibe, the question stung Tyghus for a moment, jolting his stomach. "You are past her... right?"

He didn't answer. "How'd you hear about it? You left weeks before it..."

She responded with an immediate look of sympathy as he trailed off. "Her brother's stationed here; he told me months ago."

The General shook his head with a tinge of exasperation, recalling a man with whom he'd shared little good favor. "Varlox?"

She nodded.

"Well, cheers to stumbling into him this evening," he said, before finishing his cup. "But aye, I'm past it; past her. I feel good; focused on Avergon, the Dyron..."

"Glad to hear it," Tygha said doubtfully. "I hope you're saying that from the heart and not your drink," she said as she flicked his cup. "So you two – you're friends from the Sixth?"

"No," Tyghus replied. "I didn't know the old man until two moons ago, but now it's hard to remember my life before that given what happened."

Tygha grimaced. "What happened? What did you do?"

Tyghus chuckled and shook his head. "I wouldn't know where to begin. Let's save it for another time."

"Fair enough. I thought you were referring to Kyrus."

"Kyrus? The Lorrio, you mean? You should have seen him the night he was –"

"Lorrio?" Tygha's eyebrows scrunched. "No, I meant the succession."

Tyghus paused for a moment. "Succession?"

"You've heard the announcement, haven't you?"

Tyghus shot a glance at Treos, who looked equally baffled.

"I guess not," she said, eyes looking to the ground before back to her brother. "Khorokh Rynsyus is dying. We first caught word a little more than a week ago. He's named Kyrus... *Kyrus* as his successor to the throne."

Whether from the drink or otherwise, the General suddenly felt off-kilter. "*Kyrus?*" he finally managed to blurt out.

"You heard me. Assuming what we've been told is true, of course, though word was delivered by Imperial courier."

Tyghus was dumbstruck. "Gods above."

"Indeed. And I'd be lying if I said Nar-Biluk wasn't a bit on edge as a result."

Tyghus's mind spun still, but managed a reply. "Why?"

Her eyes shifted from his for a moment. "You know his past. So do the people here."

"So?" Tyghus questioned defiantly. "So he was angry at times growing up, angry at the world or whomever."

"And now? You're telling me he's put all that grief behind him? The moods, the brooding, all of it?"

Her brother couldn't answer right away.

She swallowed hard. "The things they say he did to Valogarian prisoners here are… are things I can't even *repeat*, let alone imagine."

Tyghus scowled. "So *don't*."

"Are they true?"

Tyghus looked away from her. "War is war… I *don't* think they're true but even if they were, many men lose themselves—"

"Don't do that," she said sternly. "Don't talk down to me. I don't ask out of some sort of morbid curiosity, I ask because if he brooded as a boy, if he tortured men as a general… then what are we to expect of him as *Emperor*?"

Tyghus threw his hands out. "What do you want me to tell you? I'm no seer. *I* believe he's a good –"

"Do you trust him?"

"Trust him with what?"

"With maintaining this *peace*, Tyghus."

"*Yes*. But it's not *his* peace to maintain anyway, it's the *Empire's*. The Empire signed the treaty, so the Empire will honor it. What's an Imperial pledge worth otherwise?"

"Well, rumors are already spreading that –"

"I wouldn't pay any attention to the rumors that make their way here," the General interjected.

Tygha's face softened after a tense few moments of silence. "Let's not delve into this tonight; it's not the time for it. I'm sorry I mentioned it, I just… I just thought you knew."

Tyghus regretted his sharp rebuke. "No, I understand, I understand," Tyghus said before sighing. "I often think about he's faring up there too, 'specially after the last I saw of him was as he was being whisked away by Reds over a month ago, right after he told me I'd inherited the Sixth –"

"Did you?" Tygha interrupted, eyebrows arched.

The General remembered she hadn't received his letter informing her as much. "I did. I'm Dyrator now," he said, pulling out the necklace Kyrus transferred to him.

"Congratulations, brother," she said, though with a smile that bordered on apprehensive.

"My thanks. Still sounds odd to say," he replied shortly, put off a bit by her reaction. "But since that time, no, I haven't heard a word from Kyrus. I've sent couriers to him – couriers when I was in Dray'gon Rokh, couriers from posts along the way down here – but nothing, no response, or none that have found me yet. But perhaps this explains it."

Her face shifted from concern to reassuring. "Well again, let's not mind it tonight. It's supposed to be a night of celebration."

Still reeling, Tyghus forced another smile. "Agreed. No point in indulging the rumors and speculation at this point."

Tygha smiled in assent. "I have to leave for the time being and finish preparations, but take comfort in the city or the Hill, whichever you'd like. You won't find a people that know how to... 'celebrate' better than Valogarians. I'll see you at the ceremony?"

"You will," he said weakly as she embraced him and departed.

Tyghus turned to his friend. "What the hell is going on up there in the Capital?"

The Lakeman lightly rapped the General on the arm. "Ya' heard ya' sister, lad. Grab another drink and forget about it. She said somethin' about 'celebrating', didn't she?"

A passing priestess saw Tyghus's empty cup and immediately offered him a full one. With a deep sigh he took it, swigged down the whole serving and handed it back to her. He watched the green-eyed priestess suddenly emerge from one of the "mushrooms", then glanced at Treos. Swiping away the drink from his mouth, he said,

"Aye."

* * *

Berry spirits flowed freely throughout the night. Libations were limited to no one and indeed no one turned them away, be they clergy, townsfolk, or Rokh. All indulged in the great celebration.

The actual ceremony being celebrated had been quite abrupt, unsurprising for the proudly austere race. With little pomp before a hushed twenty-person congregation, Tygha joined Andran before a plain berrywood altar. With the Great Stone as a backdrop, a priest offered a brief invocation in exotic tongue upon the Rokhish princess and Valogarian king. The burly Lij tied a gilded ring of leaves around his slender woman's wrist, and in just moments, they were wedded – likely in less time than it would take for a Rokhish bride to walk the procession of a temple's hall in Dray'gon Rokh. Thus, were kingdoms wed.

For all the simplicity of the ceremony, however, the city exploded in music and revelry afterwards as the inner gate swung open to welcome the general citizenry. Scents of boiling stewpots wafted throughout the fete, tempting peoples' stomachs as much as the drinks stoked their ardor. It wasn't long before men and women exchanged drunken embraces, dancing to the simple yet infectiously rhythmic tunes of the Valogarian lutes and chimes – nor was it hard to find more base desires being sated.

Tygha was right about these people, Tyghus thought hazily, amusedly watching the debauchery unfold around him. Valogarian townswomen soon sought him out as a dance partner, and though they were aggressive in every respect, from intense blackish-brown eyes to their blunt propositions, the General politely declined their advances. Treos, however, was not so chaste after his seventh mug of jiupan, and after flashing Tyghus a cockeyed smile, he nonchalantly took a stocky woman on each arm to a darker recess on the Hill where they no doubt became better acquainted.

"You enjoy yourself, brother?" a booming voice said, startling Tyghus. Turning groggily, he saw the commanding figure of Lij Andran XVIII, husband to his sister. Even as he neared his fiftieth year, the King looked remarkably youthful, no doubt thanks to his ageless – if heavily tattooed - Valogarian skin stretched over a broad frame more common to the Rokhs in his blood. Unlike Tyghus's escorts, he was adorned only from the waist down, revealing a powerful chest painted shades of violet; also unlike the escorts, he stood eye to eye with the General, something not many of any race could claim, save for the Stolxians. The simple crown that sat atop the shiny curls of hair hanging past a bearded jaw seemed inadequate for a king.

"Of course, Lij," the General said, extending a forearm and hug to his new kin. "Welcome to the House of Tygh."

"I regret not speaking with you before ceremony," Andran said in respectable Rokhish. "You understand things are, how you say, 'hectic' today." Although his smile suggested otherwise, the Lij's dark black eyes, ringed with veiny ink, gave off an intense gravity to everything he said.

"My Lij, my Lij, please don't think of it."

"Brother you call me, yes?"

"Brother, then. Don't think of it."

"I *do* think of it," the King said strongly to Tyghus's surprise. "That you come to my land, my kingdom, is sign of great respect. My own blood brother in Nar-Biluk, his six wives – *none* of them show me same respect."

The General looked around him. "I wasn't aware you had a brother by blood –"

"I have five older blood brothers – only Siran still alive. The rest die before I take throne," Andran said solemnly. As he looked away, his forehead wrinkled thoughtfully. "Siran always hated me as Lij but with today's insult – he as dead to me as rest."

The brother's name rang faintly familiar to his foggy mind. "Why would he hate you?"

The Lij turned to stare straight through the General. "Because thirty-five years ago, your people chose me."

"I see," Tyghus said awkwardly.

"Take walk with me, Tyghus," he ordered, his head gesturing a direction away from the crowds.

They soon found themselves on the opposite side of the inner ring, away from the ceremonial grounds at what initially looked to be another "mushroom". This one, however, was much larger, to the extent that five poles held up its lengthy canopy, instead of the usual one. Pulling back a flap, the pair entered what Tyghus assumed was the Lij's household, but if it was at all noteworthy, it was only because of its size; otherwise, there was an utter lack of any of the regal trappings known to Imperial buildings or even proventors' dwellings. Animal heads, horns, wooden carvings and reliefs, yes, but little if any precious stones or metals.

A fire burned in the home's center, its fumes spiraling out a precisely placed hole in the canopy top. Smoothed logs were positioned around it, on which each man took a seat.

"These leaves, brother, they clear the mind," the Lij started, crushing a handful of dried leaves into the cylinder of an ornately carved pipe. "Lets leaders talk as leaders. Lets them see outcomes to decisions ahead, see paths." Reaching his bare hand into the fire's flames, Andran plucked a tiny ember and dropped it into the pipe's chamber. Immediately inhaling, his eyes closed as sweet-smelling smoke floated from his nose and parted mouth. In a moment he looked at Tyghus.

"You try."

The way the berry spirits coursed through him, Tyghus couldn't reject anything at that moment. "Hand it to me," the General answered, taking the pipe awkwardly.

"Close your eyes until you complete breath. Take in clarity of leaves."

Tyghus dutifully obliged, and whether it was clarity he felt or not, his head was suddenly abuzz, his arms and legs lighter than air. He couldn't fight a smile overtaking his face as he looked at his levitating hands, then to the elaborate pipe they held.

"Potent leaf, it is," the Lij said with a grin.

"Quite," Tyghus replied with a chuckle.

"Now we talk as leaders of men."

"You really shouldn't refer to me like that."

"That's what you are," the Lij said, waving his hands dismissively. "How else I call general of ten-thousand men?"

Tyghus leaned forward, elbows resting on his thighs before tilting his head towards the man. "Ten-thousand *foot*," he said with a smile. "Thirteen thousand with horse and siege – twenty-six if you include the Ninth Dyron in Avergon, though technically that one's not mine."

Andran gave no response except an almost imperceptible nod. Tyghus laughed.

"In any event, you make me out to be a king when I'm actually at the mercy of my Khorokh like any other subject of the Empire. It's my duty to do what he orders me to do, nothing more."

The Lij was undeterred. "You *are* leader of men."

"Call me what you want, then," Tyghus said with upturned palms. "I must say you know a great deal about Rokhish news; I only learned of my promotion a few weeks ago."

"I must know things that will affect my people. My duty as king."

The Rokh grimaced. "Why assume the Sixth will 'affect' your people?"

Andran's eyes narrowed. "'Six' history here too long to ignore."

"The Sixth isn't here anymore," Tyghus said defensively. "The treaty's been signed for years, it *will* be honored, so gods willing, my command of the Sixth will only be a *good thing* for Valogar."

"Never said I must only know *bad* things, brother," the King said, his mouth a firm line.

Tyghus nodded as he looked to the ground, his mind's "clarity" increasingly fleeting. "Aye… aye, I see. All things, not just – I see."

"Yes, all things. How else will Andran be respected as Lij, instead of scorned as reminder of Rokh occupiers?"

The General glared up at him. "Aye, I see."

Andran gave a grunting nod.

"Truthfully though, I think there's always going to be those that think of you like that," Tyghus continued. "Many swear no truce between our lands—"

"True people of Valogar always want peace with Rokhs!" the King replied defiantly.

"Not talking about Rokhs and Valogarians like you and I, brother," Tyghus said woozily. "You know exactly who I mean."

Andran broke eye contact and inhaled deeply on the pipe again. "Threat to peace comes from *your* lands."

Tyghus coughed as his eyebrows arched. "Aye? What about the Chibin? What about the godsforsaken Chibin that-that've made threats on your life from the moment you were crowned? What about –"

"I know what said!" the King suddenly bellowed in heavy accent. "I know! But here I sit, thirty-five years later – Lij of independent Valogar!"

"Aye, but the Chibin take credit for that independence! And now – now they see you without a dyron to protect you for the first time *ever!* How will you – what will you do to fight that? How do you convince –"

"*I have the blood of kings running through me!*" the mighty Native roared, eyes bloodshot red as he leapt to his feet. "Kings, not peasants! I am *eighteenth* Andran of my line, Valogar's throne was *always* mine by right, yes? Yes?"

Tyghus nodded in an effort to placate the king.

"I don't need Rokhs to give me throne and I don't need blessing of

Chibin! Chibin *murdered* father, true Lij of land!"

After a long stare, the heaving Valogarian finally seemed to reclaim his emotions, lowering himself slowly to his seat. "Rokhs think they understand Valogar but it is not so simple," he said calmly in lower tone. "Many *hate* Chibin. Many *'pure-blooded'* Valogarians hate Chibin. Valogarians honor strong leader, and strong leader needs *no* Rokh support! But if I were to – die by hand of Chibin –" he paused with mouth open, the first time he betrayed uncertainty. "— my death worth it if my people know I died for *them*. That I'd die a *thousand* deaths for them."

Tyghus struggled to recall where their discussion took such a raucous turn. "I agree with you, brother, I do," he said, further pacifying the Lij, who replied with a curt nod. "I agree. But –" he resumed carefully. "— but then why do you see my lands as the greatest threat? What's the threat?"

The King's demeanor softened further. "From Rokh Emperor."

Tyghus's face wrenched. "This is the Emperor's crowning glory, Andran. He's touted it for more than a decade."

"Not him."

"Then –" the General started, before stopping abruptly. "Kyrus."

Andran was motionless.

Through mugs of the berry drink and the smoke in his lungs, Tyghus had almost forgotten about the startling news he'd received earlier in the night. "I uh... my sister just told me of the Khorokh's health tonight. Doesn't seem possible, he's the only ruler I've ever known, longest the Empire's ever known... but Kyrus as successor is even more unbelievable," he sighed, running a hand down a numb face.

"You see? You admit he is threat?"

"No, no, I was not saying that. I just... just... you never expect a man you've known your whole life to suddenly get named to the highest... the highest..." the General's head spun like a top, causing him to trail off. "No, I'm saying he's a friend and as good a man as you'll find, there's no reason to fear him."

The Lij failed to respond, to which Tyghus took offense. "Well, at least tell me why you think otherwise?"

The King took another deep pipe inhalation before replying, "news from your city was not good, brother."

"What disturbed you so?"

"The successor is said to have lost father to Chibin attack. This is true, yes?"

Tyghus grabbed the pipe from the Lij and took in the sweet burn again. He answered through a cloud of smoke. "Aye. A brother too, in fact."

"And successor is said to hold grudge for losses," Andran continued, before boring his eyes into his brother-in-law. "He's said to seek vengeance on all Valogar for them."

The General looked perplexed. "This is what you've been told?"

"Can it not be believed?"

"On those grounds alone? No!"

"Avenging death of father and brother? Perhaps you overstate friend's forgiveness."

"And perhaps you understate it," Tyghus snapped, eyes fighting to remain focused on Andran. "Perhaps you shouldn't think he's so weak that he would… that he would send our country to war to soothe his vanity. He wouldn't do it. Nor would our Khorokh now choose such a man!"

"He doesn't –"

"And for that matter, I suffered just as much as he did from the Chibin! Me, my sister, your *bride*, we lost a father in the war too, fighting alongside Kyrus's. The same day, the same hour, the same bloody bush! But tonight *I* watched *that* sister, Rokh that she is, take the hand of the Valogarian king. Tonight I sit with you and smoke whatever this is. So don't assume the worst of the man, is what… is what I am saying…"

"But we must prepare for worst even as we pray for best, yes?"

The General sighed again, hands massaging his temples, the haze in his head growing thicker. "I'm of the mind – whatever's bloody left of it – that obsessing over the worst only ensures that it'll happen."

The Lij conceded a smile at this. "A wise saying."

"My father's."

"Wise man. Then what will you do… should worst happen?"

"It's not going to. The Capital wouldn't betray –"

"But if it did?"

"I won't let it."

"But if it did!"

A pause lingered for several moments as the lids of Tyghus's eyes weighed shut. "If it did, I'll do what I'm ordered to do. I'm a general, Andran; I'm a leader of ten thousand men, remember?"

"Thirteen," Andran corrected somberly as his head fell to his chest. He dumped the ashy remnants from the pipe into the fire, watching it turn to smoke.

"This is night of union," the Lij said quietly as he rose. "Night of happiness. We should take heart with people, celebrate with people. With your sister. You come?"

Tyghus was losing the battle to stay awake. "I may join you shortly. May I rest here for a moment?"

"Yes, brother. Rest now."

Almost on command the General's eyes closed, succumbing to the pipe and drink. Soon he was asleep by the crackling fire.

He never heard the Lij leave.

* * *

"*Mondid?*"

A mellifluous voice cut through the cobwebs of Tyghus's dreams.

"*Mondid?*"

An eye opened. It was dark. Cold. Wet.

His head rolled toward a source of light above him. His vision was blurry, and a steady stream of liquid pounded his head.

"Who – who's there?"

"It's raining, Mondid Tyghus."

Suddenly conscious of the damp ground around him, the General tried to hoist himself up. An arm gently hooked around his to assist.

A delicate arm, he realized. His head turned towards the helper's, and in the faint light of a torch, he saw her face.

"Mik – Mikolo?"

Her brilliant green eyes were barely perceptible in the dimness, the outline of her tiara even less so. "Mondid."

His vision slowly grew sharper, and he found that even in his grogginess his eyes longed to pore over her pristine face. Catching himself, he said, "what are you –"

"It's raining, Mondid… must close *gakin* for Lij," she said, gesturing above them.

Tyghus looked up and felt the rain pouring through the canopy opening which had squelched the fire and soaked the rug he dreamt upon. Self-aware, he felt his hair and attire, finding them both drenched. "Aye, it is. Raining on me."

She smiled awkwardly. "Yes. I must close it – will you hold?"

He nodded, taking the torch from her as she retrieved a dowel that reached as high as the ceiling. With surprising deftness, she swiped the dowel through the canopy hole, slipping a covering flap over it and sealing off the interior.

"What hour's this, my lady?" the General asked, steadily regaining his bearings – and enough to feel his heart begin to race from the Valogarian's presence.

She offered another polite smile. "Late."

"Aye," he said with a laugh, running his hands through his hair.

"Thank you for help, Mondid," taking the torch from him as she turned to leave.

Tyghus wracked his dizzy brain for something to say. "Mondid… that's, uh… General, isn't it?"

She stopped and looked back at him, hair whipping as she turned. "Mondid is, yes, General. Warrior."

"Ah, yes. I was uh… I was in and out of your country for five years, but I never picked up many words. Never really tried, I guess…"

"Now you know one, yes?"

He smiled nervously. "Aye," he said, eyes drifting to the floor. Between two jugs of berry wine, he caught sight of the pipe that rendered him unconscious. "Ah, the 'clarity leaves'."

She stepped towards him to look, stifling a chuckle. "*Rantazo*…"

"The leaves?"

She nodded.

"How do you say it?"

"*Rahn—tah—zoh*…"

"*Rantazo*. Well, it got me good, anyhow," he said, smiling despite himself. "That or the jiupan."

"You know three Valogary words, then," she replied.

"So I do – all the important ones?"

"Yes. For those that can use them…"

"Oh, I thought all – I thought all shared the drink… tonight at least," he said, reading her discomfort. "You didn't, then?"

She shrugged but then looked away with a coy smile.

"What?" he asked curiously, before grinning back. "You *did* try it, didn't you? You tried the jiupan?"

"No," she said, her breath in the close quarters suggesting otherwise.

His chest pounded like a stick to a drum as he eyed the jugs at their feet. "Well, would you like to, then?"

"That's Lij's… forbidden."

"Aye."

"That's *Lij's*, Mondid Tyghus."

"And I'm the Lij's brother."

"I can't…"

"Why not?" he asked, his eyes begging her to say yes.

She looked back at him, suddenly shaking hands folded in front of her.

"No harm's going to come to you… I promise."

An awkward silence ensued. "Dry," she finally croaked out.

"What?"

"Um… if we… st-stood somewhere dry?"

Her response caught Tyghus by surprise and a laugh escaped. "I can agree to that," he said, picking up one of the jugs. "I'll give you dryness if you can show me to my –" he looked around him, searching for the proper word for the 'mushroom'.

"This –" she started with a sweeping gesture. "—*ahovy*."

"Ahovy – four words," he said with fingers raised. "To my ahovy?"

He offered his arm, which she immediately eyed with alarm.

"Ready?" he asked gently.

She relented initially, her bare arm dwarfed by the General's armored sleeve, but by the time they got to the exit flaps, she quickly withdrew it, watching the opening apprehensively. "No one can see me... us."

Tyghus recalled his sister's earlier warnings. "Very well," he said, pulling the flap back to see the steady rain outside. "Rain on a wedding day – in my land that's a sign of anger from the gods."

"In Valogar, it rains every day," she said, looking out as well. "We pray to the gods that it never end."

The General smiled. "After you, *manam*."

She eyed him briefly before leaving. "Five words, Mondid?"

Tyghus, what the hell are you doing?

* * *

Simplistic as the ahovys looked from the outside, they were just as sparse on the inside. A small, elevated bed of leaves and straw topped with a woven blanket was tucked into one quarter of the circle; a pit of coals for heating and cooking opposite it, smoke escaping through a canopy opening or cracks in the doorway flaps. The ground was adorned with plain but soft rugs, made from as fine a thread as Tyghus had ever felt.

The General changed quickly before Mikolo came in. His dry, beige tunic, opened loosely at the mid-chest to reveal his silver Dyrator brooch; coupled with his worn trousers, he felt volumes lighter and warmer, despite bare feet and long soggy brown hair. A fire raged on the coal pit in moments, and he reclined in front of its radiance as he tried to look relaxed.

Inside though, his heart pounded as he watched the slender figure enter, her hair and clothes damp and clingy from the walk over. *What are you doing, Tyghus*, he asked himself again, mouth suddenly running dry. Echoing his anxiety, her hand shakily accepted his offer of a blanket to dry herself. She smiled weakly.

"You can sit," he suggested, demonstrating to a spot in front of the pit, as rain intensified its pounding against the ahovy's canopy. "Not so damp there."

He poured them both a mug of the jiupan as she sat, removing a brooch to pull her hair to one side. Strands of it dangled between eyes that glinted in the firelight.

"Better?"

She nodded quickly, meeting his eyes briefly as she took a mug from him. They listened to the pit crackle for a few moments as he watched her take a sip. "You must be the last person in Nar-Biluk to be taking their 'first' drink of the night, manam."

A grin spread over her face as she looked down at the mug she cradled in her lap. "Maybe so, Mondid," she said softly. "Priestess not supposed to

120

drink jiupan."

"Has it been long since you have?"

"Very."

"Then I'm glad you're having a chance this evening," the General said, imbibing himself. "It's been a long time for me as well."

Her brow furrowed as she turned towards him. "You drink jiupan before?"

Tyghus chuckled. "No, far from it," he said, picturing the filthy groghouse in the East Gurums. "I met a friend of mine for a grog – er, a drink from different uh... 'berries' – in my land's capital several weeks ago."

"Weeks!" she cried, which came across as a shout for her. "Had been *years* since I had jiupan. Many, many years..."

"To your first drink in years, then," he said warmly, holding his cup up to toast hers. She looked at it curiously. "In my land, we tap mugs to celebrate things."

Bemused, she awkwardly reached her mug out to touch his.

"You're a Rokh now," he said, winking at her as they both consumed more.

She turned her body to face him, still covered in the thick blanket. "Your capital, it is like Nar-Biluk?"

"A little. But instead of wood, everything is built from stone. Blue stone, white stone, white as the Great Stone itself."

Her eyes narrowed. "Where do you find such stone?"

"From the mountains to the north and east of the city. It's surrounded by stone really, born of it. Legends say my people descended from Bregnomen, the god of the mountains."

"And it is big as Nar-Biluk?"

"Bigger. A million live within its walls."

Her mouth gaped. "So many... I can't picture such things."

Tyghus couldn't help but smile at her wonder as he felt the drinks calm his nerves a bit. "Perhaps you'll see it someday," he said, marveling in his own right at her face, still bearing faint blue streaks of paint. "It's a magnificent sight to behold."

Her smile faded a bit. "Your words make it seem so."

"Have you ever left Valogar?"

She shook her head slowly. "No. Will never be allowed."

Sensing sadness in her voice, he quickly tried turning the conversation back, but the jiupan was already jumbling his thoughts again. "I uh... I hope you didn't think I was rude earlier."

"When?" she asked, looking at him quizzically.

"When you first approached me with the drink next to Tygha. I just wasn't prepared to see, uh –" he stumbled as her emerald greens stared right through him. "Well, to see someone so – so beautiful."

She immediately flushed and looked away from him again. "Don't - can't say such things."

"Why?"

She tilted her head back in his direction, eyes misty.

"Because I shouldn't be here," she said, shaking her head. "Shouldn't talk to you, shouldn't *look* at you... but I am. I don't know why, I –"

"Why do you say that? Why can't you be here?"

You know damn well why.

"I'm... priestess. I'm..." she trailed off with a sigh and swallow of her drink.

Tyghus smiled softly at her. "It's a night of celebration, we're sharing a drink, that's all."

She shook her head. "Not that, Mondid. I'm, how you say, 'marked' by my people."

"I know that."

Her head spun towards his. "How you know?"

"Manam Tygha," he said, sipping his mug.

She looked away, drinking some more. "I'm danger to you, Mondid."

"Tyghus."

"Tyghus?"

"My name."

"Tyghus, I'm danger to you."

"All this because of your green eyes?"

She nodded with chin held low. "You don't understand my people. Just being seen with me is –"

"Miko', I want you to look at me."

She resisted, tear droplets forming at the sides of her eyes.

"Please look at me," he said again, reaching out to touch her blanketed leg. She jumped, but obliged.

"Your... 'marks'. Your 'curse'... your eyes... whatever your people want to call them... they're the most amazing things I've ever seen."

A tear streamed down her face.

"I mean that."

Tyghus, by the gods above, what are you doing?

"The Chib— the how you say, 'pure bloods'... they've killed those that pursue me. This talk right now is most any man has talked to me in years besides Lij."

"I don't fear them," he said, tenderly rubbing her knee.

"I do," she said quickly, eyes still watery. "They've... said terrible things happen if I'm with man. Say they will pluck my eyes out. Cut off nose."

"But you're safe in Nar-Biluk, aren't you?"

"Your people kept Chibin out of Nar-Biluk. Now they almost all gone.

Lij is brave, proud... strong even... but he can't stop Chibin. No one can," she said, letting more drink drain down her throat. "They'll kill me someday. They *want* to kill me."

"They won't. They won't touch you."

"I sound like fool, I know," she said, clearing her eyes with her hands. "I just... just can't believe I'm here."

"On that we agree," Tyghus said lightly, pulling his hand away from her to refill his cup. "To tell you the truth though, I'd – I'd believe anything is possible after the way the last few months unfolded."

She sniffed as she wiped her eyes again, makeup smearing. "Tell me about these months. All village only know you as queen's *kiry* brother."

He confusedly wrinkled his brow. "'*Kiry*'?"

The inklings of a smile came over her. "How you say – 'handsome'."

"Oh," Tyghus said, flushing a bit. "Well, the Queen likes to embellish, doesn't she?"

"No," she said without hesitation, gaze fixed upon him. His eyes broke away as he took another gulp.

"The last few months then... where to begin..." he sighed with a laugh. "First, my love left me—" he started, before catching his recollection of Vara and looking back up at her. "—*first*, my closest friend was appointed to the High Council of Dray'gon Rokh and I've hardly heard from or seen him since. Meanwhile," he continued, chuckling in disbelief at his own story. "Treos and I were ambushed by hundreds of bandits on these horrible, desolate plains in the west of my country; I nearly died a half-dozen times... still can't believe I survived. *Then –*" He took a drink. "—then I ride into Nar-Biluk to watch my sister wed a Valogarian king, er, *the* Valogarian king, only to find out that my closest friend, *the very same one who hasn't responded to a word I've sent*, has been announced as the heir to the Rokhish Throne," he finished, shaking his head in wonder.

Her eyes were wide – and drying. "So many surprises, Mondid."

Tyghus continued as if he hadn't even heard her. "And now... now on the Winter's Ebb, I meet someone who makes me forget all of that."

He hoisted himself up nearer to her, so near that he could smell the wet flowery petals she wore in her tiara. She stared at him with heaving breaths, seemingly frozen in place. He could hear his heart pound in his ears.

Don't do this, Tyghus. It's not right what you're doing.

"*I mean that*," he whispered, mouths tantalizingly close. She recoiled, but only an inch.

"*You don't have to be afraid, Miko'... I don't want you to be af—*"

Their eyes closed and lips met, her body shuddering.

He backed away ever so slightly, meeting her eyes once more. His hand floated up to her jaw and stroked it gently, savoring its smoothness.

He kissed her again.

She let out an almost imperceptible gasp, one tinted with the smell of berries. *"This is bad..."* she whispered, lips breaking with his, before setting her drink down and throwing her arms around his neck to kiss him deeper. He rose to his knees, wrapping an arm around her slender waist to pull her close, while his other hand removed her tiara to better carress her long black hair.

"This is bad..." she purred again, digging her fingertips into the opening of his shirt, a charge racing down his spine.

The sound of her accent drove Tyghus mad, feeling her hot breaths even moreso. As he moved from her lips to kiss her neck, he'd never felt skin so soft.

"I know," he answered, hands searching for the knot behind her neck. *"It's not right..."*

"No, Mondid."

"I'll stop..."

"No, Mondid..."

With a pull, her blouse fell away and her blanket with it, revealing velvety smooth skin interrupted only by petite breasts. As his hands explored them she carefully brought his tunic up and over his head, allowing her lips to press up and down his bare chest.

She looked up at him coyly. *"I stop..."*

Tyghus couldn't help but smirk. *"You'd better not..."* he replied, before slowly allowing her to push him onto his back, propped up with only his elbows. She stood suddenly, and as she pulled out the brooch, her waist-dress fell to the floor.

The General's eyes devoured her naked body, his excitement fueled by the intoxicating brew they'd consumed so quickly. His head spun round with each passing second, any voice of better judgment having departed. With a gentle tug, his trousers slid off easily. She dropped to her knees and drove her face into his, soft tongues darting in and out.

She pulled back a moment to look him in the eyes, pupils clearly aroused, rain pounding ever louder against their abode. *"You'll protect me..."*

"Of course I will..." he said. Seconds later she sat back, and he was inside her.

Time seemed to stop in that moment, in their moment. He didn't know what tomorrow would bring; he didn't care. All that mattered was that one dizzying instant.

Their passion and cries of ecstasy ran deep into the night.

* * *

Dawn.

Light crept into the ahovy through small cracks in the canopy wall.

One beam traced its way across the face of General Tyghus of Tygonium, Dyrator of the Sixth Imperial Dyron in Avergon. As it crossed over his eye, he suddenly awoke, head pounding with each heartbeat. His mouth smacked as if all liquid had been drained from his body, his eyes bloodshot as if in the throes of battle.

He heard sounds of a village awakening outside of the ahovy and he turned to his side to block them out –

Only he couldn't turn.

For atop his left arm lay the "marked" Pureblooded priestess Mikolo, nude as the day she was born into her life of hardship and despair. Her front was to him, though she showed not the slightest hint of stirring with mouth slightly agape, small breaths smelling of berry jiupan. Black strands of hair masked her eyes and chest. He stared blankly at her for a moment, struggling to make sense of the sight before laying his aching head back down. As the ceiling spun above him, the prior night began floating back to him in tiny bits.

Shit.

Chapter XII

"8th D., 10th Mo., Y. 371:

Straggler come into camp today, crack of dawn. The men were right in the middle of their morning parries when someone saw him. Poor lad looked terrible, like he'd been crying and hadn't eaten for days. His armor and tunic was shredded, had blood caked all over his body. Hasn't said a word to anyone yet, but we plan to watch him closely. I myself don't recognize him…

9th D., 10th Mo., Y. 371:

…Turns out that straggler was Kyrus's son! Kyrus the Younger's what we finally got out of him and his story's beyond belief – his father's entire foraging platoon's been wiped out as we feared; well, almost all of it. According to him, Kyrus's son is the only survivor of yet another bush massacre, but only after putting at least a dozen to the sword. I didn't believe him, but he described every single kill he made in detail – location of the wound, weapon used, number of strikes 'til death. Still won't talk about anything else. I've men riding out to the grove where it apparently happened…

10th D., 10th Mo., Y. 371:

Remarkable. Scouts confirmed the battle, said it looked horrific. Natives and Rokhs piled on top of each other so thick the path's almost unwalkable. Said they found a pile of ashes outside the grove with Rokhish armor lying next to it. Wondering if it's what's left of Kyrus's body after his son burned it, set him free, gods bless him. The Younger wouldn't say what happened to it, and the scouts weren't able to find it otherwise…

War Journal of Vaccarius, Former Dyrator of the Imperial Sixth

Dyron

Dray'gon Rokh, Khorian Brex, 30th Day of the Twelfth Month, Y. 383 P.C.

It was cold in the Tower. Maddeningly cold, and it'd been so for the better part of two months. Didn't seem to matter how many logs were thrown on the fire.

His room was small, mirroring the proportions of the Brex chamber he'd met the Emperor in. Where the other room's table would have been, a bed layered in down-stuffed blankets took its place; instead of barren walls, there were shelves of books holding reams of Rokhish tales and legends. In front of the fireplace was a small couch atop a sprawling rug soft as velvet, while across the room sat an immaculately carved wooden chair before a window in place of a balcony.

But it wasn't the cold or cramped quarters that chipped away at his wits, his composure. It was the solitude – the weeks of solitude he'd been confined to since the day of that frantic Lorrio session, a torture hardly broken by servants sliding trays of food through a slot in the iron-barred door. He was "too important to leave the chamber", Jarax told him as he was locked away that fateful day. "Too susceptible to venture the city's grounds" now that he was heir. It was a stinging insult to a man baptized in blood and steel.

So instead, he sat and waited. Day after day, staring jealously at the citizens milling freely about the grounds fifteen stories below. The dearth of human contact led him to seek comfort in odd places, most notably with a crow that landed on his sill each day. The first few times it would study Kyrus, but fly away at his slightest movement; after a month or so of its daily visits, however, it fearlessly hopped about the sill, listening to the man's ramblings and gobbling up scraps of his leftovers. The bird never stayed long, and every time he watched it fly off into the cold air, he did so with a touch of envy. Still, there was a strange comfort in the regularity of the bird's arrivals.

At night, Kyrus would count the stars if they came out, growing steadily more fascinated with the shifting patterns that took shape each time. He'd of course been raised with the seers' teachings that the lights were the spirits of men past, dining at the Table of the Gods until the deities saw fit to return them to the worldly realm. It wasn't until now, though, that he realized how right the seers were – for if the stars were not the spirits of men, what else could produce such radiant beauty?

But the bird, the stars, the meals – they were mere distractions. Momentary diversions from his confused and growing anger at his confinement, at privileges lost, at freedom stolen. The vast emptiness of his days served only to fan those flames, and he had no indication from anybody as to when his plight might end.

Would it go on until the Emperor died? he'd ask the gods. *What if the healers are wrong? What if he lives for a year — or* years*? I'll throw myself from this window before I suffer that long…*

And the letters. He wrote scroll after scroll, dutifully sliding them through the door slot with the servants' promises they were being delivered, just as they swore they'd received no correspondences for him in return. Nothing, though — not from the Emperor, not from Jarax, and especially not from Tyghus, whose bewildered face in the Gurums was the last recollection Kyrus had of the world outside the Arxun.

As the days turned into weeks, the weeks into months, his thoughts grew more and more desperate and suspicious. *Why?* he often wondered aloud or to himself. *Why won't they respond to me? The Khorokh, the Rubator, I shouldn't be surprised at their betrayal… but Tyghus? How could I have so offended him that he won't even bother to ask about me? Then again, almost twenty years I've been waiting for him to forsake me, maybe the moment's finally here… No… no!*

But the more he replayed his last moments with Tyghus in his mind, the more he narrowed down what had changed since he'd returned from the Dead Plains — it was the Lakeman, whatever his name was. Yes, it was the Lakeman he'd been suspicious of from their first exchange, the Lakeman who'd happened to arrive just as Tyghus was ambushed, the Lakeman — a bloody commoner! — that thought he was entitled to just sit in on discussions of the State at his leisure…

Why couldn't — no, why wouldn't the Lakeman try to turn Tyghus against me? Surely, he harbors a grudge against me… certainly jealous of me…

Other nights he reflected more upon the gods, pondering whether they were punishing him for some earthly offense that angered them. But for what? They saw him lead the men into battle without fear time and again — charged across the Red Creeks, stormed the Chibin hideout in the Bluffs, put down the raid on Nar-Biluk itself; and he'd always served the Empire faithfully, always kept an honest tongue… so what could it be? The only thing that it could *possibly* be is…

The Valogarians would suddenly stare back at him as he looked into the fireplace's flames, as if it were five years ago all over again. The boy and his father, eyes brown as dirt, sitting and squatting in their pit, eyeing Kyrus in terror as he stood looking down on them. It'd been too risky to meet with prisoners in Nar-Biluk, not with the rest of his dyron scared of inciting riots among the Natives. So instead, he'd smuggled the two Natives to a deserted village not far from Valogar's capital, a place hardly monitored that he could slip away to whenever the urge suited him — and it suited him often.

They'd dug the hole they squatted in; dug it at the point of Kyrus's sword. It was barely a few feet wide but plenty more deep by the time they'd finished, far deeper than either one could climb out of. The boy broke down in tears more than once, but the only thing Kyrus saw was the man in the pit with him — a skinny man like the one who'd skewered his father in the bush. With that thought, Kyrus actually relished the boy's tears, relished the helpless horror the Native man endured as a result, or the fear he quaked with when Kyrus would question him about his own father.

"Do you remember him?" Kyrus would demand of the Valogarian. "Do you remember stabbing him through the *fucking back?* Do you remember not even giving him the dignity of facing the man who took his life? Do you!" Kyrus's own tears sometimes appeared without warning, which only made him angrier towards his prisoners. "Answer me, you animals!"

Over the weeks to come, Kyrus watched their plight worsen with a mix of disgust and delight. The daily rains gradually filled the hole with water to the extent that the Valogarians' limbs were soaked at almost all times, causing their skin to peel and turn sallow. And while the rains provided them with drinking water, they'd nothing to eat, whittling their frames away to mere skeletons. When they were in their final days, curled in fetal positions and half covered in soiled water, Kyrus made sure to urinate on them or lightly stab them with a spear to jar them awake, drawing blood that brought even more flies to the fetid pit. He didn't know when they passed exactly, nor did he care.

Other Rokhs warned him against torture. Many of his kordettes were vehemently opposed to the entire practice of it, Tyghus most of all. Said there was no honor in it, nothing to gain from it, and that the gods would punish those who practiced it in kind. But Kyrus never understood the logic of those that spoke out and covertly expelled some of those sergeants that did. To begin with, the *Natives* picked the fight with the Rokhs – *they* chose to rebel, *they* declared an unwarranted independence. Even more fundamental, do the Natives even qualify as humans that need be given such courtesies? What about the Chibin warriors who were known to delight in all forms of hideous mutilations of Rokhish captives, what about *them?* That didn't stop Tyghus from declaring that the Empire was the light and should be better than that, and it was that naivete that made Kyrus sometimes wonder how long he could ever truly trust Tyghus when their views were so completely opposite from one another; Rynsyus's peace had buried the issue for the time being, but... To Tyghus's credit though, he would note that Kyrus was leaving Nar-Biluk on those nights he'd head for the village, but never made him confess where exactly he was going. The younger man didn't want to know and Kyrus didn't want to tell.

But now, as Kyrus sat in his own "pit", he wondered if this was the divine retribution he'd been warned of. Sure, he wasn't sitting in his own waste and sure, he had food but still... could it not end up being worse if he's confined to these four walls for months, if not years? Not speaking to a soul, forced to watch the Arxun's denizens walk free on the grounds below the tower, all while questioning whether Tyghus had finally turned against him as he'd ruefully expected? Such were the thoughts he'd been relegated to, day in, day out.

It   was   a   lonely   fate.

Chapter XIII

Fate pays no mind to the most rational thought, the wisest action, or the safest path – and if it did, what boring lives we'd lead.

Rokh Proverb

Kregea Province, Southeast of the Converge, 30ᵗʰ Day of the Twelfth Month, Y. 383 P.C.

Tyghus smiled as he tucked the letter under the folds of his cloak, watching its deliverer gallop off into the distance against the waning light of day. Wrapped comfortably in a blanket before a raging firepit, he gave a gentle nod in the lekey rider's direction.

The Lakeman strolled over to his campmate. "If I didn't know ya' better, lad, I'd say that's a smile on ya' face."

The General looked up. "But you do know me better..."

"Aye, must be me aging eyes, then," Treos said with a laugh, looking off towards the horizon. "So he brought good news?"

"He did, my friend. He certainly did."

They'd traveled hard for nearly two weeks since their dalliance in Nar-Biluk, and were just beginning to come upon the rocky red soil leading up to the Converge. The Mesan city was still two or three days away via the desolate northwesterly route they took, the departed horseman being the first sign of life they had seen in over a week. Their trip notwithstanding, the whirlwind of the Valogarian excursion was still fresh in Tyghus's mind; his thoughts, and perhaps much more, still resided on that rainy peninsula. He closed his eyes as the events replayed yet again...

* * *

The pounding in Tyghus's head did little to mask the reality of the morning he woke up next to the Valogarian priestess. Looking at the naked Mikolo, that reality quickly gave way to a feeling of panic that began in his head and traveled all the way down through his toes. A quick glance down at his own body, clad in only his necklace, reminded him of the prior night's intimacy.

"Shit," he remembered saying.

His body's tenseness woke his bedmate in short order – the first green eye appeared lazily; the second sprang open in horror.

"Shit," he remembered saying again.

She scampered back from him, oblivious to her bareness. Mouth agape, her sternum heaved up and down as she searched for breath. As she drew a hand to her chest, a gasp escaped her and blankets were quickly brought up to her chin.

"Mondid!"

They stared at each other in shock as sounds outside their ahovy became more pronounced.

"Mondid..." she muttered again as she shook her head tightly in disbelief, tears welling at the sides of her eyes already smudged in makeup. "They'll kill me. They'll kill me, Mondid."

Tyghus struggled with even the basics of a reply. Looking around the room, trying to make sense of it, he caught sight of the empty jiupan jug near the entrance and cursed himself. He ran a hand over his face. "Miko'—"

"They'll kill me!"

Her comment made him recall a moment from hours earlier...

"You will protect me... Of course I will."

He sighed and looked at her again, annoyed that even in her distress, he found her lovely as ever.

Focus, you cretin! How could you have let this happen!

His heart pounded harder the more he gathered his wits. "Miko', no one's going to kill you. I promised you that and I-I... *meant* that."

She sobbed into quivering hands. "Mondid, you not understand."

"No, I do Miko', I do," he said as he reached a hand out to her, only to see her recoil further and search frantically for her simple attire. "Miko', *do not* worry, I'll see to it that you're safe. If anyone so much as... as lays a finger on you, or says..."

He trailed off as she clearly ignored him; she was busy slipping back into her waistcover and blouse, before running fingers through her satin hair.

"Miko', please stop. Just for a moment, *stop*."

Moving to kneel at the ahovy's entrance, she eyed the flap with trepidation, body primed as if about to sprint. Suddenly, she took a deep breath and closed her eyes, her expression turning eerily serene; resting her left hand on her temple with the right over her heart, she began whispering words that rang foreign to Tyghus's ears.

"Miko'."

She never broke from her trance. When her whispering finally ceased, she shot a quick glance back at the General, then silently dashed out of the ahovy's entrance.

Then he was alone.

Alone with a silence he didn't want.

Alone with not an idea what to do, waiting for a Valogarian eruption at any moment.

Alone.

The seconds ticked by with agonizing sloth.

When will they come? When will I pay for what I've done?

* * *

Yet the unexpected reigned – no screams, no yells, no furor. After an hour passed staring at the entry flap, braced for the worst, he cautiously pieced his own armored suit back together, but just as he finished, another female startled him by her appearance – Tygha.

She beamed in her bearskin robe as she poked her head into the abode, her mood entirely alien to the General that morning. "The gods lit the day hours ago, brother, you're still in here?" she said cheerfully. "I thought you'd already be headed off by now. Not a fun ride ahead of you."

Tyghus gave her a cautious look. *She doesn't know? Tell her, then... don't hide it.* "Uh... no... no, it's not going to be a fun ride."

She eyed him curiously. "You well? I was kidding of course, I just wanted to catch you before you left. Pity you can't stay longer."

"Oh, I agree," he replied, sweat beading at his hairline. "Very much so. The thought of riding today is, uh..."

He didn't need to finish his sentence as her scanning eyes soon found the empty jug. Flashing a bemused look back at her brother, she said, "I see you enjoyed yourself last night. You look like an absolute wreck."

"Aye... I enjoyed –"

"What's that?" she asked, expression shifting in an instant. Tyghus followed her eyes to a Valogarian brooch – a priestess's brooch – resting atop his blanket.

His neck burned as she looked him in the eyes again.

Just tell her, already!

"Tyghus, what is that?"

"Tygha..."

"Gods no... Tyghus, tell me you didn't."

The General could barely face her as he ran two hands over his eyes and through his hair. He sat down with a graceless plop, legs bent in front of him.

"Tyghus, tell me that's not a priestess's brooch."

"Tygha, listen."

His sister's eyes widened further. "Gods above, tell me that's not *Mikolo's* brooch."

"Tygha, *listen.*"

Her eyes closed as hands gripped her head. "No... please no..."

"Tygha, what happened last night... it was foolish... *beyond* foolish –"

"Foolish?" she asked incredulously. "Foolish? Tyghus, have you lost your mind? Honestly!"

"I know –"

"What – *by the gods high and low!* – what did I tell you last night! How could you *not* have understood the *importance* of what I told you? Of – of – of the *gravity* of what you've now done!"

"I know, dammit! I know it was wrong!"

"Oh, you do? Do you?"

"Aye! But no one'll find out, Tygha. No one will tell – certainly not me, certainly not... her..."

"No one has to tell anyone, Tyghus! Everyone knows each other's business here, it's only a matter of time! You have sentenced this poor girl to death!"

"No! That's not going to happen. I won't let it."

"You won't? You're a god, now?"

"I promised her, Tygha! I promised I'd protect her, and I don't care what the circumstances are, our house *keeps its promises!*"

"Indeed, like when you promised me you understood what I'd told you last night, hm? Or does that one not count? Is it only *some* promises, chosen at your leisure?"

Tyghus couldn't even look her in the eye anymore.

"So tell me, how will you protect her as you take off on a thousand-mile trek?"

"Work with me, Tygha," he begged, shame in his voice. "I'm in this now, whether we like it or not so help me. Help me help *her.*"

"Tyghus…" she seethed as she paced the room, shaking her head with a disbelieving smile. Finally, she threw her hands up. "What, is this about Vara? That girl so rattled you that you'd throw all your better judgment out the door for a match between the sheets? You've a bloody broken heart, it heals! You don't forget who you bloody are in the meantime!"

Tyghus's brow furrowed, a surge of his own anger bubbling within. "No, I –"

"I just don't understand it. You're a Rokhish nobleman! A general even! You could surely marry any woman in the Realm in time, to say nothing of the hundreds, *thousands* of Valogarian women around here last night. Yet you bed the one person, *the one woman* in the world that I expressly said you were *forbidden* to!"

"Aye, you did and as I keep saying, I *know* I did you wrong… but this is *not* about Vara."

She whirled to face him again with doubting eyes, hair whipping like a pennant. "Aye? Is it not?"

"It is not."

"Then what is it?"

"Does it matter now?"

"Yes!" she shouted fiercely. "Tell me what drove you to do something this – this *absurd*, only to then stand here and proclaim your desire to 'protect' her. Please!"

Tyghus swallowed deeply, closing his eyes for a moment as his stomach nearly rebelled. "I –" he stopped with a sigh, wiping more cold sweat from his brow. "I shouldn't have allowed what happened here to happen. *But –*"

"Oh, don't you say it."

"– it *did*. And right or wrong," he started, licking dry lips as his sister pierced into him. "She's remarkable, Tygha," he finally said with conviction. "She's remarkable, she's beautiful, she's… dammit, I felt

135

something with her, I swear it to you."

"You *felt* something?" Tygha cackled in astonishment. "You don't even know her, Tyghus! She barely speaks Rokhish, by the gods, how could she —"

"I know it sounds ridiculous, but —"

"And your pining for Vara had nothing to do with it? This *brew* had nothing to do with it?" she demanded, pointing at the empty jug. He started to answer before Tygha simply about-faced, showing him her back. "Tyghus, stop. The jiupan hasn't worn off of you yet — I *pray* that it hasn't," she said sharply, before sighing loudly and bringing hands to her hips. "I — I..." she finally gave up with a shake of her head, angrily swiping the entry flap aside to storm out, leaving Tyghus alone with the silence he'd come to despise so much.

* * *

Hours passed by the time Tyghus retrieved his horse and his cohort Treos in preparation for their exit. The latter had the look of a man with stories of his own when the General found him stumbling through the dark recesses of a "mushroom" cluster beyond the Hill; given their libationary fogs, however, neither was up for trading tales just yet. As they fastened supplies to their steeds at the Hill's gate, the General eyed the royal ahovy with consternation, knowing he had to make the trek.

He found the Queen near the spot where he'd napped the evening prior, adorned in a plain tan dress that fell to her ankles, its top tying off behind her neck. Her hair was pulled up into a tight bun held in place with two golden twigs, her hands busily working a wooden sandal's broken strap. The garkin above her was open to the sky again, letting the sun bathe her in a beam of light.

Silly as he knew it was, Tyghus somehow found her more approachable with this changed look and environment; indeed, he saw the stern eyes she greeted him with as an improvement from the angry ones in his dark ahovy. Looking around her, Tyghus was thankful she was alone.

"Tygha..." he started, allowing a hint of a smile.

She looked away from him, he hoped out of fear that she may return the expression. "I don't have time for this. I'm leaving to give my locks to a priestess now that I'm wed."

"Mari'd be sick if she knew you were losing that beautiful hair of yours today. I remember —"

"What do you want, Tyghus? I told you I've little time."

Tyghus flinched at her tone and sighed. "I'm sorry, Tygha," he said gently, to which she simply shook her head. "I'm sorry, but I still need your help."

She threw the sandal to the ground and looked at him with a mixture of annoyance and helplessness. "What, Tyghus? What should I do?"

"Well, you're a queen now. Can't they do what they want?" he quipped, trying to elicit a smile.

"Don't make light of this."

"I'm sorry," he said, knowing he was succeeding, inch by inch. "I don't know what you should do, but you're all I've got."

"You know Andran," she said darkly. "Why don't you ask him? Sure he'd be pleased."

"I'll keep that in mind," he said, a wave of panic shuddering through him at the thought of the Lij finding out. "Just... just keep eyes on her, I don't know. Stay alert to any sign that word's gotten out... that'd mean more than anything."

"Tyghus, I –"

"I know you *can't* promise anything, and I wouldn't want you to. I don't want to put you in any danger, so *always* place your well-being first; if she dies..." he sighed. "If she dies, she dies, it'll be a burden and a disgrace I'll carry. Just – just do what you can. I can't ask more than that."

"You can't. You literally can't, because I don't know if I can even do what little you're asking."

"I know."

She stared hard at him, a thin line of a mouth bearing the faintest inklings of a smile, albeit an exasperated one. "You're so fortunate to be blood."

Tyghus returned her look. "Don't I know it. Believe me, the shame I feel even asking you this is beyond anything I can describe."

After a brief silence, her face turned compassionate. "I'll do what I can for the poor girl."

"That's all I ask," he said. "Should I sacrifice to the goddess of mercy, the patron of wisdom, or..."

Her eyes widened above an expanding grin. "You've found the gods again, have you? I can't imagine they'd recognize you."

"I mention them now and again..." he said sheepishly.

"Doesn't mean much if you're saying their names like they're just another word," she said pointedly.

"Maybe so, but since they seem to be tolerating me at the moment," he started as he pulled a folded piece of parchment from his cloak. "I'll push my luck and ask you one last thing..."

"Oh, gods above... I'd take that luck and flee this city as fast as possible if I were you."

"You were always the smarter of the two of us."

"What is it, then?"

"Can you write the Valogary tongue?"

"The basics, aye," she replied suspiciously.

He looked to the parchment then back to his sister. "Can you translate this to her?"

"To *Mikolo?*"

He nodded.

She closed her eyes. "What've you done now?" she asked, taking the parchment from him.

"Just... please."

"And what am I going to be translating when I open this?"

Tyghus looked behind him, then around the room again as he pondered her question. "It's an apology... for what I've done to cause her fear, to put her in danger. She doesn't deserve that and it's not right that I've done it. It lets her know that my promise to protect her is an oath I'll take with me to my grave; that it's one I stake my House's honor upon." He took a deep breath. "But it also lets her know that what happened between us – whatever the hell it was that happened between us – I don't regret it. It says... it says never did I expect to travel halfway across the known world and stumble upon someone so beautiful, so... captivating, and I hope, I *pray* it's not the only time the gods let us cross paths. But if it is, well, I ask her to forgive me... but not to forget me."

Tygha's eyes narrowed on her brother. "Tyghus, feeling sorry for this woman or about what you did, or thinking that you somehow need to set things right is only going to make this harder and more dangerous for her – and you."

Tyghus blanched, a bit of a scowl creeping onto his face. "Did you hear what I said?"

"I did, did you hear me?" she replied without delay. "Do you realize you'll be a target as much as she is if you keep this up? More so?"

The General nodded quietly.

"Why doesn't that concern you?" she questioned with confusion. "You've always been so rational, so careful as long as I've known you – even when you were a little boy. Always doing the 'right' thing as pari would say, always the safest path... and now this? I just don't recognize you."

Tyghus thought about her comment for a moment, before finding himself in complete agreement. "It's not the safest path; probably not the 'right' thing either, only time will tell me that," he said, then shrugged. "I guess... I guess sometimes it pays to just do what feels good, not necessarily what *is* good. Heard that once, never lived that way before and I can't say I'd do it again... but it is what it is. It felt good..."

"To one of us, maybe."

Tyghus smirked.

"You're *really* serious about this?"

"I am."

Her stare lingered on him for a moment before clasping her hands together. "Very well," she said through pursed lips. "I'll take care of what I can, but promise nothing more than that. Safe travels, brother. You'll be in my thoughts and prayers... you'll need them, I fear."

"Thank you, love," he said, moving closer to embrace her in a deep hug. "And cheers to the new queen of Valogar. Pari would be proud."

"Of me? Perhaps. Of you?" She rolled her eyes at him. "Goodbye, Tyghus."

"Goodbye, Tygha."

After mounting his horse to leave with Treos, he looked back towards the Tayshihan, magnificent as ever against the day's rare pale blue sky. In front of it stood a lone figure watching them – she was slender with silken black hair... and eyes green as emeralds.

* * *

As he rested now before the crackling campfire, a few days out from the Converge, Tyghus couldn't stop beaming. He tapped the courier's letter nestled snugly beneath his cloak, its contents running through his head:

"I regret nothing... would have it no other way if I did... do not forget me. – 'Miko'"

Chapter XIV

When you must take your walk with death, let three smiles
cross your face —
a loving smile for those left behind;
a joyful smile for departed friends soon re-embraced; and
a knowing smile for the dead that thought they were rid of
you.

Rokh Proverb

Dray'gon Rokh, Khorian Brex, 1ˢᵗ Day of the First Month, Y. 384 P.C.

The morning began like countless others in the hell of the Brex's confines. The night prior brought the arrival of the 384ᵗʰ year Post-Cataclysm, carrying sounds of jubilance and excitement to his open window from the distant grounds below; Kyrus, of course, could only listen with the same somber detachment that his temperament had become. Despite the night's chill, he fell asleep in his chair with his face still propped up by a fist.

A sudden rapping startled him from his slumber. He wasn't sure what woke him until another violent pounding erupted at his door.

"By the gods, what is it?" he barked angrily, wiping away drool that spilled into an increasingly unkempt beard. Daybreak had begun, but dark gray clouds kept any brightening to a minimum. A light coating of snow had settled on the sill.

The door swung open without announcement to reveal the man who locked the Heir in the chamber over a month prior – Kyrus's perennial escort, Jarax.

The sight of the Rubator caused a blind rage to overtake him, hardly tempered by his sleepy daze. "You son of a whore!"

Kyrus sprinted across the room towards the Guard, ignorant to the clods of long hair blocking his view.

"My lord! What are –"

A tackle dropped the Red with a resounding clang as his armor bounced off the stone floor. "My lord!"

"*Bastard!*" Kyrus screamed as he readied fists to pound the Red, helmet or not. "*What the hell do you think you're doing to me! Locking me up like a petty thief – like a* beggar!"

The Heir's arms were restrained as the other startled Rubitian Guards regained their composure and pulled him off their leader.

"*Do you know who I am! Who my father was!*"

The four guards could barely restrain the furious man, but did so long enough to let Jarax scramble to his feet. The Heir panted heavily, maniacal eyes still trained on his target.

"What the hell is the matter with you?" Jarax demanded, rubbing the back of his helmet with a grimace.

"You've ruined me, you bastard… you-you *whore*… it's all ruined…"

The Rubator glared back at his escortee with mouth agape. "By the gods, ruined what?"

"Everything… now let me go, Jarax, or gods' help me I'll have you fed to the pigs when I'm Khorokh…" Kyrus seethed. "Damn it all, I will…"

Jarax further re-situated his shiny plate armor beneath his blazing red tunic. "Well, you'll have your chance shortly then. I'm here at this ungodly hour on the Khorokh's orders," he said, eyes burning right back into

Kyrus's. "He takes his last breaths."

Kyrus didn't blanch at the revelation, but his body's resistance faded. "And he requests me *now*? *Weeks* of silence, of ignorance, of *complete disdain* and *now* he beckons me?"

Jarax simply nodded. "So will you walk like a man, or do I need you escorted like the petty thief you claim you're not?"

The Heir shook his arms free of the Rubitio.

Jarax eyed him suspiciously at first, but finally turned his back. "If you're going to kill me, my lord, all I ask is that you do it now. Rather a tumble down these steps than a pig feedin'."

* * *

Torches lined the Heir's spiraling descent from his room. Jarax kept a brisk pace that left Kyrus gasping for breath after so many weeks of confinement, before entering the bedchambers of Rynsyus himself.

The space echoed the Emperor's decaying health in the bed across the room. Banners and emblems once surely brilliant upon creation now hung musty on the walls; swords and shields of eras past were mounted upon marble busts, but were hopelessly corroded and useless for battle. Even the Imperial maps the Khorokh so proudly pored over in better days lay strewn about the stone floor in tatters.

The air was thick with the incense given off by sticks of wax and herbs burning on either side of the Emperor's bed. Healers had long maintained that they improved the mind and body but the sight of his withering face didn't lend much credence to those tenets. To the contrary, the scents were on the verge of making Kyrus gag.

Rynsyus's head jerked at the sound of the doors swinging shut, Jarax departing without a word. The Heir stood bewilderedly eyeing the bed until a shaky bony hand beckoned him forward. Kyrus barely trusted himself at the moment, his frenzied anger from upstairs hardly subsiding, but he let himself be drawn to the bedside.

Eyes sunken into a gaunt face peered back at him, Rynsyus's head resting atop a bloated neck and throat as he squeezed gasps from his lungs. Bloody rags littered his sheets and pillows, their crimson the only hint of color about the ruler. It was a pitiful image, even if Kyrus had exhausted his capacity for sympathy. His countenance betrayed him.

"You're troubled, my son?" a raspy voice croaked.

Kyrus's reply was slow in coming. He shook his head in his bedside chair as he looked to the ground. "I shouldn't be here," he muttered.

"My son?"

"I shouldn't be here, I said," Kyrus said in louder, angrier tone.

"Why?"

"'Why?' 'Why?' 'Why' he asks," Kyrus repeated back to himself. "Because I'm not okay with this."

The old man looked utterly baffled. "With what?"

"Any of this! Of being locked away like a rat! Of being fed like a leper! Of being kept in total *isolation!* Why would you do this –"

"It was for your own–"

"*I'm not finished!*" the Heir yelled, suddenly exploding from his chair. His frankness surprised them both, and as feeble as he was, Rynsyus's eyes widened. "You abandoned me! You drag me from Avergon, you make me heir to a throne I don't even want and then you bloody abandoned me! Now I – I –" Kyrus turned his back and paced away from the bed, followed by an explosion of the Emperor's coughs.

"I must say, your anger surprises me…"

"Well, it shouldn't," Kyrus snapped. "You betrayed me. My lord and sovereign, the man whose banners I've served all my life, and he betrays me…"

After several of Rynsyus's wheezing breaths, he heard, "Kyrus, I want you to listen to me. It's all I ask of you… just that you listen."

"I can hear you, Majesty," the livid Heir barked back.

"I know you can hear me, *but I want you to listen!*"

The Heir fumed but kept silent.

"Kyrus, anything I've done, I've done so for one reason and one reason only – the survival of this Realm. I told you that on the night we met. Not *my* survival, not even *your* survival if you must know, but the *Realm's* – your life goes hand in hand with that reason, do you understand? And between my ailments, the Arxun ministers angered by my decision in choosing you, the men that call themselves Lorrions – there was simply no other way to keep you protected from them all."

"Protected?" Kyrus said, spinning to face the bedridden man. "Protected? And what of my letters, sent out with *your* tower's servants? What of them? They *told* me they were received yet not a single bloody response! What threat were they!"

Rynsyus's brow furrowed in confusion, gray eyebrows cringing. "I know nothing of such letters. Never forbade them; never forbade their being answered either."

Kyrus's heaving breaths slowed as his eyes narrowed. "That cannot… be true… *tell me* it's not…"

But the Emperor only stared back blankly, leaving Kyrus's eyes to water. *"You have no idea what that implies, Your Highness…"* he said in near whisper, before finally looking away to compose himself. "Well, I don't need your protection and I never did. Give me a sword, give me a shield and I'll take care of myself like I always have. Let the assassins come for me if they want me!"

"That's admirable, my son, but you know I could never have allowed that, not even for a second."

"Why not? If the gods truly want me, then the gods will take me, who are you to say otherwise?"

"Because I looked upon you not long ago and saw the *future* of our land," the old man croaked out. "You *must* believe me – and it was a *good* future."

"How can you say that, though? You don't know a bloody thing about me," Kyrus retorted, throwing his hands out in wonder. "If you did, you'd realize your error in picking me. I'm a godsforsaken soldier, simple as that, I don't have the bloody mind or patience for government –"

"You said the same to me before and as I said then, you worry over *nothing*. Oratus is as able an administrator as this Realm needs; he'll inform and guide you in the tasks to be done, but that Kyrus –" the Emperor forced a bony finger in the younger man's direction. "—that's all irrelevant. You already know *all* that you *need* to know, and none of that which you don't."

"You're asking me to grovel and bribe and lie and do whatever else it is that goes on in these wretched halls in the name of our 'glory', as if the fools up here have the slightest idea what it is! I *don't* –"

"I'm not asking you to do any of those things!"

"Come now, Highness! You finally called on me, so let's speak plainly. I'm no fool to what goes on here."

"Aye, but it doesn't *have to!* What you know is the military – you know creeds, you know honor, you know obedience. So command the throne and Lorrio like you'd command your soldiers. You'll either get what you seek from them or at least keep them from doing otherwise."

Rynsyus's breath gave way to more hacks and wheezes, his eyes rolling back into his head. "Now will you just sit... and talk with me as I... as I leave this world?"

The Heir clenched his teeth with blue eyes glaring, but finally he drew near once again.

"Kyrus... I wanted to speak with you more, I really did. To tell you my thoughts, tell you my mind. To try and convey what I've learned in this life. But I told myself that to do so would have defeated why I chose you in the first place, so I promised myself that I wouldn't. It was the hardest promise I've ever had to keep, but you *need* to take the throne with a clear mind – unsullied by the Lorrio or an aged Khorokh, for even I have my prejudices. And if we'd spoken more, what if you'd been cursed with my affliction? Not much use telling you my life only to have you die 'long with me, is there?" the Emperor said distantly, before his tone turned contemplative. "Though I confess that I've wondered... I've wanted to ask what kind of ruler you'll be?"

Calming a bit, Kyrus said, "as you would have it, I guess I'll be a general. Command the Arxun rats like I commanded my soldiers. What other way could I know?"

"Ah yes… the soldiers," Rynsyus mumbled whimsically with eyes closed. "Did the soldiers beget the land or did the land beget the soldiers? I've struggled with that my whole life."

Kyrus pondered the question for a moment before disregarding it. "Will you tell me one thing about *your* life, Highness?"

"To the extent I can recall it…" he replied with a flicker of good humor.

"Just tell me this – is it true what Antinax said about you?"

"Antinax? It's such a shame he lost his way… so brilliant… so much potential for good. What does he say of me?"

"When you announced me as your successor, he said that you were chosen by Khorokh Terrius to break the Valogarians once and for all."

"Ah yes… I remember…" the Emperor said, sounding faint and far away.

"Well, that's my question… were you?"

"To finish something it must be capable of being finished, my son," Rynsyus replied, a bit more lucidly. "There's no 'finish' in Valogar – but it could finish *us*."

"But *were* you?" Kyrus persisted.

"Perhaps I was. But I realized his vision wasn't in line with what was achievable there… couldn't have brought peace and prosperity, just perpetual war… that prospect didn't burden his mind like it did mine."

"You didn't feel like you'd betrayed the man when you abandoned his vision?"

The Emperor's body blanched at the pointed question; his eyes cracked open. "I did *not* betray anyone," he said sharply. "Terrius wasn't bigger than the Realm and I wouldn't drain our blood and coffers to satisfy his ideals any more than I'd do so to placate the Nortics… or my own family." He eyes turned mournful for a moment. "My own sons haven't spoken to me since I decided for peace; I die alone for *my* decisions… but why, *why* should I sanction killing those who would trade with our own people? Share their ideas, their culture with our people like we've done with so many others? Terrius spat on that – I did not."

Kyrus glared back at the emaciated figure, irritation growing again, but Rynsyus was undeterred. "Didn't a seer once say 'it is man's folly not to stray from the errant path'?"

The Heir shrugged. "I don't know, Highness. Sounds like a battle creed to me."

The Emperor's eyes stayed cracked but his head rolled away from his guest. "I've heard of your deeds on the battlefield… tales of your bravery… your legend in the bush. You're blessed to have such courage;

you'll need it as Khorokh."

Kyrus sighed and stared off through the window across the bed. "Men see courage where they want to see it."

"That wasn't courage?"

"What is courage if you have nothing to lose? My father, my brother... they were everything to me and they were gone. And when my mother went mad with grief and drowned herself in our well, I had nothing, bloody *nothing*," the Heir said as his eyes immediately misted over. "I *wanted* to die after that... charged the battlefield with no regard for my life because I had *none*... men saw that and thought it to be courage, but I always saw it as a way to leave this world with honor... a way out of the betrayals and –"

"Why do you keep saying that, my son? Why do you keep speaking of betrayals?"

Kyrus paused and hung his head as tears dropped to the floor, his clogging nose running into the coarse hairs of his upper lip. "I certainly didn't ask for them."

"Who are they, though? Who are these people that betrayed you?"

The Heir wiped his face with his tunic's sleeve. "They're everywhere, Highness... littered throughout my life, all the way back to my days at the Academy. There was Kirodus, my instructor in swordswork... he tried to have me banished from the grounds for something I didn't even do. And Tolfiax, the first kordette I served under... he spread lies about my loyalty, tried to keep me from being given a kord in my own right..." his chest started burning more and more with each deceptive face that popped into his mind. "Then – then the men that conspired against me when I *became* kordette –"

"Calm yourself, my son... calm yourself..."

Kyrus barely heard him. "- they thought I'd never find out... thought they were *so* clever." He shook his head with gritted teeth. "It's never stopped, Highness... even my bloody father betrayed me."

"Your father? Say that's not true."

"It is. He left me. He promised he wouldn't, he promised he'd swim the Ratikan Sea before he'd let the gods take him in Valogar but he walked right into it... and I'd told him I saw something, dammit! I bloody told him but we kept on goin' into the green!" A series of sobs embarrassingly overtook him. "I'd burn every bush in that country if I could!"

The Emperor gave the Heir a moment to grieve before he offered softly, "your father did what he thought was right... even if it doesn't make sense to you now."

Why does he speak to me as if he even remembers my father's face?

"What do you even know of him?" Kyrus replied coldly.

"I know he gave his life for the Empire... gave the ultimate sacrifice."

"Aye, and what'd the Empire give him?" Kyrus said, eyes aflame.

"What'd the Empire do to honor his legacy?"

"The Empire gave his son a chance to live in *peace*," the Khorokh said with what little emphasis he could muster. "She gave his son a chance to *build upon* that peace."

"But... *he never wanted peace.*"

"What parent doesn't want peace for their children?"

"My father never asked for that," Kyrus repeated. "If you'd ever spoken with him, you'd know he'd see this 'peace' we have quite differently."

"And how would he see it?"

"As surrender," Kyrus said quietly. "And I dare say he'd see my taking of the throne as the chance to set that right."

The Khorokh's breaths became even more labored as his eyes showed signs of alarm. "'He' would say that?"

"Aye... 'he'."

"Why do you believe that?"

Kyrus looked hard at the Emperor through damp eyes that glistened in the faint light. "Because with his dying breath... seconds before the Valogarian took his life in front of me... he looked at me and said, 'Don't forget this.'"

The Emperor's squinted eyes widened further as his counterpart's bored into him.

A hint of a smile crept across the young man's face. "And I tell you, Highness, I've wondered what he meant by that my whole life. Thought about it a hundred times a day. Probably a thousand in the last two months. All I know's what I promised him, dead or alive..."

Rynsyus could only stare at him as the Heir leaned in close, hot tears streaming down his cheeks. "That I would never forget what happened... what those Natives did."

Kyrus watched the Khorokh's eyes frantically bulge from under heavy lids. "You'll be seeing him at the Table soon... will you tell him I remember? Will you tell him I've never forgotten?"

The old man's wheezing became even more pronounced, coughs more congested. *"Jar... Jarax..."* he gargled to Kyrus's shock.

"I beg your pardon, Highness?"

"Jarax... Jarax!"

Kyrus scowled at the plaintive request. "He can't hear you."

"Jarax!"

"He's not coming."

"Jar —" Rynsyus's panicked eyes suddenly rolled back, his head falling away from Kyrus. His chest filled with air one final time before his breath gave out.

Kyrus stared at the royal corpse for a bit, waiting for thoughts or emotions to touch him now that he'd passed. But he felt nothing for the

Khorokh, this man who'd seemingly given him everything. The only words he had were the ones he learned as an eight-year-old tob', that familiar battle cry that had been uttered by Rokhs for centuries.

For   the   Glory   of   Man   and   Empire.

PART II

Chapter XV

"For what could peace be, but an illusion? A pleasant illusion, of course, but an illusion all the same."

Quote from the writings of Cassyus of Kyles, two weeks before Cataclysm

Kregea Province, The Converge, 3rd Day of the First Month, Y. 384 P.C.

"I remember pari telling me that the Converge is the only place in Andervold where one can stand and see all the land's fury in one place – earth, fire, ice, and water."

"Did he, lad?" Treos said as he squinted at Tyghus. "I think he forgot about this bloody wind."

Tyghus laughed as he pulled his horse in tow behind him. "Ah, it only feels that brisk because of the Bridge, my friend."

The Lakeman took a glance over the thick, stony railings of the Vargorus Bridge to the River Clyves some sixty feet below, and his face almost instantly turned green. "Thank ya'... that's a comfort."

The sun was bright and unimpeded that morning, but stiff canyon winds indeed snuffed out any warmth the two Rokhs might have taken from it. Thousands of men, carts, and beasts that surrounded them suffered the same ordeal, all in the name of trying to cross into the Converge. The Bridge, notorious for its construction as much as its traffic, was a masterpiece of Rokhish engineering, spanning 1,500 feet across the canyon and fifty feet wide. Massive guardposts anchored the bridge to the soft stone of the north canyon wall, where Rokhs waited to register each vendor coming and going.

The view from the Bridge did justice to his father's description. To the far south he could see the fertile grasslands of the Lower Rokhlands; to the west burned the fiery sands of the Skulls Desert; to the north were the highest Mesan peaks, capped white with snow; and of course below them ran the waters of the mighty River Clyves. The Converge, then, was the logical moniker for this confluence of nature's elements, even if it was originally chosen by Rokhish conquerors centuries prior in recognition of the peoples who had already established a crossroads there. Tribes from the Desert, men of Colvery, Peninsular Natives, Clannic remnants, civilized Raizana, descendants of the Early Kings, and of course the peaceful Mesan natives had been trading at the outpost for hundreds of years before the Rokhs arrived.

Once the area fell under the Empire's control, the city's profile changed dramatically, with Rokhish investments quickly growing the Mesans' simple trading post into a settlement of several hundred thousand souls. Imperials could transport materials to southwestern Lowland towns or other fringe outposts via the River Clyves much faster than proceeding overland through the region's meandering roads. Without the Converge, in fact, there could be no fortress of Avergon to project Rokhish power across the Lowlands, let alone the Trail that supplied it.

Thus, to know the Converge, one must know the Clyves, the Imperial divider between the Upper and Lower Rokhlands. Its torrential gushing began high in the Astoren Mountains to the east, carving a deep gash across verdant Rokh farmlands. As it traveled southwesterly, however, the river's power steadily waned, fanning out to become broad and shallow, the soil around it dryer and more arid. As it did, the great red Stylian Mesas formed on either side of it, creating at its deepest a canyon of some thousand feet.

Tyghus marveled as he looked upon the Mesan homes carved into the north canyon's rockface, some as low as the riverbank and others as high as the mesa's top. They were simple, square-shaped rooms punched into the stone, leaving natural overhangs as shields against the elements. Stairways connecting the homes wound in and out of view, with one in particular linking the riverbank's ports to the main trade plaza where the Vargorus Bridge met the north canyon wall.

"Like an ant hill, isn't it?" Tyghus asked as he watched thousands of Mesans clog the stairways, heading to or from docked trade vessels.

His friend refused to reply, still too ill to speak. The General glanced at him and smiled. "Don't worry, more than halfway across now. Not that you'd feel any pain from a drop at this height anyway."

"Show me the man who can vouch for that."

"So heights are your weakness; never would have thought."

"I've hardly seen anything higher than a sand dune my whole life, ya' pig," Treos snorted back, still averting his eyes from the railing. "I should have just waited for ya' in Avergon."

"But then you'd miss the views, Treos," Tyghus pointed east. "Look at it! Look at the majestic Clyves!"

"I'm gonna have ya' swimmin' in it pretty soon."

The General chuckled when a hushed silence suddenly fell over the raucous din of the bridge's travelers. He shot Treos a curious look, then craned his neck to see over the crowd. The cause for concern wasn't apparent at first, but then he could see a pack of furious crossers at the northern Bridgegate bellowing at the top of their lungs, their yells echoing between the canyon walls. Tyghus couldn't make out the dialect but it clearly wasn't Rokhish. The Rokhish Bridgeguards roared back, but there too the words escaped the General. It wasn't until a warning horn blew that Tyghus leapt into his horse's saddle to gain better vantage.

"The hell is it, Tyghus?" Treos asked. "Get me off this thing already."

"Problem at the gate," he muttered, eyeing a mass of brown-cloaked men trying to get their four carts through the checkpoint. Covering blankets had been ripped off the carts to reveal their contents, which appeared from Tyghus's distance to be large, reflective boulders. "Looks like two, maybe three dozen trying to get through. Maybe hauling silver ore? Looks a bit too shiny, though."

Smoke billowed at the gate as the crossers waved torches.

The General's eyes narrowed. "Broad daylight, the hell they need torches –"

All of a sudden one of the crosser's words rang out clearly:

"*—Chibin!*"

Torches touched the carts.

"Treos back up! Back –"

A flash of light.

An ear-busting explosion.

The stone and wood guardhouse was torn asunder, guards and cloaked men alike sent flying over the railings of cliff and Bridge. Debris showered crowds on all sides, moving faster than any arrow Tyghus had ever seen. The entire ground shook from the blast, though Tyghus watched in horror as the ground did more than just shake – the edge of the cliff where the guardhouse once stood crumbled uncontrollably, sending nearby onlookers to their deaths sixty feet down.

Screams became more deafening than the explosions. Tyghus tried desparately to wheel his horse in the opposite direction amid bridge vendors in full fledged panic with the same thought. The General watched helplessly as the weak and elderly were trampled or knocked over Bridge railings to watery graves.

"*Come on girl, turn! Turn!*"

Tyghus glanced back at where the guardhouse had been – and saw two more flashes of light from torched carts.

The new bone-rattling detonations killed adjacent vendors instantly and made the whole Bridge sway. Tyghus couldn't believe his eyes as its northernmost segment broke away from the rest and crashed into the Clyves. Some had scrambled off the collapsing chunk, but thousands had not, their bodies soon littering the ground and water. Strong winds carried the dust away from the blast site, revealing an almost hundred-foot void between Bridge and northern wall.

"*Gods above…*"

Tyghus looked at the mass around him and pulled some of the feeble up onto his mount to avoid the stampede. Treos did the same, both steeds now pressing through the crowd, attempting to instill some semblance of order along the way. While the Bridge's collapse no longer felt imminent, the rest of the crossers clearly felt otherwise.

Another blast at the Converge. More screams.

Tyghus whirled his head rearward again to watch at least two stories of cavehomes above bridge-level collapse. One pack of the attackers had made it through the gates before its destruction, pushing a flaming cart into the market-cave thereafter. Rokhish guards funneled down steps carved into the canyon wall where the attackers greeted them with vigor, a small battle erupting on the dwindling grounds. Many attackers were cut down, but several guards fell victim to the wall's crumbling edge, their bodies soon broken upon the growing pile of dead along the river. By the time the first wave of Rokhs perished, only one attacker remained. He turned to face the retreating bridge-crossers, raising his arms as if to taunt them, shouting:

"Maheny ny Chibin! Maheny ny Chibin!"

Another group of Rokhs converged on the figure in short order, impaling him with countless blades. The cloaked body slumped forward, falling off the cliff to crash into the riverbank.

Chaos reigned.

* * *

A mass of people watched in stunned silence from the southern canyon wall. Stampeded bodies littered the portion of the Bridge still standing, and it took nearly an hour for Tyghus and the other onlookers to finish removing them. Men, women, children, and beasts – none were spared in the panic. Parents wailed as they identified loved ones.

No matter how long he stared, Tyghus couldn't believe it was real. Even from 1,500 feet away now, the damage to the Converge was incredible, to say nothing of the yawning chasm in the Bridge, rendered useless now. The Cliff City looked like a furious beehive, with thousands frantically milling about the caves all the way down to the riverbank.

Finally, the General forced himself to look away, looking instead to the people around him – the only ones who had not continued their flight all the way down the Avergon Trail. He was speechless, but knew he must say something. "My name's Tyghus. I'm an Imperial general, Dyrator of the Sixth Dyron," he yelled, to virtually no reaction. "I don't uh... I don't know where to begin this, to be frank with you. Let's just try to piece things together, no?"

A few heads around the gathering nodded, convincing Tyghus they were at least hearing him. "So tell me everything, then, every last detail. Every sound, every sight, everything."

Several desert tribesmen looked at each other with confusion, as did a group of traditionally dressed Valogarians, their bags of jiupan berries splattered on them like blood.

"Anyone?"

Finally, a middle-aged Rokh stepped forward, his beige tunic in tatters from the mad scramble. "I's only a handful of yards behind 'em, sire. I – I ran fast as I could after I saw the first one go off like it did," he said, a touch of shame adding to the grief in his voice. "If I'd stayed put, I'd have been on the part that collapsed."

"Aye, so what'd you see? Did you hear them speak?"

"Aye... aye, I did, but uh..." The man looked nervously back at the Valogarians who stared blankly back at him.

"Tell me what you heard, then."

"What 'bout them?"

"Were they with the group that attacked the Bridgeguard?"

"No... least I don't think so... but ya' never know..."

"Then let me worry about them; they didn't have to stay if they didn't want to. They dragged just as many bodies off the bridge as you or me, so just tell me what you saw and what you heard."

"I heard Valogary."

Tyghus cringed, even if he wasn't surprised. "You're certain?"

"Aye, I am... I've known quite a few of 'em in my time from working the lower Astoren mines near the Shoals in the '50s. I know the language when I hear it – can't speak it, but I know it. They were tryin' to pass through the gatehouse but the guards stopped 'em, tried to take what they were carryin', and that's when they started yelling. The cloaked folks, I mean, they were sayin' something in Valogary, somethin' about Chibin."

"You don't recall exactly?"

"I heard 'em but like I said, I don't speak it..."

"Aye, so then what?"

"Well, the man with the first cart drew a sword and got after the guards in the tower and pushed on through to the market. Then –" the man became wrought with grief, his hands shaking. A woman to his right sobbed gently as she patted his chest.

"You have to remember. I have to know what to report," Tyghus gently prodded.

"Aye, aye... the-the second cart rolled into the gatehouse and it blew it up, it did."

"And the rest? Did you see anything else about the other carts?"

"They was further back on the bridge, but I was scrambling for m'life by then."

"What about the men with the carts themselves, did you see anything about them? I could only see their cloaks, nothing about their faces or anything else."

"I saw 'bout the same," the shaking man said, rubbing his forehead in thought. "One of 'em had a crooked hand, I think, like he's missin' a few fingers... the rest of 'im was –"

Tyghus blanched at the description. "Stop – the hand?"

"Aye?"

"You're quite sure about his hand?"

"Aye... I thought it looked funny."

The mental image of the hand sent a chill down his spine, taking him back a few weeks to his entrance into Valogar.

The Isthmus... those Natives at the Gate... the man that looked at me...

"Gods above," the General said, burying his face in his hands before looking to Treos. "We bloody walked right by them."

Treos furrowed his brow. "*We* did? When? Where?"

"As we entered the country – the Gate, the Valogarian Gate. We walked right by them."

"Couldn't have been…"

"It was. Their carts were running heavy and-and the hand, I saw it too. Chopped to pieces, just like this man's saying. Sons of whores, it was them," Tyghus said, voice rising. "Sons of whores!" He quickly restrained himself at the sight of quaking, glassy-eyed children. The General re-focused on the Rokhish man. "So what was it that they lit, my friend? Did you see it?"

The man wiped his face, swallowing deeply. "Pyhr, no doubt in m'mind."

"Pyhr? You know the stuff well enough to say?"

"Aye, I do… whitish silver, tinge of yellow, green. It was pyhr they carried; large rocks of it, the size of boulders. Looked like they'd threaded ropes into 'em."

"Ropes they lit, I take it?"

The man nodded.

Tyghus shrugged as he put his hands on his hips, his worst fears confirmed.

The man looked at Tyghus pensively. "What're ya' gonna do?"

Tyghus shook his head. "Don't know yet. The Eighth Dyron across the bridge has surely turned speed riders loose already, so the Capital will know within the week. From there, I – I honestly don't know."

"So m'nephew's gaspin' for his life over there, and you don't know what to do!" a frantic woman screamed near the back of the group, blood smeared about her face and hands. "But I bet ya' know to take our taxcoins pretty quick, don't ya'!"

Tyghus looked at her sympathetically. "I understand your concerns."

"No, no ya' don't!"

"I do, I swear it. A Rokh bleeding on Rokhish lands is the worst insult I can imagine. And knowing that even one of those Rokhs is a child makes it…" Tyghus closed his eyes and clenched his fists, feeling rage boil in his stomach. "Just know that the Capital will address this shortly."

"The 'Capital'!" she scoffed with scorn. "The Capital dawdles while fookin' Natives roam worry-free 'cross our lands! No one's doin' nothin' about it!"

"My lady –"

"Ah, to the Depths with ya'! Ya' *knew* this was gonna happen, just'a matter of time, and if ya' didn't, you're as smart as the beast ya' ridin' on!"

The Rokhs in the crowd soon caught the angry tone of the ranting woman, raising a cheer with each point she made. Another bloodied

Rokhish man, older than the last, chimed in, "Twenty years I wore the grays for Dray'gon Rokh! Twenty years I spent fightin' those animals and *I* knew ya' couldn't trust 'em but m'own bloody Capital don't!"

"Well, now th'Capital knows they can't be 'lowed to walk among us!" the angry woman picked up again, spitting in the General's direction.

"You *know* what has to happen!" the veteran said. "To think 'a how many'a my men died in Valogar only t'see this day!"

"Your concern is *noted*, my friends," Tyghus said with more force.

But the crowd was already in a frenzy. "*No more Rokhish blood! No more Rokhish blood!*" they began chanting in unison. It wasn't long before one of the men became enraged at the sight of the huddled Valogarians and directed rants at them. Another caught the fervor, charged the Natives and sloppily punched one in the jaw. The crowd roared as the hapless man spun around from the blow.

"*Stop that!*" Tyghus bellowed.

No response as others joined in the 'fight', pounding the other Native with shoves and kicks.

"*I'm ordering you to stop!*"

"The gods' balls ya' do!" someone shot back.

"Gods above – Treos grab one, I'll get the other!" Tyghus said as he kicked his horse into the crowd. Swinging down to grab the skinny arm of a Valogarian, he pulled him free of the mob's grasp while Treos mirrored his actions on the right. The crowd suddenly converged on the riders instead, clawing at their cloaks, ripping their trousers.

"Ride dammit! Get out of here!" Tyghus yelled.

The Lakeman's horse panicked and began bucking at the people around it. At least two Rokhs went down from the beast's powerful kicks, clearing enough space for both riders to run free of the crowd. Angry taunts followed them.

"*Bloody Native lovers! Show your own people ya' back, will ya!*"

It was more than two hundred yards away before Tyghus finally caught up with the Lakeman's spooked horse. "You alright?" Tyghus asked his friend through heaving breaths, while his young Valogarian rescue gripped the horse's neck for dear life.

Treos nodded, his clothes in shreds, but his eyes drawn to the bloodied Native lying stomach first across his saddle. "Father an' son ya' think?" he asked, still in a pant.

"I don't know..." the General replied, still shaken by what he witnessed. "We'll ride 'em down a bit further and turn them loose, then we have to make for the Capital."

He looked his friend square in the eye. "Today is going to change everything."

Chapter XVI

"It is in these most dire of straits that we do find the true character of our king. It is then that the gods will show us whether he will rise to lead or be led himself."

Quote from <u>The Fall of Great Ambelfeld</u> by Menacus

Dray'gon Rokh, Lorrian Halum, 9ᵗʰ Day of the First Month, Y. 384 P.C.

Bedlam reigned at the Lorrian table as the doors swung open for Khorokh Kyrus I. The stunned gathering he was pulled away from upon Rynsyus's succession announcement seemed worlds' apart from the raucous group before him now – not that it made them any less detestable. Gruffly pulling his chair out to seat himself, he couldn't help but see rats crawling all over each other as he looked at his Council.

Oratus sat at the opposite headseat from Kyrus, the former's discomfort immediately apparent. One hand fidgeted with the other as beads of sweat dampened the gray hair along his forehead. For a man with such power in his pronouncements, he appeared timid as a kitten at the moment.

The Emperor hardly looked the part that day, forsaking the many Royal vestments worn by his predecessors. In fact, save for his lack of helmet, he could have been mistaken for the Sixth's Dyrator still with his ashen gray tunic over a long-sleeved black shirt. He preferred it this way, seeing no need to worry about trivialities when such grave matters lay before them.

And if I'm to command them as I would my soldiers, then I'd better dress as a commander, he reasoned.

He waited for the clamor to subside, but his patience soon ran thin; he unceremonisouly slammed the table with mailed fist, rattling silver chalices but bringing all eyes to him. To Kyrus's surprise, however, his heart suddenly pounded as he prepared to address his Lorrio for the first time.

It's your bloody dyron, Kyrus, he reminded himself. *Address them as such.*

"Thousands dead," he finally said, voice echoing through the chamber. "The Bridge… useless. That's why we're here."

Lorrions exchanged glances with one another.

"Now let's stop squabbling and deal with it."

After a motionless pause, he saw the hand of his chief advisor rise sheepishly. "What?"

"Forgive me, Your Majesty," Oratus nearly whispered with nervous smile.

"What?"

"Well… before we proceed to the more serious matters at hand, I-I must ask – what of your crowning ceremony?"

Kyrus glared at the man. Preparations had been underway for a massive celebration of the life of Rynsyus I and the crowning of Kyrus I, festivities which were many times the scale of the Lorrian ceremony Kyrus had already experienced. Their arrangements came to a halt when news of the Converge attack rippled across the Empire.

"*Thousands* dead. I said that aloud, did I not?"

"Certainly you did, and certainly I heard you, but –"

"Then it should be obvious – the ceremony is canceled until further notice. We have enough to concern ourselves with than that pretentious nonsense."

"Well, it might give the people a bit of comfort –"

"The *people* will be comforted when they've a bridge to cross again, so don't ask me again until that's the case. I'll take the crown in the privacy of my own chamber, and that'll be that."

Ignoring Oratus's forlorn expression, Kyrus scanned the table for signs of support or dissent before continuing. "Now, riders speed in with more information every moment but I'll tell you all that I know - thirty men with carts in tow forged the Vargorus Bridge shortly before High Sun. At the North Bridgegate, they drew blades, killed our guards and in short order put their cargo to the torch. They blew the damn Bridge and hell of a lot of Rokhs to the Depths."

The table felt restless but kept silent.

"The Ministers in the Converge, folks of the Eighth – they're all saying the same thing: they torched *pyhr* – boulders of it, big as an ox, all told. With that much, seems pretty clear the Bridge itself was the target –"

"Kyrus – *Highness*," Castus suddenly interjected, head resting on outstretched fingers, eyes to the table. "I beg your pardon, I honestly do, but I have to ask – how do we know this wasn't some… accident? An inadvertent explosion, perhaps?"

"An accident?" Volinex quickly parroted.

"Aye, an accident, why not? Everyone seems so ready to paint this as something malicious when it could be, it *could be*, something as simple as a chemist's mishap. Look at our own alchemists in their work with pyhr, how many times have they –"

"Hah! A chemist's mishap!" Voli' crowed again. "And I suppose our alchemists make a habit of slaying their assistants with drawn swords too, Castus?"

"Not saying they weren't madmen, I'm simply *suggesting* that we're making an awful rush to judgment here, and we're supposed to the one body of citizens above that! Why bother with this meeting otherwise? Why bother with *any* of them?"

Volinex shook his head in derision. "Typical Castus. The Empire bleeds yet he weeps for the men who cut her."

"That is a –"

"*Quiet!*" Kyrus erupted, stunned at the disregard he received. "Before this proceeds any further, one thing needs to be clear, *absolutely* clear so all of you listen closely – *I am not Rynsyus!* And this is *not* your personal theater, do we understand each other?"

Silence.

"Do we! Because whatever liberties you felt entitled to take with Rynsyus died with *him!* These meetings will function with respect or *not at all!* You can rot in your chambers for all I care!"

Castus flexed his jaw and gritted his teeth before calmly folding his hands in front of him. The rest of the room had come to a standstill – but for Wollia flicking a glance at the immobile Antinax.

Kyrus glowered at the group. "Now, if the lot of you can behave as adults, I invite you to speak freely."

Barannus looked side to side. "Highness?" he asked.

"Speak."

"Thank you... I was just going to observe you uh... you didn't say who did this."

Kyrus's fingers rattled rhythmically against the table. "Because we don't know who did this... not for sure we don't."

"Hm... no bodies? No witness—"

"The bodies of the men that led the attack were mangled beyond recognition, but those that caught sight of them beforehand said they had black hair, golden skin..." Kyrus's stomach turned. "The look of Valogarians."

"Or Desert tribesmen..." Castus muttered loud enough to be heard. *"Or Rokhs of the Southwest..."*

"Other reports I've heard said they were speaking Valogary –"

"'Reports'," the Sudo chided further.

"– and yelling things about the Chibin."

A murmur spread across the table.

"So it's early yet, that's what we can conclude," Castus offered hopefully. "That's what the Khorokh is saying, Barannus."

"I'll let his statements speak for themselves, but thank you."

"Please do, because his statements say we don't know what the truth is."

"Yet," Volinex added with rolling eyes.

Castus looked to the Emperor. "Well, am I right or wrong, Your Highness?"

Kyrus locked eyes on him, silently fuming at the Sudo's mutterings while he spoke. He swallowed a ball of anger in an attempt to restrain himself. "I've told you what I know. Take from it what you will."

"Other nations aren't going to be pleased with these developments, Majesty..." Wollia said softly, her eyes drifting onto the Emperor, face ever in a half-smile.

Kyrus sighed. "No. No, they aren't."

"To lose their own within our borders," she continued, casually as ever. "It speaks poorly of the Realm... it's going to unnerve the foreigners."

"Aye, well, whether they're unnerved or not, the fact remains that the blasts took folks from all over Andervold."

"And 'folks from all over Andervold' will be measuring our response..."

"Aye..." Kyrus said after a pause. This being their first exchange, he eyed her curiously, trying to read the double-meaning she seemed to hide in everything she said and did. "Are you suggesting a particular response?"

She gently shrugged and looked away. "Oh, I'd only note that Rokhs have gone to war over far less than this."

"Have they!" Castus exclaimed incredulously. "And tell me - who would we go to war with in this case, my lady?"

The woman smiled at Castus, calmly disregarding his sarcastic, combative tone. "I think the reports answer your question. And I also think a timid reaction to this affront would only guarantee a repeat of days like the Third."

Castus quickly turned his focus towards Kyrus. "Highness, this is precisely the opportunity we've been waiting for to show that the wedding in Nar-Biluk wasn't just a sham! We can take this moment, we can *seize* upon it, and ease the fears that many in Valogar and the Lowlands still have of the Empire," Castus pleaded as he rose from his seat. "And if, *if* these attackers turn out to be Chibin, then our support to Nar-Biluk must be *unconditional.*"

"Is that so?"

"It is, Highness, because not only will the Valogarians see that we're truly committed to the new chapter we pledged – but the Colverians, the same Colverians that have banned Rokhish merchants from their lands for nearly two hundred years because of what we've done in Valogar, *they* may even soften. At the very least, we could show our commitment to their allies, and use that as a basis for expanding trade."

Volinex scoffed. "Utter nonsense, Highness. The Colverians have made a religion out of hating Rokhs, just like the Loccycs, just like the Desertmen... Aye, we could give Colvery half the damn Rokhlands and they'd still keep us banned."

"That's a *lie,*" Castus fired at the young Nortic. "Rokhs along the River Brafford in Starrea have been meeting Colverians across the borders for years, swapping goods on the shadow markets, even with our laws against it. The ordinary Colverian *wants* to trade with our people, and I can tell you that the revenue would more than offset the losses from the Converge. That's raw *wealth* waiting to be tapped, wealth that can make the Empire more powerful than it's ever been." The Sudo's blue eyes burned with such intensity, even the Emperor almost looked away. "Power's more than just winning battles, Highness... it's winning these *moments* as well. I *pray* that you see can this."

Skilled with the tongue, Kyrus thought, reluctantly giving the man his due. Then he frowned – *a schemer of the first degree, no doubt, but skilled in his art.* The Khorokh rubbed his chin, eyes dancing from one side of the table to the other until they finally fell on the one man who'd yet to visibly react to anything – Antinax. "Antinax... all the months I've watched you, listened to you, and *now* you have nothing say?"

The old man's face scarcely stirred. "Highness, I'm quite content to let the learned young men among us lead the way here."

Kyrus scowled. "Let's pretend they aren't here, then."

Without hesitation, he replied, "I move for the declaration of war on Valogar."

Kyrus reeled.

"I second," Wollia instantly added.

Castus's mouth hung open for all to see. "This must be in jest."

"I vote for war," Volinex said.

"And I," said Barannus.

Castus's eyes burned directly at Antinax, who looked right back. "Antinax," he said in near growl. "You know the gods high and low will curse you for this. You know I'm right on this, right on what to do here, yet your godsforsaken pride won't let you admit it!"

"You call it pride, I call it common sense."

"It's common sense to eviscerate a decade's worth of painstakingly rebuilt trust between the Empire and Valogar? The fact that you even raised this vote spits in the face of *everything* Rynsyus accomplished in his time! Spits at the feet of the Ruhl sitting on the throne in Nar-Biluk as we speak!"

"So what's your vote, Castus?" the Anti' asked blandly.

"The Sudos oppose, without question. Not in a thousand years would the Lowland provinces stand for —"

"Good, so four in favor, four against, then. Spare this old man the rest of your speech and let's get on with it." Antinax slowly turned his head towards the Emperor. "Because the motion hasn't yet passed."

Kyrus had steeled himself for the Nortic's tactics, but he had not anticipated a formal war request so quickly. He scolded himself for not foreseeing the possibility and furthermore, for not having a response prepared. The prospect of war – of war with *them* – sent butterflies through his stomach, yet something held him back. Maybe it was the Sudo's remarks, maybe it was his suspicion of any request from a Lorrion, or maybe he simply wanted to wait and hear Tyghus's view of the attack, given that he was said to be en route to the Capital. Kyrus certainly hadn't forgiven his former pupil for ignoring him during his captivity – and was even less certain that the Lakeman hadn't turned him altogether – but he'd be lying if he said he wasn't intrigued to talk with him after so much time.

Whatever the reason for his apprehension, he found himself looking opposite the table at the pasty, flabby figure of Oratus. The rest of the gathering followed Kyrus's lead, one by one turning heads towards the man whose "view" would determine the proposal's passage – and the Empire's fate.

The Emperor shook his head finally. "Not today. The Sixth's dyrator will be at the Capital within weeks to give me his account first-hand. Too many questions remain in the meantime, and it's too grave a decision to make without all paths being mapped out – a general should never go to war without all the facts, that's something none of you would understand," he said, pleased with his jab.

"The restraint you exercise here will echo for decades to come, Highness," Castus said, his face less confident and visibly shaken. "Centuries, even."

"That restraint will simply show that the Empire can be cowed by barbarians," Volinex retorted. "Coming at a time in which our power has already been checked on the Peninsula when Rynsyus forced our retreat; a time when the Stolxian kingdoms gather at our Western Gateway and threaten Raizea; a time when bandits bleed the Kylean Plains dry – to the contrary, Lorrion Castus, restraint could prove devastating."

"Bicker amongst yourselves about it," Kyrus said with a hand up. "But I've had enough for today. If you feel like doing something constructive, you should visit your Provinces if you can do so in one month's time; Tessax, you above all others should depart as the Kregean Lorrion. Take the pulse of your peoples; at the very least, send couriers with updates and comfort – fear's running high that a strike on the Converge means a strike anywhere, and fear's a wildfire if it goes unchecked."

The new Khorokh rose from his seat.

"We'll hold the vote six weeks from today. On that day, the Rokhish response will come."

* * *

Kyrus found solace walking the floor of the Khorian Soelum, the mighty dining hall in which he'd been celebrated as Lorrion so many months ago. The emptiness of the cavernous room suited him better than the panic infecting the rest of the Arxun, if not the city as a whole. He gravitated towards the massive windows that awed him that autumn night, no less impressed upon seeing them with an Emperor's eyes.

Luxuries like a moment's peace were in short supply since news of the Converge attack reached the Capital. The stream of speed riders seemed neverending, each one with new details for Arxun ministers, for Oratus, or for whoever else wanted to know – details which inevitably filtered back to Kyrus. Added to the demands of taking over an Empire that stretched for a thousand miles west and south, he had little time left for his own thoughts, and the afternoon following the contentious Lorrio meeting was no exception. Oratus filled his ear with a hundred tasks to be done, even as Kyrus stared detachedly out a window, hands folded behind his back.

"… ministers from Marvelon were slaughtered in the blasts and will need to be replaced. Numerous candidates have distinguished themselves from Grynea, Tryces in particular…" Oratus trailed off. The Khorokh reveled at the sudden silence, closing his eyes in peace. But then he heard heavy metal footsteps followed by another familiar voice.

"Highness…"

Kyrus turned to see Jarax standing before him, dressed in fine red and looking ready for a scrap. It'd been tense between them since their confrontation the morning Rynsyus died; even if that seemed like a lifetime ago, it was a fresh wound that would surely be slow to heal. Nonetheless, Kyrus was no fool; he was well-aware the Rubator was integral to any Khorokh's rule and protection, and resigned himself to their co-existence.

Just another soldier in my dyron, he'd told himself.

The Emperor gave him a curt nod, nothing more. Jarax glanced at Oratus then back to Kyrus. "Highness, you have visitors."

Kyrus only grunted.

Jarax cleared his throat. "And… as visitors often do, they want an audience…"

The Khorokh rolled his eyes and turned back to the window. "Them and the rest of the Arxun. Send them away. Barely have enough time for the messengers."

Hearing no movement, Kyrus turned his head to repeat himself. "Send them away, Jarax."

"Highness, they're Lorrions."

The Emperor's brow furrowed – as did the Speaker's. "What the hell do they want with me in my tower? I leave 'em in their Hall and they bloody follow me here, it's unbelievable."

"And it's improper for a Lorrion to approach the Khorokh on his own accord!" Oratus hissed. "If it should happen, it should *only* happen in the Halum…"

Jarax replied calmly, "I've no issue with telling them that… though I can't imagine they're unaware of the protocol they're breaching." He looked back at the doors behind him. "Your orders, Highness?"

The thought of more Lorrion meetings made Kyrus nauseous, though at the same time, he had to wonder – what could lead a Lorrion to so brazenly flout Rokhish custom?

"Let them in, Jarax – just be ready to escort them out in short order."

"Your will, Majesty."

As Jarax went to fetch them, Oratus moved in close to Kyrus, his whispering breath reeking of the pungent cheese the Emperor saw him gorging upon minutes prior.

"Highness, this is a flagrant disregard for Imperial law! And the mere rumor of such a meeting is –"

"Oratus, stop," Kyrus said, recoiling at the man's stench. "This is going to be quite simple – I get an explanation for this that suits me or they're immediately expelled, that's all there is to say about it."

His advisor looked around nervously. *"But people will already be talking –"*

"Let them talk! Better yet, tell them to talk to Jarax if they have an issue with it."

"Highness –"

"Now, I want you to leave."

Oratus drew back at the instruction. "Majesty, I'm happy to stay."

"Duly noted and thank you," the Khorokh said, patience withering. "But I want you out of here."

In a huff, the corpulent man made his exit, passing directly between the two approaching Lorrions – the elder statesman and stateswoman of the Nortic faction. Anti's simple gray tunic looked as old as he did, even with the thick, brilliantly violet sash that overlaid it; the robe Wollia adorned, however, looked immaculately cut from the finest gray furs of the Karanaks, her priceless Lorrian purple seamlessly stitched in.

With an intentionally loud sigh, Kyrus took a seat at one of the empty banquet tables, sunbeams from the giant windows silhouetting his figure. "I told you both to get out of Dray'gon Rokh, so by the gods, why are you here?"

Antinax hobbled plain-faced to take a seat at the opposite end of the table from the Emperor; his partner smoothly disregarded the question as well, appearing to take an interest in their surroundings instead. "Quite a change from your introduction to the Capital, isn't it, Majesty?" she asked lightly.

Kyrus rested his head on a fist. "I *prefer* it without the banquet," he replied, to which the woman smiled. "Now answer my question."

Her smile diminished a bit as she looked to her seated colleague. She strolled over towards a sill to lean lazily against it, Kyrus's eyes following her until she was behind him. "Well?" he asked again. "I don't have the patience for this."

"What's to say?" Antinax finally said with a shrug, drawing the Khorokh's attention away from Wollia.

"Something would be a start. I don't appreciate you getting my advisor in a fix; just one more headache for me to deal with."

"Fair enough, we can apologize for that, can't we, Wollia? As for our being here at all, I'd say to you that these are unusual times, so you should expect unusual visits."

Kyrus continued thinking of the Lorrions as simply subordinate officers, but he was suddenly nervous not having had time to prepare for Antinax's wiles. He tried not to let his tone reflect that. "It's not so unusual, I think – you conspired when Rynsyus sat at this table, now you conspire when he

166

sits at the gods' Table."

Though his expression changed little, Antinax seemed genuinely stung by the jab. "I regret my reputation's been sullied to the point that you would say such a thing. Really, I do."

"Aye? You didn't seem so regretful as you berated the dying man in the Halum not long ago."

"Well, I am," the old man said ornerily, before resuming more calmly. "Listen, I worked with that man for more than four decades, Highness. I knew his mind as well as he knew it himself, and to be fair, he knew mine just as well. That familiarity lent itself to a level of bluntness that could strike others as disrespect, something I often forgot in the moment." He shrugged again. "I'm old. I forget things."

It was the first suggestion of weakness Kyrus had ever heard from the man. But if he did mean it in jest, he revealed not a hint of a smile, nor did his dark eyes suggest any sort of levity.

"We didn't come here to cause a stir, Highness, much as it may look that way. We've got no interest in that. We came to ya' because you're young, let's face it."

Kyrus's cheeks flushed indignant. "It's a relative term."

The Nortic quickly put his hands up in deference. "Certainly is, you have us there. A day of your service in the Sixth trumps the three years I spent in the Second before the gods gave me this nasty limp."

"Certainly true."

"But that's not important. What's important is that Rynsyus kept ya' locked up all those weeks and it was *wrong*. He should have been talking to you, should have been telling you everything – the good he's done, the bad – though I'm sure he didn't."

The Khorokh glowered. "You have an interesting way of showing concern, then. I sent letters from the Brex to all the Lorrions asking for news, asking for *anything*."

"Ah, I got your letters, Highness, but me telling Rynsyus he was wrong would have only convinced him that he was right. He had his reasons for keeping you cut off, but the end result is that to this point you've only heard what he wanted you to hear, and even there, not much I imagine. We're here because we thought it was only fair that you hear the rest, the things that he simply didn't want to face when he held the throne."

The Khorokh studied the veteran Lorrion, calculating how the latter was trying to manipulate the former. "And you couldn't say all this at the Halum?"

The old man's eyes widened briefly. "Come now – you saw it in there. Lorrions break out in hives if they engage in civil discourse at those meetings."

Kyrus was quickly tiring of the dialogue. "Well, you're here now, anyway. Just go ahead with it."

"Thank you," the Lorrion said, clearing his throat before continuing in a hushed tone. "Highness, we have an opportunity in our hands the likes of which we may never see again. The savages have *declared war against us*. They've declared war and they've shown they're not afraid to do so on Rokhish grounds. It's a logical step, really – they've mocked our leniency ever since Rynsyus embarked on his campaign to win the hearts of every nation."

"I don't need to be told this, Antinax. I've had every horse and rider in the Empire telling me for a day now."

"Aye, so where does that leave us, then? It leaves us with a country united in hate against the savages. Finally, *united*. Hate's not a good thing, Highness, but it can be *used* for good things when channeled towards the proper purpose. So that's the question – what's the proper purpose here?"

Kyrus's face sank and he nearly looked away, disappointed with the message. "Which you say is war? I already heard this from you in the Halum and I gave you my answer on it."

"No, Highness, it's different. It's *completely* different."

"Different or not, you're wrong - where's this unity? Every Lowlander in that room today opposed a war, how many different ways can they say it?"

"The villages of southern Morremea? Towns along the River Brafford? Aye, I actually agree with Castus, the young lion – they'd never support war against Valogar. But –"

Kyrus threw his hands up. "See?"

"—*but*, it's a mistake to say those regions speak for the Lowlands as a whole. That's a lie Castus has put forth for more than a decade, when the reality is that the other Provinces *could* be turned – part of *Morremea* could be turned! – *if* they thought we could win."

The Khorokh closed his eyes as his head began to throb. "Aye, so Castus lies to you, you speak the gods' truth, and I'm left with the mess of it all, I understand it now."

"No! That's not what –"

Kyrus stood abruptly. "You can have the room to yourselves, I can't listen to any more of this non—"

"Highness, did you ever wonder what sustained those Valogarians fighting against our troops all those years?" the old man asked sharply.

Kyrus paused.

"*Your* troops should I say?"

Kyrus stared at the man.

"It's a question for you, Highness. Where did they get the money to keep up the fight, to buy new blades, maintain their supplies? Hm? Valogar's not a rich land, not in minerals anyway. They haven't been a conquering nation in centuries, so they don't draw upon any tribute, so where?"

"Just say what the hell you're getting at, Antinax."

"Castus."

"What about Castus?"

"Castus, Your Highness. Castus has been channeling his fortune to Valogarian lands for years. *Years*," the Lorrion said through gritted teeth. "Did Rynsyus tell you that?"

Kyrus felt an unfamiliar burning in his chest when he heard the accusation to which he had no response. Antinax noticed.

"I'll assume not, then. These are the types of things I warned you about, things the good Emperor knew and kept from you, things you had a right to know. The truth is Castus has probably matched Colverian support coin for coin over the years! So instead of fearing our swords, fearing our soldiers, they basked in Rokhish wealth, can you imagine? Strengthening our enemies at the expense of his own people," Antinax said with disgust.

Kyrus grimaced, horrified but forcing himself to consider the source of the news. "But to what end? Why –"

The Lorrion grunted. "He's a man of the Shoals, Highness, all the Borderfolk in Morremea sympathize with the Valogarians; surely you saw that with the Sixth. Their highborns share the same bed, always have. He didn't *want* us to be successful there, he wanted a peace and he would bloody do anything he could to get it. To him, the heavier our losses became, the closer he got to that peace by showing the Lowlanders that we couldn't win there. And – to his credit if that's what you want to call it – he succeeded: the rest of the Lower Rokhlands bought into it, willingly or otherwise, and followed his line without so much as a batted eye."

"Why didn't you bloody tell somebody then?" Kyrus demanded with a growing anger. "Why not tell the Emperor or raise it before the Council?"

Antinax paused, his droopy eyes narrowing. "*Rynsyus knew it*, Highness. Knew it all along, but he didn't care. In his mind, he'd cracked the code for bringing peace to our lands; *he* was the one man who would single-handedly re-write almost four centuries of animosity. He never believed in our troops, never thought they could end the war. So naturally, he was happy to let Castus run his schemes, more than willing to trade Rokhish lives for that Lorrio 'balance' that let him pursue his 'vision'," Antinax shook his head ruefully. "Four for war, four for 'peace', while poor Onzy handed him the keys to it all. A disgrace."

Finally, Kyrus managed, "I see."

Antinax proceeded in quieted tone. "Now, let me be perfectly frank with you: I have no direct heirs. Not a one. My branch of the Antinid line dies with me, after centuries of its sacrifice to the Empire. So in lieu of full-blooded heirs, I looked to my nephews, budding soldiers and warriors out of Avergon." The Lorrion wavered a bit, and a hint of emotion broke in his voice. "And they were slaughtered. All of them. All of them lost to Valogarians in the '60s. My hatred for those savages is… beyond description, but all the moreso from the thought that *Ruhl* money may have helped spill *Ruhl blood*, may have killed my nephews, my heirs, my *family*—"

Kyrus twitched.

"—maybe yours too."

"*Don't speak of them!*" Kyrus suddenly snapped. "Do not bring them into – into your games!"

The Nortic's hands went up in deference again. "Apologies, Highness, I just meant to –"

"I know what you meant! Don't ever, *ever* mention them again," the Emperor said through gritted teeth, looking away from Antinax. He was angry he let his guard down, but simultaneously proud of himself for not snapping the man's neck on the spot. He took deep breaths to calm himself. "So your suggestion's what, then?"

"Break them by any means necessary."

"The Valogarians."

"The Valogarians, the Chibin, whomever. If one gives sanctuary and one does the killing, what's the difference?" the old man leaned forward. *"They don't fear us, Highness.* They've got unbridled access to their pyhr mines, they have Castus and Colvery lining their treasury with gold, why *should* they fear us? Would you?"

Kyrus's eyes were drawn to the mosaics beneath his feet, head giving barely more than a nod to Anti's question.

"*We need those mines,*" the Lorrion implored. "Not just to keep the Natives out of 'em but for our own sake. By the gods, we've the best weapons in Andervold, now imagine if we coated them in pyhrric poison? Imagine if we could launch pyhrric boulders from our catapults? Why the hell have the bloody Colverians been fighting to keep us off the Peninsula all these years? They know damn well the repurcussions if we succeeded, that's why. With Valogar broken, we – you – could bring Colvery to their knees. The Stolxis – every damn one of their kingdoms! – they'd be forced to bow to your throne should you wish. Rokhish prestige could be restored!" Antinax's voice hit a crescendo that sent his last exclamation echoing throughout the empty hall. He stared intensely at Kyrus, but the latter still looked away. "Great men, Highness… great men and great *legacies* are made in such ways and in such moments."

A pause lingered. "Tyghus," Kyrus finally said. "Can't make a decision until I've spoken with Tyghus, nothing's changed there," he said.

That's a lie, he told himself. *Things have changed. The appalling allegations against Castus… the lies of Rynsyus… and as for Tyghus, who knew what –*

"Oh, and how is lord Tyghus?" asked a soft, feminine voice behind him.

He shifted towards Wollia, having almost forgotten about her. "He should be here within a few weeks, what of him?"

"Hm," she said nonchalantly. "Rumor has it that he's been all over Valogar and the Lowlands with that friend of his —"

"Not much of a rumor," Kyrus quickly interjected, irritated at being reminded of the Lakeman. "His sister's wedding was hardly a secret."

"Oh, of course it wasn't, Your Majesty, of course... he's just been quite silent for some time now... that's what I hear anyway."

"You 'hear'? You spying on an Imperial general, my lady?" Kyrus snorted, embarrassingly aware that the only reason he knew of Tyghus's impending arrival was from the sheer luck of his Converge riders catching sight of him.

"Maybe we should if he's so quiet," she said more seriously before chuckling through a full smile. "No, no, no, Majesty. But I do have colleagues serving throughout the Lowlands, both in Marvelon and closer to Valogar that'd wished to fetch a word with him, offer their congratulations on his good fortune and the like. They just mentioned that they were... surprised... at how difficult he's been to find, and, if I'm being honest, a few were quite offended when he ignored their couriers..."

Kyrus's stomach burned at the couriers' mention.

Her serpentine smiled broadened. "What's this friend of his been saying to him? And who *is* this friend? No one seems to know..."

"I don't know," Kyrus said frustratedly. "I don't know who he is. He's from Loccea Province... a man of the Lakes, that's all I was told."

"The Lakes?" she asked with arched brows. "Hm..."

"Aye."

"Always been a hotbed for rebellion, those Lakes," Antinax said. "You were just a boy when Glannox stomped out the last one, but the province is always roiling; always a thorn. There's a reason we keep the damn Seventh stationed smack in middle of the province."

"He was a soldier too, I think Tyghus told me."

"Even still. Probably a man worth watching; not someone I'd be quick to trust..."

"And now the General's so *quiet*..." Wollia cooed. "From this Lake fellow? Someone else? *Both?*"

"Well..." Kyrus started, struggling to find a coherent response.

"Apologies, Majesty," she gushed, placing a hand on his shoulder. "I only meant it in jest... simply playing off the old adage about those that visit the Peninsula... that it's known to corrupt a man's soul, no matter how pure it may have been."

"Aye, so unanswered letters and a man whose name you don't even know means corruption to you?"

The Emperor watched her with suspicion as her eyes jumped to Antinax for a second. "Has he not answered your letters, either?" she said with a tone of surprise.

Kyrus felt his face flush. "No it's uh... it's not your business! I already told you no one's responded to any of my letters," he said, immediately embarrassed at his revelation.

"Oh... well, he's failed to answer ours as well, but that wasn't what I was referring to..."

"Gods above, what more is there?"

"Highness..." Antinax started.

"Just bloody say it, I've heard enough of you two by now to know that you say nothing without purpose!"

"Agreed," the Nortic replied bluntly. "I just know how suspicious —"

"Say your piece!"

"It's conjecture," the Lorrion said after a pause, still sounding reluctant. "But some of our... contacts in Nar-Biluk —"

"Who?"

"Soldiers... some soldiers in Nar-Biluk sent word that Tyghus has fallen for a Valogarian."

The Emperor fell silent once again. *No.*

"A Pureblood Valog', actually. A Chibin priestess."

No!

Kyrus paced away from the table to the next window over from Wollia's, letting himself be distracted by Arxun ministers shuffling by outside. They no doubt came from more back-room dealings, but at the moment, they provided a welcome respite from the Nortics' assertions.

"Hope *that's* not the cause for his silence," Antinax added. "They say he did his best to keep it secret..."

"That's treasonous."

"No, it's stating what we know."

"It's *conjecture*, by your own admission!"

"True, Highness, very true. I'll let the situation speak for itself, then, you're probably right."

Kyrus gave no reaction as he felt the Nortics exchange looks behind him.

"Perhaps we'll take our leave now, Majesty, a lot's been said," Antinax offered. "We appreciate the audience. They say it's a sign of a great ruler when he can —"

"If you're leaving, then leave."

He gratefully heard the Nortic's chair scrape the floor as he rose, followed by the sounds of sandaled feet.

"Have a good evening, Highness."

The doors slammed shut behind them.

Kyrus was finally alone with his thoughts – but by then, he didn't want to

be.

Chapter XVII

"PRISONER LOG

...

Prisoner No. 34 – man, father of P35; MISSING; escaped?
Prisoner No. 35 – boy, son of P34; MISSING; escaped?

...

Kordette Kyrus said he'd look into P34 & P35 disappearances."

Tyghus Notes from Camp Eagle records, Outside of Nar-
Biluk, Y. 377 P.C.

Clyvea Province, North of the Tersic Pass, 23rd Day of the First Month, Y. 384 P.C.

"*Get help! Anybody!*"

"Tyghus!"

The General screamed still.

"*Tyghus!* Wake up! Wake up, lad!"

One of Tyghus's eyes cracked, enough to see the darkness of the caravan. Treos gripped his shoulders.

"Ya' up? Gods above."

The General's heart pounded as he regained his bearings. When his breath finally slowed, he let his head fall towards a flap in the wagon's canvas siding with a sigh. It was stark white outside, though packs of Rokhish workers busily kept the slate of the Tersian Som snow-free.

"Gods above, you said it."

"Makin' me feel like I'm back in the Jungle, wailin' the way ya' been."

"Aye, I imagine so," Tyghus said, rubbing his eyes. "How long's it been since the Pass?" he wondered aloud. Trekking back towards the Capital, they'd stopped at the great fortress spanning the River Clyves after the snows picked up, tethering their horses to a covered wagon and hiring a driver for the rest of the journey. Seemed like only a moment ago he was admiring banners whipping proudly from the Pass's towers as he settled in to rest in the wagon bed.

"Probably hours back, by now; must be gettin' towards eve," the Lakeman said, watching the General with concern as he re-wrapped himself in plaid blankets. "Same dream ya' been havin'?"

Tyghus slowly nodded. "Same one. Same boy, same brown-hair, same emerald eyes."

"Someone ya' know?"

"I don't think so... but I'll be damned if I don't see him falling off that damn bridge over and over again. Never seen anything so clearly," he said with a shake of his head. "The hell's it mean, you think?"

"Couldn't tell ya'... maybe nothin' – it was a hell of a thing we saw at the Bridge."

"Aye."

Treos crunched on some dried minnows he purchased at the river crossing. "Maybe ya' nerves for where we're headin'..."

Tyghus chewed his upper lip in contemplation for moment. "Maybe... maybe both. One thing's not helping the other, that much I know," he said with another heavy sigh. "Still can't believe it's even true. Five months ago we're grunt soldiers, and now he's... I just don't know what to expect when I see him."

"'Bout the Converge, ya' mean?"

"Aye, the Converge, the fact that he's now the bloody Khorokh, the... I

175

just wonder how he's handling it all."

"Ya' always said he was a good man, didn't ya'? Good all the way around?"

"He's a good man in a lot of ways but in others…" the General looked silently at Treos for a moment. "Treos, I gotta tell you something, something nobody really knows beyond a few in the Sixth – but Kyrus wasn't well by the time we left Avergon for the Capital. Maybe he's never been well – gods know the uh… the rumors of the things that he did to Valogarian prisoners – but he grew even worse. It'd gotten to the point where I was the only man he'd speak with, everyone else was too suspicious, too conniving, he'd say."

"Didn't know it was that bad…"

"Aye. And then when we met in the Capital that last time, sometimes he'd look fine, but more often he looked scared. Angry… more so. All that in a position he'd absolutely no desire for to begin with. And now he's gone silent for all these weeks. Who's he been talking to? Who's talked him down when he needs it? What the *hell's* happened to him since then, you know?"

Treos watched him for a bit before offering, "ya' don't believe the rumors about him? The prisoners' rumor…"

Tyghus had to look away. "I'd like to think he did the right thing. But I can't say that I know."

The men fell quiet as the cart rattled on at a quick pace, horse hooves pounding the stone tradeway in rhythm. Even though they were still about two weeks out, Tyghus couldn't help but turn back towards the view out of the wagon and wait.

Wait for the great Southern Wall of Dray'gon Rokh to materialize out of the snow and fog.

Wait   for   the   Emperor.

Chapter XVIII

"Come not with the question lest ye come too for its answer."

Creed of the Seers

Dray'gon Rokh, Gardens of the Arxun, 26th Day of the First Month, Y. 384 P.C.

He heard the voices echoing down the corridor.

They were coming. After more than two weeks of waiting, more than two weeks of replaying his conversation with the Nortics over and over again in his head, he could finally, *finally* get the answers that were owed to him.

He leaned motionless against a pillar in the portico gardens. Just above him a ceiling lined with diamond-shaped tiles cut away in the shape of a rectangle to let cold winter sunbeams spill onto withered plants. A small marble altar to the floral goddess sat in the middle of the garden, its gray stone a stark contrast against room walls green with painted trees.

But Kyrus was oblivious to his surroundings. All he saw was the sandy-haired man bundled in tan spotted furs walking into the portico alongside Oratus, little puffs of smoke emanating from their inane banter. All he felt was his quaking chest.

This man is nothing but your *subordinate,* he reminded himself for the twentieth time. *Give him no further due than that.*

"... *with the Lorrio's approval of course, Castus.*"

"*Obviously. A celebration that large would —*"

The Lorrion stopped in his tracks as he suddenly saw the Khorokh's eyes awaiting him across the room. Slowly his head turned towards Oratus, a sly calculating grin forming as the heavyset man cowered beneath his gaze and retreated whence he came. "Well then. Good afternoon, Your Highness," he finally said, looking back to Kyrus. "Guess I'll presume I'm not here to talk with Oratus about your coronation..."

"Coronation's canceled. Said that two weeks ago."

"Mm-hm," the Sudo said, scratching a scruffy chin as he walked closer from the shadows. "So may I presume I'm not here to talk with Oratus at all?"

"You may."

Castus looked around the pillared venue. "I don't have to tell you that this is a public garden, no? Anyone could walk in here and see this."

"The Arxun's deserted at this hour."

"Even still, this is *not* a private garden."

"It is for the moment," the Khorokh replied with a nod of his head towards the corridor. As if on cue, two Reds sealed off the entrance at the far opposite end. Castus took only a brief glance.

"They're Reds but they still talk."

"Then so be it."

Castus chuckled, shaking his head with hands folded behind his back. "It happened so quickly, I almost missed it."

"What's that?"

"The city. The way it's changed you. You're still a young pup here, really, but it's already happened."

"I don't see that I've changed at all. Not in the least."

"Oh, I do. *Lying* to set up *secret* meetings?" Castus asked dramatically. "A Khorokh meeting with a Lorrion beyond the Halum? None of that's you. At least, it didn't *used* to be you. So what prompted this, hm? Or is *who* prompted this the better question?"

The burning in Kyrus's stomach welled with each smarmy comment by the Lorrion. His thick red winter cloak felt needless at the moment and even with the icy chill his forehead beaded in sweat beneath dark unkempt hair. His mouth had gone dry, however, and he found himself simply staring at his guest with barely concealed fury.

He's yours to command, Kyrus! Bloody ask him what you will!

Castus looked away eventually, pursing his lips as he dragged a bare finger along a winter vine snaking around a pillar. "Nice of the snows to stop the minute I get back from Marvelon, just my luck. Still made it there and back at a fast clip, so I can't complain too loudly, I suppose. And the squalls are never more than a few days away this time of year, so it was really just a matter of..."

Kyrus remained silent, his mind tortured.

Castus's tone soured. "Well, you wanted me here apparently, so don't let me waste your time with pleasantries. What is it that you want?"

"Did you give coin to the Valogarian rebels?" Kyrus finally blurted out, jaw clenching feverishly. "Do you still?"

To his surprise, Castus only smirked. "Ah, so *that's* who talked to you. You've already had one illicit Lorrion meeting."

The Khorokh glared, bigger puffs of smoke shooting from his fuming nostrils. "Did you or didn't you? Has even an *ounce* of your gold crossed the Ratikan Sea?"

"Of course!"

"Of course?"

"I'm from Morremea, Highness. I'm from the Shoals. We've been trading with the Valogarians as long as the Empire's been there."

"That's not what I'm asking. I'm asking –"

"Listen to me," Castus said calmly, smiling as he put a hand on Kyrus's shoulder. "There are three things people will always do – drink, fuck, and trade. Make laws against 'em all ya' want, but it's nonsense to think otherwise."

Kyrus shook off the Lorrion's hand. "I'm not asking that! I'm not talking about selling a fish to a basketmaker or a basket to fisherman."

"Well –"

"I'm asking who *you've* been giving money to, Castus. You and you alone."

"Aye, I know what you're asking," he replied, no less congenial but with blue eyes narrowed. "And I know who made you want to ask it, too."

"Is there someone else you'd rather concern yourself with right now than me?"

"No. Just a simple word of caution not to believe everything you hear or see. Trite, but time-tested advice."

"So? Answer me."

"I've traded with them," he said, smile finally fading. "Along with the rest of my fellow men of the Shoals."

"You've been accused of far worse than that."

"And those brave accusers had nothing to gain from you believing their tales?" he replied with an arched eyebrow.

Kyrus's teeth clenched again. "You did this during wartime?"

"Peacetime. Wartime." Castus shrugged. "All times."

The Khorokh's eyes widened, temper slipping away. "Twelve years ago?"

"*Traded* with them, Highness. With *nobles.* Families more ancient than the Empire's entire existence. Nothing more, nothing less."

"Trade with *any* Valogarian was bloody *forbidden* during the war! It's forbidden *now!*"

"Rynsyus was aware of it, never objected to it. He endorsed it, really... fit with what he was tryin' to do."

"Rynsyus is dead."

"More's the pity. Is there anything more tragic than the death of an Emperor?"

The men stared coldly at one another for a moment, until Castus's grin inevitably returned. "I treasured the relationship I had with him, even if we didn't always agree. He left me free to do what I knew to be in the best interest of the Empire, and I let him do the same."

You arrogant son of a bitch. "You *let* him?"

"Aye," he said, throwing another hard look at Kyrus. "That's the way relationships between Lorrions and Khorokhs *work.*"

Kyrus's hands balled into fists. "Is that right?"

"It is. And I hope for that relationship with you, Majesty. I really think we *can* work together."

"You never spoke a word to me the entire time I sat with you as a Lorrion, so don't stand here and pretend to know what kind of man I am."

Castus frowned in thought. "That's true, I don't know what kind of a man you are."

"And I don't know *you,* so let's not –"

"And you're very slow to trust those that you don't know, aren't you?"

Kyrus paused with mouth open. "I thought you don't know me."

"Well, I know what I hear, of course."

"Aye, so what's that? What, that I'm no politician? Or that I'm a hated man for my politics? I heard that from Rynsyus myself months ago! I *expect* to be hated by the Arxun filth! So tell me."

Castus glanced away with a lick of his lips. "Candidly?"

"If you're able."

"I hear you're mad."

Kyrus reeled back, hands relaxing. "What?"

"That you've lost your mind, that's what I hear. Heard you've been that way since your father's passing... that you're only getting worse."

Kyrus turned away from him, his stomach suddenly queasy with knots. "Among the Arxun, you mean... among the politicians..."

"No, I mean the people and the politicans both... but aye, it's the commoners that should concern you."

"You're lying."

"You said candidly. I indulged you."

He vacantly stared at the garden altar. "How many think this?" he croaked out.

"Among the commoners? Hard to say. It's out there, though, and it's certainly not a reputation you want spreading, I obviously don't have to tell you that. Memories of the Mad Emperors still burn fresh after all these years... all these centuries."

"And those in the Arxun?" he asked, looking back at the Lorrion almost plaintively.

Castus shook his head. "Some've heard the rumors, some have not... nothing in the Arxun stays secret for long, though. You're the Khorokh, by the gods... everyone talks about you."

The Khorokh felt a nervous defensiveness shoot through him. "So Rynsyus's endorsement meant nothing, then? *He* called me here, *he* —"

"Had it been the Rynsyus of ten years ago? Possibly. The Rynsyus that just passed?" Castus simply shook his head again. "He did you no favors by locking you up in the Brex as soon as you were chosen; that only raised more questions, 'specially since he wasn't much of a communicator by the end. Frankly, many thought he was mad by then, too."

Kyrus leaned back against the pillar again with closed eyes, feeling the cold stone through his unbraided hair. A maelstrom of emotions swirled inside of him, from his despisement of the Sudo for talking so nonchalantly about his Valogarian dabblings to utter helplessness at his reputation among the people. *What am I to do? Curse the ministers to the Depths, but the people? If this is true, if I'm really seen as a madman, what the hell am I doing here? What am I doing anywhere? I don't even know where to —*

A hand touched his shoulder again. "Highness..."

Kyrus's eyes opened.

"Highness, *I* don't believe the rumors about you," Castus said, face stone serious with brow furrowed. "And I don't believe you want those rumors to define you. I believe you want to remain on the throne, but the reality is that as long as those rumors persist, you'll always have to be looking over your shoulder. Hated for your politics is one thing... but the people simply won't stand for a mad man, and there aren't enough Reds in the Empire to stop the people's will."

The Sudo knelt down to keep eye contact with Kyrus, whose head dropped ever so slowly towards his chest in a vacant gaze. "Highness... I want you to hear me: you can have an ally for life with me. I'll be a bigger patriot for your throne than you could have *ever* asked for, and I'll bring my Lorrian allies along with me. All I ask is that you trust me; that you leave me with the freedom to do as I've always done, that's doing what's best for the Empire." He nodded. "That's it, I'll take care of the rest of it. *I can make these rumors go away.* I'm the *only* one who can say that and mean it. These impressions of you, Highness – they can get better..." Castus's voice lowered, his lips in a tight frown as he stood upright. "Or they can get *worse.*"

A chill ran down the Khorokh's spine. His head tilted up until his almost watery eyes locked on the Sudo's. His breathing labored as much as he tried to control it, while Castus simply squinted at him with one hand clasped over the other and smiled.

"Highness, we can help –"

"How 'bout I just rip your fucking tongue out right now?"

Castus's mouth froze.

"How 'bout that? Then you can't say anything. Then you can't make things better but you can't make things *worse.*"

"Highness," Castus finally said in a menacing voice, eyes still wide in shock. "You really, *really* should *not* threaten a Lorrion."

"And you should not try to blackmail an Emperor," Kyrus seethed.

A scowl came over the Sudo's face. "There's no blackmail about it, I'm *offering* you my help! I'm offering you a way out of the hole that's been dug for you with Rynsyus's treatment, with the Bridge attack, with these awful 'rumors' of madness that circle your name! You can't rule without the people's backing and I have that to give to you – the Lowland Lorrions *back* me! My friends and kinsmen manning posts throughout the Arxun *back* me! And after all the grain I've given to the Gurums over the years, the bloody *commoners* back me! I can give that all to you! I can make them all *love* you! *No one else can promise you that!*"

Kyrus only glared, saying nothing.

Castus shoved aside the hair that had fallen over his eyes. "You don't believe me," he sighed with a shake of his head. "Part of you understands what I'm telling you, Highness, I know it does. You've come too far in this world, you're too smart not to. So I'll do my best to forget your threat, your *insult*," he said bitterly. "And instead I'll just *pray* that you see what I'm telling you before it's too late; that you understand how I can help you, how we can help each other... because like I said, that's the way it works in the Capital."

With a look of exasperation, the Lorrion turned his back on the Khorokh, heading towards the corridor he entered through. The sight of the Reds at the end of it apparently left him undeterred.

Don't let him leave you like this... he's your subordinate!

"Castus, wait," Kyrus called out weakly. "I'm not through with... with you."

But after a muffled exchange between the Reds and Castus, the former parted to let him free. The soldiers looked back towards their Khorokh with confusion.

"I'm   not   through..."

Chapter XIX

"Alas! Would the Fates have only told man he'd reached a crossroads, what misfortune could his kind have been spared!"

Spoken word of Kolionos Speratus, Rokhish muse and poet

Dray'gon Rokh, Khorian Brex, 1ˢᵗ Day of the Second Month, Y. 384 P.C.

Tyghus's heart pounded as the Brex's door slammed shut behind him. Not from the climb up a seemingly endless staircase, nor the hauntingly silent Red that had escorted him.

No, it was the prospect of seeing his long-silent friend for the first time in what seemed like years – and quite simply, he feared what he might find.

The room was dim and empty, the fireplace a barren, ashy cove, despite the howling blizzard outside. He shivered as vicious winds blew snow in through the opening to a balcony.

"Kyrus?"

No reply. He stepped towards the balcony.

"Kyrus?"

Puzzled, Tyghus wrapped himself tighter in his wolfskin cloak, bracing himself for the storm's fury.

And there he stood at the balcony's railing – Kyrus the Younger, for almost two decades his friend, his mentor, his commander. He appeared perfectly serene gazing at the city below as icy flakes peppered his beard and ponytail. The same brilliant crimson winter cloak that Tyghus saw him adorn as the Sixth's Dyrator draped over his back and shoulders.

"I'll be damned," Tyghus said, smiling despite his nerves. "Kyrus the Khorokh, that can't be right. Didn't believe it when the riders told me at the Converge and I still don't. I mean Kyrus the bloody *Khorokh!*" Tyghus said with a grin, before spreading his arms wide. "Embrace me, dammit!"

But Kyrus remained motionless, back still to his friend. Tyghus stared curiously. "Well, face me at least. I just traveled a bloody month through every kind of ice, wind, and shit you can imagine to see you."

At last, Kyrus finally turned, bloodshot eyes meeting Tyghus's but hopelessly distant. He looked worse than Tyghus could ever recall seeing him – his skin devoid of color, face sunken even with his full beard. The General's smile faded. "Gods above, you look terrible. Are you well?"

"No," he muttered. "I'm not."

"What's wrong?"

"What's wrong?" Kyrus scoffed. "What's right?"

"I –"

"I mean, I'm imprisoned for months, I get out and the Bridge is in shambles. The throne is dumped on me, and my own bloody Council I-I-I think they'd rather me dead if they weren't so busy trying to manipulate me, *lying* to me…"

"Did you say you were *imprisoned* –"

"I've tried just telling myself that they're my subordinates," the rambling Khorokh continued, gaze falling away from Tyghus. "Thinking of them as soldiers in my Dyron but somehow I always end up feeling like I'm just a

185

guest passing through their homes, their lands... and a mad, hated guest at that."

It was a worse version of his friend than even the worst scenario Tyghus had envisioned.

"So now there's a vote for war on the table... a-and I don't know what to do with it."

"Well, what do you want to do with it?"

"I don't know. Is it even true what they're saying it is? Are they right?"

Tyghus sighed. "If 'they' are saying it was a Chibin attack... then I think they're right."

"You saw it?"

"Saw it. Heard it. Haven't slept right since."

After a moment of quiet, Kyrus shook his head. "Half the Lorrio wants a war, half wants peace... but if I choose war then the bloody Lowlands may break away altogether. If I choose peace, then – then... well, I don't know what the Uplands would do. Hang me?"

Tyghus rolled his eyes. "No one's hanging you."

"You don't know these people. You don't know the *pit* that I'm in here..."

Kyrus turned back to look over the balcony again, hands propping his body up against the railing. "It's like the snowfall... all the land's coated in this blanket of white, hiding all the imperfections, all the struggles, all the *lies*. Even the blood-soaked sands of the *Styliun* are covered. So it is with the Empire. So it is with the Capital. So many imperfections, so much –" he paused as if searching for the perfect word, then sneered. "—*rot*. It was there all along, we just chose not to look, but now the Converge attack has laid it bare."

Kyrus fell silent for a bit, Tyghus choosing to let it be as his own thoughts turned distressed. Even if he knew it was only natural that some would call for war, it made him nauseous to hear Kyrus say it, to *know* that it was formally proposed. He saw images of his sister and Mikolo as if they were standing before him.

"So now I find myself on this godsforsaken tower. Standing like a fool in the middle of a blizzard, all because of my father."

"What about your father?"

"He used to say that 'the cold keeps the liar's tongue at bay'."

A pang shot through the General's stomach.

"It was a stupid expression; made no sense then, makes no sense now – why the hell would the cold turn a man honest? Yet here I am all the same. A fool amidst a storm."

"Because you think I've come to lie to you," Tyghus said irritatedly.

"Because everyone else already has. What else can I do? I'm desperate for answers."

"Aye," Tyghus said quietly. "So let's talk it through, just you and I."

The Khorokh's body flinched. "*Now* you want to talk," he said, a sudden anger in his tone as he faced the General. "Almost three months of silence, three months of *nothing*, and *now* you want to talk."

"Nothing? I should say the same of you!" Tyghus protested. "I sent dozens of letters –"

"I received *nothing!*" Kyrus scolded. "You had ways of getting through to me, you know you did, but you did nothing!"

Tyghus tried to rein in his frustration, knowing from years of dealing with the man that it would only inflame things. "*Dozens* of couriers, Kyrus. Visits to the Halum's gates. *Everything* I could conceive of –"

"And you received nothing of what I sent you? Everyone I sent my letters to received them, but you?"

"*No*, Kyrus. I never received a thing from you. Not in the Capital, not –"

"Rynsyus himself *swore* it to me that he allowed them. Swore it!"

"So him you believe?"

"He was on his deathbed when he said it!"

The General suddenly felt speechless. "I don't know what to tell you. Treos can tell you, I-I tried every way I could to reach you."

Kyrus frowned deeper. "Treos... the Lakeman?"

"...Aye."

"Why is he still riding with you?"

Tyghus grimaced. "We bloodied swords together; I very well may not be here right now if it weren't for his bravery on the Plains. Why shouldn't he ride with me?"

"Because he's a *Loccean*. Locceans have been rebelling against the throne since the Early Kings –"

"Oh for gods' sakes, I already told you he's a Rokh, not a Loccean Lordist! A Rokh who's served twenty years in the Jungle of all places!"

Kyrus's chest heaved up and down, eyes wider than ever, voice carefully measured. "Where... have the two of you... been for the last three months? *Don't* lie to me."

Tyghus looked around in bewilderment. "You know damn well where we've been; or at least me you do. Why the hell would I lie to you about any of this?"

"Because you *have to lie!*"

Tyghus shook his head. "I don't understand."

"You're either hiding something... or my Lorrions have lied to me yet again. And honestly, I don't know what's worse any more, so I just... I just need to hear it from you."

"By the gods, hear *what?*"

"What happened in Valogar?"

A chill ran through Tyghus and it wasn't from the snowstorm… it slowly dawned on him that there were other factors – other people – at play. "Who've you been talking to? Who's putting these ideas in your head?"

"Just tell me, Tyghus. Tell me so I can put the lies to bed."

The General swallowed deeply, eyes blinking away a torrent of icy flakes. "What do you want to know?"

"The truth."

"The truth is I rode to Nar-Biluk," Tyghus said, trying to remain locked on the Khorokh. "The truth is… I met with my sister, met with her husband, the Lij. Watched them wed."

"Aye, and that's it, right?" Kyrus asked with nodding head.

You already know the answer to that, Kyrus, Tyghus thought. *Just tell him.*

"No, it's not," he said, losing eye contact, guilt suddenly eating at him.

"No?"

"I drank a fair bit. A lot of that uh… I forget what they call it, but it was powerful, very powerful…"

"Mm-hm."

"And I met this…" Tyghus breathed deeply as he forced himself to look upon Kyrus again. "I met this Valogarian woman. She drank, I drank and we uh…"

"Who was she?"

"Pardon?"

"You *said* she was a Valogarian. So, a commoner? A noble's daughter?"

You already know, dammit. "She was a priestess, actually."

"A priestess."

"Aye… and for honesty's sake, I think she was actually a… a Pureblood."

Kyrus's jaw dropped, teeth appearing from behind his bushy beard as his eyes closed. *"They were right,"* he muttered in near whisper.

"Listen, I… I know you…" Tyghus searched for elusive words before he said in frustration, "I mean I'm not the first Rokh to bed a bloody Valog'!"

Kyrus let out a loud exhale before reopening his eyes. "And that's the end of it, then?"

Tyghus looked to his feet.

"Tyghus!"

"Well, I don't know that it is."

"Why?"

"Does it matter?"

"Yes!" Kyrus erupted, hands exploding out to his sides. "Yes, it matters! The Chibin attack our lands and you're out there bedding one of them? Then you say it's not the end of it!"

The General had no response as Kyrus surveyed him up and down.

"I'm trying very, *very* hard to ignore what I've been told, to-to *trust* you still, to believe that nothing's changed here but instead I find myself looking at a man who for no good reason ignored me, ignored everyone for *months* -"

"Everyone? Kyrus, I told you I tried to reach you!"

"— and I'm looking at a man who's been riding for months with a Lakeman who's done nothing but fill his mind with poison against me, against his country!"

"He's never said a word about you!"

"*He did!*"

"Kyrus, *stop this!*"

"And I'm looking at a man whose *sister* sits on the Valogarian throne, a sister he may very well be at *war* with in a month's time —"

Tyghus fought to keep his hands at his side. "I knew that when I accepted your offer of the Sixth! Do I think we can use her to get revenge for the Converge while at the same time keeping the peace? Of course! She knows the tensions here, the Lij hates the Pure —"

But Kyrus continued on as if he didn't even hear the General. "And now... *now* I'm looking at a man who for some reason, unbeknownst to me or the gods above, won't bloody tell me his dalliance with a Valogarian *whore* is over!"

Tyghus fumed but held his tongue with all his might.

"It ends here, Tyghus!" Kyrus raged, one hand pointing at the other. "Do you understand me? I'm ordering it to end *here!* Do not see, do not *speak* to that woman *ever* again!"

The Khorokh brusquely showed Tyghus his back, stalking back towards the balcony's edge. "And I don't want that Lakeman within a hundred miles of you anymore. Send him back to the Lakes where he came from, he's no business in a Rokhish army, let alone tagging along with the most important general in the Realm! It's an embarrassment!"

"If he goes back to the Lakes, those bandits will hunt him down like a dog for helping *me!*"

"He could be hunted down like a dog *anywhere* in the Empire," Kyrus said coldly.

"'Could be'?" Tyghus echoed, concerned for Treos as he heard no response. He spoke as calmly and sincerely as he could. "Kyrus, I'm worried about you. I haven't seen you like this since... I don't know if I've ever seen you like this. You're not well, and I —"

"I don't want to talk about this any more. You've heard what I said, heard my orders, haven't you?"

Tyghus sighed. "Aye."

"So return to Avergon and follow them. *Please* follow them," Kyrus said almost mournfully. "Or…"

"Or?"

"Or that's it, Tyghus. That's it."

The General could only stare at the Emperor's vivid red outline against the white snow, not wanting to know for certain what he meant. "Guess there's not much left to be said, is there? I can't argue you into believing I'm the same man I've always been."

"That's true, you can't. Your actions will tell me all I need to know, just as they've done these last three months."

After the final stinging remark, Tyghus placed a gloved hand on the Khorokh's shoulder. "Pains me to see you this way, brother."

His chest burned as the words left his mouth. With a rueful turn, Tyghus headed back out the way he arrived, the heavy door taking all his strength to wrench open. Two Reds stood on either side of the doorway, silent guardians of the Brex.

He couldn't help but look over his shoulder as he began his descent.

Chapter XX

"It is man's curse that a smitten foe should warm the coldest heart."

Speech of Khorokh Rynsyus I to the Lorrio, 373 P.C.

Dray'gon Rokh, Lorrian Norum, 3rd Day of the Second Month, Y. 384 P.C.

"He goes alone?"

The eldest Nortic watched Volinex perched by the window of his Norum, spying the Emperor fleeing south from the Arxun on horseback. "The word 'alone' lost all meaning once he took the throne. Rubitians will follow him to his grave."

"Aye," the young one said with a smile. "Where do you think he goes?"

"Depends."

The young Lorrion looked back. "On what?"

"On where he decides to go," Anti' said glibly.

Voli' rolled his eyes. "So old, so wise. Where do you *think* that is, then?"

Antinax grunted. "If fortune stays with us, then Kyrogon. To those precious woods he's spoken so often of, lately."

"Aye, and if we're not so fortunate?"

"Such a pessimist, aren't you?"

"I'm only asking."

"He's going to Kyrogon, two sources confirmed it," Wollia suddenly interjected, before looking to Antinax with a stern expression. "Don't agitate the boy."

Anti' couldn't help but let out a derisive snort as the young man looked away in annoyance.

"And the rest of the sources?" Barannus asked from a chair across the room. Even reclined as he was, Antinax could see he was pale and unsettled, nails whittled to nubs, lips chapped from constant licks. "When will they tell us what happened with General Tyghus? Two days he's been gone already; two days and our 'sources' have said nothing. No one knows yet?"

"What difference does it make?" Antinax scolded.

"It makes a big difference!" the chubby Lorrion said. "*I'd* like to know so —"

"We'll get our information when it's safe to get our information," Antinax cautioned. "But we already know what was said: either Tyghus admitted to his affair with the Chibin animal or he didn't. If he did, it speaks for itself — he's busy mounting Chibin women while their men slaughter thousands of Rokhs; if he didn't admit it, the Khorokh thinks him untrustworthy."

"It's that simple?"

"Certainly. When Wollia and I saw him, all we had to do was *hint* at Tyghus's infidelity and it sent him flailing like a toddler, like he'd worried about it all along. There's nothing that Tyghus could have said that would have *improved* his standing with the Khorokh. Think about it, Barannus."

"Aye, and the General's sister?"

Antinax quickly grewed irritated at the younger man's worrying. "What about her? Everything we've been told says that Kyrus thought her marriage was meaningless at best, a fraud at worst – and that was *before* the Bridge attack. Certainly not –"

"I don't mean that, I mean what if Kyrus lets the General negotiate with her? What if they reaffirm the peace?" Barannus croaked, beads of sweat dotting his forehead. "Or if they start questioning why their correspondences keep disappearing –"

"Gods above, enough!" Antinax said, scowling at the nervous Lorrion. "You know that nothing about the couriers leads to this room; you know we've seen to that."

But Barannus just shook his head. "The only thing I *know* is that we're relying on *men* and *women* to give us information *and* to keep secrets. Men and women can be turned!"

"*These* men and women are being handsomely rewarded for their efforts," Antinax said as patiently as possible.

"And if someone outbids them?"

"Then they'll have outlived their usefulness and will be done away with," the old man replied coldly. "Don't complicate things – *nothing* leads back here."

The younger Nortic looked away but didn't protest.

"And even if the Khorokh thought talks with the queen would be worth his while, *even if* he thought she had an ounce of clout on the Peninsula, he's not going to entrust them to someone he's at least suspicious of. But at worst, Tyghus negotiates a 'peace' with his sister – what's the worry? It'd be easy enough to have it breached – the Purebloods would probably do it for us! Did it for us at the Converge, no?"

"But if that's true, then how could he let this man, this *same* man lead his troops to war?" Barannus cried. "The Sixth, no less, he leads the *Sixth!* They'll be the first troops into the fray if we invade –"

"Precisely," Antinax said, devoid of emotion. "The Sixth's command is too important to entrust to just anyone, isn't it? You have my word that Tyghus won't sit long in that position."

The younger Lorrion's cheeks flushed finally, a hint of a smile taking root. "Perhaps," he conceded with a nod.

"This all ends the same way, Barannus. The destination's fixed but the paths are many. So? It's about *patience* then. Flexibility. Look at me, I'm practically at death's door and only now do I see the fulfilment of my life's dream on the horizon," Antinax implored. "Ultimately, it'll be Kyrus's pain that leads him to his decision, that and that alone. The hurt that lingers inside him is plain for anyone to see; he'll get there in due time, but we can help speed him along that path as we have been..." his eyes bounced to

Wollia's. "Like today for instance, if it *is* Kyrogon he heads off to..."

Barannus's small grin faded as he looked to the ground. "What we've done there... I cannot believe."

"Had to be done, have you heard what I said?" the elder Lorrion said with a glimmer of defensiveness to his voice.

"Aye, but the gods... they frown on such things..."

"No one ever said it wasn't a high stakes game we play, brother," Volinex offered, breaking his silence.

Antinax's eyes fell on young Voli' with approval, something he rarely granted. Beyond his silhouette, the beauty of the blustery snow provided a welcome respite from their talks. He sighed. "Leave nothing to chance."

* * *

The two-day journey to his homeland had served Kyrus well thus far. It was a freedom he hadn't felt in forever when he kicked his horse into a sprint outside the walls, every deep, freezing breath making him feel that much more refreshed. He rode the dappled beast hard but it maintained a healthy trot far longer than many of the warhorses he rode as Dyrator; in fact, it was Kyrus's back and shoulders that soon ached from months of inertia, clearly not the mount's.

He'd vainly tried to hide his escape from Dray'gon Rokh through the drab brown colors of a commoner, but the mighty steed and the large rider atop it made him conspicuous – at least to those that kept track of such things. With the blizzard yet to subside, there was no other route to take from the city but the Tersian Som, which only made his pursuers' jobs that much easier. Every so often the weather would break and he would look behind him to see the fiery red of his protective Guards. It wasn't until he camped the first night in a sleeping hut along the Som that he realized it was a full dozen, but to their credit, they kept a respectable distance.

As he cantered into the Kyrogon outskirts, he saw the distinctive Bannaman's Creek, a shallow run that wound to the south and then east around the village, creating an elbow-shaped moat. A simple bridge forged the creek at the elbow's bend, where a rudimentary stone road took its visitors the rest of the way in. Once across, it was clear why the Kyrogon name meant "people of the woods", as a thick grove of trees sprang up within the area protected by the moat, with the town itself in a man-made clearing.

Gentle puffs of smoke floated from brown-tiled roofs, the homes beneath huddled around the town well as if warding off the cold and snows. Even though the town square appeared to have been recently cleared, not a person stirred about the village, not a footprint could be seen in any direction.

Bet they're reclined by the fire with soup in hand, Kyrus thought nostalgically. *Probably praying for sunnier days. Hopefully, they'll get them.*

Ringing the village were the estates of Kyrogon's Ruhls, and while he was tempted to pay visit to his own or his relatives' for the first time in years, the Khorokh had only one site to see if he wished to make it back to the Som by nightfall.

He briskly dismounted from the horse at the well and tied it off at a nearby post, only then seeing the first signs of the town's life, curious children appearing at the windows. Parents too were soon drawn to ogle the strange man in brown. The Khorokh glanced back at his trackers still down the tree-lined stone road, barely visible in the snow and fog.

"Gentlemen," he yelled to them. "Your pursuit's been admirable – even if I never asked for it – but your presence here will needlessly disturb these folks. Just stay on the fringe and leave me be – I don't need you at the moment and I won't be gone long, anyway."

The soft trots slowed to a halt, the Reds murmurming conflictedly. Satisfied they tred no further, Kyrus deftly took his leave, dashing north through the village until he was in the ring of trees again.

He was almost there.

* * *

Atrophied muscles made stomping through snow piled up to his knees a brutal task. Even worse, his leather boots did nothing to keep out the ice, nor did the commoner's cloak and the cloth wraps around his face and neck ward off the chill. But in the end, those were only minor distractions, because the closer he got, the more lost he became in the thoughts consuming him – the same thoughts that sent him fleeing from the Capital in the first place.

Guide me, he begged silently. *Guide me in this decision… tell me what to do…*

Once he arrived, he'd get the clarity he sought. He'd be in the company of people he could trust, the *only* people he could trust, where he could ask much wiser minds than his what the proper path was. He'd update them on everything that'd transpired since his last visit, the five months of hell that he'd gone through.

He shook his head ruefully as he swatted away barren branches in his path. *I shouldn't have ignored you like I have. I should have come more often like I promised, but I didn't. No excuse for it. If I had, I wouldn't feel so lost as I do… so lost in that city of snakes. I don't even know who I am anymore; I'm pushed down paths with no reasons given, no time to figure them out. No one to confide in. Everybody wants something there, no one's just there for me. Not even Tyghus… Tyghus of all people! Riding with a turncoat, sleeping with a godsforsaken Pureblood – in love with her if that crusty Nortic is to be believed. Why? How? How can that be?*

195

"You knew it'd happen eventually," Kyrus inadvertantly said aloud. "Knew it since you were young."

Aye. Aye, you did. And the Lorrio's no better. Castus with his unimaginable arrogance, his treachery – yet flush with power, so he says. And Antinax... well, at least he can claim to've been right about something... right about Tyghus, right about Castus... but then, Rynsysus and how many others have warned that there's no greater manipulator than Anti', so – so...

He squeezed his eyes shut and bared his teeth as he felt familiar pressures crushing him. *Why am I bothering with this? Why do I bloody care what Antinax wants or what Castus wants or what Rynsyus wanted or what anyone wants? Why! I've been ready to give up on this world so many times since the Bush yet every time I step back from the edge, and every time I regret it.* Well, this time I'm ready, Kyrus thought, smiling weakly as his eyes watered in emotion. *I've waited – begged for the gods to take me on their own but I'm tired of waiting, I'm ready to do it myself if you'll only tell me.* Tell me, *dammit,* and I'll join you at the Table. In a moment's notice I will, then we'll dine and drink 'til we're all drunk and full. We'll wait together for the gods to send us back.

He patted the knife underneath his ragged clothes; he'd have his answer soon. He would have resolution. "*Almost there,*" he whispered, recognizing a particular fork in the nearly invisible trail through the trees. As usual, he turned right.

Surely, you want me to join you? I don't serve any purpose here. Only thing I ever did right was pretend to be a brave soldier and the gods saw fit to snatch me away from even that. So what else is there? The Empire'd be better off, I'd *be better off. The people don't need –*

And suddenly he stopped.

Footprints marked the snows in front of him.

Footprints that led his eyes to an image that simply couldn't be.

The delicate silence of descending flakes was shattered by the Emperor's unearthly bellows. Sounds of sheer grief as the man saw the pile of rubble before him.

The once majestic obelisk, the ode to his father, mother, and brother commissioned and built over a decade prior by master artisans, lay smashed in a heap of priceless black stone.

Kyrus stumbled forward towards the wreckage, running its pebbly remnants through his frozen hands. Dropping to his knees at the monument's base, he looked up at the trees it used to punch through and found it impossible to tell anything had ever been there. Falling ice stung his eyes, prompting more tears to well at their corners.

"How could – who would –" he muttered helplessly, but the tone soon turned angry. "How could this have happened!" he screamed. "*How could this have happened!*"

He stood, every yell echoing longer. "*Who did this? Who in the name of the gods did this!"*

Enraged, he violently kicked the ruined base, sending a spray of powder into the air. The base's blackness refocused him, dropping down again to find his family's names inscribed. But as his shaking hands brushed the snow away, it wasn't their inscriptions he found.

Defacing the stone, obscuring the inscription, were characters of a language far from Clyvea Province, far from the Upper Rokhlands.

Kyrus's face wrinkled for a moment as he tried to make sense of this newest shock. He brushed away more. The carvings vandalized nearly all of what remained of the base – and then it struck him like a catapult.

"It's Valogary."

The distinctive looping styles…

"It's *Valogary.*"

He never heard the Rubitio sprinting up the path to find him. It never occurred to him that his cries of agony reached their ears. All he could see were those characters. Those distinctive, *grotesque*, looping characters.

"My Lord!" a Guard called out. "My Lord, are you okay?"

The Emperor never bothered to face the men.

The footsteps slowed as they neared him. "My Lord, are you hurt? What is this?"

Kyrus's face was almost immobile, jaw hanging slightly, discharge from his nose coating his upper lip, eyes refusing to blink. But somewhere, deep in the back of his mind, he heard the Guard's question. And to no one but himself he whispered a plaintive two-word reply:

"*My*   *answer.*"

Chapter XXI

"If I may implore one thing of my brothers before I leave this life, it is this – do not let this throne dictate the will of the Rokhs; let the will of the Rokhs dictate the throne.
It is only by the latter can one rule."

Last words of Khorokh Cassyus I to the Lorrio, Y. 33 P.C.

Dray'gon Rokh, Lorrian Halum, 21st Day of the Second Month, Y. 384 P.C.

"Good gentlemen and ladies of the Lorrio, we gather here today to cast our votes on the resolution proffered by Lorrion Antinax of Antillion – the declaration of war and full-scale invasion of the Valogarian Sub-Realm."

Kyrus sat erect in his chair with hands folded neatly in front of him, perfectly serene as he watched Oratus address his Lorrio. To the Speaker's left were the four Nortics; to his right, the four Sudos. His voice rang majestic in the open arches of the Halum, though the Ruler doubted anyone but him was taking time to savor it. While Kyrus had already "advised" Oratus which direction his vote should take, certainly no one else knew; thus, the table remained gripped in palpable tension.

"The Khorokh's hope is that you all have had time to take stock of your constituents' wishes," the Speaker continued. "And that you've searched within yourselves for the proper path to take at this crossroads. So with that said... I believe the time has come."

Kyrus eyed the Lorrions carefully, searching each face for reaction as Oratus carried on.

"Antinax, you made the motion, so you'll have final word on it. But first, the floor's open to anyone else who would like to address the table."

Eyes moved but heads didn't, all waiting to see who would seize the moment. Inevitably, Castus became the focus of attention, but it was clear the handsome young Sudo appeared quite the worse for wear – a spotty beard grew on a normally smooth face and dark circles hung loosely below his eyelids. Whether the weariness stemmed from taxation of the mind or body was anyone's guess.

Castus hunched over and stared at the table at length, as if summoning thoughts or inspiration. After a deep sigh, he brought himself upright in his chair and spoke, his tone low and grave. "Oratus, I thank you for that. If it hasn't been said to you already, then I welcome your presence in this Halum amidst all your other duties. You're a man of many trades, but few could ply so many with such skill. I applaud you, as we all should."

The corpulent Speaker appeared touched by the kind words, his eyes immediately shooting to the Emperor's. Castus continued.

"Friends and fellow Lorrions, your Highness Kyrus, I... I fear for the Empire. We are an old people but a young nation by Andervold's standard. In the four centuries since Cataclysm, we've pushed our borders to natural divides along the River Anonga in the west, the River Brafford and Ratikan Sea in the south, conquering the people we've encountered along the way. No one can dispute our supremacy on the battlefield – it'd be foolish to do so by words; it'd be suicide to do so by sword. And that view of the Empire works for the commoners, it works in the Gurums, maybe even works for our children. Why shouldn't they believe that we've always been this strong, that we'll always *be* this strong?'"

The Sudo paused before turning his head directly towards Kyrus. "But we're the Lorrions. *We* need to see that such a simple view overlooks the infirmities lying beneath the surface – we control as far west as the Anonga, yet the Plains are ravaged with such banditry that even the Stolxian kingdoms are in an uproar. We control as far south as the Brafford yet the Lowlands are full of Rokhs who feel the Capital's forgotten them – the same Rokhs who'd bear the brunt of any Colverian retaliation for attacking Valogar."

Immediate shuffling could be heard on the other side of the table as the two younger Nortics looked for a response from from Antinax, sitting immediately to Kyrus's right. But the old man did nothing but stare.

"Now, this is *not* to say we can't proceed with this vote, send our troops back into the Bushlands. This is not to say we could not succeed there – of course we could. I'm simply suggesting that perhaps we should embrace a new phase as an Empire – perhaps the more *noble* phase; where expansion by the sword has brought us the Realm we now rule, *sustaining* that Realm should be our focus going forward. *That* focus would address the Plains' disaster or Colverian distrust. *That* focus would give Nar-Biluk the chance to prove *they* are the faithful allies *they* pledged to be, *and* that *we* are the faithful allies *we* pledged to be."

Castus licked his lips, blue eyes darting around the table. "Lest it be forgotten – the common Valogarian *despises* the Chibin as much as the common Rokh; the common Valogarian no doubt bleeds with us for the disgrace those radicals have brought their country yet again, if they are indeed to blame. The common Valogarian wishes only for peace, only for prosperity, only for *trade* with the Rokhs – *not* to sow discord between our lands."

Castus paused, voice running ragged. He took a sip of his chalice, its water running down his chin; he didn't bother to wipe it as he stared straight ahead again, seemingly focused on nothing but each word that left his mouth.

"If we do attack," he started, swallowing deeply. "We *destroy* that base of trust that we've built. The buds of new trade outlets. The goodwill of neighboring nations. The Lowlanders will feel that much more detached from their Khorokh in Dray'gon Rokh, a man already weeks away by horse but even farther away in mind. And let's not kid ourselves – *there will be blood.* Rivers of needless, fruitless blood, if we do this.

"While I pray that the elder statesmen and women across from me will hear what I'm saying, that they'll back away from the path they've proposed, I recognize my pleas will fall on deaf ears..." He sighed as if finished, when suddenly he looked right at Volinex and Barannus, sitting side by side. "But Voli', Bari' – *you do not have follow those two in lockstep, do you*

200

hear me? The Lorrio was never designed to be Uplands against Lowlands, 'Nortic' against 'Sudo', whatever those cursed terms mean. That's a dysfunction that you and I inherited, but have the power to change! To unite for the proper vision, not what's been handed down to us! *We* can give back to the Empire the Lorrio it was *meant* to have if you'll just… *listen* to what I say and think for yourself what makes sense here!" Castus's eyes burned into his younger counterparts, who both flushed at the unorthodox direct appeal. "I am Castus, and… this is my word."

Kyrus watched the Sudo close his eyes and lean forward again in his seat, chin dropping to his chest. It was a calculating, well-crafted speech by any measure, a calmer, more sincere side of Castus than he had ever seen either as Lorrion or Emperor. Opposite Kyrus, Oratus stood.

"Lorrion Castus, we thank you for your words. Will anyone else be heard?" the Speaker paused, furtively casting a glance at the two young Nortics. "Hm. I see none. Very well. Antinax, I cede the floor to you."

The stone-faced Nortic remained fixated on Castus even as Oratus sat down, and when he spoke, every word seemed directed towards his adversary, dripping with antipathy. "That my 'friend' Castus wishes to portray the Empire in a state of stagnation, rather than one of ascendancy, only goes to show how truly far apart we are here. That distresses me," he said with a sharp nod. "It absolutely distresses me, much as I'm sure that'd surprise some of you to hear. It's as distressing as the shameful act that brings us together today, but that *act*, my friends, warrants concern far beyond simple power grabs or land expansions – we should be so lucky! No, we have been *attacked*; a tradeway's been destroyed, families *that we pledged to protect* – fathers and mothers, sons and daughters, husbands and wives of the Empire – they've been destroyed. Shattered, never to be pieced together again."

Kyrus flinched.

"So with all due respect to good Castus, I am not ashamed to suggest that a response to an attack – an attack on this *scale* – involve the sword rather than a trade agreement. Distinguishing between a 'common Valogarian' and a Pureblood is a fool's errand, because where one gives sanctuary to the other, there *is* no difference. Certainly Rokhish law punishes the thief as harshly as the abettor, does it not? More simply then, if the Valogarian king is not *actively* campaigning against the Purebloods, if he is not actively rooting out any sympathizers, it means one of two things – he either lacks the power or he lacks the will. *Neither* reason excuses Imperial inaction here."

The old man spoke with a quiet intensity, effectively mirroring the tone used in opposition moments earlier. "Now, good Castus makes much of the affairs and postures of our Colverian and Stolxian friends; well, let's address that. The Rokhs, for all our troubles subduing the Jungle

Beastmen, are virtually beloved by them compared to their feelings for the Stolxians. Rynsyus might have said my history's hazy, but I'm quite certain it was the Stolxians that destroyed their homeland west of the Anonga, was it not? The Stolxians that drove them to the point of near extinction?" The Lorrion sharply nodded, underscoring his sarcasm. "I'll check the scrolls after we're through here, but I believe that's right. So the Tenth Dyron in the Jungle may be unappreciated at the moment, but should even one giant Stolxian pass through the Gateway with arms drawn, that Dyron will find itself with a Jungle *full* of allies. Whether we can control them or not, they'd be allies all the same. I don't fear the Stolxis, and you shouldn't either."

He paused and let his eyes survey the table before continuing.

"Colvery. Valogar's faithful allies south of the Brafford owe their strength to the massive trees in which they hide, a strength they've managed to convince others of is *power*, but *we* need only look at the facts to know better: they hide in their trees because they don't *like* to attack! And even if they did, they've one feasible crossing in the south to do so and *we* control it! If they want to forge a fortified bridge against the most powerful troops in Andervold, then quite frankly, *I invite them to* – saves us the trouble of burning down their forest!" he said, pounding the table and rattling his jowls. "Or if they'd prefer to bring their bows to Valogar and join the Natives in open battlefields, then our cavalry will have a merry go at them! So the Lowlanders need not worry about being a bulwark against anybody. If the Sudos wish to ease their fears, they can remind them that when the Peninsula is properly subdued again, the first area to benefit from its resources and slaves will be those Lowlands."

"The Lowlanders don't *want* Valogarian slaves, Anti'."

"You can speak for the Shoals and the Shoals alone, Castus," Antinax scolded. "I'd say your characterization of their sentiment being the Lowlands' as a whole is a *fraud*, though I know you'd never let your fellow Sudos here say as much."

Castus's face immediately darkened. "You –"

"*But regardless*, I have the floor!"

Castus silenced with a look at Kyrus, as Antinax pressed forward. "People, we've *fought* and *beaten* these enemies before. There are any number of reasons why the last war wasn't as easy as it should have been," the Nortic said with a glare at Castus. "But that's the past and this is now. And *now*, you can't let the presence of other problems blind you to the most pressing: a savage, *brutal* attack on one of the Empire's most vital trade routes. You can't let the presence of other problems blind you to the *repercussions* that will come should this atrocity go unaddressed – first and foremost being more pyhr bombings! Valogar's access to its pyhr mines carries far graver risks than even I realized. If we forsake the lesson given at the Converge then we are destined to repeat its folly, there's simply no other way to see it.

"Now, I've thought about this at length; I've prayed to the gods, begged them to tell me if I'd gone astray – but I heard nothing to suggest I'm wrong. So now, I'll beg my fellow Lorrions – even you good Castus – to unite behind our war banners. Show them a united front. I am Antinax, and this is my word."

A deathly silence fell over the room, as all knew the vote was at hand. The portly Speaker nervously arose once more.

"Thank you, Lorrion Antinax. I... well, brethren, I-I suppose it is time. As the last appointee, I will cast the final vote." Oratus licked his lips with trepidation before turning to Volinex at his left. "We'll proceed in circular fashion. Will you begin, Volinex?"

Castus shot a pleading glimpse at the man directly across from him. The young Nortic did not miss it – but his face scowled. "For Loccea Province and Raizea by steward – I vote for war."

The deflated Sudo let his head sink.

"Barannus?"

The pasty Nortic gnawed at his cheek for a moment until a look from Antinax. "Astorea Province votes war."

"Wollia?"

"For Draygonea, I vote for war."

"Antinax, can I presume –"

"Kylea votes for war."

"Desiria?"

"Grynea Province opposes."

"Tessax?"

"Kregea – *and* the Converge," the one-eyed old Lorrion said pointedly. "We oppose."

"Holiokus?"

"For Starrea Province, I oppose."

"Castus?"

"I choose peace. I choose logic, I choose sense –"

"Your bloody vote, Castus!" Antinax barked.

"Of course Morremea opposes."

"We have four in favor and four opposed then," Oratus started, eyes locking on the Emperor's silent yet imposing figure. "Well I... um... as Speaker of the Rokhs, I'm the uh... temporary Lorrion for Clyvea Province. As such, it is my... duty... to vote in lieu of deadlocks. And here we stand in deadlock at four votes apiece..."

Sweat poured down the sides of the man's face, rushing down his many chins.

"On the motion of Antinax for war with the Valogarians... I vote..."

Antinax's eyes widened as he watched the Speaker; Kyrus bored into him the same.

"*War.*"

A collective groan went up on Oratus's right, while the Nortics clearly forced themselves silent. The Speaker didn't seem to know what to do next when Castus leapt to his feet, straight sandy brown strands of hair flopping over blue eyes.

"Damn it all, damn you to the Depths, damn you-you – *you have have condemned our peoples to ruin!* You *imbeciles* have no feel for sentiments in the Lowlands, *they don't want this!* You have *wasted* this chance to prove that all those that died in the name of making and maintaining this fragile peace did not do so vain!" he wheeled to point at Antinax. "I always felt that men like you were a dying breed, I really did. I thought your ideas were so far beyond reality they couldn't *possibly* take in anyone else, but you've done it! You arrogant, deceitful, *evil* man, you've gone and spread your venom to a new generation of pawns with no idea of life beyond this cursed Hall or beyond the Clyves!"

Antinax stared back at the Sudo with a hint of amusement to his face. "Are you through?"

But Castus still raged. "The gods will hold you to account for your actions someday, Antinax; you'll have no hole to crawl into when they ask you why the blood of thousands of innocent Rokhs and Valogarians stain your hands red! Oh, how they'll *laugh* when you seek a seat at their Table!"

"Lorrion Castus, please!" Oratus pleaded, looking to the Emperor. Kyrus's face had yet to change but upon meeting the Speaker's eyes, his head nodded ever so slightly, even as Castus ranted on.

"No! There's no good in this room, not while it has the stench of –"

"Lorrion, please sit, this meeting is not adjourned!" the Speaker bellowed, drowning out the young Sudo's increasingly grating voice. In a near pant, Castus glared at Oratus with confused contempt.

"Nothing else need be said here, Oratus. I bid you a good day."

With an enraged kick, he sent his chair crashing into the table.

"*Castus, sit! This meeting is not adjourned!*"

The angry Lorrion didn't even look back as he stormed towards the exit – until he was stopped dead in his tracks.

Jarax, with five Rubitian Guards, blocked the door.

"Step aside."

No movement.

"*Step aside.*"

No movement.

The skulking Lorrion did an about-face. "What in the name of the gods is this?"

Oratus's voice suddenly took on an eerie complacency. "Castus, you stand accused of high treason against the peoples of the Rokhish Empire and her Ten Provinces."

Though his back was to him still, Kyrus could hear the shock in the Sudo's voice.

"On what grounds?"

"On the grounds that you have openly violated the ban on trade with Valogar; on the grounds that you have actively and unlawfully aided and abetted the Valogarian resistance in the process. Do you deny the charges?"

Kyrus felt the eyes of the Lorrions on him in stunned silence as Castus stammered a reply.

"I – I – of course I deny the charges. This is madness—"

"Then you will be held in the appropriate lodgings until the time of your trial before the Court of Inquisition."

The Rubitio quickly apprehended the Lorrion, jerking his arms behind his back.

"What is this! *I am a bloody Lorrion of the Empire!* Highness! Highness, you can't let this happen! Say something to these fools!"

The Khorokh sat still as a statue, with just as many words. Oratus remained his voice.

"Your innocence will be determined in due time, Lorrion, and you will have the chance to prove it. But the Emperor does issue you this reminder," Oratus said, cutting through the sounds of Castus's struggle. "Should you waste the Court's time by hiding the truth, then you'll be treated just the same – just as painfully – as any other Rokh that knowingly lies before the Court."

With that, the Guards hauled the Lorrion by each arm out the door, notwithstanding his desperate protests. "You don't know what you're doing! *I am a Lorrion!*"

His cries grew fainter and fainter. At last, the remaining nine were in silence again.

After receiving the Emperor's approving eyes, Oratus finally said, "Lorrions – I believe that concludes our business here."

Chapter XXII

"Avergon is no longer just a fortress or keeper of troops.

No, if Dray'gon Rokh is the head of this Empire, then Avergon is its very beating heart.

It is a shield against the Desert, Colverian, and Valogarian foes that border the Lowlands on all sides, just as it is a sword that strikes the same.

Ergo, the soldiers guarding it should be of the highest stock, the man that commands them the most valorous.

Anything more is the gods' blessings of course, but anything less invites disaster."

Speech of Emperor Terrius to the Lorrio, Y. 348 P.C.

Starrea Province, Fortress of Avergon, 27th Day of the Second Month, Y. 384 P.C.

"Repeat!"

Hundreds of swords flashed in the sunlight as they swung up in unison, arms poised to strike.

"High-low!"

Arms swung down across bodies.

"Step-shields!"

The line of soldiers surged forward on left feet, same side as their black shields.

"Draw back and lunge!"

Sword-hands cocked back before thrusting forward to impale invisible foes.

"First line, fall back!"

The leaders of the "attack" peeled off to take their place at the back of twenty ranks.

"Repeat!"

The rhythmic slashing, blocking, and thrusting repeated for nearly an hour, high sun beaming down on the men in the fortress's sparring yard. The air carried a typical Lowland winter mildness, though the men gushed sweat like it was midsummer. If any were fatigued, of course, they were smart enough to hide it behind a mask of gnashed teeth and relentless effort. At last, their instructor had mercy on them.

"Alright enough, you bastards," Tyghus said with a grin and a wave of his arm. He was sans helmet in gray and silver battle regalia, having not yet taken the crimson cloak of the Dyrator.

"Give us more!" a lone voice cried out over a chorus of gasps and exhales. More soon took up the challenge.

"You let us off easy, Dyrator!"

"You think we're weak, sire?"

The ritual never failed to make Tyghus smile. "Weakest bunch I've ever laid eyes on! 'Bout to head out to the Desert, find some men pickin' sand who can actually scrap!"

The men returned his insult with laughs.

"Take a knee, brothers. Catch your wind."

Towards the end of the Campaigns of Unity in the century that followed Cataclysm, Khorokh Pistoniux had methodically liberated the Lowlands of Clannic remnant kingdoms – and kept them liberated through the installation of small strongholds throughout. His successor by a hundred years, Khorokh Cassyus III, found the arrangement to be unwieldy once peace had taken hold, and opted to consolidate the outposts by designing the "perfect fortress", one destined to be the finest training ground the Empire had ever seen, one that would draw in the brightest, bravest, and strongest of the Empire's citizens; and indeed it was everything he'd hoped for and more. Shaped like an eight-sided star with a tower at each point, its twenty foot walls were rigged of foreboding rock and wood, its ramparts manned night and day. The famous Academy rose upon a hill as a massive keep in the middle of the star, replete with four more towers of its own, while barracks ringed the walls' inner perimeter. Within those troophalls lurked the mighty Sixth Dyron, the only Imperial unit to make no distinction among the Uplanders, Lowlanders, or Westlanders in its ranks.

By the gods, did it feel good to be back within the walls! Tyghus thought, especially so compared to the long, miserable ride from the Capital. Painfully dwelling upon the inexplicable ill-treatment Kyrus had given him was compounded by suffering through the ordeal in solitude. The meeting with the Khorokh left him little choice but to leave Treos –

Tyghus shook his head at the thought of his departure from Dray'gon Rokh, guilt creeping in yet again. *"No,"* he muttered to himself. *"You focus on the good. You have a job to do now, and that job is here."* He sighed. *"You made your choice, you did what you thought was right... if he makes it, he makes it. Out of your hands now."*

He nodded, looking around at the one place he felt he could count on for things to follow some degree of order. Shieldsmiths make shields. Swordsmiths make swords. Directions are given, men obey, and it's on to the next task, that's that. The simplicity lightened him a bit.

One benefit of Tyghus's agony was forgetting about the awkwardness he expected in commanding kordettes he so recently had been commensurate with. No one had shown him the slightest bit of disrespect since he'd arrived two days prior, but even still, it was bound to be a peculiar arrangement – after all, he'd known most of them since his first days at the Academy in 371. He'd made lasting friendships with some during those training years, fought as boys do with others. He'd shed blood with still others in the years following their Runs, when they found themselves sent to the fringes of the Skulls Desert to punish the Corulesh tribes there.

And now he stood as their Dyrator.

Two of his sergeants and oldest friends stood at his sides, both having returned with their kords that morning from a week and a half of simulated marches. They were massive men, mirror images of each other at well over six feet in height, arms and thighs thick as tree trunks. Indeed, they were the lauded golden-eyed Fyrid twins, and had they not hailed from the legendary welding city of Fyrogon in Astorea Province, they could have passed for Stolxian men – small Stolxians, but Stolxians all the same. To distinguish themselves in battle, Fyrustus wore his blondish-brown hair in the lengthy Upland style, while Fygonus wore his in the sides-shaven Lowland style with a beard that traced along his jawline. Both were of ferocious stock and champion wrestlers of the Imperial Games, dominating all challengers they faced – except each other. It wasn't often and never planned, but whenever the twins squared off against one another, the camp stood back and watched.

Trying to further clear his mind, Tyghus clapped Fyrus' on the back. "Did well with 'em boys, nicely done. They seem very sharp."

The big man grunted. "Worked 'em as hard as we work ourselves."

"Took it easy on them after all, then?" Tyghus joked.

Fygonus chuckled. "They held up alright. Itchin' for a fight, but they held up."

"Aye, 'specially once word of the Converge spread around camp. Half the time we wake up to find them training on their own before the sun's even risen."

Tyghus nodded. "Good. Very good. Lot of them haven't seen battle in some time, so they're going to need that discipline. How'd they take to the marches?"

"Could barely contain 'em," Fygo said proudly. "Mud, grass, hills, stone – damn them all as far's they were concerned."

"Better men than I. Did them all the same, but I bloody hated those Academy marches."

Fygo' laughed. "You sayin' ya' like 'em now?"

"You didn't see me trying to find you out there, did you?" Tyghus replied with a smile.

"Must have missed you."

"Must have."

Fyrustus looked at the General. "That ride to the Capital must've been hell. Rather be out here marching through swamps and shit than eight weeks there and back on a damn horse."

Tyghus gave morbid smirk. "You have no idea."

"The hell's he know?" Fygo' added. "He'd sooner eat a damn horse than ride one."

"A good point, Fyrus'."

"He can kiss my ass, Ty- uh... what the hell we callin' you these days, anyway?"

"It's 'General' now, isn't it?" Fygonus answered with a mischievous smile.

"Aye? Not jackass?"

"I'll answer to either," Tyghus said, crossing his arms with an uncomfortable grin. It was the first chance he'd had to talk with them about his promotion, and he'd hoped there wouldn't be any pushback from the proud Twins – apparently there wasn't. "Let's say that on the march, it's General. When we're not, it's Tyghus, agreed?"

"He won't remember that," Fygo' said with a baritone laugh. "But I will, don't worry."

"My thanks to you."

"I have to say, though," the Twin said in a more serious tone. "When we'd heard Kyrus left for Dray'gon Rokh, we thought he'd give the Sixth to someone from his class. We knew you two were friends, but "

"I'd have guessed Reverus, if anybody," Fyrus' interjected with a shrug. "Same class, already commands our cavalry – probably the best damn rider in the Empire."

"Aye, he is," Fygo' agreed. "Thought it'd be him too. Think *he* thought it'd be him."

"Well, gods forgive me, which of you should I console first?" Tyghus replied in annoyed jest. "Or should I start with Reverus?"

"Just sayin' he might a bit prickly towards ya' with you being picked and all."

"If he is, he is," Tyghus said curtly. "I'm sure we'll have it out if we need to." But after a pause, he shook his head. "Truthfully, I'd no more idea Kyrus was appointing me than anyone else. Never discussed it at all really, we just dived into this shithole of a groghouse in the Capital a few months back and that was it."

"He told ya' in a bloody groghouse?"

"Told me right then, over a mug of their slop. Said I was to be the Sixth's new dyrator and apologized for not doing it more formally." Tyghus shrugged. "That was it. I protested, told him I wasn't ready –"

"Not *ready*?" Fyrus' said, glaring at him in disbelief.

"Aye. We – well, *I* just haven't seen the kind of battle, *true* battle like some of the older kordettes have. Not like Grantax or Nikolux or Rev–"

"No one's seen the hell Niko' has, can't hold yourself up to him, by the gods," Fygonus said.

"I do, though. To do what's right by the Sixth, I have to."

"Bah, you're breakin' yourself over nothing," Fyrus' said with a snort. "You'll know what to do when the time comes."

"Aye, it'll be the same as the drills we run here as far as I'm concerned, 'cept with a helluva lot more blood," Fygo' added, coaxing guffaws from his brother.

Tyghus nodded but felt no urge to laugh. "Aye, probably right. In any event, it was just a damn peculiar day in the Capital."

Fygo' grunted. "That *sounds* peculiar."

"Though there's little that man does these days that reeks of logic," Tyghus sighed, recalling their talk on the Brex again despite his best efforts not to.

"You slanderin' our Emperor, General?" Fyrus' said with feigned warning.

Tyghus faked a chuckle as he pictured his wayward friend staring vacantly from the Brex's balcony; staring at everything and nothing all at once. "Never."

"Slander the bastard all ya' want, I just want him to give me my war!" Fygonus said excitedly. "When's the order gonna come? Got soldiers asking me every day for a month now."

"Just waiting on the Lorrio's vote," Tyghus replied quietly. "Should know any day."

The big men could hardly mask their delight. "Gods let that be true. My first prayer in the morning and my last at night has been beggin' them for our chance," Fyrus' said with burning intensity.

His child-like excitement finally made the General laugh again. "You boys that anxious for Valogarian whores again, eh?"

The three of them laughed as they watched the soldiers regain their breath and start rising from crouches. "That's enough in daylight," Tyghus said with a nod. "We'll drill 'em again tonight, I want to see them fight under the moon. Two of you can join me in my quarters if you'd like."

"Of course, Gener – er, Tygh – agh!" Fygo' threw his hands up in frustration as the other two men laughed some more.

As they headed off the training fields to the sounds of soldiers venturing towards midday meals in the dining lodges, a hand grabbed his shoulder.

"General."

With a start, he saw an assistant to the fort's Quartermaster at his side, but the fresh-faced lad never waited for a response.

"Quartermaster Bostonos asked me to tell you that uh… the fish has been placed in your chambers."

After initial confusion, a grin slowly widened across Tyghus's face. "Well, I'll be damned."

* * *

After the three men had doffed their armor in favor of beige tunics that tied off at the chest, they reminisced for hours in Tyghus's torch-lit quarters atop a keep tower, each trying to top the other with their tales. Like the time an Academy instructor caught the three of them, all of ten years old, bloodying themselves in the armory from playing with steel weapons instead of their training woods. Or the time the Valogarian caught his daughter atop Fygonus during the first year of his Run, proceeding to chase the nude Ruhl clear back to his camp. The stories they relished the most were the ones about their campaigns in the Skulls Desert, when they scrapped with the wily tribes in their post-Run years. The memories had them smiling ear-to-ear as they sipped spicegrass teas before a toasty fireplace.

Fygonus set his mug down and snatched up the pile of armor he'd removed. "Alright, to the dining lodges. Wanna get a full belly before the night trainings."

"I'll find you there, I need to have this report sent out by this evening," Tyghus replied as he pulled an unfinished piece of parchment to lay on the desk in front of him.

The Twin looked at the paperwork in disgust. "And you *wanted* to be Dyrator?"

Tyghus grinned at him. "Never said that."

"Leave the bastard to his scribin'," Fyrus' said with a stretch. "Gonna be left with that porridge slop if we don't get down there soon."

"Perish the thought."

As the door slammed behind the Twins, Tyghus waited to hear their footsteps fade. Then his head tilted backwards towards a backless couch in a darkened corner of the room. "Welcome to Avergon, fish."

With a shuffle, a figure arose from the corner's shadows. "I thank ya' for the courtesies, lad."

Tyghus chuckled as he stood, extending an arm towards the voice. "'Fish'?"

A dirty, brown-hooded Treos accepted the General's offer of a shake. "Clever?"

"Quite," Tyghus said, whacking the lanky man's shoulder with his free hand. "Good to see you, my friend. You made good time, didn't expect you for another week – if at all."

"Parallel to the Som all the way to the Clyves, half day's ride to the crossing at Barlerion, then due south through Grynea 'til I hit Marvelon's trail to Avergon," he replied with tired eyes but an easy smile. "Ya'r directions were spot on."

"No... issues?"

"Not a one. Kept outta Lowland towns best I could, pitched camp on the outskirts. F'course, didn't make for the best sleepin', so I tried to get goin' early and turn in late. Never saw anyone on m'trail..."

"Good... sorry to keep you waiting here in the dark so long, been a long time since I caught up with these folks."

The Lakeman shrugged. "Heard some good stories, at least. Seem like good men, those two."

"They are," Tyghus said, before his grin faded with a sigh. "And under other circumstances, I'd of course want you to meet them. But..."

Treos nodded. "Aye. Fewer people knowin' I'm here, the better."

"Aye... For what it's worth, I'm sorry it's come to this."

The Lakeman shook his head. "Nothin' we hadn't already talked about, lad. Nothin' to feel sorry for."

But he did anyway. After he'd met Kyrus on the Brex, Tyghus told Treos everything – the Khorokh's instability, his suspicion, but most importantly his direct order to banish the Lakeman to his fate in the Lakes – an order which meant almost certain death, be it by Rom's hands or the Khorokh's own agents. And though Tyghus knew, *he knew* it wasn't right to disobey an Imperial order, in that moment, he just couldn't abandon the man who'd laid down his life for him on the Plains. How could *that* be right? So they hatched a scheme to have Treos take his chances travelling solo to the fort in Avergon; with luck, he wouldn't be tracked; with luck, Tyghus had overblown Kyrus's veiled threat altogether…

"You sure I'm not more of a hindrance to ya' than I'm worth? I've no problem hackin' it out there on my own."

"Death doesn't bother you for a moment, does it?"

"Nor should it. When it's time, it's time."

"Aye, well, you may not care about your life, but I do. It's not… it's not right what Kyrus asked of me."

Treos's voice turned lower and serious. "It's what the *Khorokh told* ya'."

Tyghus thought over his disobeyal yet again before finally throwing his hands out. "What's done is done."

"This safe-keepin's a debt I can never repay."

Tyghus cringed. "I wouldn't call it safe here just yet."

"Safer than the Lakes, then?"

"Aye, I'll grant you that."

The two men went silent for a few moments. Treos walked to a window and watched troops milling to and from the muddy training fields. "Nothin' from the Council yet, lad?"

Tyghus shook his head. "Nothing."

"Hm… gives me shivers hearing those drills down there again."

"Ah, you could still swing blades with the youngest of them, I bet."

Treos snorted. "Aye, I can swing 'em. Swing 'em right? Now that's the issue."

Tyghus laughed. "Looked pretty damn good on the Plains. On horseback at least."

"We were lucky there," Treos said with an uncharacteristically sharp tone. "Those men were rats. Lower than rats, prob'ly – rats will at least turn and bite if ya' agitate 'em enough."

"How dare you taint our great victory?" Tyghus teased with a bemused smile.

"I'm just sayin'… what you'd be facin' in Valogar is far beyond rats."

"High praise, I suppose."

"Not meant to be praise, just the facts. They'll be fightin' on their own lands, their own grass, their own hills. Men're desperate when they see their own homes at stake," Treos said as he turned to look at the General. "Saw it in the Jungle, swore I'd never see it again."

Tyghus ran a hand through his long hair, suddenly feeling tired. "Gods above, Treos, I was just paying compliments to your work on the Plains. I wasn't going to ask you to take up arms with us."

"Just in case."

"I wasn't. I promised you how long ago now that I'd never ask you that?"

No response came from his friend silhouetted against the window's light.

"Lining your old bag of bones up with the Sixth would only encourage the Natives anyway," Tyghus said lightly.

The Lakeman's face softened over a laugh. "Pardon m'tone, lad. Memories of the Jungle aren't good ones, much as I know–"

A sudden rapping shook the door.

Tyghus's eyes jumped from Treos's.

"Who goes there?"

"It's Bostonos, General," his Quartermaster's voice called back from behind the door. "There's a messenger from Dray'gon Rokh here… word from the Khorokh."

The General quickly slipped his army gray over his tunic.

"Shall I leave, Tyghus?" Treos quietly asked.

"Just… keep to the side…" Tyghus said uncertainly as he stared at the door. "Come in, Bostonos."

The door opened, however, to a gang of six men clad in crimson surrounding the portly quartermaster Bostonos Curtanus. Tyghus's brow furrowed. "What the hell is this?"

"I'm sorry, my lord," Bostonos said shamefully.

A man on his right donning a shimmering cloak stepped forward as his comrades fanned out behind him. Each of them was armed and helmeted.

"The Khorokh sends his regards, General Tyghus. My name is Dronos Dekatur, one of his trusted couriers."

Dressed like the Emperor himself, Tyghus thought as he looked him over. He was a handsome man despite the sneer on his beardless face, with long, light brown hair pulled back. He stepped into the room with a royal gait, left arm clutching a tied scroll. His gray eyes pored over the tall General.

"Care to introduce your friends, or –"

"Protection. Couriers have had the bad habit of not reaching their targets of late."

"Maybe so, but you're here now. You reached your target. Still feel like you need protection in the most fortified piece of land south of the Capital?"

Dronos's sneer deepened. "I prefer it this way."

Tyghus fought an urge to let his swordhand fall to his weapon's hilt, waiting instead for the man to extend an arm in greeting. "Well, welcome to Avergon, then," he said, trying to gloss over the tension. "I'm glad to see Kyrus had –"

"Khorokh," Dronos quickly corrected.

Tyghus glared at the man. "I'm glad to see the Khorokh have better luck with his couriers than I have."

Dronos gave no hint of amusement. "Do you know what's happened in Dray'gon Rokh, General Tyghus?"

"I've been waiting to hear along with the rest of the Empire. I presume you're here to tell me the Lorrio's decision, no?"

"Decision on what?"

Tyghus looked to either side of the man in annoyed confusion. "Are we going to war with Valogar or not?"

"Ah," the man replied. "The vote. I've news of that as well."

The General's brows arched. "Is there something else I should know?"

The courier started to answer but then he paused, eyes scanning the room with suspicion. "Are we alone here?"

The back of Tyghus's neck began to burn. "Clearly not... you've brought quite the entourage with you."

Dronos scowled. "And who do *you* keep in here? That's my question."

"Why?"

"So there are people here," Dronos said as he boldly walked into the room to Tyghus's anger. At length, he found Treos standing in his darkened corner. "You," he said with a point.

"He's of no concern to you, Dronos," Tyghus said with rising temper.

"If that's true, why didn't you say so to begin with? Why keep it a secret?"

"Because it's not your business who I keep as military council."

"Military council?" Dronos said as he looked back at Tyghus with a surprised face. "Do you keep all your retainers so filthy and ragged? Hiding in dark corners?"

The man's tone irked Tyghus further, his face flushing red but words escaping him.

"And as it happens, where's the rest of your 'council'?" the courier continued. "This man's wise enough to speak for them all?"

"I'll leave," Treos suddenly offered as he emerged from the shadows. "'Pologize for m'appearance... just got back from some hard ridin'..."

"Mm, of course," Dronos said, before his eyes narrowed on the Lakeman. "Won't you stay?"

Treos froze on the question, eyes shooting to Tyghus's. The General finally grabbed the unfinished parchment scroll and handed it off the Lakeman. "No, the courier was right in the first place, he's here to meet with me. Run this down to the stables, will you?"

"Aye..."

After a bit of hesitance, the Lakeman pushed towards the line of guards.

Tyghus's hand itched towards his sword again, but to his massive relief they let him through without incident. As the door slammed behind him, Dronos eyed it for a moment before locking on Tyghus. "I don't recognize that man."

"I didn't realize you'd served in the Sixth."

"I haven't."

"Then why the hell would you know who he is?"

The courier seethed in unmasked contempt. "Peculiar accent for a Lowlander. Who is he?"

The General glared back. "Do you have a message for me or not?"

"*Who* is he? Do I need to remind you that my eyes and ears are an extension of the Khorokh's?"

"No more than I need to remind you that you're a *courier*, a deliverer of His messages, nothing more."

"You don't know who I am," Dronos growled.

"Then correct me. Have you been given license to interrogate me like this? In my own bloody chamber?"

A tense moment ensued, the courier clearly not expecting the rebuke. "General Tyghus, Lorrion Castus of Cassitigon has been imprisoned on charges of treason against the Empire. He's set to be tried before the Court of Inquisition and one hundred of his Peers at a time of the Khorokh's choosing."

"Very well," Tyghus said, too angry to even focus on the revelation.

Dronos appeared perturbed by Tyghus's response. "You surely recognize this is the first time in the Empire's history that a sitting Lorrion has been punished in this manner."

The General gritted his teeth. "I do."

"Do you? Because the Khorokh wishes to send a message – to everybody – that any acts of betrayal in days past or days to come will be punished appropriately. It's important to him that *no one* feels they are above the Empire's laws."

The threatening tone was unmistakeable. "And nor should they," Tyghus offered calmly as possible.

"Indeed."

Tyghus was loathe to ask his next question. "Dronos, what has the Lorrio decided?"

"War, General Tyghus," the courier replied without hesitation, eyes never breaking hold. "Your orders are to proceed with the invasion of Valogar at once."

To Tyghus, the silence that followed said more than the courier's words. "That's it?"

"What else were you expecting?"

"This is a *war* we're talking about Dronos, not a bloody trip to the

Tanokhun. What the hell are the logistics? Who else is joining the invasion and when? The Khorokh can't expect the Sixth to win this war on its own, I'm assuming. Could be upwards of a hundred thousand Natives waiting on us!"

"Obviously not," Dronos replied with irritation. "General Glannox plans to join you—"

"An *Uplander?*" Tyghus exclaimed incredulously. "The man's never set foot on a battlefield south of the Clyves."

"The man's steel and unbroken in the Uplands," the courier scolded. "But that's not your concern. He will meet you on the Peninsula – following your breakthrough on the Isthmus, of course."

"When?" Tyghus questioned with a hint of skepticism. "With how many?"

"He's preparing to depart Marvelon with the First, Second, Third, and Fifth Dyrons in the coming weeks, General Tyghus."

"My men can be at the outskirts of the Isthmus after barely a week's march. Whenever Glannox leaves Marvelon, he'll be at least three weeks out from the Shoals with a baggage train for more than 50,000 men."

"Nevertheless –"

"And from there, what? He boards the fleet at Port Hovium to invade by sea? Another few days – assuming the fleet's even gathered."

"*Nevertheless*, those are matters beyond your concern. *Your* campaign is based on stealth and swiftness, striking hard at the Natives before they have time to gather in strength."

"With no idea of when to expect reinforcements? How can I run a campaign in such a way?" Tyghus demanded before pointing in a window's direction. "How can I, how can the *throne* ask these men to give their lives in such a way?"

Dronos sighed contemptuously. "By the time you've pushed onto the Peninsula, Glannox will be landing on its northern coast, *that's* the timetable he's been issued by the Emperor."

That's nonsense, Tyghus thought, but he forced himself to move on. "And what of negotiations?"

The courier grinded his teeth, but replied calmly. "So long as they don't interfere with preparations for your attack, He'll allow them, but under these terms and these terms only: that they surrender their lands and permit Imperial troops to stamp out the Purebloods and their vile supporters."

"Some diplomacy," Tyghus said regrettably.

"This war isn't about preserving the independent kingship of the Lij, General Tyghus. That's a Rynsyan policy hereby abandoned – Valogar is a rightful province of the Empire whose 'Lij' therefore is Khorokh Kyrus I." Dronos's eyes ran up and down the General again. "Of course, if any of this is too great a burden for you, then –"

"Don't finish that sentence," Tyghus commanded, his temper's restraint all but snapped. The courier stared back in silent fury, his mouth a pressed line; from his vision's periphery, the General watched for any sudden movement by the "protection". His heart pounded as breaths deepened.

"Tell the Emperor," Tyghus finally said. "Tell him I'm heading straightaway to the Isthmus while the Dyron readies itself for the invasion. If I leave tonight, I can be negotiating within a week's time, and –"

"Just do it quickly," Dronos interrupted with a clasp of his hands. "Remember, stealth and speed, General, those are the only orders that matter here. The rest is for you to work out."

"Indeed," Tyghus replied firmly. "Safe travels, courier."

"By   your   leave,   General   Tyghus."

Chapter XXIII

"Do not bewayl that whych thou fyndest cruel or wythout reason, for thyne
lyfe be less 'bout choyces thyne mortal bodyes makest than 'tys following
th'path set out for thee by thyne gods.
Yea, bewarned – strayest yn'thys world, be'damned yn'th next."

Scrolls of Seer Tokh-talus, circa 500 years Ante-Cataclysm

Mid-Point of the Isthmus, 4ᵗʰ Day of the Third Month, Y. 384 P.C.

"Too much, brother," Tygha said. "You risk too much coming here."

The General stood dismounted from his trusty stallion Fidipodus, staring at his tightly bundled sister with glazed, red eyes. A thicket of brown beard stubble covered his face, and heavy misty sea winds whipped his hair and cloak violently about.

"I probably do… but it's upon us now, Tygha."

"I know," she said with a sniffle.

He didn't have the energy to ask how she knew. "Well, thank the gods you've come," Tyghus said. "I barely thought your people at the Valogarian Gate would let my messenger live, let alone fetch you so quickly."

"They wouldn't kill him, Tyghus," she said sadly. "They don't want this to happen; they can't believe that it is, not three months after they thought they'd made eternal allies with the Rokhs."

Tyghus nodded as he looked down at his brown boots. "You can speak for him?"

"I can. What am I speaking to?"

Tyghus sighed before he looked at his sister again. "They're coming."

"Who?"

"My troops. The Sixth. They're coming and I… I can't stop it."

Tygha's lip quivered. "You don't have to tell me this."

"Doesn't matter now," he replied with a shake of his head. "What matters is that we're down to our last chance to avoid…"

"Just say it."

"Hell."

She nodded with moistened eyes. "Okay. Then what's this chance?"

Tyghus swallowed deeply. "To submit. To-to convince the Lij to peacefully submit to Rokhish rule again. Open his gates to us. Give us free rein to search the countryside for Purebloods and maybe… maybe that'll be enough to avoid a massacre."

"Tyghus, I can't –"

"I'm begging you, in the name of the gods above, the gods below, the gods of the Valogarians… *any* gods. I – I don't know what's happening in Dray'gon Rokh, what's happened to Kyrus, but I swear to you I didn't recognize him last month. He looked broken, broken beyond repair. His thoughts, his orders, they made no sense. He's throwing his own bloody Councilmen in jail!"

Tygha cringed. "What?"

"Aye! And truthfully, I can't tell you whether he sees me as a friend, foe, or something worse. But listen to me… I *can* tell you that if Valogar resists the invasion, they'll be conquered by force. And once conquered, the terror he'll unleash will far outstrip any blow to Andran's pride by surrendering."

"He's said as much? About this terror?"

"I can't tell you how I know, Tygha, I just do. You asked me months ago whether I trust him, well… no, I don't, there's your answer. Not anymore, I don't."

A silence reigned between them for a moment before Tygha shook her head, eyes darting left and right of her brother. "Tyghus, what do you expect me to say to Andran?"

"Tygha, say anything, did you hear what I told you? You have to at least try. *Gods above*, you have to!"

Her arms flailed upwards. "And what? Rokhs come marching over these peoples' homes and families, and Andran simply bows to them?"

"He bowed once," her brother implored. "He wouldn't *be there* without the Rokhs."

"That's certainly true, brother, but it's a funny thing – when you make a man a king, when you tell him he's a king, when you let him rule as if he's a king, *he bloody well may think himself a king!*"

"Listen to me –"

"I am! And I'm telling you he doesn't care that he was appointed by a Khorokh, Tyghus; he considers the kingdom his by right and blood! And in truth, it is just that!"

"But if he steps down –"

"If he steps down, what?" she demanded. "What, Dray'gon Rokh will just let him walk away? They'll let a man with a blood claim to this throne 'retire' to a life of – of – of what, exactly?"

Tyghus looked away, having no answer for her.

"You're being naïve, Tyghus," Tygha continued grimly. "The minute he steps down, he's a dead man."

"And what is he now?" he asked coldly.

Tygha recoiled, her voice low and grave. "He's preparing the country for war; he's gone village to village rallying every Valogarian with a beating heart; he's…"

"What, Tygha? What else?"

She looked away from him for a moment. "He's just doing *everything* in his power to *win* here."

Tyghus shook his head. "Delays the inevitable. He's still a dead man."

"Well, if he is, he is, but that's not on Andran; that's on *you*."

"On me? *Me?* You know I don't have a choice in this! I'm not the Khorokh, I'm not a Lorrion! The vote's been cast, the order's been given; if I'm told to fight, then I have to fight! This meeting, this talk – this is the extent of my power to do anything!"

"Demanding surrender isn't 'power'. An errand boy could do that. If you believe you're no more powerful than an errand boy, then I'm not sure what else I can say to you other than I think you vastly underestimate yourself."

A pause ensued as Tyghus helplessly watched his hopes vanish into the Isthmus mist. The siblings' faces laid bare their distress.

Tygha took a deep breath before gesturing behind her towards a body of men one thousand deep in Rokhish military regalia. "I've brought my Imperial Guard to turn over to you. They're not safe in Nar-Biluk anymore; riots in recent days have already claimed three of them."

The thought of the Guard's fate hadn't crossed his mind, but as he'd approached his sister, their image made him shiver – Tygha would be beholden to Valogarian protection alone going forward, if such a thing existed. "I can see that," he muttered. "You're safe without them?"

"No," she said with a weak smile. "But I wasn't safe with them, either. Their presence was doing more harm than good."

Tyghus closed his eyes. "They barely protected the Lij from Purebloods all those years... and now you—"

"Stop," she said gently, hand grabbing her brother's. "It's done. Time to let fate have its day with us."

The General nodded as he brushed away hair with his hand. "Never was the philosopher that you were," he said, lightly as he could manage.

She smiled softly. "I... of course, have another matter to turn over to you..."

Tyghus's eyes, already wincing off wind-blown drops, crinkled further as Tygha looked behind her. "*Avonga!*"

From around the side of the troop line a hooded figure emerged, as bound in brown garments as Tygha. The figure walked towards them with lowered head, hands keeping warm in opposite sleeves.

"Tygha... what..." the General mumbled, sparse minutes of sleep he'd enjoyed the last few days catching up with him. But Tygha only looked to the ground without response.

The figure came to her side, its head slowly rising.

He saw a woman's face, pristine and vibrant, a stark contrast against the gray skies hanging overhead. Brown hair fell just below her ears while a few strands danced across her forehead. Her eyes glowed an emerald green.

Mikolo.

Tyghus's mouth gaped. "Tygha... you brought her *here?*"

His sister looked up, though his eyes never left the priestess. "You made a promise to her, then I to you. You pledged to keep her safe and I did the same so long as you were unable. Remember?"

The General's heart pounded in his chest. "Of course I do."

"Well, I can't hold up my end of the bargain any longer. I did the best I could, but the people – the priests – they've been suspicious since –"

Tyghus's hand floated up to touch a wispy tuft of hair by her ear. "Her hair?"

Tygha sighed. "She's been suspected since you left, Tyghus. She's never wavered, never said a thing, but the head priests question her relentlessly through words, and —" she said, pulling back Mikolo's hood to reveal deep purple and black bruising on her neck. "— through force. They seek to shame her into confessing her sins. Torture her."

Tyghus felt as if he'd been struck in the stomach. "Gods above."

"With my guard gone, I no longer have eyes I can trust to watch over her — not that her bruises don't say all that need be said. So I approached her before I left, asked her about lopping her hair, dyeing it with root oils, then getting her out of the city. About turning her over to you. I can tell you that leaving the worship was crushing to her, despite her treatment."

The General finally looked back to his sister in shock. "How'd you do this without the priests' knowledge?"

"I don't know that I did frankly, but she's here now, isn't she? Hopefully, they'll think she took her own life; it's not uncommon for priestesses."

Tyghus's jaw clenched, feeling a surge of anger. "The brave priests make their lives that miserable, do they?"

"Some, not all. The greeneyes get it the worst."

"Gods above," Tyghus said again, staring in awe of his sister. "I can't believe you did this. I'm honored to share your blood; you honor me by your very breath."

She shook her head with closed eyes. "If I'd done it right, she'd never have been beaten in the first place."

"You did the best you could with the situation I created. You're a goddess, Tygha."

A stiff wind cut through the three of them, and the General shivered. With watery eyes, Tygha embraced her brother. "I don't want this to happen."

Tyghus fought back tears of his own. "I know."

"How'd we get here? How's this happening?"

Tyghus could only bite his upper lip. He thought back to his conversation with Treos atop the wagon laager, rain beating down up them, when he openly pondered his purpose with such distress; he thought about how the world, how that purpose had finally seemed to take shape when he was given the Sixth upon their return to Dray'gon Rokh.

And now the world was seemingly crumbling again, but in ways he could never have imagined.

Tygha finally pulled back and wiped her eyes with a sniff. "I love you, Tyghus. Loved you since the day you came into this world, I remember it like it was yesterday," she said with a heavy sigh. "Be safe, will you? Safe as a brute can be, anyway."

223

The General smiled softly. "And you do the same. You'll be in my heart."

As they parted, Tygha took the hands of the priestess, whose cheeks also steamed with fresh tears. "You're safe now, Mikolo."

Miko's pursed her lips as she nodded. "In Fate's hand, no?" she said meekly.

Tygha smiled as she looked at Tyghus. "Let me thank the men for their service, then I'll be on my way."

At that moment, all the General could do was watch his proud, brave sister, Queen of Valogar, give thanks to the Rokhish guards. In the distance, relentless waves pounded the cliffs' bottom below, and even a rumble of early-season thunder rippled through the howling gusts.

"Gods protect her," he whispered.

* * *

At a score of miles from the Seas, the salty winds began to wane. All the better, as a damp chill blanketed the trotting General ahead of Tygha's kord. Tyghus, however, burned iron-hot from the petite figure wrapping her arms around his waist as they rode. A Chibin priestess's arms no less.

Tyghus had pictured his next encounter with Miko' a thousand times, pictured her face, her words, her smile; yet here she was, her very body attached to his, her entire being surrendered to his good judgment, only to have his voice escape him. The words he'd recited in his head were a garbled mess now, replaced by fears of what to do. And after realizing Kyrus knew about their first dalliance, he couldn't help but worry about others finding out about this one; about *Kyrus* finding out...

Someone in Nar-Biluk had to have reported it back to the Capital... was it a Rokh? Was it one of these Rokhs? The General turned his head towards the marching men. As he scanned the front ranks for familiar faces, a soft-spoken voice startled him from his thoughts.

"Mondid..."

Tyghus faced forward. "Yes?"

"You say so little."

The General's face reddened a bit. "I know... I uh... I've a busy mind right now, I apologize. Not much sleep, either."

"'Busy mind'?"

"Aye, I uh... I've many thoughts. Hard to express them, you know?"

"You tell me, yes? Tell me these thoughts."

Tyghus smiled weakly, feeling the heat from her breaths against his neck. "Well, now that you're here, I... I don't know where to start."

He felt her snicker. "What is it?" he asked.

"You said same thing to me in your ahovy, do you remember?"

Tyghus grinned wider as he tried to recall their late-night encounter so many months prior. "Aye," he said, almost lying.

"You talk more in ahovy. You tell me thoughts in ahovy."

"That's true, I guess."

"With jiupan, no? With jiupan, you talk."

The General laughed. "What can I tell you, Miko'?"

"Can I know where you take me?"

"Of course," Tyghus said, as the road began curving into a grove of scattered, leafless trees. "Avergon's where we're headed, a city a few days west of here once we pick up our pace. My army's waiting there."

"Waiting for what?"

"For me."

"And what will you do with army, Mondid?"

The General sighed gently, feeling even wearier from his dearth of sleep and the directness of her question. "We'll see, Miko'."

"More you won't tell."

"I said I'd protect you, Miko'," he said lightly. "Not that I'd make good conversation."

"Oh," the priestess replied softly.

"I'm joking, I... meant that in jest."

"Joke, okay."

Silence fell between them as Tyghus listened to the horses' hooves clacking off the worn stone road. His head turned back to her at last. "I want you to know that I'm... I'm sorry they beat you. I'm sorry I put you in that kind of danger."

She gave no immediate reply, though Tyghus thought he saw an eye begin to well up.

"No sorry. I'm punished by gods, Mondid. I'm –"

"No, I don't want to hear that."

"– marked by gods. We exist at their will, in the ways that they will, yes?"

"*No*," Tyghus said again with conviction, growing angry as he pictured the crotchety priests raining blows upon the woman.

"No?"

"Listen to me – maybe the gods put us here, Miko', *maybe*. But no man should be speaking for them in this realm, not a one. And no honorable man of any creed should be doin' it to justify beatin' those weaker than him."

"But my eyes are –"

"Eyes be damned, they've no right to touch you," Tyghus barked, growing even angrier. "*I've* green eyes, let's see 'em get to beating on me. Run 'em through with my sword before they'd thrown a punch."

Mikolo gasped. "Never hurt a priest!"

225

"Yet you're a priestess and they hurt you," Tyghus said defiantly, before catching himself and reining in his temper. "I'm just trying to say I couldn't stand back and watch them hit you. No man's ever doin' that to you again. You're *not* cursed."

He felt her sigh and lay her head upon his back again. "Your people very different from mine."

"How so?"

"Your people say man cannot speak for gods."

Tyghus smiled. "No, *I* say that. My people, the Rokhs that is, they feel quite differently for the most part." Tyghus gave a dark chuckle. "My views are criminal in my lands, so I keep them to myself."

"Oh... but you –"

"I've struggled to find the gods' places in my life. When my parents were taken from me, I uh... it took something else from me that I've never gotten back, even with all the family I have that remains in Tygonium. The gods never made sense to me after that, and it just..." He sighed. "I don't know. Maybe there's a place for them; maybe they'll reveal it to me when the time is right."

"I can't imagine life without knowing gods' presence," Miko' said in disbelief.

Tyghus looked back to her. "Must've been difficult to leave the worship, then."

Releasing one hand from the General's waist, Miko' reached down the front of her wrap and pulled out a piece of twine threaded through a stark white pebble, a black blemish the only sign it was chipped away from something larger. "Tayshihan still with me," she offered with a smile.

Tyghus smiled back. "Miko, you're a thief?" he teased.

Just as he felt her smile against his back, a doe and several fawns suddenly dashed across the path in front them, catching Fidipodus and his riders by surprise. Mikolo's arms squeezed tight.

"It's alright," Tyghus said, gently patting her arm.

"I'm sorry, Mondid. I—"

"It's okay... it's okay."

She turned her head to try to follow the deers' path but they were quickly out of sight. She inhaled deeply for a moment, before saying, "I've never seen these lands before."

"What lands?"

"The Drylands. Your lands."

"You've never left Valogar?"

"I've never left Nar-Biluk."

"Your life's barely begun, then," the General said as he stroked her wrapped arm. "You have much to see."

Her tension slowly subsided. "Thank you for keeping promise."

The   General   nodded.   "Of   course,   Miko'."

Chapter XXIV

"It is with this first step do you set out to avenge your fathers and mothers that died before Cataclysm! Died while Valogar dawdled!"

Speech of Khorokh Mercius the Blind to Troops Departing Grynea
Province for Valogar,
Y. 196 P.C.

Dray'gon Rokh, The Hovikum, 9th Day of the Third Month, Y. 384 P.C.

Deep within the well-laid streets of the Arxun's northern reaches stood a one-room circular building. It was hardly an imposing structure, yet it had long been the venue for the Empire's most critical decisions and debates; it took the nickname *Hovikum*, or "War Room", for good reason. This damp late winter eve found it inhabited by the most powerful of Rokhs with the most pressing of matters before them – and that's to say nothing of the fact that a member of the Lorrio sat in a Rokhish dungeon for the first time in recorded history.

The Khorokh strolled about the small room admiring the tiled, domed ceiling. The candlelight was fairly dim at the top, but it didn't take much to make out the perfect craftsmanship of the dome's swirling patterns. The floor was sheer beige marble with a large circular representation of the known Andervold world etched into it, revealing in greater detail the areas under Rokhish domination. Kyrus couldn't help but smile as he looked at the jutting piece of land representing Valogar.

Jarax, Antinax, and Glannox could only sit on the whitestone benches ringing the Andervold carving and watch. The Khorokh was well aware their anxiety must have been growing with each quiet second that ticked away, but he wasn't concerned. They'd waited over two weeks for this moment, they could wait a little longer. They could wait until *He* was ready. *He* was the Emperor, *He* was the one about to embark on the grandest conquest in Imperial history.

They're simply means to an end, he thought coolly.

Kyrus's horror in the Kyrogon glade had proven oddly cathartic for him. As he'd fallen back into the snow that day, as he beheld the inexplicably shattered totem to his family line, that hallowed portal to their souls, a great calmness overtook him. At that moment, all the events of his life – his struggles to conform in the Academy; the butchery of his father and brother before his eyes; his rise through the military's ranks while skirting death at every turn; his taking the Lorrian purple, his taking the throne – they all suddenly made sense.

It was the gods' work. It was their singular answer to the questions he'd been asking all along.

It was clear now where he'd made his mistake since he'd been beckoned to Dray'gon Rokh. He'd fallen into the Capital's trap of elevating men's wisdom above the gods'; it was a place where a privileged few wielded such immense power that they probably fancied themselves gods in their own right. In all his despair, he'd sought men to explain his predicaments when it was the gods he should have reached for. He'd ignored the tapestry they were weaving before his eyes, the lot they'd *chosen* for him.

Why else would they let everything be taken from him, snuffing out even the last vestiges of his beloved family?

Why else push him to the brink of taking his own life time and again?

Why else would his closest friend suddenly turn unrecognizable and speak poison to him?

To clarify his vision, of course. To thrust him forward. He'd been so busy looking backwards that he missed the destiny laying ahead of him – a destiny of vengeance; for his family, for his country. Pure, unadulterated vengeance.

Such arrogance to think I was ready to sit at the gods' Table! he thought with an embarassed shake of his head.

So now here he stood, the room rapt with his every step, aching for his words, his vision. For his part, Kyrus could look at them now and see them for what they really were – tools for implementing that vision. He had no illusions, for instance, that Antinax was any less of a conspirer than he'd heard and seen him to be. Nevertheless, he was a powerful conspirer and one that shared the view that Valogar had to be crushed; that made him a necessary pawn for the time being.

Jarax he had known since he first stepped into the Khorian Soelum, and he had proven efficient, blunt, and well-seasoned in the machinations of Dray'gon Rokh dealings ever since. Their earlier tensions notwithstanding, he knew he needed the Rubator's iron will to quell the internal discontent said to be swelling with Castus's jailing. Thus, he became yet another to whom Kyrus was wedded by circumstance.

The Emperor had only met Glannox, the bulldog-jawed general of the north, one month prior, but his list of martial accomplishments for the Empire was testament enough to the man's ruthless drive. At nearly sixty years old, the hardened warrior from Glostium had campaigned and smashed foes all over the Upper Rokhlands – rooting out raiders in Draygonea's lower Karanaks and western Astorens, routing Baraleshic uprisings in the northern Skulls Desert, annihilating the plotters and their army in the latest Lords' Rebellion in Loccea. All his campaigns were meticulously plotted down to the man and sword, and he was notorious for staying up all hours of the night calculating his foes' next move. By the late 370s, he had proven so thoroughly effective at keeping order in the Uplands that he was appointed the title *Gelator Questalrokh* – Supreme Commander of the Upper Rokhlands, a position that had no parallel south of the Clyves and one that many emperors were too wary to even assign or recognize.

Tools, all of them, he thought again proudly. The wisdom, the sword, the enforcement – none to be trusted too closely, but when used properly…

Kyrus finally stopped pacing.

"We're going to war," he said crisply with a vacant smile.

Glannox's crystal blue eyes bulged from their sockets in focus upon the

Khorokh, his head nodding sharply. His mouth was a thin, pressed line within a groomed, silver beard.

Antinax watched the Gelator's bobbing head too, before bouncing his eyes to the Emperor's. "And cheers to that, Highness. A moment long overdue, is it not?"

Kyrus paused for a moment, smile fading ever so slightly. "Moments happen when they're meant to happen, Antinax."

The Nortic recoiled at the rebuff. "Indeed... well said," he said, before clearing his throat. "The war, then..."

The Khorokh stared at him for a moment before continuing. "The Campaign will begin with the Sixth's invasion of the Isthmus. As you may or may not already know, my couriers have sent word to Avergon to launch the attack at once."

"And leading the Sixth —"

"Will be the Sixth's Dyrator. After all, Dyrators lead dyrons," Kyrus added drolly to Glannox's snort.

"My battlefield lore pales beside yours, Highness, but that much I know," the Nortic responded with a bite. "Are we to presume then that the Sixth's commander remains Tyghus of Tygonium?"

The name still gave him chills. It brought him right back to the despair he'd felt when his spies told him Tyghus hadn't banished the Lakeman at all, but instead sent him clandestinely back to the very heart of his camp. It brought him right back to hearing he'd gone alone to meet his sister on the Isthmus, where he could have said anything, *anything* at all to her in the name of these "negotiations" he kept pushing for. Or hearing he'd left the Isthmus with a mysterious accomplice...

He's godless, Kyrus thought sadly. *If he fears no gods, why would he —*

"Highness?" Antinax asked again.

The Khorokh shook his head again and sighed. "Your presumption's correct."

Antinax's brow furrowed. "Well, that concerns me."

Kyrus fixed eyes on the old man, looking sullen as ever. "Does it, Anti'?"

"It does. I think the man's proven himself inaccessible at best, unreliable at worst considering it's his sister's adopted realm we're asking him to attack."

"We're not asking him, we're *ordering* him."

"Even still —"

"Even still what?" Kyrus growled, annoyance quickly rising.

"Apologies Highness, I'm not-not trying to —" Antinax seemed perplexed as he fell silent for a moment. "He's just said to be close with the woman, that's all. Taken with the other rumors we've discussed, should we be entrusting him —"

"I don't think they are just rumors anymore, Antinax," the Khorokh interjected. "In fact, I think you were right about him, right about all of it, from the Lakeman, to the Native wench to – to all of it."

The Nortic's active eyes continued shifting around the room. "Aye, so if we're already questioning his competence, if not his loyalties, then why not remove him –"

"Because be that as it may, Tyghus was still chosen to lead the Sixth, and that is not an order wisely or easily undone, do you understand me?"

"I –"

"No, you *don't* understand, because you have no concept of the brotherhood that's formed among the dyrons – *especially* the Sixth. Listen to me –"

"Highness, I understand –"

"*Listen to me!*" Kyrus barked with gnashing teeth. "The Lakeman, he can be killed! The Native woman, she can be *killed*. Even his bloody sister can be killed! But you can't do that to a Dyrator! The dyron's loyalty is stronger to its general than it is to the crown, that's simply the way of things, and even if Tyghus is new to the leadership, he's still well-liked among the men. He's talented, he's a *leader*. Now, if he refused to attack, if he refused to move against Valogar as ordered, then of course I could strip him of his title, but not before. The things he's done to lose my trust simply aren't enough to sever his ties with the Sixth, and the last thing we need on the eve of war is a mutinous dyron!"

"So we're sending him in with the Sixth," the Nortic responded after a pause, looking no less baffled.

"Aye, we're sending him in," Kyrus replied with a nod. "His goal's to be on the Valogarian doorstep as soon as possible with his 13,000 men, then to keep right on pushing into the interior."

Antinax grunted, clearly perturbed. "He can push, but the Valogarians can field numbers in the tens of thousands, possibly the hundreds. He's only going so far 'til he gets help."

"He's taking the Sixth. *Only* the Sixth."

"Aye, so… until Glannox arrives in support, then?"

"No. Glannox won't be arriving for some time."

The old man's eyes closed to a squint, jowls shaking in wonder. "Highness, do you *want* the Sixth to succeed there or not?"

But as soon as Antinax finished his question his eyes immediately jumped to the Khorokh's. Kyrus offered no words, only a deep stare into his deep brown eyes, willing him to understand.

"You wish him to fail?" Anti' said at last.

"*That's* how you eliminate a Dyrator, Antinax. You do it on the battlefield."

The bewilderment gradually drained from Antinax's face. "So he'll *think* there're reinforcements coming, but…"

Kyrus looked away with a nod, pleased that he stumped the great schemer himself. "Aye."

"But the Sixth? The dyron itself will be as much a sacrifice as Tyghus, no?"

The Khorokh frowned. "Should the dyron fall, it'll be a great rallying call across the Empire, will it not? We can tailor the reasons for its failure as we see fit."

"Aye…"

"Regardless, another *will* rise, and in the meantime, Glannox will fill the void left behind."

"And if he *does* succeed?"

Kyrus blanched momentarily. "A nonsense question. But if true, then we've conquered a nation without losing a single dyron," he finally said with a grin. "But he won't. Not with one, he won't."

"And what of the rest of the Lower dyrons?" Glannox's deep voice questioned behind him.

The Emperor turned to face the Gelator, who looked like a caged dog as his knees ticked up and down, thumbs fidgeting up and over each other. His red-striped cloak rippled with every bounce. "You're taking the Uplands' First, Second, and Third Dyrons to Marvelon where you'll link up with the Fifth there as well."

"Marvelon's not going to like you taking its dyron…" Antinax muttered.

"It's not the Fifth *Marvelonian* Dyron, it's the Fifth *Imperial* Dyron - and anyway, when's Marvelon liked anything Dray'gon Rokh does?" the Khorokh scoffed, having no moment to indulge Marvelon's traditional grudge towards the Capital; for its feeling that *it* should have been the Empire's focal point once the Clans were defeated, not Dray'gon Rokh. It hadn't helped that once the Clans sacked Marvelon and conquered the Lowlands, Upland Rokhs were all but cut off from their southern cousins for more than a hundred years. Nevertheless, history was history, and Kyrus despised the agitators who still raised the issue after three hundred years.

He focused again on Glannox. "I'll leave it to your discretion whether you require any further troops than that. From Marvelon, you'll wait while Tyghus is brought to bear by the Valogarians, but whether he succeeds or not, he'll have softened them up for your seaborne assault from the Shoals."

Glannox's head bobbed once again. "Agreed, Majesty. Whatever scraps are left, we'll devour them."

Kyrus placed a hand on the general's shoulder in acknowledgement, before tilting his head towards the ceiling again. "In the midst of all this, *I* plan to oversee the creation of *ten* new Imperial dyrons. I'll pull men from across the Provinces, so that before the campaign season's over we'll have armed at least 100,000 new troops, training to commence immediately."

Hearing no response, the Emperor smirked. "Nothing to say, Anti'?"

"I'm afraid not, Highness…"

"Well, it doesn't matter anway, it's being done all the same."

"And… the, uh… the coffers can provide for such an undertaking?" Antinax asked with deliberate tact. "Naturally, it's going to tax the treasury just to win the war in Valogar –"

"Naturally, but winning the war in Valogar will more than pay for the venture," Kyrus said dismissively. "Now's the time to do it, though. The people are united in rage, as *you* said, and we'll need them if we're to continue the Empire's expansion beyond these stale borders."

"Aye… and what bold venture –"

"Valogar will be broken within the year," the Emperor said as he positioned himself over the Andervold map again, stomping the Valogarian outcrop. "By the first day of the first month of 385, it will be over, and we will begin preparations for the following campaign…" Kyrus dragged a foot over the darkened swath below the skinny line representing the River Brafford.

"The invasion of Colvery."

He scanned the faces of his three guests before mirroring Glannox's tight smile. "Again, it's time. For three bloody centuries we've been dealing with their schemes, their bowmen; three centuries they've felt safe because no one'd dare attack them in their forest, but it's time! We're going to settle things and show them that their trees and their river *and their bloody sea will only protect them for so long!*"

The room echoed with Kyrus's red-faced shouts, a realization which led him to calm somewhat. He left the center map and walked behind the benches, tracing the perimeter. "That'll be easy, really, once Valogar's taken and her pyhr mines are under our control. The keystone for everything to come, then, is a complete and lasting victory there, and to achieve *that*, we must eliminate the reason the country manages to be the recurring thorn that it is – the *Valogarian people*."

The Emperor paced in a wide circle around the gathering, deep in his own thoughts and words. "*The people*, after all, can't be distinguished from the Purebloods. And the people, as Antinax so eloquently put it in the Halum, have had their chance to deal with the Purebloods on their own and they've failed. So there'll be no more deals. The Purebloods will cease to exist, but more than that, for every Rokh soldier that dies in Valogar, we'll execute ten Natives. And if that means the land is barren as the Astoren caps in one year's time, then so be it! But the Valogarian blight *will be resolved*."

The room was silent, a beautiful sound to Kyrus. He could feel the spirits of his family in the room with him as he laid the foundations for their retribution. He sniffed beneath watery eyes at the thought of how proud they would have been, at this opportunity bestowed upon him by the gods. He quickly wiped them and stood before Glannox.

"General, we have much to plan, do we not? We'll meet on the morrow to discuss logistics and alternate supply routes in light of the damage at the Converge, agreed?" he asked, extending his forearm. Glannox rose, gripping it firmly, his eyes belying the calculations already being made.

"Agreed, Majesty. It is my *honor* to serve you in this; you've given more to my family name by this day than all my years prior put together."

"The honor and thanks are all mine."

Glannox's jaw clenched repeatedly. "We *will* break them. On my word and legacy, we'll break them all."

Kyrus smiled softly. "I know."

The Gelator gave one last sharp nod and Kyrus turned towards the conspicuously silent Jarax sitting with an arm resting atop his thigh and helmet. The man's long graying hair hung messily past an equally ratty beard.

"Jarax, I want more spies watching Tyghus's every move, do you understand me?" the Emperor's face suddenly morphed into a scowl as he heard the door slam behind Glannox. "*Fifty* spies. And fifty spies following those fifty. I want to know every step he takes in fulfilling my orders, am I clear?" he demanded, pounding one first into the other.

The Rubator gave little reaction but to rise and say, "of course, Highness." He turned to leave before Kyrus's hand landed on his shoulder.

"There's more, Jarax. I want your men in every Lowland village, hamlet, city or shithole, but especially in Morremea. I want to know the moment any word of insubordination is uttered. Examples will be set should any Rokhish city plead sympathy for the Valogarian filth."

Jarax gave no reply.

"Are we clear, Jarax?" Kyrus asked.

"Aye, Highness, we're clear," the Guard said finally, turning to face the Emperor. "Let me depart, though; it's going to take a massive overhaul to put your orders into effect while still keeping watch over your safety in the Capital."

Kyrus eyed him, searching for weakness, but at length gave a masked grin. "Very well. Let me know when things are underway."

Jarax promptly sprinted for the exit, and within seconds, the room was down to two. The door may have closed, but Kyrus fixated on their exchange for a moment – Jarax had hesitated. Just a bit, but he did. The Emperor felt it and immediatly made note.

Still staring at the door, he said aloud, "Antinax, do you have men you trust? The same that you've sent to spy on General Tyghus?"

The typically unflappable Antinax grasped for words. "Highness, I—"

"Let's not delude ourselves, Anti'. Do you or don't you?"

The Lorrion swallowed heavily. "Yes."

Kyrus clenched his jaw. "'Yes', he says. Good. I want Jarax followed. And you are responsible for it."

"Followed? Follow *Jarax?*" the Nortic stuttered.

"Aye."

"You want to have the leader of the Rubitio *followed?*"

"I thought I was clear," Kyrus replied, before sighing in annoyance. "These are the things that must be done to ensure that no one subverts the Empire's rise, her goals, no?"

The Emperor could feel the Nortic's eyes on him as he walked back to look at the center floormap. "Now please, leave me to myself."

"Very well… goodnight, Highness."

But Kyrus was already deep in thought as he looked at the Valogarian Peninsula. He hadn't even realized Antinax was still there until his one last question came from the door.

"Highness, what's to be done with Castus?"

The Emperor paused for a moment, before dismissing the thought with three words:

"Let   him   rot."

Chapter XXV

"Tyghus of Tygonium, First and Only Son of Tygustus (deceased) and Marria (deceased):

A tough soldier to gauge. Skills with the sword superb, though not supreme; shieldwork of above-average means for a Bull. Above-average strength; tall build, needs muscle. Shines with his acumen on the field, tactical understanding. He's a thinker, this one.

Assuming he survives his Run, biggest worry I'd have before making him Kordette is the same I had for his father – will he wilt? Is he prepared to handle the rigors of the campaign, the terrible choices where there's no right answer, the burdens of leadership? Making those decisions, living with those decisions, it breaks a lot of men, a lot of 'thinkers'. Look at Tygustus – he was was of sound mind and a superlative soldier but his rigidness put off a fair lot of his colleagues. Hope his son doesn't follow suit.

Young Tyghus's Run should be telling."

Final Assessment of Tyghus of Tygonium upon completing the Academy,
as given by his Academy Instructors Y. 375 P.C.

Starrea Province, Near Avergon, Eleventh Day of the Third Month, 384 P.C.

"Gods above, Tyghus, you look like shit."

A bleary-eyed General looked up from hammering a tent stake to see the Fyrid twins approaching in their silver armor, cloaks billowing behind them. With an exhausted grin, he tossed his mallet to the ground and rose to greet them. "I want to see you after almost two weeks with a few winks of sleep."

"Ah, listen to you, bleatin' like a sheep," Fygonus scoffed.

"Sheep sounds delicious about now."

With a little more than a day's march left to reach Avergon, Tyghus had seen his Valogar-bound troops' approaching on the western horizon. He dismounted to build his four-posted sheepskin tent near a hill's copse that overlooked a grass field, while sending Tygha's kord ahead to Avergon. The dead, gray moss that hung from low tree branches provided welcome insulation from the late winter chills while the wood itself burned strong and bright.

Thousands of hammers echoed around the three men, a hollow cacophony ringing deep into a still, clear night. Remaining within Imperial territory let the men forego the perimeter wall they would typically build, but it was still no small task to pitch camp for over 13,000 men and beasts. Horses whinnied and men laughed as circles of firelight popped up in the checkered pattern typical of Rokhish army camps. The Sixth Dyron was on the move.

"So? How'd Tyghus the diplomat fare, then?" Fyrustus said. "Did ya' snatch peace from the jaws of war?"

The General's smile faded somewhat, his cavernous eyes turning away from the twins. "No, my friend… the war's still on track."

His somber tone must have been more noticeable than he'd intended. "Didn't mean to be callous, brother, I know you worry for your sister," Fyrus' said.

"Aye, it's an odd spot you're in," Fygo' added.

"No, it's not," Tyghus replied defiantly. "I knew it'd be a possibility when…" But he was too tired to speak to his broken heart, trailing off instead with a shake of his head, eyes fixing on a far-off firepit. "You made good time," he offered distantly. "I'm beginning to believe you have this kordette business down, after all."

"The men are ready to go, I told you," Fygonus said proudly. "Coiled snakes, the lot of them. More'n two months they've been waiting to be turned loose; the Clans themselves couldn't hold them back right now."

"Aye – and you?" Tyghus asked, already knowing the answer.

The Twin paused before answering, when the massive man's eyes surprisingly misted over. "I've waited my whole life for this; for a campaign that truly meant something. Something more than the Desertmen who'd break at the first charge if they stood at all…" He shook his head with a tight grin, head looking to a star-filled sky. "Every man and woman of our House will be watching this one, I just hope the Natives will make a show of it…"

Tyghus followed his eyes to the stars. "Well, you're going get your wish, I've no doubt about that."

Fyrus' looked at him in silence for a moment before putting an arm around the Dyrator's shoulders. "I know you're frettin' about your sister, brother. But –"

Tyghus rolled his eyes. "I told you –"

"Just listen, you stubborn clod! You're worried about her, and that's fine. But the best thing you can do for her – and *yourself* – is sharpen that blade, scrub ya' shield, and get ready to run through as many Native bastards as you can. Because –"

"I don't need –"

"*Because*, dammit, the sooner we break 'em by the sword, the sooner you get that peace you couldn't talk 'em into."

Fygo' whacked Tyghus on the back. "He's right, ya' know. The Natives are fighters, you knew they weren't going to cave without a battle… even with your sister's touch, gods love her."

Tyghus quit protesting and let out a deep sigh. Fyrus' turned the General's body to look him in the eyes. "So get your head in the right place, aye? Get some damned sleep and come ready to bring the hell of Stygus like you know you can. Like we've seen you in the Deserts."

Tyghus smirked and brought his hands to rub his grizzled face. The Twins were born to kill men, but he had to confess it was their advice at the moment that impressed him more than their ferocity. Maybe it was a conclusion he would have come to on his own, maybe not, but the overgrown Fyrids had done something he'd failed to do ever since he'd left Tygha on the Peninsula – look ahead to a solution, not behind at the problem.

"And with any luck, my brother'll be takin' his own advice."

"Me?" Fyrustus asked with a look of disgust at his sibling. "I didn't need my best to beat back those Desert cowards, you know damn well that's true."

"'Desert cowards'," Fygo' mocked. "You'd have fled to the walls if you didn't have Tyghus and I by your side against those 'Desert cowards'."

"Aye?" Fyrustus asked, releasing the General's shoulders to square off against Fygonus. "Anything else?"

"Aye. I think it was Tyghus that cut his way through to ya', wasn't it? Cut his way through *on foot no less* after you lost your horse in a charge?"

"Bah! That speaks to a fragile beast, says nothin' about me! And I *still* took more heads that day than you as I remember it!" Fyrus' shot back, before yanking the ponytail of his long-haired brother. Wheeling about violently, Fygonus planted two palms into his taunter's chest. Curious soldiers nearest to the hillock drew closer to the growing fracas, eager that one of the legendary Fyrid grapples was at hand.

Tyghus was relieved for the amusement but quickly interceded between them. "Grab a grog and stand down, you animals. I can't have either of you injured at this stage. Plan your fights during peacetime."

The brothers circled each other even still, reluctant to be the first to stand down. Their eyes burned bright until finally Fyrustus let a smile creep over his face. "Just testing him. He knows our House would be better off if I went went before him."

The tension in Fygonus's arms ebbed. "Aye, 'cause you'd spend our fortune on whores and drink."

"Aye, if I could be so lucky!"

The three men shared a hearty laugh, as disappointed bystanders filtered back towards the camp.

Fygonus kicked Tyghus's mallet resting on the grass. "So why you settin' up so far away from camp?"

Tyghus looked at the Twin for a moment before his eyes found the moist soil beneath his feet. His hesitation wasn't missed.

"Difficult question, brother?" Fygo' said with amusement.

The General closed his eyes and shook his head. "I'm not travelling alone."

"Aye? You mean that lot you brought with you?"

"No... no, that's Tygha's kord. They were more trouble than they were worth I was told, so she released them to us. I sent them on to Avergon."

"Aye..." Fygo' said slowly.

"So who else do you run with here?" Fyrus' asked with a puzzled look.

"Did Bostonos come with you from the fort?" Tyghus asked without looking up.

Fyrus let out a chuckle. "The hell you cookin' up this time, Tyghus?"

"*Nothing.* Is Bostonos here?"

"Aye, he's here. He came to take any last orders from you while you're away —"

"What the hell's it matter?" Fygo' interjected with a grin. "Why you askin' for him?"

Tyghus suddenly heard soft footsteps approaching from the rear. He glanced anxiously behind him. "Look, this stays between the three of us, aye?"

"By the gods, what?"

"Well, when I met with my sister —"

"*Sah-dy nonara... nonara sah-dy...*"

A light, feminine melody floated towards them, and the three men instinctively turned in its direction.

From the darkness, the slender figure of Mikolo wrapped in a bear's fur appeared, her face and hair glistening in the moonlight from her cleanse in a water pool amidst the trees. She stroked her short strands with each hand before gasping at the six eyes fixed on her.

"Oh, Mondid, I –"

"'Mondid'?" Fygonus repeated.

The General let out an anxious laugh. "Brothers, this is Mikolo."

"Mondid?" Fygo' said again.

Fyrustus only stared at the woman frozen before them. "Tyghus, who the hell did you bring back with you?"

The General turned towards the Priestess. "Miko', give us a moment, won't you? I'll have your tent ready shortly." She nodded curtly before fading back whence she came; Tyghus about-faced towards the Twins. "She's Valogarian. Tygha gave her safe-keeping in Nar-Biluk 'til it wasn't possible any longer... so she turned her over to me."

The Twins exchanged baffled glances. "Safe-keeping *here*?" Fyrustus asked in surprise. "Is she aware we have 13,000 men frothing to tear into the first Native they see?"

"They might make an exception when they see her, though," Fygo' added.

"No," Tyghus said sharply. "No one's to touch her. She's under my protection."

"Protection?" Fygo' replied quizzically. "From whom? For what?"

"She just *is*," the General said with a sigh.

"Gods above," Fygonus uttered as the realization appeared to hit him.

Fyrus' looked to his brother then the General before his eyes widened. "You jesting, Ty'? You really shagging a Valogarian on the way to war?"

"No, she's just –"

"Well, why the hell not?" the bawdy Twin said with a guffaw.

"Just leave it be," Tyghus said more harshly, tiring of the discussion. "You're sworn to secrecy, that's all you need to know. I'm sending her back to Avergon with Bostonos in the morning, that's why I was asking for him."

"You picked the right man to escort her back then, with those belly and teeth of his," Fyrustus said, continuing to laugh. "I pity the woman he ever falls in with."

Fygonus shook his head with a faint look of bemusement. "Greatest campaign the Empire's seen in centuries would be danger enough for most men, but not Tyghus!"

Tyghus had to chuckle with him. "Alright, alright, get out of here. Send Bostonos up here when you see him, then get some sleep. The sun rises quickly."

"Indeed it does, you lusty bastard," Fyrustus said as he exchanged forearm grips with the General. "Indeed it does."

* * *

For the last five days, Tyghus had taken to the pillow long after Miko and awoke long before. Most of the nights he lay awake anyway, waiting for danger to arise or for his busy mind to finally tire itself out, whichever happened first. But today was different. Even though he woke with the first rays of sunlight yet again, he simply lay on his bed of fur and moss gazing – gazing at her.

Though she slumbered only a few feet away each night, he'd only indulged in the exotic scents of her native oils, never her touch. Any time he'd felt the urge to reach out to her, a crushing guilt weighed on him; especially so when her robe and blanket pulled away enough to reveal the purple lines and welts across her otherwise bronzed neck and back.

You caused that, he'd tell himself. *Your recklessness, your lack of control, caused all of this.*

He sat up from his bed, arms wrapping loosely around knees. He ran a hand over his stubbly face as he considered whether she still slept, but the rising noise of an awakening camp beyond their tent forced his hand.

"Miko'?"

"Yes, Mondid?" she immediately replied.

"Look at me, manam," the General said, head askew as she rolled over to lock eyes.

"You not leave this time?"

"No," he replied with a smile, amused that he wasn't as furtive as he thought he'd been in the mornings. "Did you sleep well?"

She nodded with a smile of her own.

He chuckled. "It was raining on me by the time I came in last night. Rained throughout the night, I think."

Even through the tent it was evident that the clouds that brought his midnight shower had long burned off, replaced by brilliant sunrays. Miko' gestured towards the outside. "Gods looked after me for night, Mondid," she said lightly. "Gods look after you today."

Tyghus laughed as he broke eye contact, chin falling to his chest. "Or yours frowned upon me last night and mine frown upon you today?"

The sound of her laughter kept the grin on his face. "I meant to ask you," he said as he looked back to her. "What did that song mean that you were singing last night?"

"I can't tell," she replied with a sparkle in her green eyes. "You will be angry with me."

"Will I?"

"*Uny...*" she answered coyly.

"Tell me... *sah-dy no* – what was it?"

Miko' smiled further as she raised herself up to her knees, sitting lightly back on her heels. "'*Sah-dy nonara... nonara sah-dy...*' Means '*rains will come, oh, rains have come...*'"

The General shook his head in feigned disgust. "So *you* were to blame..."

His eyes fell on hers again and she did not waver. He laughed.

"Why you laugh, Mondid?"

Tyghus threaded a hand through his messy hair as his mind spun. "Just... just being here, having you here, it... it doesn't seem real. It's unbelievable."

"How you mean?"

"Because..." he started as he brought his head closer to hers. "I meant what I said in my letter to you; I did with all my heart, but even so, I never believed I'd see you again. That's what's 'unbelievable'..."

"Ah, 'unbelievull' to me too, then."

"How so?"

"Because no one ever care about me before Mondid and Manam Tygha. Always spit on, always beat on by my people. *Nobody* cared. My life..." she started, before eyes wettened. "My life said to be punishment for sins of my past lives... so I expected nothing."

Tyghus felt his guilt resurging, his eyes finding her bruises again.

"Don't feel bad about these, Mondid," she said softly as her hand touched her neck. "They are not first time."

"I don't," Tyghus lied with a grimace, before catching himself. "I mean I did, I hate what they did to you, and you have the most spirit despite it all, but – but no I don't –"

"Then why you not touch me? All week you not touch..."

"I – uh..."

"I thought from ahovy night and letter that you... that you would," she said as she tilted her head towards him, eyes hardly dry. The nearness of her lips made his earlier hesitance begin to wane. Her back stiffened with his as she glanced from his eyes to his lips and back.

"*No, it's not that,*" he babbled in a whisper, hardly hearing his own words. As their mouths danced tantalizingly close to each other for a moment, he –

A horse's piercing whinny outside the tent made them both jump, shattering the tension.

Tyghus instinctively looked at the tent's entry flap in exasperation, suddenly taking deep breaths. "The camp rises..."

"*Uny,*" she said as she sat back and looked at the flap herself. "Where does camp go today?"

The General looked to the ground with clenched jaw and a sigh. "Miko', we haven't spoken of where you are headed with me –"

"You say Aver-gun, no?"

"*You* are headed west to Avergon," he said, finally placing a hand on her bare shoulder. "The camp – and me along with it – head east."

Her crestfallen face spoke volumes, but she was resolute. "I see."

"My quartermaster Bostonos will escort you the rest of the way to Avergon with a writ of my authority. With that, you'll receive every level of care that you could ever ask for."

"I don't know what 'Avergon' is, Mondid," she said disappointedly.

"It's a safe place, that's all you need to know," he said with a caress of her shoulder. "Safe from those that would harm you. Like I said, you'll have everything you want there."

"I want to be where *you* are…"

"It's too dangerous, Miko'. Even now, we're camped amongst a field of killers, and right now they're ordered to kill Valogarians. They're my men, but they're killers all the same," he said, going quiet for a moment before adding, "I wish I could do more."

Mikolo nodded as her hand reached up to Tyghus's on her shoulder. She ran a thumb over his weathered knuckles. "And what will you do, Mondid?"

Tyghus looked away. "You don't need to know about that."

"You make war upon my country?" she questioned plainly.

After a pause, he nodded. "I'm the 'Mondid'."

"But why you make war?"

"A terrible attack was made on my lands by your people… probably the Chibin. I saw it with my own eyes, but I still hoped it wouldn't come to this."

"Manam Tygha cannot make it right? She is Valogarian Queen –"

"I know," he interjected ruefully. "But it's far beyond that now, Miko'. Blood must be shed."

The Priestess's eyes searched Tyghus's face. "I do not understand, Mondid," she said, shaking her head. "I do not understand this part of you."

Tyghus smiled weakly. "My family's given warriors to my land since its birth. Fighting wars, fighting battles… it's in my blood."

"But you seem so happy when at peace."

Her comment gave him pause. Since his whole life had been geared around war, he never really took the time to consider whether he was happy at peace or if it was simply a gap until the next fight. He smiled in thought. "You know, I'm not sure I am happy at peace…" he started, before shaking his head. "But I do think I'm happy at peace with *you*."

Miko's infectious smile returned, along with reddened cheeks. "Well, I hope you find peace again then, Mondid."

"I do, too. In this life or the next."

She watched him for a moment before taking his hand in her own. "Before my people fight, they must bow in direction of Tayshihan and make amends with gods. *You* need to make amends with gods before you fight."

Tyghus squirmed a bit, ever uncomfortable seeking out the gods. He'd always preferred to think that they were just – if anywhere – 'there', and didn't need to be bothered with the conceits of men and women. But in this moment, he just nodded his head. "Aye."

"Promise me," she demanded with vigor, tightening her grip. "*Promise me* you make peace with gods or else I never see you in next life."

"I promise you, manam."

Gripping the loose flaps of his shirt, Miko' pulled herself into his chest to rest her head below his chin, locking themselves in a suddenly silent embrace. The camp's rising clamor and horses' snorts outside the tent reminded them it was time for her to leave, but they both clung to that elusive last moment.

One last moment together.

* * *

She was gone with Bostonos long before the camp finished packing. Their horses trotted steadily into the distance, heading north before cutting due west per Tyghus's instructions. The Quartermaster's squat figure contrasted amusingly with the demure Mikolo, but amusing or not, the General's chest clenched upon seeing them go. Even though he knew he could rely on Bostonos – who was devastated about being strong-armed in the Dronos incident and eager to atone – it was still unnerving to be powerless in her protection once again. He'd asked the Quartermaster to work with the "Fish" as best as he could in keeping the "Emerald" safe... whether he returned from Valogar or not.

It wasn't until a gust of wind brought salty scents to his nose that he finally looked away to face east. Suddenly, the Valogarian Peninsula so far beyond eyeshot felt nearer than ever.

Gusts notwithstanding, a picturesque day blessed he and his men, as not a cloud marred the blue sky and the air was slowly milding. It was perfect marching weather for an army nearly ready to head out. But first, Tyghus had a promise to keep.

He let the breeze fill his lungs with eyes closed and head tilted up. In hushed tone, he said, "*Mighty gods above, guardians below, Tyghids past and watching... you know I've been... remiss, I suppose, in seeking your counsel or giving thanks when I should. I don't know why that is, I honestly don't, and if I've asked you anything over the years, it's for an answer to that question. I've never meant any disrespect, I've just... well, you sent me here as a man of reason. I look for the logic in life, so when you took my parents from me, when you – when you didn't even let me say goodbye to them, I..."* He swallowed hard for moment before continuing. *"Anyway, if my prayer falls on deaf ears, I'd understand... but if your ears are ever to be open to my words, please let it be now.*

"I haven't sought this war, it's been given to me. Whether the war's just or not I'll leave to your divine judgment, though I'm not sure it matters now anyway. If you see fit to end my days in the shrublands of Valogar for taking the sword to an unjust war, I'd hold no grievance. But whatever your judgment may be of me, I beg of you one thing – spare those men I lead today. They march under my banners, they wear the Stygan Bull out of a love for their home, a love for their Empire, a love for their familes that dot the night sky – a love for you, I reckon. If the seers construe your will correctly then that loyalty is to be lauded. I'm hoping they're correct."

Tyghus wavered for his moment as he searched his soul, closing his eyes tighter. *"I'm afraid,"* he finally offered. *"Afraid that I'll fail these men, that I'm leading them into an abyss with no idea where our reinforcements will come from... afraid that Kyrus was wrong to appoint me, or worse, that he already agrees... I'm afraid for my sister, one of the best people I've ever known – I mean,* why gods? *Why would you put her through this?"* He demanded in sudden anger. He sighed and reined himself back. *"I know fear is an asset when used properly – I've preached it, I've embraced it, but... this time just feels different."*

He swallowed hard. *"So guide me. Guide me to do what is right – right by me, right by them, and right by your Table. I will remain open to your blessings."*

Another salty wind wafted through, which only reminded him of something – or someone – else.

"And if you do speak to us through the Tayshihan... I'll see that no harm comes to it."

The General paused after he'd finished, almost expecting to feel the gods' touch. After an uneventful moment passed, however, he shook his head at himself, somewhat embarrassed. "Forgive my vanity," he said aloud.

He opened his eyes and gave a sharp nod. His hand had instinctively drifted down to the hilt of his blade and his gaze soon followed.

"Now, let's bring them the sword."

PART III

Chapter XXVI

"Justice is defined and enforced by man —
therein lies the folly in lauding its sanctity."

Speech of Leonig, Leader of the Fifth Loccean Lords' Rebellion,
to the Court of Inquisition, Y. 361 P.C.

Dray'gon Rokh, Court of Inquisition, 18ᵗʰ Day of the Third Month, Y. 384 P.C.

The gavel smashed its block and Kyrus could feel the air escape the gathering. No time for breathing as a disgraced Lorrion stood chain-bound in the middle of the Court, plaintively watching clerks finish counting the votes that would decide his innocence. The boyish face people remembered was replaced by gaunt, sunken cheeks and eyes. His blondish-brown hair appeared filthy and matted, his gait upon entering the courtroom carrying a limp. Bloodshot eyes combed the shocked Peers on either side of him, Inquisitors looming menacingly above.

A smile crept over Kyrus's face.

It is time.

* * *

"Highness, you realize the trial of a Ruhl is no mere trial of a Rokh," Oratus had cautioned the Emperor a month prior, in the days leading up to the Valogarian war vote. "And the trial of a powerful Ruhl is no mere trial of a young pup learning his way."

"I'm aware," the Khorokh replied distantly as he peered out his Chambers window.

"Then perhaps it will resonate when I tell you that your desire to put a *Lorrion* before the Inquisitors is utterly unheard of. I've not seen precedent for it *anywhere* in the Rokhish annals and I can *assure* you I gave it my diligence."

"Aye?" Kyrus asked innocently, when in fact, he wasn't only aware of the scarce precedent – he *relished* it. But he didn't want to distress the portly man any further; he needed him to look and sound as resolute as possible at the Lorrio meeting, so he calmly engaged him upon the particulars that the Speaker thrived. "So we've no process for doing so, then?"

"Oh, it's not that, Highness, it's not that at all," he said with a determined shake of his head. "It's just –"

"Well, that's a relief, isn't it?" Kyrus said with as little sarcasm as he could manage. "So tell me the protocol."

The Speaker adjusted the folds of his black robe uncomfortably as he ploddingly paced the room. "I really hate to be seen even *remotely* encouraging this…"

"I don't need your encouragement, so indulge me, anyway," Kyrus said with a scowl. "You're my advisor, unless you've tired of the burden."

Oratus looked back at him with pursed lips. The Khorokh knew well that the man's morality always fell in line behind his love of the power and prestige of his office. "The procedure, if you're so inclined to use it, isn't so different from the one for common Rokhs. He's still brought before the three Inquisitors, still subjected to their questioning. And as with a commoner, he can still pay an Advocate to argue his cause, summon evidence, witnesses, and the like. The main difference I suppose is simply the size of the audience casting judgment on his innocence – a commoner would see fifty common Peers, while a Lorrion would see that fifty plus another fifty in Ruhls."

Kyrus smiled vacantly as his eyes scanned the castle grounds below. "Wonderful, then."

"The *problem*, though," Oratus continued, as if he'd never stopped. "Is that that protocol was etched into scrolls more than three hundred years old, and their mettle's never been tested. *Every* prior Khorokh's found the stakes, the legacies, the repercussions to be so unforgiving that they'd never risk it."

The Speaker's tone steadily irritated Kyrus. "Then it's been more an issue of willpower than it has actually doing the right thing when circumstances demand it?"

Oratus's face flushed. "*No.* It's been an issue of not upsetting the balance of Imperial governance, the Arxun most of –"

"Balance?" Kyrus asked incredulously. "*Balance?* Correct me if I'm wrong, but it's that 'balance' that created the monster that Castus became! It's that 'balance' that turned a blind eye while he paid off our sworn enemies with coin and weaponry and only the gods know what else! If he can convince a hundred Peers that that's somehow just, then I must say I've been misled about Rokhish law all these years!"

"True, Highness, very true," the Speaker replied with a lighter, more conciliatory tone, hands outstretched before him. "*But*, be that as it may, Castus has been an immensely powerful figure in the Capital for some time now, and his roots and the roots of his House here run deep – *very* deep. He's a champion to many for pressing Lowland rights – a champion or an overlord of sorts… you've seen the way he's cowed the other Sudos to his whim, Grynea included. Even many that would argue against him are drawn in with his charm."

The Khorokh rolled his eyes. "I've already had a lecture from Castus himself about his power, I don't need you giving me another. Gods above, the way the two of you talk, it's as if *I* should fear *him!*"

The Speaker said nothing at first. "He's just… extremely power –"

"Oh, gods spare me, I beg of you!" Kyrus yelled, finally turning from the window to face the advisor, who lowered his head in deference. "Listen to me, Oratus! Listen, because I'll only say this once – *are you listening?*"

"Yes, your –"

"If you'd been through one handful, one *thimble* of what I've been through in my life, if you'd seen what I'd seen, fought who I've fought, lost what I've lost, *you would know I don't fear a gods-forsaken soul in this world!*" the

Khorokh erupted. "Do you hear me? Not *one!* And certainly not some wolf in sheep's clothing whose only talent is manipulating imbeciles and calling it 'power'!"

"No, certainly not, Highness –" the flustered man stumbled.

"*Quiet!*" Kyrus barked. "Now, the gods placed me on this throne for a *reason!* That's why I'm here! And whether you understand that reason or not, just remember they did so *knowing* my mind and *knowing* I will govern matters as I see fit!"

"Certainly, High –"

"Now *I see fit* to have Castus thrown in our dungeons and await his bloody trial before his bloody Peers, and *you* are going to deliver that message the moment the war vote is complete. He hasn't earned the right for it to come from me! Now get out!"

"Forgive me, I didn't mean to upset –"

"*Out I said!*"

The Speaker shuffled hastily out the door without even bothering to close it, prompting Kyrus to storm over and slam it himself. "'Balance'!" he bellowed to no one in particular. "*Is this not an Empire of laws? Am I not the bloody Emperor?*"

* * *

And so the day of reckoning finally arrived.

From the very outset, the courtroom had been abuzz with its hundred Peers, as much for the trial as for the attendants themselves. Indeed, commoners rarely sat shoulder to shoulder with Ruhls, even in the Arena duels; but this day was one of them. Judging by clothes alone it would be impossible to tell one from the other, as all were required to come dressed in drab beiges and grays to the house of justice. But in reality, most everyone recognized the faces of those hailing from legendary family names in the pews. Lords of all the important neighboring towns had turned out to be seen among the Peers.

The room itself took the shape of an egg, but its every detail was designed to focus upon one individual: the accused. Along its deep brown wooden sides were five rows of curved marble benches, each successive row retreating higher than the one in front of it. At the front sat the three Inquisitors, with the Khorokh and the Lorrio – the Nortics being the only ones that dared presently attend – seated behind them to enjoy the show. And what a predictable show it was, with Kyrus being treated to the Lorrion's self-made defense, a tortured, drawn-out rendition of the justification Castus gave in the gardens two months ago. He talked for almost an hour about how his coin never made it to those that it shouldn't, how he was some great bridge-builder between Valogar and the Empire,

251

how the Nortics had arranged the entire hearing as a means for his humiliation. But in the end, he had no answer for the Inquisitors' query as to how he *knew* where his money ended up; no answer for why he took it upon himself to be the bridge-builder in total secrecy from the Lorrio.

Now we see how powerful you really are, you little rat... he thought vindictively. *The people have heard your crimes for themselves, so if you are who you say you are, if that power isn't just the mirage I think it is, they'll set you free.*

The back and forth banter between judges' and accused made the silent voting that followed particularly poignant. Each Peer made the solemn procession to deposit his or her clay chit in one of two ceramic containers stationed at the entryway – for guilt or for innocence. The deposits rattled hauntingly throughout the room, magnified by the silence of the Peers being shepherded back to their seats. Castus remained standing as his fate was decided thirty feet behind him.

Kyrus's heart beat faster the moment the last chit clanked in. Clerks descended upon the containers like wolves to a kill, the Peers, Inquisitors, Lorrio, and Khorokh alike watching as the contents were pored over, then pored over again. After a third counting, a figure was etched onto a piece of parchment meant for one man's eyes: the Khorokh's.

The gathering remained hushed as the scrap was handed up to the Inquisitors first, then to Kyrus I. He took it nonchalantly, his cold eyes fixed on the enfeebled Ruhl some twenty feet below him.

His stomach warmed as he saw the figures and a smile appeared despite himself.

"Guilty."

Murmurs spread immediately.

With a clear of his throat, he happily elaborated. "Castus of Cassitigon, your Peers have voted 68-32 in favor of your guilt on these accusations. In light of this condemnation, you are hereby declared treasonous and collusive against the Empire."

The tumult grew louder.

"For violating your sacred oath to uphold Imperial virtues, for failing your colleagues on the Lorrio, the Arxun, and the Rokhs you're meant to represent in the Province of Morremea, I decree as follows: the House of Cas is hereby stripped of all land and title, to be sold at auction at a time and place as the Lorrio sees fit. In addition, for as long as your now-existing heirs are alive, your House is hereby forbidden from holding office within the Realm, and during that time, an Imperial garrison will monitor all couriers coming and going from Cassitigon."

Castus's blood-red sunken eyes widened. "You disgrace me."

"According to your Peers, you've disgraced yourself. And for your crimes against the Empire and your fellow Rokhs, you are sentenced to death by archer volley upon the breaking of this assembly today."

The tumult spiraled yet rowdier, rival supporters in the gathering shouting to be heard over the other.

The Ruhl defiantly shot back at the Emperor, "oh, I am?" He cackled wildly. "You, *you* overstep yourself, sir! You seem to think your silly title, your little throne give you power? It doesn't! It never did and it never will! Power's earned here, you'll see it! You'll see it when this 'war' of yours is rejected outright and openly along the Borderlands! You'll see it when the Lowlands link arms against it! Opposition won't end with my death, I swear it, no matter how you try to disgrace my House!"

Kyrus was unmoved but answered the challenge anyway. "Then it's my hope that any other Rokh who's funded enemies of the Empire will step forward and identify themselves so that justice may be meted out accordingly. It's to be a country of laws again, Castus, so if there's any part of you that still embraces the Empire, you should take pride in knowing your death makes clear that *no one* is above those laws!"

Shouts from the benches rang out from an unruly crowd that was devolving into an orgy of shoves and punches.

"Don't do this, your Majesty!"
"We'll bleed for you, Castus!"
"Kill him for m'brother!"

Jarax suddenly appeared as planned with a squadron of Rubitian Guards, packing the Courtroom floor to restore order in the pews. Several more Reds approached Castus from behind, who feverishly continued his railing.

"It all appears so simple now young one, but I warned you before, that's the haze of Dray'gon Rokh! You're mad – you're mad as the day is long and you're naïve! You've no idea you're just a pawn in a craftier man's game! You'll outlive your usefulness just like all the others, I swear it!" he bellowed, before turning his vitriol to a man at Kyrus's side. "And Antinax - you may have avoided my retaliation in this life, but it'll come. Whether by another's hand or by the spirits above, it will come! Your life's not long for this world, I promise you that!"

Though barely audible over the rising din, the old Nortic was blunt in reply. "They say a man's true character is revealed in his final worldly moments, Castus. I pray that you stay strong."

"Strong?" Castus cried, as Guards gripped either of his arms to take him to the execution grounds. "You'd never know strength! Strength is morality! Strength is choosing the righteous path when the rest choose evil! Your gods are *deception, greed –*"

His protests grew fainter and fainter as he was hauled away. He flailed all the way, but finally his cries were outside and beyond earshot of the room. By that point, the room was in a virtual riot, but Oratus attempted to make himself heard regardless:

"Peers, the Khorokh thanks you for your service. Go now in peace and be fruitful! For this day is young, and much can still be done!"

* * *

If not for those three wooden posts, it would be a beautiful little courtyard.

Gray stone walls standing ten feet high formed a rectangular yard twenty yards deep and half as many across. Ivy climbed the length of the walls, nearly covering the barred door leading onto Arxun streets at the far end of the courtyard. A beautiful fountain of blue-cut marble lay close to that door with an oversized statue of Tip-Netus, god of justice, as its centerpiece.

But those posts, Kyrus thought. *Those lonely wooden posts.*

In the center of the courtyard, three wooden posts were driven into the tiled floor. The left and right stakes stood no higher or wider than a child, while the middle was tall enough to look down on any man. It had to be – it was the only way to ensure a "clean" death.

From the shadows near the Court's exit, the Khorokh watched the wretched figure dragged into the courtyard's daylight. Castus's entire being had seemingly surrendered itself to its fate, his bony frame standing listlessly as crusty, watery eyes looked around for the one to deliver him to the gods. The chains rattling about his feet seemed needlessly excessive.

Kyrus did not ask the Lorrions or Peers to witness the Ruhl's death, and none of them but Oratus joined him at his side. Some gathered at the courthouse's upper floor windows to watch, however, and looking behind him, Kyrus could see the hunched figure of Antinax spying down. Judging by Oratus's green expression, he'd have preferred to be with the Nortic or not at all had his Speaker duties not drawn him to the yard.

The four Reds that presented Castus took their place at the Khorokh's side, leaving the teetering Ruhl pitifully alone, and giving way to ten more ominous figures arriving in single file – the "Browns", they were called, or more plainly, the executioners. They wore drab browns from head to toe, magnificent bows and quivers slung about their back and chest. With chilling nonchalance, they set about cleaning their weapons of death, completely ignoring their intended victim.

Kyrus couldn't help but shake his head as he watched them prepare. "They say the executioner either has the most honorable job or the most detestable one, Oratus," Kyrus observed, before frowning in thought. "Guess it depends on which side of the killing you're on."

Oratus, pale and clammy, smiled weakly. "Never…"

"Never what?"

"In all my years, Highness… in all my years I've never seen this…"

The Khorokh scowled at the wilting, dry-mouthed Speaker. "What? An execution?"

254

The word looked like a trigger to the fat man's vomit. He nodded his head vigorously with closed eyes.

"Hm," Kyrus grunted. He'd seen them. Plenty of them, in fact. In the shrublands of Valogar, captured spies were executed on the spot, but he'd often taken liberties with other captives as well – as was his right. He'd always found the execution to be the most ignominious way to die, but then again, were the Valogarian animals entitled to anything better? Certainly not. In any event, he took much more pride in this day's execution than any savage killed on the Peninsula.

"You're soft, Oratus," Kyrus said scornfully. "This is the way the world *really* works, not the fantasy world half the Arxun walks around in. In the real world, the traitors, the vanquished, the liars, they all die; the saviors hold the sword, it's that simple."

"I-I-I know, Highness... I-I'm sorry..."

"Just see the day for what it is, then – a magnificent one!" the Khorokh said, whacking his advisor's sweaty back. "This is the first step towards purging the blight that's brought this city and *Empire* to its knees. Easily as important as any battle in the wars to come, no?"

But Oratus had no response. Instead, he appeared to be taking deep breaths to calm himself.

Kyrus shook his head in shame. "Just read him his bloody death warrant, by the gods."

The Speaker gave an uncertain nod and took a few steps out of the Court's shadows. Castus huddled but forced his eyes to watch. *"Oh gods..."* the wretch muttered.

"Castus of Cassitigon, you have been sentenced to die for your crimes against the Empire and its peoples. By the grace of your Khorokh, you've been granted a clean death –"

"Oratus... Oratus, please... will you promise me something?" the Ruhl whimpered, catching Oratus off-guard.

"Proceed, Oratus," Kyrus ordered.

"Oratus, I beg of you by the gods above, below... will you see that my ashes are returned to the Shoals upon my death?"

The Speaker looked back at Kyrus with wide brown eyes.

"Proceed, Oratus!"

"A-a clean death requires the hands and feet to be bound to the posts on either side of you," the Speaker stammered.

Castus glanced back and forth in horror. "Why? Why do you—"

"This shows the gods you approach them unarmed and in humility for your... for your disgraces. Th-the head and torso are secured to the middle post. This ensures you do not cower before the gods' wrathful glares..." Oratus said through labored breaths.

No... it's to keep you from cringing when the arrows are launched, which would only

255

make it worse for you, you filth… May the gods honor the mercy I show to you for that.

"Such is the 'clean death'… such is your fate this day," Oratus finished, looking to the nodding Khorokh. "May the gods embrace you and may they… may they forgive the worldly transgressions that wrought your dishonor."

With a glance to the Browns, he receded back into the shadows. As one hooded figure strode towards Castus, bow and quiver bouncing with each step, the Ruhl instinctively recoiled and stumbled away from him.

Kyrus shook his head. *Antinax was right – you learn all there is to know about a man when the rest of his life measures seconds rather than years. Pari died with a blade in his hand, fighting to the end; Kylius too. Rynsyus died clutching his lies, his deception…*

"Come, sire," a voice thundered from beneath the brown hood. "Come with me to the posts."

"Please… *please…*"

"*Come!*" the executioner said, grabbing Castus's rail-like arm and forcing his body up against the middle post. "I swear to you, my lord, resisting only makes it worse."

As if the last of his fighting spirit finally departed, the Ruhl's body went limp again, and the hooded man went about roping his throat and waist to the center pole. Methodically, he disconnected Castus's chains to spread and tie off his legs on the far posts.

"Will I feel anything?" Castus plaintively queried the man kneeling at his feet. "Will I feel any pain?"

The executioner, having finished both legs, raised his head slowly. "No."

Kyrus smirked, then leaned close to the Speaker's ear, already thinking about the wars to come. "*When this is over, I want to review the conscription figures with Glan –*"

"*Majesty!*"

It was a blur.

The Brown whirled, drew his bow, and unleashed three strikes before his baffled brethren knew what hit them.

Castus sprang to life, his "tied" feet scarcely bound – and sprinted to the far door of the courtyard.

"Protect the Khorokh!" Oratus bellowed.

Four Reds dived atop him, as arrows killed three more Browns with ease – they were trained to shoot, not be shot at.

Seizing the shock, the rogue bowman spun around and dashed after the fleeing Ruhl who struggled with the worn wooden bar sealing the door.

Kyrus's head spun. "*Get off of me! Get him, you bastards!*"

Two Reds leapt up in obeyance when the courthouse doors swung open behind them – five men in gray rags identical to Castus's stormed out, racing towards the yard's Arxun exit. The guards were startled but immediately gave chase.

Oratus dashed to the court entrance. "Jarax! Send every guard out here immediately!"

"Bloody door!" Castus screamed as the doorbar creaked ever so slightly while his "executioner" guarded his back.

"Move aside!" the Bowman yelled out.

Parting on command, the line of charging "gray-rags" gave the Bowman a clear line of sight at their pursuers, but the Reds closed too quickly. One arrow found a Red helmet's eyehole, dropping him immediately. But the other crashed ferociously into the shooter, their bodies hurtling into Castus and the door. With a great thud, the aged lockbar shattered into pieces, and the door wheeled open onto the Arxun's streets.

Behind Kyrus, Jarax's men flooded out of the courthouse, not quick to see the struggle at the opposite end.

Kyrus frothed with rage as he stumbled to his feet and pointed to the courtyard door. "Get them! Bloody kill them all now!"

The Red rained mailed fists upon the Bowman, but the gray-rags were soon at the latter's side. The guard gutted one with a short dagger, but the rest overran him, stabbing him repeatedly with a spent arrow.

The Bowman scrambled to his feet, hoisting Castus up with him. "Come on, my Lord! We have to run! To the Gurums!" He glanced back at the gray-rag decoys. "The lot of you – scatter! Two west and two east – *now!*"

Reds were soon at the open door – in time to see six figures sprinting off into the Arxun.

Castus   had   fled.

Chapter XXVII

"I will rely on no drink, no man, and no god for the strength to battle;
For drink is illusory,
Man is fallible,
And the gods are fickle.
I will be steel before, during, and after the fray, so long as I shall live.
On my name, honor, and legacy, do I so pledge."

Rokh Military Credo

Starrea Province, the Rokhish Gates, 19th Day of the Third Month, Y. 384 P.C.

"Look around you, brothers. We stand at a divide, a divide between civilization and barbarism, order and lawlessness; a divide between the Empire of the Unified Rokhs and Valogar. Beyond these gates we march into an abyss, we march to meet hundreds, thousands, perhaps hundreds of thousands waiting to give battle on the Isthmus, at the Valogarian Gate, and their homeland itself. Vicious warriors, every one of them, ready with their foul poison to kill at the slightest cut."

Tyghus let his eyes sweep over the crowd hanging on his every word, his entire dyron gathered forty feet below him as he stood atop the front of the double-walled Rokhish Gates. Against the clouded sun of the evening twilight, he was a regal sight, the crimson and black teardrops of the Imperial coat of arms emblazoned on a tunic of gray, wind rippling his crimson cloak enough to reveal brilliant silver ribbed armor underneath. Feeling a rush unlike anything he'd ever experienced before, he resumed his pacing between the gatewall's two massive parapets, each as broad as the gateway itself.

"And what do we go to meet them with? Thirteen thousand on a good day. Reinforcements days away if at all, all while knowing the only friendly faces we're to see are those we imagine or the ugly curs standing at our sides."

He paused again as his last word echoed from the high wall, before challenging his men with, "so do we run?"

"*No!*" came the collective roar of the soldiers.

"Do we cower behind these walls and let others take our glory?"

"*No!*"

"No, we do not! Because *we* are the Bulls of Stygus, the Cursed Few, the Bloody Brigade!"

Massive bellows shook the ground beneath him.

"We are Rokhish power, utter hell taken shape as men!"

"*Huzzah!*"

His long hair whipped in the misty breeze, his eyes a fiery green. With a charge coursing through his veins, Tyghus swallowed hard through pursed lips, seeking to gather himself.

"Now, some of you know me well, and some of you know me hardly at all. To the latter I tell you this – the history stones, the scrolls, what have you – they'll all say I am Tyghus, son of the House of Tygh, born in Draygonea at Tygonium. And aye, they may be right – but in my *heart* and in my *soul*, my birthplace is *Attikon*, my home *Avergon*, the cities I came to as a tob'. I've walked with a sword in hand ever since, and what an honor it's been – but it's *nothing* compared to leading you with it, *leading* the Sixth, the most feared group of bastards the world's yet seen!"

"Huzzah!"

"You see, I'm a student of history. I am, always have been. And I proudly recall that almost two hundred years ago, your forefathers and mine bled these grounds red against the Natives. Tens of thousands died – some by Valogarian spears, some by Colverian arrows; some of 'em never got their due of being burned after battle, keepin' 'em from the gods' Table while the crows did their nasty work. It was a *six year* nightmare on this horrible stretch of earth we call the Isthmus, yet through it all, it was the Bloody Brigade that led every charge, the Bloody Brigade that finally broke through at the Valogarian Gate – and it did so happily!

"Fifty years ago, the Purebloods chose to deny their rightful rulers, plunging the Peninsula into a war that Rokhish arms had to quell, and again it was the Cursed Few that led the sixty-thousand Rokhs to victory.

"And when they rose once more, brothers, near enough in time that some of us still –" Tyghus's voice choked as visions of his father suddenly flooded his thoughts. He momentarily brought a fist to his mouth before continuing. "Near enough that some of us can name fathers, uncles, and brothers among the dead – even then, it was the Bulls of War called upon to hunt down the Purebloods. Village by village, house by house, man by man…"

A quieter, more solemn roar rang out after he finished this time.

"And now it comes to us. How will we answer Stygus's beckoning? How will we match our forefathers? How do we answer that horrible attack on Rokhish soil? The ones that came before us never shied away from their duties, never turned from their heritage, and neither now can we. So we'll answer them with steel; we'll answer them with fury; we'll answer them with *blood.* Brothers, if Avergon is my home, then *you* are my family. You give me your all, your everything – and so help me gods I will give you life, glory and victory!"

A massive cheer rose up from the crowd.

"Cherish this final night, because then we'll pass through these gates. And when we do, I want you to listen for the echoes of our great history, because *we* have been tasked with mirroring its triumphs. For the gods, for the throne, and for the glory of man and Empire!"

The raucous crowd yelled back in echo, wracking the General's body with chills.

"For man and Empire! For man and Empire! For man and Empire!"

* * *

"Fine speech, General," Fyrustus said with questionable seriousness.

Tyghus ignored the hulking kordette as steel feet clanged off the stony floor. He'd called twelve men to the Gatemaster's dim quarters atop the northeast parapet, all but two of them commanding a thousand men. The eleventh commanded 2,500 horsemen – he was the *Stuqatta*, or master of cavalry; the twelfth, the *Belagette*, directed the Sixth's twenty massive catapults. All circled a wooden table, its dozen candles sparkling off silver armor beneath ashen tunics; all eyes drawn to the tall commander.

"Fine or not, the time for speeches is over," he said bluntly.

"Oh, don't say it," Fyrus' said with a smile. "There's always time for speeches."

Tyghus scowled at his friend. "I'm serious, aye?"

The brute gave a deferential nod. "Aye… just –"

"Aye, well I'm in no mood for it. We attack in the morning yet we've *still* almost no information to act upon. No reports of how many Valogarians have rallied on the Peninsula – if at all; no reports on whether Colverians have joined them."

"Have the Gatemen here seen –"

"The Gatemen here haven't seen a damn thing with the fog being as thick as it is, let alone signs of Natives gathering on the Isthmus. Our scouts are probing as we speak, but the fact is we're going to have to march blind if we're to stay apace."

It was hard for Tyghus to hide his irritation. The Gatemen's failure to keep a close watch on the Isthmus infuriated him, even if he understood their limitations. It was true they were soldiers, but primarily those considered ill-fit for the rigors of regular campaigning or extended marches. Some were veterans of the dyrons, too lamed to go on but too proud to admit it. Asking them to scout the grounds on foot in blinding fog would only make them prime targets for predatory Natives. Nevertheless, traveling sightless along one of the most blood-soaked lengths of earth the Empire had ever seen would irk even the most optimistic general.

"Alright, we're marchin' blind, then; so we keep a skirmish line one, maybe two hundred yards ahead of the rest," a bald man named Nikolux offered. He was the oldest of the kordettes by more than a decade, and with his scarred face looked every year of it. He'd declined offers of generalship elsewhere in the Empire to remain with his Iron Kord of the Sixth, preferring future scars come with the same brigade as the rest. Hailing from the rough Starrean frontier town of Nikium, he was blunt, rude, and ornery – just the type of man Tyghus found relatable at the moment. "I mean to the Depths with it, let's just stretch *my* kord from cliff to cliff as we march – I can get you a hundred damned volunteers to charge the Valogarian Gates alone if we have to."

"Aye, Niko's got it right," the General said in deference to the weathered man, fully aware of the narrow front the Isthmus presented him with. "It's not ideal, but I don't think we have much of a choice now. If the skirmishers hit something – *anything* – then Reverus, I want your horsemen immediately up the sides while they engage. Flank 'em early, and we'll feed more kords into the fight as fast as we can."

The Stuqatta gave an expressionless nod. Of all the kordettes he had greeted since he returned as Dyrator, Reverus had proven most distant. Given his familial prestige and what the Twins had told him about his expectations of inheriting the Sixth, he wasn't terribly surprised, but it still bothered him — not the least of which because of the sheer power and importance of Imperial cavalry in battle. There was such pride in the cavalry kord that it sometimes acted like a dyron unto itself, and as a man who hailed from the "horse plains" of Draygonea, Reverus was its perfect leader. For better or worse, however, Tyghus had simply too much to do in preparation for the invasion to spend much time soothing the Stuqatta's ego.

"Gimme one of the front kords, General," Fygonus barked from across the table, his body made even more imposing in his armored shell. "If Niko' wants the skirmish line, that's fine, but I want the kord backing him up."

"No objections, I take it?" Tyghus asked with a glance around the table.

"No objection, so long as I get the front too," said Kinistus, a wiry warrior from Loccea who reminded Tyghus of what a young Treos might have looked like, thinning pate and all. Like Treos, he had an easy, kind way about him, one seemingly inapposite to the killing of his trade — until the charge was called upon. Then he underwent one of the more startling transformations Tyghus had ever seen in his days in the Dyron.

"Aye then, to the both of you," the General said, recognizing only two kords could march abreast at normal depth on the Isthmus. "Grantax, Golaxus — you'll back up Fygo' and Kini'," he continued as he looked between the two agreeable Upland Ruhls. They were distant cousins from Kylea's Grolligon, but their silky coal black hair and thin pursed lips made them seem like more immediate kin. From a distance, only their height distinguished them, with Golaxus holding a full head over his relative.

"Now, we're either in for a slog on the Neck itself or we caught 'em early enough that they'll be holding back to make a stand at the Valogarian Gate; regardless of which it is, Napodonax?"

"Aye, General?" the Belagette replied crisply.

"I'm placing your catapults as the fourth line, understood? Any problem hitting men, hitting the Gate in this bloody fog? Don't imagine it's lifting any time soon."

"Of course not, General," Napo' said, who beamed with such pride that the question must have offended him. He was a short, hot-headed man of the northern Lowlands who kept largely to himself. He was a man of numbers, after all, who could be seen at all hours of the day and night tracking distances and measuring trajectories for his plethora of projectiles.

It was rumored that he'd split a sapling at two hundred yards with a ten-pounder – and the stump left behind with a five. "I've had the ranges for the Isthmus well-mapped for years. Only a driving rain could keep –" he started, then stopped as a frown appeared with a shake of his head. "Actually no. No, not even rain could keep our boulders from staying true."

The General tried not to smile at his quirks. "Aye, well the wall's a pretty damn big target whether you can see it or not."

"It'll be dust, General," Napo' said coldly. "Only a matter of how fast you want it so."

Tyghus nodded in his direction. With a sigh, he reflected upon the Gate for a moment. "It's gonna be bad there… at the Wall, I mean."

The table was quieted too, until a blond-haired kordette named Siderius spoke up. "S'pose that could be true… guess that assumes Napo' leaves us anyone to fight, though."

The table of men let out a low rumble of chuckles to which Tyghus was not immune.

"'Dust', he said, General – how the hell we fighting dust?" Siderius added to more laughing.

Tyghus looked to the straight faced siegemaster. "I think he's challenging you, Napo'."

"Aye, he is. And it'd be a pity to see a stone slip and hit 'im in his ass," the siegemaster said. The men laughed louder.

"So we take the Wall," Reverus said over the din, hands running through his long, auburn hair looking scarcely amused. "What then?"

"What then? Well, once it falls, we're bringing the bulk of the gateguards here up to man what's left of it."

"And the Sixth?" the Stuqatta asked quickly, smacking of impatience.

"I'm getting there, brother," Tyghus replied, a bit tersely. "The Sixth will swing south along Valogar's lower highlands – south and *fast*. Our goal's to reach their port of Bakia, because if the Colverians have any plans on returning to the Peninsula they'd have to land there. To my knowledge, there's no other suitable coast or harbor within a hundred miles of it to disembark in strength. A group of –" the General stopped as he saw puzzled expressions on several faces. He focused on a man directly across the table named Pydonus, an awkward looking fellow bearing exaggerated jaw, nose, and ears with eyes gray as ash. "Problem, Pydonus?"

The kordette blanched under the direct address. Pydo' had served with Tyghus in the Tenth Kord, and the latter was happy to name him as replacement kordette upon becoming dyrator. Tyghus knew he had the fighting skills, but even still, he was young; he wanted to see if Pydonus had the mental resolve as well. "No, not a problem really… I–" he started initially. "I just think a lot of us thought we'd be targeting Nar-Biluk…"

"Why?" Tyghus challenged.

His subordinate's brows furrowed. "It's their Capital..." he replied innocently, to the chuckles of some of his comrades.

"Aye. So?"

"Well, it'd be a hell of a statement to sack the beatin' heart of their country, wouldn't it?"

"Agreed," Reverus suddenly offered. "Nar-Biluk *is* Valogar."

Tyghus's eyes bounced to the Stuqatta, annoyed at the timely statement. "No, it's not, actually – if anything, it's an island in Valogar."

"No, it's –"

"But regardless, say we brave the fortress, say we carve our way into Nar-Biluk – then what?"

"It can be done, General," Pydonus protested.

"It's not whether we can, it's whether we *should*. We'd have a hundred thousand angry Natives on the inside to keep us busy, while Valogarian militias gather outside."

"Or the militias see the sacking of their capital, and lose heart," Reverus suggested pointedly.

"The moment we enter those city walls we become trapped by them, Reverus."

"So *burn* it and leave."

Tyghus bored deep into the Stuqatta's eyes. "Burning Nar-Biluk is not an option. Who would you have surrender to us afterwards? A hundred different militia leaders, all with different aims?"

The horsemaster started to reply but then stopped, defiantly looking away instead. Tyghus returned his eyes to his former kord-mate. "Look, with another dyron or two, Pydonus, I'd consider differently – but the reality is we don't have them and we don't know when we're getting more. Nar-Biluk has to be out for now."

A Coastal Ruhl named Noccus looked around the table before asking a question certain to be on more than a few minds. "No word on the other dyrons, then? No word on Glannox?"

The General sighed, more peeved that he didn't have an answer himself. "No. What I know is what I've told you all, I've kept no secrets – we're to invade immediately, while Glannox is supposed to be landing in Valogar's northern reaches."

Noccus's eyes danced away from the General's for a moment before meeting them again. "Where's he intend to drop fifty thousand men in the northern reaches? Straight cliffs on all sides there..."

Tyghus sympathized with the kordette's suspicious tone, as it gave voice to one of his own concerns. "That wasn't part of the orders I was given, Noccus, but frankly, we can't worry about Glannox's plans. From this point forward, it's the men in *this* room against the whole of Valogar, that's how we have to think of this campaign until proven otherwise. Agreed?"

He noticed a broader range of nods this time. "So then, we cut off Bakia from the rest of Valogar. It's doubtful the Lij has rallied his troops in strength, but if he has, he wouldn't have done so in the lower hills; the men answering to him will be coming from the villages near the capital. As for the militias, they won't attack us piecemeal –" Tyghus paused as he looked to each of his men. "– but once Bakia's ours, we *will* attack them. Plan's to hunt down as many of 'em as we can until we link up with Glannox to smash the Lij's main army. To that end, we'll have speedscouts scouring the countryside, traveling fast and light, keeping eyes for the Lij and Glannox alike." He looked to the table, suddenly feeling tired. "So that's it," he concluded, reclining back into his seat to measure the room's silence.

The Twins glanced at each other for moment. "Wise plan, General," Fyrus' said with a plain face. "Hope it lasts past the first arrow."

The table laughed again, a hearty, relieved laugh.

"How could it not against a hundred to one odds?" Fygo' yelled as he gave his brother a slap on the back.

As the laughter faded, Tyghus scanned the men surrounding him, running a hand through his growing beard. "Brothers... I hope you realize that I *know* I've never led you in war. And I know the last few months have been a whirlwind for us all – gods above, just last year I was riding with Dyrator Kyrus to the Capital; now I'm him and he's Khorokh," Tyghus said, eliciting some shaking heads. "But the fact is, the part I didn't say to the men, is that the odds we face go far beyond what our forefathers faced... and the only way we survive this is by sticking together. I know that's been said to death, said by so many others that it's lost all meaning, but for the Sixth, it's absolutely true. But with every ounce of my being I truly promise you that I *will* be with each of you to the very end... no matter what happens."

All eyes were drawn to his, when suddenly his voice turned quiet. "To the Bloody Brigade."

Nikolux nodded proudly. "To the Cursed Few."

Tyghus gave a nod in the veteran's direction. "Rest up... tomorrow we march to hell."

* * *

Long after his kordettes left him he still found himself sitting at the table, distantly eyeing the dying candles in the room's fading light, a window's light breeze cooling bearded cheeks. He replayed the last week of marching, the speech atop the Gate, the meeting with his men...

Through it all, he'd never mentioned her. Not even once, even though she was all he could see as he prepared to conquer her kingdom.

He never expressed his impossible dream of striking the Valogarians so hard and so fast that they'd break and give up the fight before it worsened; that he'd somehow bypass a war and be able to protect his sister from the Natives before they turned on her – or before angry Rokhish soldiers did. He didn't care whether Dray'gon Rokh would approve of her rescue or not, he would be doing what was *right* – whatever 'right' meant anymore.

This dream wasn't the men's burden to carry. For them, he'd said what they wanted to hear, what they needed to hear. No, this burden was his and his alone – by his House's honor, he couldn't lose her too…

In the end, only one thing really mattered, one thing from which all else could flow.

The   only   thing   that   mattered   now   was   victory.

Chapter XXVIII

"Perhaps it is not your hubris being punished my King,
Perhaps it is your enemy's bravery being rewarded."

Quote from <u>Tales of the Wandering Kings</u> by Massulax

Dray'gon Rokh, Khorian Brex, 20ᵗʰ Day of the Third Month, Y. 384 P.C.

"Gone?"

"He's gone, Majesty."

Jarax stood listlessly inside the doorway of the Brex just past High Moon. His body was shorn of armor, his face a filthy, sweaty mess; his stench almost overpowered the reek of Kyrus's wine that permeated the room. The Khorokh could do nothing but give his head an angry, helpless shake. "*Gone.* Gone *how?*"

"I don't know, Highness."

"Gone *where?*"

"I don't know, High –"

"Well, why not!" Kyrus shouted with a pound of the table. "What the hell *do* you know!"

The Rubator's hand ran through a grimy beard and sighed. "We've given chase for two days now, haven't slept a wink."

"Nor should you!"

Jarax sighed again. "Aye, I'm just saying there's not much more we know now than we did when they... when *he* escaped in the first place..."

Kyrus closed his eyes above gritted teeth. *"Escaped,"* he muttered.

"There were five of 'em. Five scrawny bastards that ran out of the courtyard – six I s'pose if you count the Lorrion."

"He's *not* a bloody Lorrion."

"Apologies," Jarax said with a nod towards his leader. "But aye, we chased 'em into the Gurums, ended up killing all but two... but Castus was one of those two."

"Splendid work," Kyrus mocked with a wave of his wine chalice. "You kill four fools that could have talked, could have told us something –"

"They *attacked* us."

"— while the only bastard we needed runs free."

The proud Rubator hardly even blanched at the derision, so deep was his shame. Seemingly oblivious, he plowed forth with his account. "Awilix and I searched every square inch of the Gurums and didn't find anything 'til he saw the Drayan Creek, the part carrying the smiths' wastes beyond the South Wall. He noticed that right where the wall grate would have been, right where the creek passes through, the grate had been wrenched aside. We galloped south of the wall to the creek's wastepool, and gods-be-damned, we saw footprints leading away from it. I –" he stuttered. "I wouldn't have believed it lest I'd seen it. Fish can't even survive in that wastewater, let alone a man..."

Kyrus looked at him silently for a moment. "Yet here we are."

Jarax's gray eyes looked down, mired in disgrace.

The Khorokh let out a sigh of disgust as he turned away from Jarax and swallowed a glass of spirits. *Must everything be a battle?* he wondered. *Do I bloody have to do* everything *myself?* "I should just make Awilix my Rubator."

"Awilix is a fine soldier."

"I should have *you* flayed for this."

Jarax stared at Kyrus for a moment before suddenly drawing a dagger from his belt and slamming his free arm down on Kyrus's table.

"Jarax!" the startled Khorokh exclaimed.

With cold efficiency, he pulled his tunic's sleeve back to run the edge of his blade straight up his forearm. Curls of skin peeled back like rinds to an apple, his arm instantly a blood-soaked mess.

"*Gods above, what is this!*" Kyrus bellowed after recovering from his initial shock. As the Rubator continued unabated, Kyrus finally smashed his knifehand with a fist of his own and sent the dagger skittering across the stony floor. Jarax started after the blade, but the Khorokh leapt to his feet and shoved the Red to the ground.

"Gods above!" he said again as he looked from the dagger to his guardian's arm and back. "What are you, mad?"

The Rubator stared back through the peppery hair scattered across his eyes, chest heaving as blood coursed onto the floor. "You... said..."

"I said I *should* have you flayed, you imbecile! *Should!* It's not *your* decision to make!" Kyrus paced around the room, his wine-induced fog blown asunder.

"You..."

"You couldn't tell I was angry? You've made it this bloody far just doing what any man says in passing?"

"No –"

"Any man just tells you to stick a knife in your chest, and you just, you *do it?*"

"No!"

"No *what?*"

"Not for any man! Not for you!"

"Oh, is that right? That's why you're lyin' there looking like a wolf kill, is it?"

"I'd do it for the Empire! I bled my palms upon the Swearing Stone some twenty years ago for the *Empire!* And *you* are the Empire!"

"You should –"

"And if *you've* lost faith in me, the *Empire's* lost faith in me, so let me take it! Let me take my life and sit with the gods!"

Kyrus recoiled, suddenly reminded of his own similar thoughts not so long ago; thoughts that had haunted him all his life. "You won't have a seat if you take your life and you know it."

"If my Khorokh orders it, I will!"

"Well, I'm not ordering it."

"Why? I've disgraced you. You've lost faith in me –"

"By the gods, Jarax, I never said I've lost faith in you!"

"Then why the hell are Antinax's men tracking my every move!"

Kyrus felt a sting shoot through his stomach. He had no immediate retort.

"What, you think I'd not see 'em, Highness?" Jarax brazenly continued. "The way his fools stomp about in the shadows with the grace of an ox? Mirroring my steps, my family's steps?"

"That's my business," Kyrus finally mumbled.

"It's my *insult*."

Kyrus scowled at the crumpled Rubator. "Dress that wound and take a seat," he said tiredly before collapsing back into his own gnarled chair and refilling his cup.

The silver-haired Red gingerly stood and approached, wrapping a grungy rag tight around his arm. The Khorokh watched the rag darken. "It hurts far more when someone else's doin' it to you, I assure you," he said darkly.

Jarax just looked at his arm and nodded.

Kyrus's brow then furrowed as he spoke in measured tone. "Jarax, you – you more than anyone should understand the folly in relying on one man for information, for my safety. I'm new to Dray'gon Rokh; I don't like Dray'gon Rokh; I hate many and I'm *hated* by many. There's not a soul in this city whose word is worth the very clothes they wear but against all that, I'm supposed to run a bloody Empire. Do you understand what I'm saying?"

Jarax gave no eye contact, let alone a response.

"If it puts your mind at ease, Antinax has had nothing but good things to say of you."

The Rubator smirked. "I've seen that man at work for decades now, Highness. And I know damn well my oath to protect the Realm is an oath to protect the Lorrio within it, but I'll tell you this – the man's a manipulator of the highest order. If he's saying 'good things' now it's because it suits him *now* to say good things."

"Well, thankfully it's not your place to question the mind of a Lorrion, is it?" Kyrus scolded.

"And gods be praised for that," Jarax said as bloodshot eyes locked on his counterpart. "I never cared about Rynsyus's politics, and I don't care about yours. I only, *only* care about the Realm – *your* Realm. So I'll beg of you one last time, either you trust me or you kill me, but don't drag me into these games. And I'm telling you now – if I ever see a spy within twenty feet of myself or my family again then *by the gods I will slit his throat!*"

Kyrus's heart raced as a silence fell between them. He simultaneously despised the man's audacity while admiring his unflinching – his fanatical? – devotion to the throne. He gently swirled the liquid in his chalice.

"Just let me do my job, Highness."

"I see now the folly in the advice Rynsyus gave me," Kyrus said in a calmer tone. "He said to rule like a general. He said to 'treat the Lorrio' and my ministers like my soldiers in Valogar. Command them like soldiers, he said."

"And where's the folly?"

Kyrus's eyes raised from the cup to Jarax. "The folly's that those men I commanded carried out orders when given," the Khorokh said, each of his words rising in volume. "The folly's that not once did I *ever* have to sit with a subordinate and rationalize to him why I take the actions that I take. And you say what you will about Antinax, but the reality is that I've as little reason to trust you as I do him."

"So then you trust no one?"

"Aye, and I'm better off for it!" Kyrus snapped.

Jarax stared hard at him for a few moments before letting his eyes drift down to the chalice. "You're going down a very dangerous path if you choose to trust no one."

"And why is that?" Kyrus demanded.

A wide grin broke out across the weathered Red's face. "Because you'll make enemies of *every*one."

Kyrus contemplated the words for a moment before turning to his drink again. "Trust," he said with scorn, water irritatingly creeping up the sides of his eyes. "Look what it's brought me, look what it brought my father? I raised Tyghus like a brother only to see him... a-and my father... my father trusted that the Rokhs in the very Capital he was fighting for weren't sharpening knives for his back like 'trustworthy' Castus. It's a useless commodity, trust is. It's a fiction."

Jarax coolly shook his head. "But you have to, Highness – you have to trust *somebody*."

The Khorokh searched his counterpart before mockingly raising his cup in his direction. "To trust, then."

The Rubator replied with a grim smile.

Kyrus's conscience faded farther and farther from the table, his eyes distantly staring at the ground near the Tower door while the table's candles popped and sparked. "How could this have happened? This –" he struggled for the word. "*Coup*. How could it have happened right under my nose? The planning, the support –"

"All the Lorrions are powerful, all of them have massive webs of allies and people that kiss their feet, both in the Arxun and out of it, but Castus even moreso. On top of that, he's a very wealthy man and he had a long time in those dungeons to let that wealth do its work."

"No," Kyrus retorted defiantly. "This is more than coin. I've seen paid men on the battlefield, I've fought mercenaries; I *know* when a man is doing something for coin, but *those* men, those vile traitors that risked their lives for Castus did so for something more." He paused reflectively. "Is he *that* loved below the Clyves? Is he so revered that the people there just accept his treason? Or am I truly that hated?"

The Rubator awkwardly looked to either side of his master, despite the Khorokh's still distant expression. "He's very powerful."

"Oratus warned me," the Emperor said in a near whisper before falling quiet. "Well, he's been sentenced to die," he finally said matter-of-factly, as if to convince himself. "The only question now is who else need die for aiding his escape, aye?"

Jarax nodded, albeit warily.

"*Aye?*"

"Aye, Highness. I—" the Red leader started before stopping abruptly.

Kyrus' head tweaked and turned towards him. "You what?"

"Just remember, the more you kill, the more enemies you make. Everything has consequences..."

"Jarax, this *cannot* stand – you know that, right?"

"I know. Just... just remember," the Rubator cautioned. "Rynsyus might have described it to me best some twenty years ago – he said 'people new to Dray'gon Rokh see only the tree that is the Lorrion; veterans of Dray'gon Rokh see only the roots thrust deep below the surface.'"

The Khorokh stared at him as a smile appeared on his face. "And so emperors are wise to respect those – 'trees' and 'roots' – as Rynsyus put it? Avoid putting the axe to them, he might say?"

Jarax shrugged. "He might. He might say the Capital is what it is."

"Which dyron did you serve before joining the Rubitio, Jarax?"

The Rubator blanched. "My dyron?"

"Aye."

"I was at Alemyles, Highness. I served in the Second."

"Well, let me ask you something. Imagine you and the Second are marching to battle under my command. And imagine we come across a foe lined up in a wall of pikes – massive pikes, the way the Early Kings fought. Now imagine I tell you to charge those pikes head-on with every ounce of your being – would you do it?"

"If that's the command, that's the command. Of course I'd do it."

"Of course. Now imagine by the gods' graces you survive the slaughter. We line up against the same foe a month later, and gods above, I tell you to charge those cursed pikes again."

"I'd –"

"And the next month, and the next month, and the next month, until one of the battles finally takes me to the Depths, leaving you to inherit the Second."

Jarax stared at the Khorokh in silence.

"You're telling me, as the gods watch us now, that you'd continue charging that wall of pikes? You're telling me that you wouldn't change a thing, you wouldn't find a *better* way to break those spearmen?"

"Highness, I'm only trying to tell you the reality of the city, I'm not –"

"As *you* see it, Jarax!" Kyrus erupted. "From the moment I stepped foot into Dray'gon Rokh, all I've heard is how I can't or shouldn't change one thing or another. As a Lorrion, Rynsyus told me to vote as Onzero did and don't cause a stir; as Emperor, our bridge is nearly annihilated yet half my Lorrio proposed doing *nothing!* And tonight I'm reminded yet again how I shouldn't dare attempt to change things."

"I'm –"

Kyrus scoffed. "What you say may be true, Jarax. The 'trees', the 'webs', all of it. But treason is treason. And if Castus is just a treasonous tree with treasonous roots, then we'll have to keep cutting and cutting until the tree collapses. We've got enough enemies outside the realm to worry about, we shouldn't have to worry about enemies from within."

Jarax simply nodded this time.

The Khorokh poured himself more of the spirits before continuing. "No more. I can't have this distraction anymore; we're at war, by the gods - the holiest of wars. So first, you're to make me a list of every person within the Arxun's walls holding ties to the Lowlands; then, your one and only goal is to *find Castus*. Every coffer, every requisition that you need to take, it's yours," he said, with pointed finger. "And if your numbers start to thin, I'll send word to have five thousand troops of the Fourth Dyron in Fyrogon placed under your command, to station throughout the Lowlands as you see fit. *Find me that blood-sucking traitor.*"

After a nod, Jarax rose from the table. "Your will, Highness. If you'll indulge me, though, I'd ask that you stay in the Brex until we're certain everything's secure in the Arxun."

Kyrus let out a morbid chuckle. "I'm used to being a prisoner in the Brex by now, I think."

Jarax's face seemed to lighten but as he turned towards the doors he stopped, looking back one last time at the Khorokh. "And Antinax's men?"

Kyrus averted meeting his eyes at first. "Don't let them keep you from your duties."

The Red gave the very slightest hint of a smile as he bowed his head in Kyrus's direction. "Understood, Highness."

"Good luck."

Kyrus sighed in exhaustion as the door slammed behind Jarax. He closed his eyes after finishing his cup, forehead coming to rest upon the table. *"Just let me have my vengeance, gods,"* he whispered plaintively. *"I beg of you,   just   let   me   have   it."*

Chapter XXIX

"It was a slog today... a vicious, bloody, terrible slog. Natives everywhere, spears forward, arrows above... nowhere for us to even move, just charge then brace for countercharge all day... I'm utterly exhausted. Hopeful a few more days of this will break them, but I confess they're faring far better than I was led to believe..."

Letter from an Unknown Soldier,
Day 1 of 2,134 days in the First Valogarian War, Y. 197 P.C.

Isthmus, 20th Day of the Third Month, Y. 384 P.C.

"Where the hell you painted bastards hidin'?" Tyghus muttered anxiously to himself. *"The hell you waiting for?"*

He could see nothing through a fog thick as soup and heard little beyond plodding boots and turbulent waves lapping at the cliffs' bottoms. But it wasn't until they'd been on the march for several uneventful hours that something began to feel amiss. Maybe it was because he was so sure the Valogarians would pack the Isthmus with spearmen like the wars of old, or maybe it was because the scouts he sent out had simply been gone for far too long. Whatever the reason, he grew warier with every unchallenged step. After they'd passed the "Choke" – the skinniest part of the Isthmus, well past its midpoint – the General spurred Fidipodus to join his kordette at the forefront.

The grizzled veteran Nikolux trotted atop his warhorse a few yards back from his skirmish line. His helmet dangled from his horse's saddle, revealing a shaven head criss-crossed with scars, including one that went clear down the back of his head and neck. As Tyghus materialized out of the fog, he gave a curious glance at him, followed by a quick nod.

"This wind's gotta be hell on that noggin of yours," the General quipped as his eyes flicked to Niko's head.

The man didn't crack a smile, and in truth, Tyghus was no fool as to the reasons for Niko's hairstyle. He was a member of the much-romanticized religious knighthood called the "Steccio" – "men of the divine death" – that gave no message to the outward world about their affiliation beyond their shaven heads. Though the institution dated to those first years Post-Cataclysm, the Steccian Knights were expressly banned by Rokhish law and despised as heretics by the clergy. Nonetheless, Niko proved the Empire was wise enough not to enforce *all* of its laws.

"Concerns, General?"

"Don't know if I'd call it a concern yet, but…"

"If you're sayin' 'but', there's a concern."

"Maybe so," Tyghus said with a nervous laugh. "It's just… the scouts. Wish we'd seen them back by now."

"Aye," the Kordette nodded, as decaying Rokh materiel broke beneath their horses' hooves.

Tyghus's thumb ran over his sword's hilt. "Thinking about sending more out on a swift ride, try to figure out where they've gone."

"Oh, I wouldn't bother."

"No?"

Nikolux gave Tyghus a cold look. "You know they're dead, General."

The Dyrator looked away. He didn't 'know' they were dead but… "If they're dead, then we've got Natives at the Gate… at *least* the Gate."

"So it'd seem, wouldn't it?" Niko' said, eyes straight ahead.

"I just don't understand it. We'll probably be in catapult range within the hour. Why the hell would they just forfeit the rest of the Isthmus?"

Niko' wrinkled his nose as if a foul odor overtook him. "The cowards have never possessed a mind for battle; it doesn't surprise me at all."

"They'll fight."

"Aye, they'll fight, but they fight mad, they fight reckless. You're not going to find any logic in their approach," the Kordette said with disdain. "Cowards, the lot of them. Foolish cowards at that."

Cowards they may be, Tyghus thought. But he wouldn't concede their foolishness just yet; his sister's ominous comments about the Lij's 'preparations' stuck with him.

"Could be that the mirami haven't answered the Lij's call in the numbers we thought," Nikolux added. "He's a false king after all."

"But they've all been false kings since the First Conquest, no?" he asked, shaking his head. "And even so, they've still held sway with the people."

"A bit. But none were handpicked like this one. I never heard Natives singin' songs about him, telling tales about him; I'm sure you didn't either."

"Aye, and that's just it," Tyghus said, eyes straining through the clouds. "He's finally got his chance to seize the reins of his country if he proves himself against us. Can't imagine we wouldn't see his best —"

"We'll find them, General," the kordette barked, seeming to tire of the conversation. "If it's on the Neck, it's on the Neck; if it's at the Gate, it's at the Gate. Wherever the gods-forsaken roaches are hiding, we'll —"

Niko's line of men suddenly rippled, followed quickly by the sound of armor hitting grass. Curses floated through the fog. They glanced at each other before Niko's face reddened into a scowl. "Soldiers!" he hissed.

But Tyghus knew the men in Nikolux's kord wouldn't risk their sergeant's legendary wrath without good reason. A few more steps proved him right.

A Rokhish scouthorse lay on its side, wheezing terrible breaths. With virtually no armor, the arrows that riddled its body had met no resistance, but the beast was cursed enough to lay suffering. Tyghus's eyes drifted up to the stark white face of its rider, a young Rokh he'd met before leaving for Dray'gon Rokh the previous autumn. An arrow had driven into his lightly guarded chest, staining his gray tunic a blackened red. The shaft was a putrid colored green, evidence of the pyhr in which it had soaked. Several more arrows littered the ground around them, their gnarled, hooked heads betraying their deadly goal: pierce Rokhish flesh and let the deadly poison do its work.

Several of Niko's men gathered around the fallen scout, drawing the kordette's immediate rebuke. "*Stay in formation!*"

Tyghus's neck suddenly burned. "We're in range Niko'… raise shields —

raise shields!"

Whistling sounds suddenly pierced the wind and fog.

The first soldiers dropped in front of Tyghus as if faint of breath, green shafts protruding from their mail.

"Shit – shields *up!*" the General bellowed. "We're within range!"

In an instant, the skirmish line was alive.

"Get 'em in line and draw back, Niko'!" Tyghus shouted as Nikolux leapt off his horse and donned his helmet in one fluid motion. "I'll get the rest and have the catapults brought up!"

"*Shields up and face the fore!*" Niko' demanded. He pounded the golden bull of his black shield before looking into the abyss. "And come on you bloody bastards! You don't break Rokhs with twigs like these, you break 'em man to man!"

Tyghus raced back in a gallop to Fygonus, whose kord marched to Niko's rear. The arrows' whistling was interrupted only by their clanging off metal shields or plunging into flesh, to say nothing of agonized screams in-between.

The Twin's eyes were fiery as the General approached. He smiled. "It's time, isn't it? Tell me it's time!"

"It's time," Tyghus replied shortly. "Their archers are firing; gotta be the extent of their range here, even atop the Gatewall, but march shields up anyway. We need cover so Napodonax can prepare. Tell Kinistus."

More whistles and richochets echoed through the thick air as Tyghus bolted down the gap between Fygonus and Kinistus's kords. Soldiers maintained a gritty silence, allowing Fygo's voice to thunder all around them; the sounds of hundreds of shuffling shields soon followed. He raced so quickly that he barely noticed the wide-eyed faces he passed along the way.

When suddenly the buzzing began.

Like a swarm of locusts, the buzz grew to a crescendo only to be punctuated by the swift collapses of Tyghus's men, a full fifty or sixty yards behind Fygonus. The General looked about in bafflement, unaware of how or from what direction this new attack spawned. As he saw arrows the length of a man plunge into the earth on either side of his mount, a chill ran up his spine.

Colverians.

The deadly precision of Colverian bowmen was as unmistakeable as their ammunition – a massive arrow with heavily weighted head fired over the ranks of of their enemy, farther and higher than any nation, only to plunge on vertical slope towards their victims. The buzz of the greased feather fletchings was the last thing most soldiers ever heard. Combined with the blood-curdling whine of the Valogarian shafts, the Isthmus sounded like a menagerie.

"They're already here," the General said aloud, moments later hearing several kordettes yelling to hold shields overhead. It was a standard defense, but Tyghus had seen Colverian archery in practice – while a shield could weather one arrow, it was unlikely to take a second.

He quickly realized the danger his ranks were in. "Kordettes, stop advancing! There're Colverians on the wall! Relay to the forward lines to roll back immediately!"

"Aye, General!" voices shouted back in unison through the fog and noise.

Praying he could trust them, he kipped Fidi' into full sprint as the buzzing lapsed for a moment. Surely it would soon resume.

The creaking of wooden wheels told Tyghus he was close to the catapults, and sure enough one of the massive war machines finally reared itself before him. To his left he heard the harsh voice of his Belagette.

"Now set down the holding rods – *gently Jepolus!* Check the winding cords, make sure they're tight! Bouldermen – *bouldermen I said! Where in the Realm are you?*"

The stomps of Napodonax drew closer and Tyghus leapt off his horse to greet him. Like a hurtling boulder himself, however, the squat man stormed right by the General.

"Napo'!" Tyghus called after him.

"Apologies General, but we got heathens up ahead, don't we?" Napo' yelled without turning around.

Tyghus turned with reins in hand to follow. "Aye, how –"

"And I figure you have mind to respond."

"You figure right," Tyghus replied as the siegemaster continued his furious pace along the front of his line, inspecting all the way. "How far along are we?"

"Fire-ready in less than five minutes. Range is good if they've already begun arrow volleys. Only question now is the – *Esselis, you imbecile! Lock the rear wheels in place!* – aye, only question now is the arc of fire," Napo' said, before looking back with intense wide eyes. "But one salvo and I'll know, don't worry yourself 'bout that."

"Aye, but listen to me, Napo' – "

"*I want boulders loaded in sixty seconds!*"

"Napo', listen to me!"

The Belagette locked his wild eyes on the Dyrator. "Aye?"

"It's not just Native arrows on the loose, it's –"

"Oh, I know! Our Colverian friends have joined the fray, I've heard them!" Napo' said, before letting out a raspy laugh. "I must'a done something right in my last life to get to kill Colverians and Valogarians on the same day! The gods have blessed us, indeed!"

Tyghus couldn't resist being impressed with the man's single-minded focus, if not horrified by his utter disregard for the deadly bolts. "Thank the gods after we've won – we don't know the range of the Colverians, the war machines may not be out of reach."

"Bah! Let's see what their sticks do against these!" the Belagette said with a proud slap on one of the wood frames.

Tyghus's face began to burn as the man kept walking. "Napo', *be prepared for –*"

The buzzing returned.

The General's head instinctively tilted towards the sky before dropping back down to an unconcerned Belagette, continuing to inspect his catapults.

"*Napo', take cover!*" he bellowed.

The kordette looked back at the General with curiosity or disdain, but either way he simply stood in place, raising a hand to his ear as if trying to place the source of the noise. Tyghus's stomach twisted as the buzzing grew closer. He dashed with horse reins in hand behind a man-sized leg of a machine, just as the arrows rained down.

Shafts plunged into the soil around the catapult, some not inches from the General. They peppered the catapult frames, dozens of strikes ringing out like axes chopping wood. But the hail of death did nothing to take his eyes off Napo', standing tall amidst the fire without a shield in sight, all while muttering calculations to himself. Arrows riddled the ground around him, every second of the volley seeming to stretch eons. Tyghus watched every bolt miss – but one.

Seconds after the buzzing died, a headless shaft spiraled down from the sky, harmlessly bouncing off the Belagette's helmet. The General's chest clenched for a second, until he saw Napo' look down annoyedly at the faulty bolt and stomp it with heavy boot. Tyghus burst into laughter as he charged the somehow blemish-free Napo', too relieved to unleash his pent-up fury. Only crazed guffaws came out.

"You mad son of a bitch!" Tyghus yelled, as he gripped the man's mail below his chin. "They said you're insane, my friend, but *gods above!*"

Napodonax looked at the General blankly at first, as if he knew it was only the dud arrow he'd had to worry about all along. Then, a broad smile overtook his face. "General, we can scratch the test volley – I've got the range."

Tyghus was speechless, and as he shook his head in astonishment replied, "then bring that gods-forsaken wall down so we can fight them proper."

Napo' laughed. "They won't stay to fight, General – but aye, I'll bring it down."

Towering over the Belagette, Tyghus leaned down and clanged the foreheads of their helmets together, then leapt atop his horse and listened to the suddenly sweet sounds of the crazy man barking out orders.

Crazy, but alive.

* * *

"Fire!"

In nearly perfect unison, the twenty catapult arms lurched forward with a rising and ferocious force, halting only upon crashing into padded cross-bars. The back half of the great machines bucked, and oven-sized stones, hundreds of pounds at a minimum, launched through the air as if they were pebbles. They soon became lost in the fog like everything else, and for a few brief moments, all was still, all were silent.

Napodonax sat in a squat between two catapults, squinting straight ahead, lips pursed and palms pressed flat against each other below his nose. His General was mounted behind him, ears straining for the noise that would end the arrow barrages and the screams that accompanied them.

Tyghus's horse let out a snort, and he reached forward to quiet the anxious beast when thunderclaps suddenly cascaded towards them, rumbling the ground like a crashing wave. The great blasts echoed inside his helmet and he instinctively gripped the steed's reins. A mighty cheer went up from his men, nearly rivaling that of the boulders' impacts. Frantic cries in foreign tongue chattered in the distance.

Napodonax leapt up from his crouch only to calmly turn towards the General and say, "Direct hits." A tight, almost smug smile invaded his face for a moment, his gray-blue eyes aglow even in the day's drabness. But it soon faded. "No collapse, though – wall's still standing."

"How many more do you need?"

"I could drop it with a quarter launch, I imagine – depends on how much of a breach you want."

Tyghus thought for a second before shaking his head. "Dust, Napo'."

"Without delay, then," the Belagette replied with a remorseless frown. *"Bouldermen! Full reload!"*

Tyghus nodded in satisfaction. "Bring the damned thing down, I'm headed to the front."

With a spur of his heels, he sent his mount trotting forward into the gray, careful to navigate the central seam running between the kords' ranks. He surveyed for damage on either side of him, and while many men in the second and third lines carried bolt-peppered shields, the wounded numbered far less. The two lines seemed more annoyed than dismayed at the archer volleys.

Niko's skirmishing line hadn't been so fortunate. Though it had pulled back, it wasn't in time to avoid the toxic Valogarian volleys. Looked to be a dozen men, perhaps even two, laying prostrate on the ground. Some suffered nicks, others direct strikes, but with pyhr it was all the same. The noxious salve quickly found its way throughout the body, its victims' flesh rendered ghastly white in all spots but the wound itself, which turned a rotten green. Napodonax's first barrage had silenced the threat for the moment, but damage had been done.

Tyghus's heart raced as he took position alongside Nikolux behind the skirmish line.

"Mind yourself, General – surely still some shooters up there!"

Tyghus heard him but simply shook his head, eyes wide and full of blood, before unsheathing his sword with a piercing ring. "Almost time, boys!" he called to the men. "Almost time!"

A guttural cheer rumbled the ground once more.

"*For man and Empire!*" Niko's men shouted back.

The chant spread like a wildfire throughout the ranks, as if the entire Bloody Brigade was caught up in it. Tyghus's skin drew chills as he listened with pride, the impenetrable fog giving the chants a hypnotic effect. He thrust his sword into the air in unison with the words.

Like a wind scattering dead leaves, however, the sounds of twenty catapult arms smashing cross-bars ended the chants. The same anxious bracing returned.

"*Come on… come on…*" he muttered to himself as he stared blindly.

A blast of air swept overhead.

"*Come on, you bastards…*"

A series of thuds rattled the General's very bones. The earth shook and Fidi' reared up in distress. Tyghus clung tightly to the reins with his left hand, dropping his sword hand low to balance. As his steed's feet planted back down, the echoes of the boulder collisions had stopped. Tyghus's heart pounded as his ears strained for a sound. For a brief moment, silence reigned.

Panicked Native screams soon changed that, overwhelmed shortly after by the sounds of wood splintering up and down the length of the Gatewall. They reminded Tyghus of what he used to hear when his father felled trees, when an innocuous crackle foreshadowed dramatic collapses. The Gates soon followed this pattern, the series of crashes convincing Tyghus that little more than rubble now stood between his dyron and their enemies.

A roar rippled from the ranks and Tyghus himself had to resist the urge to sprint headlong into the abyss, eager to see first-hand what his war engines had wrought. He turned to see Nikolux staring at him, begging with his eyes for an order – *the* order. The General's lips curved upwards.

"Attack."

"Aye, General," he said curtly.

"But be –"

"Aye, be careful, of course," he said with a tight grin. Facing in the Gate's direction, he yelled, "Fourth Kord! Advance at the cautious step!"

His order was relayed up and down the line, drawing cheers along the same. Nikolux adjusted his helmet and began a slow trot into the fog, his line following suit. Each soldier kept a defensive, crouched posture, poised as if the Natives might pour towards them at any minute.

Seconds later, Tyghus turned towards the men of the second line about two dozen yards behind him. "Sixth Dyron – full advance!"

The command echoed its way through the Sixth, and in a matter of moments, ten-thousand foot soldiers were on the march.

The General trotted at the forefront of his advancing army, and while Fygonus and Kinistus flanked either side of him, the three of them may as well have been alone. All strained for sounds of the Valogarians' blood-curdling war cries, Niko's steely reply, or *something*.

But then – nothing.

As they arrived at the pile of wooden wreckage where the Valogarian Gate once stood, they found Niko's men prowling about, coolly finishing dying Natives, or pulling free the lesser wounded for questioning. Others had begun the work of clearing a thruway for the oncoming troops. But nowhere did a Rokh battle a Native – nowhere could a Native warrior even be seen beyond those trapped under the collapsed Gate.

Tyghus looked about in alarm at the lack of formation in Niko's line. "Hold here, men," he said to Fygonus and Kinistus as he traipsed over the litter. "Niko'!" he called out.

The kordette stalked out of the mist into the General's view, his face flushed with anger and frustration. "They ran! They *fucking* ran, I knew they would!" he yelled as he tossed a handful of recovered weaponry to the ground by a group of wounded Natives.

"You saw 'em? How many deep –"

"No idea, we couldn't see them! Couldn't see a bloody thing!"

"Volley sizes say there must have been a thousand, maybe two..."

"They don't even have the courage to even take their weapons with them," Niko' continued ranting in disgust, kicking the pile into the prisoners. "Clouds! Clouds are the only things that spared them!" the kordette continued, stomping menacingly towards the group, when he shot a hand into the prone throat of one on his knees. "*Zia ozoman nona vanoha erefani?*"

The Valogarian gagged with tongue protruding, unable to resist with hands bound. From the awkward bulge of his left arm, it appeared broken anyway.

"*Notravona naia!*"

"Niko'!" Tyghus bellowed at the furious kordette, barely recognizing "have you no honor" in Niko's crude Valogary.

"*Notravona naia!*"

"Keep him alive, dammit!" Tyghus said as forcefully as possible. "He can at least tell us something!"

"Bah!" Nikolux replied, releasing the man to fall to the ground helplessly. White marks from Niko's grip still ringed his throat, mouth sucking air like a fish out of water. The kordette turned his back to Tyghus with hands mounted on hips. "No bloody use to this world, these worms — no use to anybody!"

Tyghus knew to let the proud man calm down a bit. "Well, we've got moist ground, don't we? So we have footprints," he offered. "We'll have horsemen track them, but even if it is a thousand men, that's not enough to concern us now."

Niko' started back towards him with hand sliding over his shaven head. "How the gods — above, below, wherever — how they stand by and permit this is beyond me," he muttered, again kicking the stack of bows. "It is, it's beyond me!"

Tyghus's eyes suddenly fell upon one bow in particular. "What is this?" he said in wonder as he pulled the man-sized weapon for inspection. It was twice the size of the other bows, and beautifully crafted — a sturdy, yet pliable piece of wood, reinforced at the mid-point with thin shreds of twine. Even in the day's dullness, it still glistened as if coated in polish.

Niko' stared at the bow then the General. "A gift from our friends across the Brafford," he said drily before turning away again.

"Indeed it is," Tyghus replied, still marveling over its quality. "But I don't see a Colverian anywhere, do you? Among the wreckage, among the wounded?"

Reason and logic had finally begun to weave its way back into the kordette's mind, looking at the bow with furrowed brow. "No."

"You hear any Colvian spoken by anyone that fled?"

"No…"

Tyghus nodded with wide eyes as he started recalling the attack his men had just weathered with surprisingly few casualties. The broken Colverian arrow that bounced harmlessly off of Napodonax leapt to mind in a new light. "And their volleys — they were crude for Colverians; I've seen them shoot."

"As have I…"

"So there's no way those were Colverians firing these bows. We'd have lost far more — *far, far* more if they were."

Niko' grimaced thoughtfully. "Maybe. Thought it could have been the wind — but I saw a lot of snapped shafts too."

"Colverians are born holding these things; the gods themselves haven't seen them snap more than a bolt or two in battle." He threw the foreign weapon to the ground and looked at Niko'. "They may not have landed yet after all, Niko'."

"Not in time to reach the Gates, anyway," Niko' cautioned.

"These bastards had the weapons but not the warriors," Tyghus said, looking down at the ailing prisoners. "Ask them. Ask them about the Colverians – sure they're eager to talk with you."

Niko' flexed his jaw as he ignored the General's sarcasm. "Agh... you," he said to a man replete in green warpaint from his face to his bleeding abdomen. "How many Colverians – uh, *lava ramo py* Colverians? *Lava ramo py* Colverians!"

The Native's black eyes stared back emptily at the kordette. "*Nihalara* Colverians..." he growled.

Tyghus looked to Niko'. "'The Colverians are their brothers'?"

The kordette nodded annoyedly. "Why bother questioning them? It's useless," he said before kneeling down before the Native. "*Lava ramo py* Colverians!"

"*Nihalara* Colverians!" the Valogarian snapped again, jaw thrust forward defiantly. "*Ysa angoty naro-lona izaya! Anasa mikopy Valogary nenerify tu* Rokh *izey!*"

Niko' rose plain faced from his crouch.

"Something pleasant?"

"'The Colverians are their brothers, and they will come in waves'," Niko' replied, still staring at the warrior. "'We will wash away the traitorous Rokh – scourge I believe he said? – wash 'em away from Valogarian lands.'"

Tyghus looked from Niko' to the Native himself, whose face was devoid of fear, despite blood streaming faster from his wounded belly. "No," Tyghus said, shaking his head as he recalled the foreign word. "*Asi.*"

The General turned from the bound Native to head back towards the rest of his army.

"Where're you going? What's the order here, General?"

"Sun's setting soon – earlier than usual in this fog. Day-marching in this slop is madness enough, we're not doing it by night. We'll clear the wreckage til dusk, honor our dead, then sleep on the grass; we'll break at first light tomorrow," he said, before looking straight up at the hidden sky. "And gods willing, these cursed clouds will be far above us like they should."

The kordette grinded his teeth but nodded respectfully. "Aye."

"'Let discretion win today; our swords tomorrow', isn't that the expression?" Tyghus chided lightly.

More teeth-grinding and begrudging nods. "Aye."

In moments, the kordette had his men doubling their efforts in clearing the Gateline and swelling the number of Valogarian dead and captured. As he watched them work, Tyghus let out an exhausted sigh, the battle surge he'd felt earlier leaving him fatigued and shaky. It was an unexpected first day on the campaign – he'd 'taken' the Isthmus, 'taken' the Valogarian Gate, but the answers to two questions remained elusive: whether the day had been a success – and whether the day was indeed over.

Chapter XXX

"You'd be better off throwin' a saddle on the wind…"

Excerpt from"The Taming of the Wolf" by Menacus

Dray'gon Rokh, Lorrian Norum, 20ᵗʰ Day of the Third Month, Y. 384 P.C.

"This is madness," Volinex said in his Norum quarters, his arm dropping with scroll in hand, eyes finding Antinax. "I mean it is, isn't it?"

"Why? What now?" Barannus squealed. "Let me see that!"

"Oh, by the gods, there's nothing to see!" Voli' snapped in his fine-furred robe. "Says the same damn thing we've been hearing for three nights – no sign of him, no whiff of him! Same ol'!"

"So give it to me, then!"

"Take it," the young Lorrion said, flipping the scroll dismissively with one hand while eying an unfurled one in the other. His counterpart's blotchy skin reddened as he reviewed its contents. "What a misery you are, you know that?"

Antinax felt the chamber's tense air, where fear had overtaken what a month ago was excitement. Beyond the back and forth sniping of the two junior Nortics, even Wollia's trademark indifference had been replaced by crossed arms and inquisitive eyes. They all looked tired, and in truth, Anti' hated meeting at the late hour as much as any of them, but lately it felt like the only safe time to hear their spies' reports.

For his part, Anti' was conflicted. Kyrus's attempt to crush the name and power of Castus was something he scolded himself for not foreseeing. He *knew* the young ruler was bound to be volatile but he should have known he'd be doubly so once he tied the Sudo to his family's fate. Then again, who the hell could have predicted the Khorokh would go as far as he did? No one, not in all of Imperial history, ever had the gumption to take down a sitting Lorrion – even the Dosid "Mad Khorokhs" of the second century knew better! The elder Nortic was quickly realizing that the new Emperor may not be inclined towards the conventional path.

He lamented Castus's loss in another, odder way – he missed his predictability. Even though his most vehement opposition was now gone, Anti' had taken comfort in the familiarity of the Sudo's tendencies over the years. And though he was loath to admit it, the utter audacity of the Sudo's escape from the courtyard three days prior – the planning, the inevitable bribing – it was... well, it was damn near admirable if the repercussions were more apparent.

"Anti' where? Where is he?" the sweaty Barannus pleaded, breaking the old man's concentration.

"'Where is he'," Volinex parroted mockingly. "Did ya' listen to what I said? Did you read the letter, Barannus? Does it sound like *anybody* knows?"

"Aye, so... so then where *would* he go? Antinax?"

"South," the old man said at last.

The sarcasm wasn't lost on the young Lorrion, who quickly wiped beads of sweat from his forehead as Volinex snickered. "I just... I just want to know..." he muttered to himself.

"If you'd wanted to know the impossible then you should be in the seers' temples, not the halls of the Lorrio," Anti' snapped.

"How could no one have seen him—"

"Bah, maybe there's nothing to see?" Voli' challenged. "Who knows if he's even alive? He's bloody well not travelin' on the Som, so maybe animals got him? Bandits? Any one of 'em could have left him for the birds and we'd never know."

Barannus's droopy eyes fixed on Volinex. "You don't believe that."

"Oh, I don't?"

The chubby Nortic shook his head and looked away. "No."

"Well, who knows what he even looks like at this point if he is alive? His clothes, his hair—"

Barannus glared at Volinex. "He was a bloody skeleton at the hearing, is a walking corpse not obvious enough? *Someone* should have seen something."

"The man *spit* on the hand of death, I wouldn't put anything past him!"

"Aye," the heavyset Lorrion said sadly as he looked again to the floor, dirty tunic darkened further with sweat. "And what's to stop him from comin' after us?"

The six other eyes jumped to Barannus.

"Right?" he continued with quaking voice. "I mean we... we have to leave these halls eventually. If he paid those bowmen to set him free in the courtyard—"

"We don't know that's true."

"We don't know it's not, either!"

Volinex scoffed.

"You know I'm right, Voli'! If he paid them to do that, he could pay men to do most anything! O-our families, o-our children!"

"Do you always flatter yourself like this? Half the bloody Empire's looking for him, you think he doesn't have better things to do than worry about *your* family?" Volinex scolded.

"You don't have a son or daughter like I do! If you did, you—"

"Quiet, both of you!" Antinax growled, finally having heard enough. "You'd make Stygus beg for peace with your bickering! The other scroll, young one—by the gods, what does it say!"

Volinex glared at the old man, who knew how much he despised the "young" moniker, before snapping the seal off the second scroll. The paper unraveled to his waist.

"Gods above," he quietly muttered, face fading from anger to shock.

Barannus's head swiveled with alarm. "What? What does it say?"

"They've identified the—the runners, the archer that aided Castus's

288

escape…"

"Who are they?" Wollia suddenly demanded.

"Squires. They were… squires to ministers in the Arxun."

"But who?" Wollia said, almost yelling. "Which ministers, Voli'?"

"It doesn't bloody say! It just – it just says they were sons of Lowland Ruhls, sent north to serve ministers as squires."

"Which Ruhls? Which provinces?"

"It doesn't say, Wollia! Doesn't say the Ruhls were involved, anyway, just their children…"

Wollia closed her eyes and put hands to her face. "Well, if they weren't before, they certainly are now."

She turned to her older counterpart. "Anti', every day Castus lives, he's going to spread his venom south of the Clyves. Some in the Lowlands haven't even heard he was imprisoned yet, let alone sentenced to death! Can you imagine their reaction to hearing their squires have been killed?"

"Squires? The traitors?"

Wollia cocked her head at him. "Don't speak to me like I'm a fool. You know they won't see them as –"

The woman's shrills triggered waves of fury throughout his body, and his eyes finally shot to hers. "Won't what?" he seethed, waiting for an answer. "What, Wollia? What, Barannus? What, Volinex?"

No response.

"What then? Hm? Castus raises an army? Leads a rebellion? Hm? Is that what you're all crying over?"

"If we don't –"

"*Do you not recall why we've been meeting here all these months?*" Antinax demanded in a rage. "Was our goal to disgrace, to *execute* Castus of Cassitigon?"

Antinax let a pause linger. "*No*. It was to set. The War. *In motion*. And that is done now!" he said, slicing his hand through the air in front of him. "This Castus charade is of no matter in the greater picture, none at all! You're all so bloody consumed with the tree you missed the gods-forsaken forest, so step back and look at it, dammit!

"In days, maybe weeks, the only other person who could have ever challenged our sway over the Khorokh will either be slaughtered in Valogar or have paved the way for Glannox's invasion – kudos to young Kyrus for that! So with Valogar conquered, its slaves and jewels flowing into the Lowlands, who do you think will be foolish enough to lend an ear to a disgraced Lorrion?"

The jowls of the old man rippled with each sudden movement, his bulbous forehead glowing bright red. Foams of spit gathered at the corners of his mouth and he breathed deeply, his body-length tunic suddenly feeling sweltering. "Now," he continued. "Is this ideal? Of course not! But that, young men, is what makes a good Lorrion! When the hunter sees the deer that he wants, he keeps his eyes on it, stays fixed on it; he ignores the twenty beasts running alongside it, the distractions in his way."

He paused, before glaring at Wollia. "And you, my lady, have lived and preached that maxim better than any man I know. I'll assume this late hour clouds your judgment."

Antinax lingered on her for a moment, then looked again towards his younger colleagues. "See the beast you want, lads. See the forest. The Khorokh supports the war, the general Glannox can win it, *and* we control the Lorrio. Let's pray for Castus's capture, but pay it no further mind than that. It's a risk we can *manage*."

The group jumped as a thud slammed against the Norum's door.

Antinax turned with startled eyes in the noise's direction. He waited. They all did.

Pounding ensued.

"Bloody hell is this?" Voli' murmured, eyes transfixed. "At this hour?"

"*It's Castus... it's him...*" Barannus whispered, eyes wide and face drenched.

More pounding.

"*Antinax!*" a voice bellowed from behind the door.

The Nortics exchanged bewildered glances.

"*Antinax, show yourself, damn you!*"

"Who is it?" Volinex shouted back.

Silence for a few moments, then pounding again. "*Antinax!*"

"Very well, then," Anti' said as he struggled to his feet. "Let's be done with it."

"Antinax – Antinax don't you open that door!" Barannus pleaded.

"Anti', stop!" Wollia ordered.

But the old man never broke his hobble towards the door, all but Barannus trailing cautiously behind him.

With a grunt, he slid the bar lock out and swung the door open.

A bloodied body tumbled through the doorway, collapsing at the elder's feet with a groan. Anti' barely had a moment to look down before a finger was between his eyes.

"This is your only warning, Antinax. Keep your whore-born, flea-ridden spies at home, or by the gods they'll start coming back to you in *pieces!*"

The old man couldn't believe his eyes as they finally recognized the grizzled figure before him in the dim hall.

"*Jarax?*"

"If you have an ounce of sense in your being, I *beg* you not to test me," the Rubator said through gritted teeth, his shiny armor reflecting what little light there was, before turning to leave.

As the shock wore off, Anti' was suddenly swept up in his own rage.

"Who – who are – *do you know who I am?*"

Jarax stopped in his tracks, barely visible in the shadows now. "Do you know who *I* am?"

"Aye, the bloody walking dead! You exist as Rubator because we've *let* you exist! You answer to me –"

"I answer to the *Empire*, the gods only know who you answer to!"

"And who the hell do you think rules the Empire?"

"Khorokh Kyrus I."

"Aye, and his foremost duty is to *protect the Lorrio*, you insolent bastard, so I'll make sure he hears of this protection! He'll have lions feeding on you in the Arena by dawn!"

"So be it. I'd *welcome* death before I'd have my loyalty questioned by a man not brave enough to do so while looking me in the eye!"

Anti' scowled. "Are you so vain as to think *I* give a shit about your loyalty, Jarax? You really think *I'm* the one that ordered spies –"

"Then tell me that's not your man, Antinax," Jarax demanded with a point. "Tell me he doesn't act on *your* orders."

"Jarax, you –"

"Go ahead! Go ahead and lie, makes no difference to me."

The man at Anti's feet let out a wet gurgling sound, drawing the old man's attention for a moment. "You say you'd welcome death Jarax, well do yourself a favor and welcome it *now!*"

Jarax let out a gritty laugh. "All the Emperor need do is ask, Lorrion."

The Red briskly showed his back to Antinax, who stood infuriated in the doorway. "You have no idea what you're playing with here," he bellowed in helpless rage. "You're a boy in a man's game!"

"*Last warning, Antinax!*" a voice echoed from a man now unseen.

Chapter XXXI

"Some say it's camping on mountain tops; some say it's the swamps on a midwinter's eve. But for me, the quietest nights I've ever known are the ones that follow battle, when every living thing seems compelled to pay their respects in silence."

Memoirs of Khorokh Jatrius the Conqueror,
Written Y. 91 P.C. following final unification with the Upper Rokhlands

The Isthmus, Valogarian Gate, 21ˢᵗ Day of the Third Month, Y. 384 P.C.

It was late by the time Tyghus and his kordettes broke from their fireside dinner of grain and dried cheese. It had been a somber meal, the time between bites spent trading tales of the thirty-one men that died that day. The dead came mostly from Niko's kord, and it seemed he could recall the name and life of every one without pause, one of the qualities that endeared him to the same. Tyghus said little, the faces of the dead – the first men to die under his command – still fresh in his mind. Dealing with death was easier when he was a kordette, as the brothers he lost then were the burden of the Dyrator – or he could at least pretend they were.

The fog had dissipated to a fine mist, but it was enough to keep the moon's light at bay. Tyghus passed through the ranks of his slumbering soldiers en route to his mount, handtorch lighting his way. The piece of wood he tied Fidi' to was near enough to keep watch over the Rokhs manning the makeshift palisades along the Gateline's remnants. While Tyghus felt assured by now that the Valogarians would launch no reprisal that night, he wanted to be the first person the nightwatch turned to if they did; it was only right.

It was not the east that suddenly drew Tyghus's attention, however, but the west. He had just reached his beast when the corner of his eye caught a figure, torch in hand, mirroring his path. The General held up a handful of grain to the horse's mouth, feigning interest in his appetite as he rotated around to get a better vantage. If the person was at all concerned about Tyghus spotting him, his quickening pace surely hid it.

At twenty paces, Tyghus could see that he was not a soldier of the Sixth, instead wrapped tight in a dark blue cloak, with hair that dangled across his face down to his shoulders. The General's heart quickened as he grabbed his blade's hilt, knowing it was hidden from the man's view by the horse. He allowed himself a snicker as he considered the prospect – and lunacy – of an assassin carrying lit torch through the Bloody Brigade's camp. Nevertheless…

"General!" the figure called out to him by whisper.

Tyghus pretended to keep focus on the grazing horse. The man crept closer, less than ten steps away.

"Gener –"

In a flash the great Rokhish sword was bared and pointed at the shadowy man. "Aye?" he replied, stepping out ominously from behind his beast. "You lookin' to see the Depths, friend?"

The figure froze. *"I-I'm a messenger!"* the flustered man whispered back.

The General looked to see if the nightwatchmen some twenty yards behind him were alert to the confrontation, but saw no sign that they were. Sword still pointed, he crept towards the man with caution. Reflexively, the man put his hands up in submission, causing the torch to light only his hair and the top of his face. But as he did, the man's cloak pulled away at the middle, revealing the Imperial teardrop emblem.

Tyghus stopped, his face a confused grimace. "The Empire's mark – where'd you travel from?"

"Avergon, General," the man said with a deep swallow. "I brought you a... I carry a... I brought you a message – a message from –"

"Stop," Tyghus ordered as the man reached his free hand into the folds of his cloak.

"Aye, of course... forgive me," he replied, pulling his hand back.

Tyghus licked his lips, again shooting a glance behind him to the nightwatch. "What's your name?"

"Seldonius."

"A Ruhl's name. So why are you sneaking around on friendly grounds, Seldonius?"

"So as not to alarm the camp!" he whispered strenuously.

The General considered the response for a moment. "Alarm them to what?"

Now it was Seldonius who looked behind him for listening ears. Locking eyes on Tyghus again, he whispered, *"my lord, the Desert tribes have risen."*

Tyghus finally let his swordhand drop as a scowl overtook his face. "You come all the way from Avergon to tell me about something a militia of boys could handle? Have the Eighth take care of 'em; better yet, send the cadets."

"My lord –"

"I jest, but truthfully, it's never taken more than a kord to scatter the tribes, be it Baralesh or Corulesh."

"It-it's not them, my lord," Seldonius said, letting his hands fall as well. The torch revealed a young face stung by fear.

Tyghus glanced down at the fold where the messenger had reached earlier. "No?"

Seldonius shook his head. "It's the Terelesh... the Terelesh of the lower Skulls."

The words struck the General like a thunderclap. Like most Rokhs, he'd heard only rumors about the Tereleshi tribe, the legends of their viciousness and cruelty that served to haunt young tobbies' dreams. Their years-long campaigns of terror would end as suddenly as they began, lying dormant as a volcano. Given that they had not been seen since Khorokh Glabulux fell victim to their hammers more than a century ago, many Rokhs were happy to declare their extinction, to the extent that Rokhish settlements in Starrea Province had pushed the Empire's border to meet the lower Skulls Desert. But Tyghus had seen the Terelesh name raised with their northern desert cousins, and be it a Baralesh or Corulesh tribesman, their eyes would widen and curse the name. They would swear the Terelesh were alive and well, that an uprising was never far off, and drop to their knees to pray that it not be so, for the Terelesh never dealt in coin – only in blood.

The General took a moment to gather himself, before sheathing his sword and resting his left hand on the side of his mount. He sighed. "It's been generations since there's been any sign of the Terelesh, what evidence do we have of this?"

"Well… they've attacked. They've struck across the border, sacking farms, looting homes. Latest word is they've pushed east to wipe out entire villages…"

Tyghus blanched. "Entire?"

"Rumor's that even Holliton's been put to the torch… every man, woman, and child, my lord, all taken in the same manner – hammer blows to the head. Many bodies have none left to speak of… it's horrible, the things we're hearing."

Such attacks were consistent with their gruesome legacy: their weapons of choice were said to be massive warhammers, the kind that would obliterate man, shield, and armor alike when they found their mark – to say nothing of defenseless villagers.

"How many deep are they?"

"No one's gotten a fair count on them yet; they've only attacked by night and the numbers we have are from those that fled. But they're saying their numbers are in thousands…"

Tyghus grimly shook his head. "Who sent you, Seldonius?"

The man looked to the fold in his cloak again. "May I?" The General nodded, and the man pulled a sealed scroll for his review. "From Quartermaster Bostonos…"

The seal was indeed from the acting curator of the fort, unbroken since its departure. Just below it, he saw the word "Fish" scribbled onto the parchment and he couldn't hide a smirk as he pondered how the Lakeman, a man seeking to evade conflict the rest of his days, arrived at yet another; it also made him realize just how much he missed his friend's counsel. His eyes jumped back to the messenger. "He sent you all this way?"

Seldonius nodded quickly. "I'm the fastest rider in Avergon," he said with a bit of pride. "Well, fastest one not on campaign, anyway."

Tyghus studied his youthful face for a moment. "You look so young to be in the reserves – where've you seen combat?"

The man looked to the ground. "Not in the reserves, sire. I'm sixteen – I'm in my final year of the Academy there."

Tyghus's brows peaked. "Bostonos sent a bloody *cadet* with this message?" he asked incredulously.

The messenger looked awkwardly to either side of the General, before offering, "Aye, but I'm... I'm quite fast."

"Aye, I reckon so!" Tyghus said with an exasperated laugh. "And quite crafty too, being able to place me without alarming my men."

Seldonius seemed to exhale. "In truth, Bostonos wanted all veteran soldiers on hand for the attack."

The General's momentary smile disappeared. "He thinks it imminent?"

"Every town that the Terelesh have burned has been closer and closer to Avergon. The entire fort's in a panic with the Ninth guarding the Brafford Bridge against Colvery and only few thousand reserves manning Avergon's ramparts... it's scary..."

Tyghus closed his eyes as his head fell into cupped hand. His fingers rubbed his temples as he bit down hard on his bottom lip. "Can you write something to bring back, Seldonius?"

"Aye, got some parchment and coal right here."

"That'll do – take down these instructions."

The cadet set his torch down to kneel and unfurl a blank piece of parchment across his leg.

"First, notify the Ninth on stand-by to withdraw a kord or two from the the Brafford. I'll leave the amount to Adulus's discretion, it's his dyron, and he's the one staring 'cross the bridge into Colvery. Second, do the same with the Eighth in the Converge – until this threat is put down, the bridge's reconstruction can wait. But I've heard that Glannox is trying to requisition any spare troops from the Eighth for his own army, so that raises the most important step – send swift riders to Glannox's army *immediately*. Glannox should be en route to the Splintered Shoals as we speak lugging a baggage train for fifty thousand troops, so he shouldn't be difficult to spot. My words and Bostonos's seal should be enough to get Avergon the reinforcements it needs."

The General opened his eyes and lifted his head. "Understood, cadet?"

Seldonius nodded as he finished frantic scribbling, then held it up to Tyghus. "Anything further, my lord?"

After thinking for a moment, he wrote on the rolled scroll, '*There is an important line between courage and foolishness – one can quickly become the other.*' "Tell the Quartermaster to say this to his 'fish'..."

The cadet mumbled it to himself in confusion. "I don't under—"

"He'll understand, I promise," Tyghus said. "Fastest in Avergon, you say?"

Seldonius looked to him confidently. "I am, General."

"Well, if Bostonos trusts you, I do as well. Now listen to me: tomorrow we march onto the Peninsula, swinging south along the southern highlands towards the port city of Bakia. We'll be difficult to find, but –" Tyghus sighed audibly. "- but you *have* to. I *must* be kept informed of what's going on in Avergon, and bloody hell, tell Bostonos I want more than one messenger next time to ensure I get the message. Always assume I did *not* unless you hear otherwise."

The young man nodded. "Understood, General – it's been an honor meeting you."

Tyghus gave a weak smile. "Honor's mine, you're very brave."

Seldonius placed his right fist over his heart then turned to leave. He paused after a step though, and looked back at the General. "Any thoughts on why they'd rise now, sire?"

Tyghus had turned to face his horse when he heard the question, but it was one that was already on his mind. Recollections of past meetings – hints from his sister on the Isthmus just weeks ago, from the Lij Andran himself some further months back – were all he could think of. He shook his head as the conversations unfortunately began to make sense, but Tyghus chose not to share his revelations with the cadet. Seldonius had enough concerns to worry about.

"Because barbarians are prone to sense weakness where there's none," he said at last, before looking back to meet the young man's eyes. "It's an Empire's burden to correct those mistakes."

The response perplexed Seldonius, but after a short smile and nod, he dutifully turned to weave his way back through the camp. The lingering mist soon swallowed him up, leaving Tyghus to himself. He dropped to the ground and leaned against the post to which his horse was tethered, but the moment his eyes closed, images of burning Starrean villages were all he could see. He could hear the the licking of the flames, the screams of the people... the screams of Miko –

He shuddered, feeling more helpless than he had in some time.

He thought sleep would never come, but it did, just as it had all the other nights he felt the same. His last thought was one of hope. *"Gods, if you hear me... protect that fort... protect those within it,"* he whispered distantly. *"For   I   cannot...   not   yet."*

Chapter XXXII

The only thing predictable about man is that he continues to fancy man predictable.

Rokh Proverb

Dray'gon Rokh, Celacio Hallokh, 1ˢᵗ Day of the Fourth Month, Y. 384 P.C.

The *Celacio Hallokh* was virtually deserted by twilight, even if the torches' glow between its pillars suggested otherwise. The high-ceilinged temple was the Arxun's northernmost structure, a setting where Imperial ministers and bureaucrats could gather under the pretenses of worship to discuss issues of the day. What began in 25 P.C. as a single-halled tribute to Bregnomen, god of stone and mountains and patron of Dray'gon Rokh, was now a massive network of connected halls, each one paying homage to another Rokhish god. The complex had grown so expansive that it was better known throughout the Arxun as the "Labyrinth".

In honor of the simple majesty of Bregnomen's room, all future halls mirrored the same dimensions and layout. That is to say, each walked two hundred steps long by ninety wide, lined all around with soaring columns. Impressive as the columns were, it was the raised pools of water in the middle of the great rooms that resonated most with their visitors, each half the size as the hall itself with a man-sized idol of its god standing in the center. Soft cushions lined the pool's perimeter, where the faithful could kneel in reverence or light floating prayer candles, all in hopes the god would hear them.

Two clandestine Rokhs were not put off by the day's dwindling light and empty halls; indeed, it was the latter that brought them there in the first place. The cloaked figures skirted silently through one vast hall after another, constantly looking to either side of them for pursuers unseen but imagined all the same.

"Do we really need travel to the *bowels* of the Labyrinth?" a weary feminine voice called. "It's —"

"*Shh*," came a man's stern reply.

On the pair marched, two more halls in, until finally, the man halted. "Here."

The woman looked to the nude female statue keeping silent watch over the water around her. Carved from priceless white marble, her right hand reached to the sky, while her left was frozen in a pardoning motion at her waist. Flowing hair covered demure breasts while legs crossed below the knees. Her posture half-faced and half turned away from those who looked her in the eyes.

"Verina? Feeling you like you're in need of mercy, Anti'?"

"No," he lied stubbornly. "I just wanted a quiet hall, I told you that from the beginning. Away from prying eyes."

"Could have had that three or four halls back," Wollia said with annoyance. "Even Bregnomen's if you'd wished, you know the Rubitio aren't allowed in the Hallokh."

"Aye, well we're here now, aren't we?" Anti' chafed, before eyeing the statue. "And maybe begging her mercy isn't the worst thing, if I'm being honest."

The old man hobbled towards the pool's lip, Wollia lending an arm to ease him onto the kneelers. A tall skinny torch stood to his left, which he used to spark one of the candle balls; with a hiss, it took light, and he floated it in the still waters towards the figure. The bobbing flame sent shadows dancing about the dim room. Antinax exhaled deeply as he rested his elbows at the water's edge.

"It's a start," he said drily.

Wollia knelt down in the same position next to him, her hood masking all but a few lonely strands of hair. "It's absurd, all this running around we're doing."

"Like thieves, don't I know it."

Wollia shook her head. "We're Ruhls – Lorrian Ruhls, no less. If my father'd seen me reduced to this... or my mother? I can only imag – "

The echoing footsteps of temple druids in a nearby hall gave them both a moment's pause, until it was clear they had only come to tend the Hall's torches. It was a vigil they were sworn to continue for all hours of the day and night. The steps quickly faded away.

"Do you remember the day we heard about Torrus's massacre, Wollia? Your husband was still with us, wasn't he?"

She nodded. "We were at the investiture of one of the Inquisitors. Perdinces, I think."

The old man scowled as he reminisced. "I see it every day still, that scrawny little messenger, breath reeking like fish. His eyes terrified and mine too probably; the news made me want to vomit then, no less than it does now."

"I remember. Potrilus was never the same after that, knowing his brother'd been taken. I'd find him weeping all hours of the night."

"He was a good man, your husband; too good of a man to be reduced to that," Anti' said angrily. "So terrible, that day. Such a complete rebuke of any idea of co-existence with those animals; it was the moment that should have given us all the justification we needed to crush them once and for all – how could it not? Surely, Onzy would see that. Surely, he'd give us the vote to force Rynsyus's hand. But nothing. For reasons only the gods know, he sided with the great peace king, that sorry, pathetic man that he is... that he was."

Antinax shook his head. "Twenty years we had to watch that fool try to cut deals with a nest of vipers. Twenty gods-forsaken years –"

"Don't speak down on the gods here," Wollia warned. "Needn't any more misfortune."

"Aye, you're right, you're right," the old man said with a deferential nod towards Verina. "I'm not sure if you need to be careful, but certainly I do; I must have done something to offend them. Just as Rynsyus's gone from the throne, just as I think my life's work is about to rewarded when Kyrus was seated –" Anti' paused, eyes almost misting as his head gave yet another disbelieving shake. "I fall into a feud with the bloody Rubator – the *Rubator!* His cretins everywhere, in the shadows, in the daylight; they follow every move I make, tracking me like I was a buck. All over a suspicion the Khorokh sensed that I never did. In Jarax's twenty-something years here, I'd never had cross words with him! The bloody poets couldn't have written something so comical."

Wollia offered no response as he stared pleadingly at the statue, almost waiting for her to give him the answer his intuition had not. After a quiet spell, he asked in a near-whisper, "what to do?"

"Call them off," Wollia answered with uncharacteristic urgency.

"What?"

"Call *off* your spies."

The old man looked to her. "I don't send them out on my behalf, you know that," he hissed.

"That doesn't matter, this *has* to end. You must make peace with him; call them off then kiss his feet if you have to, but *end it*."

Anti's hands parted helplessly in front of him. "I don't need you to tell me the obvious –"

"Apparently I do, because like you said, we still see his men at every turn. It's a matter of time 'til they run into yours, and what then? It'll be out and out war within the Arxun."

Anti's face burned with frustration. "Wollia, I *know*. But to get this peace of yours, I'd have to directly disobey Kyrus."

"Then talk to *him*. Tell Kyrus of your concerns."

"Talks that Jarax would probably know of before they'd even finished, how's that supposed to mend things?"

"You think *he* hasn't already spoken to the Khorokh about *you*? He wouldn't have confronted you like that otherwise, not a chance! The longer you wait to talk with Kyrus, the more you cede the advantage to Jarax, there's simply no way around it."

"I don't want him focusing on this nonsense with Castus still at large and war preparations so freshly underway," Antinax frowned deeper as his mind combed through his options. "I want him to–"

"I think we need to quit thinking of this in terms of wanting him to do anything, Antinax!" she said sharply. "It's a myth, a tragic, tragic myth that he's in *any* of our control!"

"It's not a –"

"It is! Every action we've 'wanted' or 'directed' Kyrus to take has led him to take two more that we did not."

"Well, we knew he was a mad man when he took the throne, did we not?" the old Nortic replied defensively. "The loon doesn't even don the robes of a Khorokh, by the gods. But you can't deny we've pushed him in the main direction we wished him to go, that's a – that's a success!"

"He's locking up every Rokh in the Arxun with ties below the Clyves. If the worst of what our sources tell us is to be believed, they're being tortured until he gets the answers he wants! Meanwhile, every Lowland town is crawling with Rubitian spies seeking 'disloyalty', you call all that success? He sees traitors everywhere, and this pleases you?"

"Of course it doesn't please me, but it's a passing mood, you'll see. And frankly, it's an understandable one given Castus's scheming; I'm not sure what Sudos to trust either after what he managed to pull off," he snorted.

"The reason we're here right now is because Sudos aren't the only ones being tracked by Reds," she said as she whipped her head towards Antinax.

Antinax blanched. "Jarax does that of his own accord, not at Kyrus's request..." he said uncertainly.

"Not yet. You think you can't be the next man to fall out of favor? And myself along with you?"

The old man wouldn't meet her look. "Nonsense – he's taken to our views, he wouldn't -"

"Would you have said he wouldn't try to *execute* a Lorrion? Would you have said that he wouldn't have wanted to spy on the leader of his personal guard? You don't know what he'd do! He's a wild boar yet you still refer to him like a faithful hound!"

Her near yell forced Anti' to face her with a glare. *"Quiet your tongue,"* he growled in a whisper.

But her position was undeterred. "Talk to Kyrus."

"A moment ago you argued for peace with Jarax, now you argue that I come out against him?"

"No, a moment ago I presented you with one solution to this mess. Now, I'm giving you another. That's two. I don't care which you choose."

She had served on the Lorrio for more than thirty years with him, and it was moments like this that made Antinax cherish every year. Her raw, practical, sometimes brutal persistence was a trait he'd come to respect. Sometimes she was ostensibly aloof, other times she took the form she had tonight, but whichever it may be, Antinax understood how she became so powerful in Nortic circles.

The pair sat in silence for a spell, both of them fixing their gazes on the flickering candle that had come to rest against the side of the statue's leg. The old man was deeply uneasy about squaring off against the Rubator, and as he envisioned the conversation with Kyrus to come, he became increasingly pessimistic. "Merely complaining about the spies won't move Kyrus so long as Jarax keeps rounding up his enemies. He's too vital."

"So what would?" Wollia asked simply.

The Nortic man was quiet as he pondered her question.

"What ultimately sent Castus to the dungeons?" she continued, her hood covering all but one eye. "It was our words."

Antinax turned towards her slowly.

"He asked you to find evidence of Jarax's infidelity," she said, before leaning in closer the man. "So tell him you *found* it."

"Aye, but we *had* proof of Castus's treachery; the whole bloody city knew," he said, recoiling at first. "We'd have *only* our word against Jarax."

But as the words left his mouth, he realized Jarax's removal was the only solution, and only if he reinforced Kyrus's suspicions could that be accomplished. His thoughts must have betrayed him, as Wollia offered no reply; instead, she casually turned her eyes back towards the statue.

"You realize if I fail to convince him of this... if Kyrus doesn't believe me... our lives will be fair game. I'd put nothing past Jarax's vengeance, in this life or the next. You understand this, right?"

The woman merely shrugged. "Given the way he's reacted thus far, I'd say our lives are fair game already, but so be it. I've private mercenaries, you've private mercenaries. They may not be Reds, but they're enough to make a show of it. If he wants a war, then we'll have a war; any attempt on our lives will only force Kyrus to act that much faster."

Antinax was only half-sold on her logic, but he said nothing. Instead, he added, "well, if it does come to the sword, hopefully Jarax will take Barannus first. Any more of his bleating and I'll be in the grave."

A loud laugh escaped Wollia's mouth, and she quickly drew a hand to the same. Looking to him, she said, "you're awful." Her eyes met his as she stared back with a crooked smile. "All these years, Anti'. Where would we be if not wedded by circumstance?"

He turned away from her. "Happy?"

She replied with a playful giggle, and their eyes fell again on the bobbing ball of wax in the pool. "May merciful Verina answer your prayer."

He nodded. "Aye. Though it's the god of fortune I need now."

Chapter XXXIII

"… And when he saw the first sword drawn,
he knew that Glory beckoned."

Quote from the <u>Early Wars</u> by Belogus

Southern Valogar, 4th Day of the Fourth Month, Y. 384 P.C.

From atop the high plateau, Tyghus scanned the northern vista for signs of the scouts he set loose upon the Valogarian countryside two weeks prior. Though a light mist hung over the General and his troops, it was sparse enough to see for miles in all directions, from lush green valleys in the northeast to the roiling Ferlen Sea to the southwest. He'd grown as anxious about the scouts' well-being as he had about the army that surrounded him, especially after seeing the fates of those he lost on the Isthmus.

"Should have been back by now..." he muttered again to himself, oblivious to Fygonus riding next to him.

"You keep lookin' for them and they'll never show," the Twin said.

"Well, not looking hasn't done me much good either, so where's that leave us?"

The Sixth Dyron had beaten a steady path along the highlands that ringed the Peninsula's coast, one column after another marching in a line that stretched a thousand feet. Even if the men didn't complain, there was no denying it was a tough route to Bakia, especially lugging the war machines up the inclines. It was one that could have been made in half the time had he taken a direct line to the port city, but with mirami presumed to be on the prowl and no scouts to warn of their whereabouts, Tyghus had been forced to the coastal high ground.

Terrain notwithstanding, these were Chibin hills overlooking Chibin valleys filled with Chibin supporters. It was the most volatile region in the country, one that had been restive since the days of the First Conquest. Even in the most peaceful of times, Rokhish influence waned the farther away one moved from Nar-Biluk, so the Purebloods' passion caught on quickly in the southern and eastern highlands. It was no secret that many had chosen to pay nominal homage to Andran while aiding the Chibin so as not to arouse the Lij's suspicion or that of his Imperial overlords.

It was unsettling, then, that Tyghus had seen neither Chibin nor mirami traces throughout their travels thus far. For almost two weeks they'd marched and camped, but while grazing wild lekeys stared curiously at the column and massive sea condors circled high overhead, there'd been no other sign of life. He suspected they fled ahead of the troops' advance, but if they did, they left no tracks to follow. Nor did his view of the valleys provide any answers, only abandoned "mushroom field" hamlets scattered throughout.

He shook his head. "And what of the mirami, anyway? Did they bloody rise or not?"

"They better have," Fygonus replied gruffly, face frowning. "I don't want to have spent two weeks smelling this shitty, salty air for nothin'."

Tyghus laughed. "It is awful, isn't it?"

305

"It's no wonder they're all so angry."

"Aye, I'd say you're right," Tyghus said with a grin, looking northwards again. "But I don't doubt they're seeing us —"

"Gods above!" Fygo' suddenly exclaimed, hand shooting to his right towards the Ferlen Sea below. "We bloody arrived!"

Tyghus's eyes followed the twin's, finding a brownish strip of earth jutting into the water that ran parallel to the southern coast — a sure sign of Bakia's approach. The breakwater known as the "Horn" extended five-hundred yards from the city's harbor, and was famed for taming the Ferlen's violent tides. The result was a nearly pristine harbor — the only such kind that Valogar was known to possess — which let trading ships safely offload their wares at port.

"Indeed we have," the General responded, slipping off Fidi'.

Fygo' cheerfully whacked Tyghus in the shoulder. "Who needs those miserable scouts, eh?"

But Tyghus was already anxiously looking at the bluff's edge up ahead. "Halt the men, then join me. Let's see what view of the city we can get — see what they have in store for us."

Fygonus nodded, then flung his arms out over head in the shape of an "X"; within seconds, the troops behind him ceased marching and imitated his motion. Like a river suddenly frozen in place, each successive kord halted where they stood.

"Quiet, now," Tyghus cautioned, creeping forward in a tight crouch towards the edge before dropping onto his belly. The General's heart pounded as he peered down, only to be stunned at the view — the ridge gave him such a complete picture of the grounds that he was appalled it was undefended.

The southern coast ran almost due east, with only a slight southerly hint. From the plateau's edge on which he lay, the terrain took a sharp eastward descent towards the outskirts of the town some four hundred yards below, where it flattened out around a semi-circular "notch" carved into the coastline. The side of the notch farthest from him jutted a hundred yards farther south into the sea than the side nearest him; from the former, the Bakian breakwater took root at nearly a right angle to the harbor bank. The rest of the notch was lined with piers, protruding out of the semicircle like teeth to a mouth. Fishermen milled about dragging nets of their catches from the simple, single-masted boats bobbing gently in the peaceful waters — a sight that made the General's spirits soar.

"Not a Colverian ship in sight, my friend," he said as he looked to Fygonus laying at his side.

Fygonus scanned the docks and nodded. "Think the gods let us beat 'em to port?"

"Would it upend things if I said they did?" Tyghus said, smiling briefly before considering otherwise. "Suppose they could have gotten here weeks ago... *someone* had to give Colverian bows to those men at the Gates."

The kordette looked away for a second, before offering, "I hope they're here. For my father's sake alone; you never heard a man curse Colvery like he did."

"Shame our paris never met then, they'd have had that in common, I'm told."

The General's eyes scanned over the town of thirty thousand Natives, seeing its "mushroom" homes radiate away from the harbor banks like rings to a tree. Meandering dirt roads connected the homes with each other and the docks, while large pylons of wood bundled together to form conical storage shelters. At the far northeastern edge of the town, where the terrain began inclining again, a path led to a large stone planted into the ground. A small wooden wall surrounded it, and Tyghus quickly recognized it as a far less majestic version of Nar-Biluk's great white stone, the Tayshihan.

Tyghus marveled at the thousands of villagers going about their daily business. "Can you believe this? War's afoot, yet they're coming and going without a care. I was sure we'd been watched all this way, but..."

"Aye, they'd *have* to have seen us, no?"

"I don't know... I don't understand this, if so – they're no fools to Bakia's importance."

His friend shook his head uncertainly. "It *was* a barren march..."

"They haven't even a wall to protect them, though it looks to be old men, women, and children anyway – I don't see any mirami. Not mustered, at least."

"Stupid, stupid bastards," Fygonus said with shaking head, before looking to Tyghus with an insatiable grin. "Think the town's ripe for the taking."

"Waiting to see otherwise, but I reckon so."

"Ha!" the irrepressible Twin laughed excitedly. "Aye, so how're we going about it? We'd have to mind ourselves charging down this slope, but the docks would be ours in minutes if we did."

Tyghus's eyes swept over the descent below them. "Aye. We could line up Napodonax's catapults along the ridge as well, cover any surprises for us."

"From these heights he could make the thunder gods jealous! Town would be dust."

"We'll try to avoid that and keep this clean – clean as we can," Tyghus said, feeling almost sorry for the defenseless folks below. "I want the bulk of our kords down this slope while the rest and the horse sweep north and east to cover the other approaches to the town. Once any resistance is dealt with, we need to knock out the docks and breakwater. You won't find a Colverian ship within a hundred miles of Bakia after that."

"The Ferlen will be a nightmare without them."

As the pair observed the town in silence for a few moments, Tyghus felt an excitement in his stomach start to well, when a maddeningly familiar worry invaded his thoughts without warning; it was yet another burden that he alone had carried among the Sixth – Avergon. He closed his eyes and tilted his head to the ground, blades of grass stroking his chin. *Nothing you can do, Tyghus,* he thought. *What will happen there will happen there... surely Glannox has some men to spare. Surely, the tribes will fall back after seeing the fortress's troops. Surely Miko'... you just win here first, then worry about –*

"You alright?"

The General's head flipped up. "Aye... aye, just taking a quick prayer."

Tyghus felt the kordette linger on him for a moment, aware that his friend knew he was not one given to the gods. "Tyghus sayin' a prayer? What's that Native of yours done to you? Where's the –"

"Quiet, you ass," Tyghus said with a relieved smile, his eyes falling back upon the breakwater.

"Oh..." Fygonus suddenly muttered.

Tyghus barely heard his kordette. "See the angle of those waves crashing there? Looks like if we knock out that breakwater stone that meets the shoreline, the harbor should flood. Not the same as destroying the whole thing, but we don't have the time or means for that; besides, coupled with the ruined docks, no ship's offloading there."

"*Shit, Tyghus!*" Fygonus exclaimed now. The soldiers around them now gasped as well.

The General's brows furrowed as he looked up. "What –"

"*Look! A hundred yards north – northwest of the town!*"

Tyghus arched up to look over the hulking body of his kordette, eyes widening at the sight.

Mirami.

"Think our plan needs to change..."

"Aye," Tyghus breathed, mouth agape. "Looks like we caught them on the move."

A teeming mass of Valogarian warriors mustered in the valley, and even from his distance, he could see the militias were a diverse lot: spearmen mixed with archers, stone throwers, and *silotys* – men brandishing fifteen foot wooden poles from plants of the same name, whose shafts were lined with vicious spines. None of the men were clad above the waist, though many faces and chests were lined with dyes of white and green, a sporadic number donning crowns made of branches extending well above their heads.

"I'm seeing nine or ten bands of mirami based on the warpaint," Tyghus said distantly, eyes transfixed. "How many you think?"

"A good twenty thousand at least..."

"Aye… I'd guess twenty-five… good odds on this venture."

"It is good odds… and I'm not seein' a Colverian or horseman among them either."

Tyghus nodded. "I wonder if there's a Lij? We'll have to find out when we get there…"

Fygo' grinned. "So we're not gonna flee?"

"Not gonna flee, my friend… though I'd love to know where this lot's headed, that'll have to wait 'til afterwards…"

The Twin gripped his shoulder tight. "We very well may win this damn war today, you realize that? We could be in poems by the time the year's out!"

Visions of a swift surrender were too enticing to indulge, so Tyghus forced himself to lose his smile and rapped the Fygo's forehead. "Win first, brute. We'll worry about the rest later."

"You show me a Native foolish enough to rally to the Lij after we leave ten mirami dead on the field. Show me and I'll name you my heir when this is over."

"You despise me that much?" Tyghus joked. "But just win – and don't lose your bloody wits in the process."

The twin looked at him with a more serious focus. "Steel – before, during, and –"

"After," Tyghus finished, as he edged back from the ridge before leaping to his feet. "Ready your men, standard formation."

"Aye, General."

Tyghus adjusted his mail as he strode back towards his army.

"It's time for battle."

* * *

"Sixth Dyron, advance!"

The Imperial wave swept down the plateau's gentle northern slope. Tyghus rode at the back of the three lines, trailing the one led by Pydonus and Siderius. Ahead of them were the front-line kords of Grantax, the Twins, and Niko'; Golaxus, Swiftus, Noccus, and Kinistus the second, while a central pathway cut through them all the way to the fore. Behind him, Napodonax readied his war machines on the plateau's edge in the event they were needed, while to his left, Reverus swung out wide with his cavalry, the perfectly synchronized movements of thousands of riders never ceasing to amaze him.

The soldiers were stripped of their billowing cloaks and marched clad almost head to toe in steel under ashen tunics. Silver helmets, poked with two small eyeholes, protected their heads while shimmering chain mail shirts draped down their arms and a foot past their waist. Trousers

309

ensconced their thighs, meeting greaves that covered the length of their shins. Their black tear-drop Bull-shields hid the left sides of their bodies, while swords drawn on their right waited menacingly. They were a moving wall of metal.

The Valogarian mass stood four hundred yards off, undoubtedly aware of the Bulls by now. That they initially froze as Rokhish troops closed the gap further convinced Tyghus there was little central leadership, and that these miramis had just recently come together. Nevertheless, he knew the window to take advantage was one that wouldn't remain open for long, and he wasn't going to miss it.

Three hundred yards, he observed of his front line, his men keeping a steady, silent pace. Reverus's horsemen had run even with the Natives, albeit several hundred yards off to their right. They soon would be angling east to threaten the mirami's rear, a maneuver Tyghus had seen practiced hundreds of times at the Academy.

The General scanned his infantry kordettes, their statuses obvious from the vibrant feather plumes sprouting from their helmets. Per custom, they had doffed their horses back on the plateau to march alongside their men, for they were to set the bar for their unit's bravery. It was no coincidence kordettes were often replaced.

Native shouts reached the Rokhs, but Tyghus swore he heard a tinge of panic. He smiled to himself.

Twenty more paces and the Valogarians finally fanned out, forming a line that soon stretched beyond his view and overlapped his own lines by hundreds of feet in either direction.

"Very well, then," he muttered, pulse starting to quicken.

Two hundred —

Arrows suddenly arced over the Native lines, coupled with a pellet barrage from swift-appearing slingers.

Tyghus fought his body's reflex to crouch close against the reins. *C'mon boys… hold formation.*

The haunting whistles of the Valogarian Gate returned, this time accompanied by a percussion of stones hitting armor and shields. The front line shuttered as the first bolts and bullets struck home. Even with the kords' middle rows holding shields overhead to protect the men in front of them, cries of the stricken inevitably came. Rokhs collapsed sporadically along the line, bolts strong enough to split mail, pellets fast enough to split helmets – but still they marched on.

"Alright men," Tyghus yelled. "At fifty yards the forward lines charge!"

"Charge at fifty!" eight kordettes bellowed back in succession over the stones' whizzing din.

He looked down to Siderius and Pydonus manning the reserve kords. "The two of you – march cautious and *eye those wings!"* he said, pointing to the overlapping edges of the Valogarian line. "The moment *they* move —"

"We move," Pydonus finished.

Tyghus nodded. Looking straight ahead, he let out a long exhale.

One hundred yards.

Alright, Tyghus, steady now.

His blood flooded with a rush he hadn't felt before, not in the Skulls, not on the Dead Plains.

Everything slowed down, every sense magnified.

Air was damp, smelled of mulch…

Sword and shield weighed perfectly in his hands…

His beast's heaving body warmed armored legs…

His eyes traced the Native's front line, catching every detail of the painted brood: chests and faces of blue, green, or white; two-foot high crowns of thorny branches; spearmen and silotys with weapons longer than the men themselves.

And though he knew he was a prime target within range of their bowmen and slingers, he simply felt invincible.

His teeth gritted.

Gods protect the Sixth… Tygha… Aver —

Suddenly the front line's swordhands went up in unison.

"Cha-r-r-r-r-r-r-r-r-ge!"

Arrows whistled and stones screamed as his front two lines broke into a sprint. Swords pointed straight ahead, each soldier moving in rhythm with his brothers around him.

Now.

Tyghus kipped his horse about the haunches and in seconds was off on a full-length sprint of his own, straight up the central path between the kords. At full speed he'd hit the Natives at the same time as the front line.

He knew it was risky; knew he hadn't attempted such a move outside Avergon's training grounds. Yet…

Native slingers fled behind their lines, the rest bracing with weapons raised, eyes wide, voices howling.

Tyghus picked his target…

And like a hammer upon anvil, Rokhs met Valogarians with a deafening crash. Native spears snapped against shields, while others shot right through. Silotys' hideous spikes came smashing down on Rokh limbs and armor, but most were hurled back without time to strike. Natives barely had room to die in place from the press.

Fear of Tyghus's massive stallion cut a divot in enemy lines without landing a blow, a breach the General immediately seized upon. On his right, his sword swept down in hypnotic succession — left, right, forward and back — Fidipodus wheeling and kicking as if one with his rider; on his left, his sharp and weighty black shield pounded bare Valogarian arms and

311

skulls. Heads rolled, limbs gashed, and bones broke as his weapons did their dances of death.

Beyond his divot, the Fyrid twins at the center of their kords used an unteachable tactic – bullrush those in front of them as if the charge never stopped.

"*Push goddamn you!*" Fyrustus roared over the raging fray.

The brothers' furious thrust shirked swordwork in favor of brute strength behind their shields, but it sent their enemies reeling just the same. Many off-kilter Valogarians were simply trampled underneath the Imperial charge, others left their chests exposed for stabbing with arms aflail. The second it appeared the Valogarians finally regained footing, the Twins' kords dropped back in good order, allowing the Swiftus-Noccus line to storm through with a fresh rush of their own. Only moments into the fray, the Native center was giving precious ground.

The space around Tyghus was littered with Valogarian dead and wounded, though he had little time to admire his work. Looking to his right, he saw Nikolux far down the line giving a ghastly display of stabbing and slashing, showering the battling lines with blood – but beyond that he could see the left edge of the Valogarian line curving inward like a fishhook, wrapping around the veteran's kord.

Dammit Pydonus get out on those –

He saw the stone a split-second before it struck his helmet.

His head rocked back, and no matter how many times he blinked, the world appeared yellow all around him.

A roar erupted from the Valogarian lines as the General staggered. Their war cries began anew, and the divot soon collapsed as they regained their nerve.

"*Protect the Dyrator!*"

Tyghus barely heard his men cry out over the deafening Natives.

Stones showered all around, and suddenly enemy hands were all over him – shield, mail, greaves – clutching, clawing at the General to bring him down. Fidi' whinnied as Native clubs and spears clanged off his armor, probing for a weak spot, and with a mad panic, reared back on hind legs. Arms mobbed, Tyghus clenched the great beast's body with his thighs for dear life.

As the horse found ground again, the General's sight began to clear, and with one glimpse he realized his peril. Natives swarmed his horse on all sides, steps away only out of caution for the bucking stallion.

No… no, not here! Fight Tyghus – fight dammit!

With a surge of power, he jerked his shield free of grasping hands, before cascading a duo of blows with shield and sword upon Natives to his left. The face of a tall warrior, bathed in white dyes, stumbled back with a broken nose; his cohort spewed blood from cloven shoulder. He raised his sword hand up for an encore – but in an instant he wasn't alone on his beast.

He was eye-to-eye with a Valogarian's green-painted face, a deft individual who vaulted aboard the warhorse from his right. He was strong, too, immediately arresting the General's sword arm high into the air; with his right, the Native wrenched the Imperial's helmet from his head, clanging as it struck the ground below and drawing more roars from the armies.

The roars were magnitudes louder, the air fresher free of the stifling helmet, but seconds later a spear gashed him behind the ear, barely missing his head outright. Smaller slingshots welted Tyghus's neck as he struggled for leverage against a frenzied Native punching his face. Though the blows were without enough force to truly rattle him, they took their toll. At last, Tyghus found the shield's weight more burden than benefit, released its grip and swung his free fist into the Native's jaw, green dye smearing on his steely mitt. The Valogarian's grip loosened on his sword hand just enough to yank it free and drive into his temple; the Native slumped off the mount with a thud.

As Tyghus regained his bearings, he found the clawing fray around him had waned and the hail of rocks had stopped. In fact, he saw a sight that few things in war could rival.

The Fyrid twins had heard their kords' cries for the General and converged at once on the collapsing pocket. Imperial steel mauled the exposed Valogarian flesh, even as silotys punctured handfuls of Rokhs. The soldiers exploited the Natives' close combat weaknesses with long weapons, mercilessly smashing them back with their shields, only to bring sharp upward stabs with their swords. Soon, Valogarians were replaced by Rokhs around Tyghus.

Fyrustus made his way to the General, his shield split down the middle and blood coating his sword arm's mail. "You're a mad man, General!" he boomed from within his helmet. "You owe me – I don't know what, but you owe me something!"

Tyghus grinned down at him with a bloody mouth. "This just settles our debt from the Skulls, no?"

The kordette laughed as he whacked Fidi' on the rump and sped off in his troops' direction.

"Did you see him Fyrus'?" Tyghus called after his friend. "Did you see the Lij?"

Fyrustus slowed for a moment to look back at the Dyrator. "Not a sign of him!"

On the far wings, Tyghus saw his reserve kords wading into the scrum just as he had ordered, stemming the Valogarians' wraparound attack. Again, once the combat came close, the Imperials' prowess could be brought fully to bear, and though the battle there had been a standstill, the steady advance on the wings was now without question.

But perhaps the sweetest sight of all was the majestic horde of Imperial cavalry rampaging through the rear of the Native lines, cutting down slingers and bowmen like grass, then charging straight into the backs of the spearmen and silotys. Caught between an Imperial vise of massive cavalry and ten-thousand Rokhish foot, the Valogarians cracked. Painted warriors tossed their weapons to the ground and broke into a frenzied sprint in any open direction. Imperials roared as Reverus's horsemen quickly about-faced to ride down the fleers.

The Native flight was soon contagious along its right wing, leaving Grantax and Siderius on the Rokhish left in pursuit. On the Rokhish right, however, he was surprised to find a melee still raging against Niko' and Pydonus's kords, moreso when saw distraught lines of Bakian women and children edging towards the fray. Leaving the center troops to their chase, he galloped along the line to flag down Noccus.

"Noccus – re-form and assist Niko'! He's not gonna like it, but he's stuck down there, not sure what the hell's goin' on."

The kordette removed his helmet for a moment to glance down at the battle at the eastern end of the line. With a surprised grimace, he looked back to Tyghus. "It's the men of Bakia, General. They're fightin' before their own at the city's edge; no surprise they're holdin' out."

Tyghus was too charged to allow even the vestiges of sympathy. "They can tout their honor at someone else's expense; make it quick."

"Aye, General," Noccus said before bellowing to his troops around him, "*Seventh Kord! Re-form! Quick-step due east!*"

In a matter of moments, the euphoric solders were on the move, and in quick order brought the stalemate to a resolution. Noccus's bloody and battered kord crashed into the backs of the Valogarian hold-outs, wavering the Native front lines enough to allow Niko' and Pydonus to finally break through. Like a python around its prey, the front and rear kords squeezed the Bakian warriors, the latter's war cries silenced by a fearsome butchery. Imperials began ripping helmets off to roar in delirium, drowning out the sobs of nearby villagers.

"*For Man and Empire! For Man and Empire! For Man and Empire!*"

Tyghus drew chills as a boyish smile infected his face. *What if this is it?* He thought gleefully. *What if the war, the Lij's army, what if it's all over? I can march straight into Nar-Biluk now! I can get to Tygha, get her out of there! I can turn Glannox towards Avergon and bring those Desert rats to bear! And Treos, and Miko, I can...*

"*Ahhh!*" he happily bellowed at the top of his lungs.

The mirami had been routed.

The day was theirs.

Chapter XXXIV

O' the schemes that men will lay,
To keep the gods from havin' their day.

Rokhish Poem

Dray'gon Rokh, Khorian Hallokhum, 4ᵗʰ Day of the Fourth Month, Y. 384 P.C.

Even at the height of his feud with Castus, Antinax never feared for his life. Not like this.

He had a silver tongue and called more men allies in the Arxun than Anti' could count, but Castus was never known to use violence in achieving his ends, not like those early Lorrions after Cataclysm. Since those turbulent first years where power was leveraged at the point of a sword, Lorrions had mostly stayed away from such methods, finding the inevitable cycle of tit for tat retributions not worth the gains. Proper Lorrions treated Arxun politics as the gentlemen's sport that it was – a battle of wits, strategy, and sometimes coin, not of hired thugs and assassins like barbarians; that was too easy, too base, too uncivilized.

But Jarax was no Lorrion. And he certainly didn't abide by any gentleman's code. So when his spy's body arrived in a bloody heap on Voli's doorstep that night, it was unfamiliar grounds for Antinax – a rarity at his age.

Ever since, Reds shadowed his every step about the city. They were furtive at first – or perhaps he just wasn't looking for them – darting in and out of alleys he'd pass by. But soon he saw them everywhere, loitering outside the Lorrian Halum or in spots visible from his Norum windows, red blots against the Arxun's white. His heart quickened just opening a door in his abode anymore, his body constantly bracing for the moment if – when? – the volatile Rubator simply snapped. The gods wouldn't let him die that way, would they? They *couldn't!*

Regardless, his new reality led Antinax down the path Wollia laid out in the Celacio a few days back, but even that endeavor was perilous these days. To get an audience with Kyrus, he was forced to go through backchannels to even reach Oratus. Given his newfound "influence" over Lorrian matters, the Speaker was a highly visible and popular fellow around the Arxun; messages could be issued to him in crowds without arousing too much Rubitian suspicion – or so Anti' prayed when he reached out to him, anyway. During his evening walk to meet the Emperor, he could tell his mind wasn't entirely convinced, even as he came upon Oratus waiting to escort him into the *Khorian Hallokhum*.

The Speaker was more opulently dressed than he'd ever been in the years he served Rynsyus, replete with a silken shawl across his chest and shimmering jewels on every finger. Indeed, no Speaker had stumbled upon such power in more than a century. With a wave of his hand and a wide smile, Oratus boomed, "and a good evening to you, Lorrion."

Antinax tried to hide his irritation with the boisterous greeting. Even dressed head to toe in a hooded robe, the Red threat made the Nortic feel naked anywhere but the confines of his Norum chamber, and certainly wanted no more attention drawn to him. "Oratus," he said quietly with a nod. "You'd do me a life's favor if you'd lower your tone, aye? As you were originally told, this is an especially *private* meeting."

The Speaker's hands clasped together in front of him as his broad smile morphed into something even more annoying – a look of smugness. "You needn't worry, Antinax. I've dismissed the Guards from the Hall per your request."

"Aye, well you'll notice we're not *in* the Hall yet, are we?" Antinax said curtly, quickly growing paranoid over their open conversation. "So can we please –"

"It was an unusual request, you know… you asking me to dismiss the guards."

"There're prudent reasons for it. Urgent matters of the state."

Oratus pursed his lips in thought. "All the more reason I'd think you would want protection? But of course that's just me…"

"Your insight is most appreciated," the Nortic said acidly. "I believed that –"

"Oh, you don't have to explain yourself to me, Antinax!" the Speaker said, with all the gravitas of a seasoned Lorrion. "I was happy to grant your request."

You are not my equal, you repulsive swine, let alone someone to be "granting" my requests, Antinax thought as he stared furiously into the fat man's eyes. Still, he remained calm but couldn't resist adding, "on the Emperor's behalf, of course."

Oratus's glow dimmed just a bit. "Well, of course."

"Then you and the Emperor have my thanks, once again," he said, before tilting his head beyond the gates. "May we?"

Oratus lingered for a moment before his congenial smile returned. "Of course, Lorrion," he said, before finally turning and pushing through the gates into the Hallokhum. Beautifully sewn carpets lined the long corridor, their brilliant crimson and gold brought to life by white walls pocked with dancing torch flames. To their right, they passed the Soelum where Kyrus had been sworn in as a Lorrion, an event Antinax could scarcely remember anymore but a time he longed for. The dining room where Oratus had arranged for the two to meet, the *Cassyan Soelum*, was further down the hall, a smaller venue than its grandiose cousin. The old Nortic hadn't been privy to it in decades, as it was typically reserved for the Emperor and his family's private use.

To Oratus's credit, there wasn't a Red in sight, but somehow their absence made him feel even less secure. *The dogs are out of sight but not out of reach*, he frustratedly noted. *Certainly not out of mind.* His hood stayed raised until they'd reached the Khorokh's dining room, when his anxiety was supplanted with bafflement – soft musical notes emanated from behind the door. He immediately scowled in alarm. "Who –"

"Your Khorokh awaits, Lorrion," Oratus said with a half bow and exaggerated smile. He opened the door for the Nortic. "Do enjoy your meal, won't you?"

Antinax barely noticed the Speaker's syrupy farewell, so startled was he by the musician apparently joining the dinner.

As the door locked shut behind him, the smells of succulent meats and pungent spices flooded his nose. Before him was a long, dark-wooded table, aglow with candles and laid out with a spread fit for a dozen people; yet there were only two chairs – one at the end nearest Antinax, the other directly opposite and occupied by a Khorokh dressed in his typical gray army tunic, a black long-sleeved shirt covering his arms. Framing Kyrus were two floor-to-ceiling windows on the wall behind him that provided magnificent southward views of the Arxun and beyond.

But it was the boy to the left of the windows that commanded Antinax's attention. He couldn't have been more than an early teen, though his long, ratty black hair made it difficult to tell for sure. He stood softly strumming a three-corded instrument as tall as the boy himself. His utter indifference to the Lorrion's arrival made Antinax even more wary.

"Evening, Highness," the Nortic offered, briefly taking his eyes off the musician. The Khorokh had matched the boy's indifference to the Nortic's arrival until he noisily broke a bread roll in half and flicked eyes up to him.

"Antinax," he said between bites.

The Lorrion hesitated for a moment as he frowned deeper at the boy. "Apologies, Highness, but I thought I relayed to Oratus that I'm here to speak with you on private matters – Imperial matters…"

Kyrus looked at him blankly. "Aye, so you're here. Sit down."

"But the boy –"

"The boy's deaf and blind," the Emperor quickly interjected before reaching for a leg of smoked fowl. "He's no bother to you."

"Well, he is, in fact," Antinax said before he could catch himself. "Who's saying he's 'deaf' and 'blind'?"

After a chomp, Kyrus threw the leg down with a glare. "He *stays*."

The eternal grimace on Antinax's face deepened as he studied the lad.

"I think you'll find his gifts with the strings beyond compare," the Khorokh continued. "His melodies soothing as the gods' voices. You'll see."

"Indeed… indeed," the Lorrion said glumly. "And where did you find such a gifted musician?"

Kyrus sat back in his chair and looked at the lad. "A finance minister raised his name last week."

"Which minister?"

"I don't recall."

"I didn't realize you'd taken such a meeting."

"Did you need to?"

"I suppose not," Antinax said with a shrug. "Do we know anything about the child?" he inquired, frantically wondering who this "minister" was – or who he was aligned with.

The Khorokh gave an annoyed sigh. "I know he bloody well plays music, Antinax, that's all that matters. Beyond that, I believe he was a pauper playing outside a groghouse in the South Gurums, if you can believe such a thing. Such talents being wasted."

Antinax could sense the Khorokh's impatience so he held his tongue, instead listening to the strumming's soft notes.

"It's remarkable really," Kyrus said. "The similarities between us."

"Between you and the boy?"

The Khorokh nodded. "The gods stripped him of even the barest of senses yet blessed him with the ability to make such magnificent sound – sounds he himself cannot enjoy," he said, looking to the Nortic with an eerie smile.

"It is remarkable," Antinax said, still skeptical of the boy's senses.

"And I, well… the gods allowed everything to be taken from me, as well," he said plainly. "Father, brother slaughtered before my eyes. My dear mother taking her own life from the grief, yet… yet *now* they've seen fit to vest me – *me* of all people! – with the power to avenge them all. That revenge won't call them from the gods' Table, but I tell you Antinax – if there *were* a price in Valogarian lives I could wager that would bring them back, I'd pay it in a heartbeat. *I'd strip that Peninsula bare and do a jig on its carcass.*"

"I'd imagine so," Antinax said as he watched the Khorokh ramble on, growing increasingly concerned with the audience he'd risked his life to fetch – and upon whom his life depended.

Kyrus lingered on the Nortic for a moment before finally turning to tear a chunk of game hen from its roasted bones. "Didn't I tell you to sit?"

"You did, indeed, forgive me," the old Nortic said as he hobbled towards the table. "And lest it go unsaid, I appreciate you giving me this time. I know you've a number of far more pressing issues than dealing with a crotchety Lorrion."

"A fair statement," Kyrus grunted.

The Khorokh fell silent for a bit, save for his continued smacks and bites. Antinax watched him with apprehension, failing to find his own voice. *Just say what you've come here to say*, he pleaded with himself. But it was Kyrus who broke the silence first.

"Cassyus himself once sat here, sat right in one of these chairs," he said, eyes still drawn to his plate. "Hm? Did you know that?"

"Aye, learned that as a tob'. The hall bears his name because of it, no?"

"Imagine the things that were discussed around this table," the Khorokh said, dropping his bone to wipe his bearded face with a black cloth. He whisked down several swallows of his drink as he sat back in his chair, right hand cradling the chalice. "From that very window he could have seen the hordes coming," he said with a jerk of his head towards the pane behind him. "Could have watched his army huddle atop the great Walls, waiting for the Clannic warriors. Can you imagine it? What a scene it must have been! What a scene when the battle was finally joined, everything hanging in the balance – *truly* everything." Kyrus's smile faded somewhat. "Pity that no emperor will ever see such a grand vision again. Even when my glory comes to pass, I'll have to imagine it. I'll have to imagine Glannox crushing Valogar."

Antinax eyed the young ruler carefully, while keeping himself devoid of expression. "Well, however you see it, it's going to be real all the same, and that's what matters."

The Khorokh gave a pleased nod, though his eyes still looked distant.

"I'm glad to see you in good spirits, Highness," the Lorrion said, encouraged by their agreement on Valogar. "I was concerned that the Castus situation would have you needlessly troubled."

The smile evaporated from Kyrus's face. "'Needlessly'? What an interesting take you have."

Antinax cleared his throat. "Apologies, I didn't mean to offend, I just meant that you should-that you should trust that we –"

"There's that *damn* word again!" Kyrus suddenly yelled as a fist smashed the table. Dishes and cutlery flew through the air only to shatter loudly against stone floors; bowls of red fruit preserves splattered the same. Antinax looked wide-eyed and speechless at his Khorokh; the boy played on obliviously. "Three sons of Lowland Ruhls lie dead at the hands of my guards, sons who rose in rebellion against *me*! Others actively helped Castus plot an escape so that he now roams my Empire with impunity! Castus, the same man condemned to die for confessed treason! Those sons and those men and those women that assisted his escape were people that I *trusted!*" Kyrus said, jabbing a finger into his chest. His face ran a deep purple as swollen neck veins pulsed from his fury, and an agonizing few moments passed as he glared at the Nortic. Finally, he steadied his breaths and calmly reclined back into his seat, chalice in hand. "So you'll forgive me if I don't trust much of anything at the moment... but I'm getting it. I'm wringing the gods-forsaken truth from this city one soul at a time."

Anti's face flushed as well, startled from the outburst; his cloak now felt stifling. "I understand, Highness."

"Do you?" Kyrus quickly replied.

"I've served the Lorrio for more than four decades. 'Trust' is a word seldom heard and rarely practiced."

Kyrus sniffed at the stone-faced Nortic's quip. "Perhaps that's the key then – simply don't expect it to begin with."

Antinax gave a deferential tilt of his head towards the Emperor.

"So why are you here?" the Khorokh asked, though less irritably than before. "At this hour, of all times."

Anti' had plotted his message carefully, but in light of Kyrus's volatility he knew it had to be even more precise. As his mind fumbled over the proper words, he finally sighed and looked straight at the Khorokh. "Well, I'll be blunt, because I don't know any other way," he started, staring at the musician as he finished. "It's Jarax."

The boy never flinched, but Kyrus's eyebrow did. "What of him?"

"Suffice it to say, he's not happy with our... arrangement."

Kyrus grimaced. "Arrangement?"

Anti' felt a flash of anger pass through him. "My spies, Highness. He knows about them and he's not happy about it."

"Why would he be happy about it?"

Antinax paused. "Pardon?"

"Why would he be happy about it, Anti'? Of course he's not happy about it! His happiness was never the point."

The Nortic squinted in confusion. "Highness, perhaps you misunderstand what I'm saying here: he and his men are bludgeoning every spy he finds tracking him – and he's found quite a few."

"Aye, so?"

"So? So I – I – I mean he *knows* he's being spied on, what's the point of all this if –"

"He's supposed to know," Kyrus replied as he swirled his cup of spirits. "Watched men are men unlikely to act out of turn. Same reason we march troops through conquered lands – people aren't inclined to rise up when there's a dyron looming about."

"Then I'd say that that purpose has been served. He knows he's under watch now. Nothing else can be gained from sending my men into harm's way against him."

"I disagree. Your men shall continue their watch."

"Highness, he's threatening me *personally*, do you understand this? He's essentially declared war not only against my men, but *me* –"

"I *do* understand that, but that's a reality of the position you are in," Kyrus quickly barked. "The Lorrio was designed to work in service of the Khorokh, so you work in service of *me*. When you work in service of me, it means you accept that there might be risks to you personally."

Antinax inwardly recoiled. *We weren't 'designed' to be your martyrs,* he thought angrily, but tried with all his might not to let his countenance reflect it. "Then I misjudged our conversation in the Hovikum, Highness."

"If you misjudged our conversation, it's because you failed to see the bigger picture, the *larger* war that we're fighting. Valogar's but one battle in that war. My officers must be kept honest, the city still has to be purged, Castus has to be brought to justice. You're a soldier in *all* of those battles, Anti'. A soldier, for the first real time in your life... and soldiers die."

The Nortic fumed at the ruler's patronizing tone. "I *never* said Castus should be taken down –"

"You did! You did by your actions! You knew what had to happen to him when you told me the depths of his betrayal," Kyrus said with a point before throwing the cup's contents down his throat and tossing it to the ground with contempt. "Now as for Jarax, *if* you found proof of his disloyalty, it'd be an unexpected benefit. But a welcome benefit, certainly."

"Well, as it happens, I have found proof."

The Khorokh's eyes immediately narrowed on the Nortic. Anti' clenched his teeth and hoped his face did not flush again, as manipulating the truth came easily to him, but outright dishonesty did not. The soft notes in the background ironically proved a welcome distraction.

"Have you, now?" the Emperor asked in a menacing tone.

"I have," he replied, pushing ahead with his fabrication. "He's found many of my men, but not all of them. And not before one of them saw him arrest but then release a man in the West Gurums... after taking a bag of coin."

Kyrus offered no response other than his searing look.

"Did he have cause to be in the West Gurums?" the Nortic asked innocently. "Well, either way, we have nothing more than that, but he felt it was worth telling me."

"Hm... and this spy of yours, he's a man *you* trust?" Kyrus finally questioned.

"Of course. Paying spies doesn't make much sense if you can't trust them."

"So you could call him in here *right now* and he'd say the same thing you just told me?"

No, Antinax thought. "Aye," he forced out instead.

"Without hesitation?"

"Aye."

"Hm..." the Khorokh grunted as he ran a hand through a wooly beard. "I find it odd that you didn't tell me this first," he offered calmly.

"I thought the offense of threatening a Lorrion was as egregious as bribery. But taken as a whole, his actions more than warrant his dismissal, do they not?"

Kyrus grunted again as his hand stroked the thicket of hairs on his chin more vigorously. "Are you lying to me, Antinax?"

Yes. "No," the Lorrion replied, feigning insult.

The Khorokh took a deep breath and exhaled loudly. "Well, I'm not going to act on your spy's word alone. Not to go so far as removing him."

"Taking coin in the middle of Castus's pursuit doesn't alarm you, Highness?"

"So you knew why he'd be in the West Gurums after all, didn't you?" Kyrus asked with a sneer.

Anti' blanched. "Of course I knew. Half the Arxun knew. Every Red in Dray'gon Rokh was canvassing the Gurums, east, west, south –"

"He's too vital, controls too many men," the Khorokh said as he rose from the table to face one of the windows. "Get me more and you may get your wish."

"I think this is a mistake," Antinax said quickly.

Kyrus turned to give the Nortic a side-view of his face. "I hope it is. As I've said since I took the throne, we have far too many goals abroad to be distracted by more betrayals here at home. I think I've shown that there's nothing I want more than to weed out the infestation of deceit in my Capital."

"Then –"

"But with Jarax, *I need more.*"

Antinax nodded to no one in particular. "Aye... I see. Well, that's all I had to discuss. If there's nothing else you want with me this evening, I suppose I'll depart."

"Nothing more, Anti'," Kyrus said distantly as he peered out over the city from the window. "I'm sure we'll reconvene soon enough."

"I'm sure we will."

As the old Nortic shuffled creakily towards the door, he took one last look at the boy in the corner, seeing vacant eyes without a hint of comprehension. With that, he flipped his hood back over his head, bundling up for what was sure to be the longest walk of his life.

Chapter XXXV

Take stock of the best days so as to draw upon them during the worst.

Rokh Proverb

Bakia, 4ᵗʰ Day of the Fourth Month, Y. 384 P.C.

If the Bakian breakwater took years to build, it took only hours to tear asunder. If the Bakian harbor was once a safe haven for offloading trade and troops, it was now a raging torrent. And if the Bakian people thought their woes ended with their losses on the battlefield, they were sadly mistaken.

One by one boulders nearest to the coast had been wrenched away through raw Rokhish manpower. Natives watched in baffled horror as ropes sent the giant rocks plummeting to watery graves, and with each plunging stone, the Ferlen Sea's waves came closer and closer to breaching the wall. When the rockwall finally gave way, ravenous waters crashed into the harbor, and in moments, its waterline was on the rise. The wooden docks jutting out from the Bakian "notch" were quickly submerged, sending Rokhs scrambling off the coastline's "Horn" to avoid being swept up in the surge.

Leaving the soldiers to their port destruction and garnishment of Bakia's provisions under the day's fading light, the General headed back to their camp on the field. His head still throbbed, neck still lined with welts, and eye had nearly swollen shut, so he hoped some time away from the shrieking Valogarians would ease the pain. Mainly though, he didn't want the men to see his body tremble the way it did whenever the rush of battle had passed. His arms shook the most, but none of his body was immune to it.

The field, however, proved to be a haunting experience in its own right.

Masses of Bakians lurched about the quiet battlefield in search of dead loved ones. Some knelt to grieve at the sides of lifeless bodies while others solemnly proceeded towards the whitestone monument north of the city with corpses in tow. In the distance, Reverus's horsemen kept silent watch in a vast ring around the field, their shadows looming larger as the sun dropped behind them. The Stuqatta was openly displeased about giving the Natives free range of the field; it was "a privilege they wouldn't have given us," he said. But Tyghus didn't care. On a day where Rokhish losses were lighter from catching their enemies off-kilter – catching them before they had soaked their weapons in pyhr – he saw no harm in giving the Valogarians a chance to clear the fields. The thought that maybe, just *maybe*, Miko's gods might appreciate the courtesy played a part in decision.

If not her gods, then Miko herself anyway, he thought with a smile.

A horse breached Reverus's ring, followed shortly by two more. Tyghus gave their approach passing attention, the bucket of water at his tent far more alluring. It never occurred to him they would be anyone but messengers from his Stuqatta, and certainly no one of import. His error grew more apparent as the riders closed in on his tent.

The lead horsemen rode with an awkward gait, keeled to his left side as if nursing a wound. A tattered cloak fluttered from his back while a torn Imperial tunic hung loosely across an otherwise bare chest. As he drew closer, Tyghus saw a bloody, young face taut with anguish. A blackened bald patch marred his forehead amidst an otherwise stringy mess of brown hair. The rider closed so quickly Tyghus couldn't identify him until he violently reared the beast before his tent, tumbling off the saddle to the ground with a thud.

Tyghus dashed over to the fallen body in confusion, rolling the rider over with a groan.

Seldonius.

The poor boy's face was more battered and bruised than many of the General's soldiers. He raised a hand to the cadet's swollen cheek.

"Seldonius, my boy! What happened to –"

But Tyghus couldn't even finish his question without the cadet breaking into a spate of wheezing coughs. Blood trickled from his lips.

"*General…*"

As Seldonius moved his hands aimlessly, Tyghus saw the true source of his anguish – a left side gored with a deep puncture wound, blood flowing unvexed into the shredded tunic.

"You got it good, didn't ya' boy? We'll find you a healer," Tyghus offered as he started to rise.

"No! No, General, please…" he pleaded with closed eyes. "There's no time. It'd – it'd be a waste…"

Tyghus stopped and knelt back down at the cadet's side, gazing upon him helplessly. "What the hell happened to you?"

The cadet just shook his head. "General… Avergon… it's – it's under siege…"

That the mighty fort could be besieged was inconceivable. Tyghus's brow furrowed as he shook his head. "How's that possible? How could – well, there have to be reinforcements en route by now, aye?"

"No."

"No?"

"There's no troops," Seldonius repeated, with a tinge of shame in his weakened voice. "There's none… none to spare."

The General's eyebrows arced downward. "What do you mean?"

Seldonius wheezed and bore his bloody teeth before continuing. "The Colverians… have attacked the Ninth at the Brafford Bridge… Adulus is barely holding them back… he can spare no troops… he's even called in the village militia…"

Tyghus swallowed hard. "And the Eighth at the Converge?"

"Converge dyron… is with Glannox…"

A burning sensation flooded Tyghus's chest as his next question spilled from his mouth. "And Glannox? He's been spoken with?"

The cadet, even in his mortal state, seemed hesitant to respond as his face fell to his side.

"Seldonius, don't you leave me, boy," the General begged, gripping the cadet's chin with his hand. "Look at me, look at me! Don't you do it!"

His eyelids creaked open. "He…"

"Yes?"

"He hasn't even left Marvelon… he's weeks away from Avergon… prob'ly even more from here…"

Tyghus's jaw dropped without realizing it. "What?" he uttered, his eyes absent-mindedly reviewing a pile of Rokhish dead not far away. "You're certain of this?"

"As the gods watch me, I swear it…"

His heart pounded. "Why? *Why* hasn't he moved?"

"I don't know… I'm sorry, General…" The boy's face had turned a greenish white as he lay dying at Tyghus's side. His bloodshot eyes gave a flash of life as they met the General's. "I'm scared."

Tyghus took the cadet's cold hand in his own. "It's alright, boy. The gods'll have a special place for such a brave warrior. A spot next to all the heroes of Rokhish lore."

"I'm sorry…" Seldonius muttered faintly, tears welling at the corner of his closing eyes. "I'm sorry."

"Nothing to be sorry for."

The slight grip against the General's hand gave out, the little fight left in the boy's body along with it. Tyghus closed his eyes and sighed deeply, countless emotions surging through his body.

When he finally looked up, he realized he had more visitors. The two riders that trailed Seldonius dismounted from exhausted, froth-mouthed horses, and Tyghus recognized them as two of his long-lost scouts. As they approached the kneeling Dyrator, they saw the cadet's lifeless body and removed their helmets in deference.

Both men were short and slight-framed, clad in the lighter gray tunics and armaments characteristic of scouts; the smaller of the two spoke first. "That boy, he – he moved like the wind on that beast of his. Like the gods themselves carried 'im," he shook his head glumly. "May they take him now, aye?"

Tyghus nodded with pursed lips as he stood with a creak. "Did you see what happened to him, Neos?"

He shrugged his shoulders, looking to his companion. "Recius saw it better."

"It was Chibin, my lord," the taller scout said without hesitation. "We'd swung by the Valogarian Gate to get a fix on your whereabouts when lo and behold we saw this flash of brown –" he continued with a nod to

Seldonius. "- fly by us headin' southeast-like. Seemed fine 'til a line of Chibin – had to be a dozen or so – sprang out of the grass and knocked him from his horse. They hadn't seen us somehow, but they pounded the boy good. Gored him with a spear, scalped a lock. Awful things."

Tyghus clenched his teeth. "I see."

"Neos and I decided to take a chance on rescuing him, even with just a couple daggers between us. Figured we could spook the Puries' with our mounts and by the gods it worked. Scattered like roaches."

The anger in Tyghus's belly rose again, and he shot a glare at the scouts. "You should have brought him to the camp at the Gate after that, not here! You had the bloody Gateline within reach!"

Recius threw his hands up in frustration. "Damn it all if he didn't hop back on that beast of his and take off like it never happened. We couldn't keep pace with him, 'specially in the rain. The one time we thought we'd caught 'im it turned out to be –" The scout stopped mid-sentence as he looked to Neos.

Tyghus wasn't gaining patience. "What, dammit?"

Neos shot a wary glance to his partner before eyeing the General. "Well, we found it... we found the Valogarian army."

"Aye, as did –"

"The *Lij's* army."

Tyghus's heart dropped as he gave a slight nod, gaze falling to the ground at Neos's feet. "Aye? And where is it?"

The scout cleared his throat. "They've gathered in strength at the Sunken Fields, 'bout a day's march north of here. Prob'ly two or three with the siege engines."

The General gave no response. Recius took the interlude to add, "they saw us, sire... their troops. Didn't try to attack us... just said that he awaits you there... the Lij, I mean."

The General continued his nods before asking quietly. "Their numbers?"

"We circled 'em trying to find a way around. They'd been movin' west towards the Gateline, trying to block entry to the Isthmus, I suppose. He's rallied many mirami, men ran as far as I could see..."

"How many deep are they, Recius?"

The scout sighed. "We counted at least thirty-five, forty mirami flags – sixty, sixty-five thousand, I'd say?"

Tyghus's eyes suddenly shot up to Recius's. "Sixty-five thousand? Sixty-five thousand soldiers or soldiers with women and children in tow?"

"Soldiers," Neos said. "Sixty-five at the least. Fair amount of their lekeys, as well. I'll say though, the Chibin controlling the lands near the Gate didn't appear to be fighting 'longside the Lij..."

"Aye, and no sign of Colvery either," Recius offered hopefully. "So

328

that's... that's something."

Tyghus turned and paced away from them with hands squarely on hips. His eyes combed the dark skies for a sign of the stars he loved so much back in Draygonea, but tonight they'd seemed to have forsaken him.

"So what are we doing then, General?" a scout called from behind him.

Tyghus never turned around, maintaining his slow, steady walk away from them. "We finish off Bakia. We take care of our wounded. Give honors to our dead," he offered, before stopping at last.

"Then prepare to give battle on the Sunken Fields."

* * *

The camp was alive with soldiers' movements deep into the night. The spoils of war, acquired en masse from Bakia's sacking, gave the men fresh food and full stomachs – neither of which they'd had in weeks. Apart from the sated soldiery convened the General and his twelve kordettes around a raging fire, where the officers were already trading tales of the day's glory.

But Tyghus couldn't join them in their revelry. He already felt like a fool for letting himself feel such unrequited glee following their victory; he should have known better. In the wake of his scouts' revelations, gone were his hopes that he'd see his sister again; gone were his plans to thank the Lakeman for all he'd done; gone were his aspirations of ever gazing upon Miko's beautiful face, of hearing that intoxicating accent. Perhaps worst of all, he now had to share the news with the jovial men – news that amounted to a death sentence.

"Ah, it was a good day, a warrior's day!" Fyrustus said with a tired smile in Tyghus's direction. "So what the hell you lookin' to counsel about now?"

"Ready to counsel with a cup of grog and a warm blanket, aye?" Fygo' added to the approving chuckles of the group.

Tyghus gave a tired grin. "It's a fair question," Tyghus replied calmly. He inhaled deeply before pushing forward. "Believe me, I've brought you here for good reason..."

"Well, you're gonna make us nervous now," Fyrus' said with a joking tone.

"We've located the Lij and his army."

The circle exchanged bewildered glances as a long silence followed.

"You mean those dead painted bastards on the field?" Noccus finally said to some anxious snickers. "They weren't it?"

Tyghus simply shook his head.

"Well, where are they, then?" Fygonus asked gruffly, all trace of humor departed.

"About two days' march north of here. He waits for us at the Sunken

Fields."

The Twin gave a contemptuous snort. "Waiting for *us?* It's his bloody country, he's too scared to join the fray down here?"

Tyghus's eyes shot to him. "Perhaps."

"Perhaps what? The king coward would rather let his Bakians do the dying than the king coward himself. And after today's results, I wouldn't blame him for keepin' clear of us."

Tyghus folded his hands in front of him, forearms resting on his knees. "Brothers, we know the creed that a single Rokh soldier is worth ten of any other, do we not?"

"A most hallowed creed," Nikolux responded proudly.

"Aye," the General nodded. "Well, now we have to prove it."

The group was silent at first, before Kinistus asked casually, "how many are they?"

Tyghus's gaze fell on the wiry warrior. "Our scouts report that he marches at the head of some sixty thousand men."

"*Sixty* thousand?" Fygonus gasped in astonishment.

The General nodded. "Maybe sixty-five."

Reverus's head shook quickly. "Why should we even consider offering battle on such terms?"

"We're not cowards, Horseman," Niko' barked.

"Aye, and I thought we weren't fools, either, hopefully you don't argue with that?"

Nikolux grunted in response.

"General, you can't seriously be considering answering the Lij with these numbers, are you? We have what, four dyrons on the way as we sit here? Let the Lij chase us around the country if he wants, then we can repay him in kind when he has to defend the north against Glannox. True?" the Stuqatta questioned, clearly impressed with his assessments. "Why would we —"

"Reverus, Glannox isn't coming," Tyghus stated bluntly.

Frozen expressions on the men's faces told him not to expect a response. He continued.

"Not coming; hasn't even left Marvelon. And even if he departed this hour at the quick-step, paying no mind to his siege or baggage train, it's two or three weeks to the Shoals, days or weeks more to requisition ships, and a full day or two at sea — assuming the winds favor the sails. He could be here in four weeks or as many as ten — if he was coming at all."

Reverus's bafflement spoke for all of them. "You told us he'd be meeting us on the Peninsula, Tyghus!"

"General!" Niko' angrily corrected.

"'General', then — you *told* us that by the time we broke through the Gate, he'd be coming ashore in the north!"

"I know what I said, Reverus," Tyghus replied with a quiet intensity. "And what I said was exactly what I was told. Tonight's no different."

"So he just decided not to come?" Reverus asked sarcastically. "This has been in the works for weeks so – so *why?*"

"Maybe he had no intention of comin'," Fygonus said with a darkened look.

The Stuqatta turned to glare at him. "That's not what I meant. That's bloody treason, you saying that."

"How you could *not* say it? Everyone and his brother knows that Glannox's opinion of himself could consume the whole Empire, so why wouldn't he want the glory of conquering Valogar for himself?"

The General shook his head at the thought. "It doesn't matter right now, we need to dwell upon what does. The reality is that we don't have the supplies to dance through these hills for weeks on end; and frankly, if Andran's truly fielded this many already, any more delay would only swell his ranks. Beyond that, I was told that not only is the Lij moving to block off retreat to the Isthmus, but the Chibin are already there."

"The Gateline will hold," Fyrus' said defiantly. "The Purebloods would never attack an army dug in."

"As I said, it's the Lij's army that's headed there too."

"Well, damn it all and let them have the Gate, then! We'll loot the country bare if we have to, then you'll see 'em move. They think we *want* to leave yet?"

Tyghus looked at the kordette for a moment before turning his gaze vacantly beyond the group. "We may have to for Avergon's sake."

The circle was slow to reply. "Avergon?" Swiftus echoed. "Since when's Avergon at risk?"

"Since the Tereleshi tribes rose in the west and carved a path of destruction all the way to the fort's walls. Since the only reinforcements they could have called upon were commandeered by Glannox or are fending off Colverian attacks at the Brafford Bridge."

"The Terelesh?" Kinistus queried rhetorically.

Tyghus nodded. "They've besieged the fort... I don't know how they plan to break it, but they're besieging it anyway." His stomach twisted in knots as he said it, the horrified expressions of Miko among others running wild in his imagination.

"There're only reserves at Avergon," Noccus added quietly.

"Indeed. When we set out to march under the assumption we'd be meeting Glannox, the attacks hardly seemed a threat since his reinforcements should have been within a week's march. Yet here he is having never moved a foot in all this time, and here we are on a bloody battlefield, nearly a thousand miles from Avergon," he said, allowing a brief pause to swallow a sudden rise of anger. "I didn't want to burden you with these concerns; they're a general's bother, not kordettes', but I felt you had a right to know given these circumstances. If anyone's going to relieve Avergon, we're the best shot it has – and I say that fully aware that we've sixty thousand troops awaiting us."

A contemplative pall fell over the circle until Niko's gruff voice intervened. "Then I think the answer's pretty clear," he said, eyes scanning the group. "We smash the Valogarians at the Sunken Fields."

The circle, Tyghus included, gave a delirious laugh at the blunt assessment, as much from its absurdity as its boldness. He saw his comrades differently as they shared their chuckle, knowing that in another few days or so, the group would never again sit in such a meeting, at least not in its current makeup.

"The old bastard's right," Tyghus said with a smile.

"More's the pity…" Kini' added drily, drawing more laughs.

"It's no pity, lad," Niko' said with a straight face. "The legend of the Sixth wasn't born from weavin' baskets, it was born from moments like these, dammit!"

"Aye, Niko'," Kinistus said in amused conciliation. "Indeed it was."

"Talk to your kords," Tyghus said. "Prepare them. Steady their nerves, tell them that once we arrive at the Fields, they get only a minute to be afraid, because when we face the Lij's army, we're not going just to make a show of it."

"And our plan when we face them, General?" Napodonax asked from across the fire.

Tyghus looked at him through the flames. "Before I take to the pillow, I hope to have that worked out," he said, already using a stick to sketch formations into the dirt.

"With due respect, General, I'd like to stay with you 'til it's done," Napo' said, catching Tyghus off-guard.

"Unnecessary, Napo'. You're best off taking to your bed –"

"We'll all stay, aye?" the Belagatte said stubbornly. "Better that we all know the plans from the first phase til the last if we're going to prevail against these numbers."

Heads bobbed in agreement all around Tyghus, and his pride in the group swelled. "Very well, brothers. Then let's get to work so the poor twins here can get their rest."

With a grin, the nearest twin shoved the General aside as the group laughed at his expense. Before long, the dozen huddled around Tyghus, debating the strategy and tactics of the coming fight. They would work deep into the night, but hours passed like seconds even with the aches and pains wracking his body. The brilliance of their minds provided all the distraction from the wounds that he needed on these, their final hours together.

332

If my prayers — no, if my men *mean anything to you, my gods, then welcome them when the time comes,* he thought to himself. *Welcome them to your Table.* He drew a contemplative breath. *And if it's my fate to die in these lands, the very same that took my father, if that's my purpose such that the Dyron lives on or gives Avergon even a mite of a fighting chance… then by all means, let me do so with grace.*

Let me do so with courage.

Let   me   do   so   without   fear.

Chapter XXXVI

"Peace of mind comes at the expense of many."

Writings of Khorokh Kyrus I, Y. 384 P.C.

Dray'gon Rokh, Khorian Brex, 5ᵗʰ Day of the Fourth Month, Y. 384 P.C.

My dear *pari, mari,* and brave *Kylius —*

Your son and brother writes to you from the Khorian Brex of Dray'gon Rokh, capital of the Rokhish Empire. From my throne I can see all four sections of the capital and the great market at the centerpoint of them all. I can see the white walls that have warded off enemies for centuries. I can see the grasslands and villages that paint the horizon. And with my hand stretched out in front of me, the whole view fits right into my palm. As if it's all there, all mine for the taking.

Well, dear family, I'm taking it. Perhaps you won't recognize the man writing you this letter. Perhaps I don't either. But I've never seen things so clearly in my life.

For almost thirteen years now I've been without you. Thirteen years of memories never made, accomplishments never realized, promises never filled. And for thirteen years it all seemed so senseless to me, why I was chosen to suffer so greatly, why you were chosen to die while I was forced to live. But as I consider it now, do I finally, finally understand? Is it truly as simple as the impossibility of life tasting sweet without the bitter? I think it might be, I truly do.

All the days and nights of my life since the day in the patches, all the tears I've shed at the Kyrogon grove, all the years I had to stand idly by and watch your killers roam free, they've all led me to this moment. A moment where the gods conspired to place me in the most powerful seat in Andervold in order to avenge you, a moment where a Lorrio supports it. But would this vengeance taste as sweet without the bitterness prior? I think not. It's difficult for mortals to recognize their logic, but sometimes one must simply trust that the gods will bring us low — or make us think we're low, perhaps? — before taking us to heights unimagined.

The signs have always been there, even when I was locked in this Brex all those weeks and months. Back then, a bird used to fly to my sill everyday. It was a hideous thing — feathers askew, eyes encrusted with pus. Yet everyday it came. I never thought it to be more than a curious little creature, as wondrous about me as I about it. But of course it was more than that, it was a sign! A sign from Stygus, god of war! Just as legend says he sent a flock of crows through the town of Kyles to alert Cassyus to Clannic hordes on the march, he placed that lonely crow on the sill to tell me: the time is coming. War is coming. An honorable, righteous war. A war that vindicates man and Empire. And that it will all be worth it.

Look forward, not backwards, that's what the gods have been telling me. But to make it so, they took away the last vestiges of my prior life, my life before being reborn as an instrument of their destruction. An instrument of your redemption. Tyghus was the most painful sacrifice they demanded, of course. We'd gone through so much together, shared so much pain together, bled together. By the gods, I bore witness to his father's death before my own! Were these not the bonds of fate? How could I ever fail him? How could he ever choose a traitor's ilk or a Chibin whore over a friend who'd given him so much?

But again, the signs were there all along. He's godless, plain and simple. And in *the godless man's heart, what does honor truly mean?* What could *it mean?* What *could friendship ever mean? I could never be bound by fate to such a man, as fate is a construct of the gods themselves, not something simply declared by men, something hoped for. Through Tyghus's betrayal, the gods were simply reminding me of the folly in putting one's trust in man instead of putting it in the infallible gods. It's the gods that grant us life and fortune, not man. Would one ever pray to a man or woman for deliverance? Certainly not, so why was I?*

The symmetry of Tyghus's fate is so beautifully perfect that it brings tears to my eyes – but tears of joy, now, no longer despair. After puzzling me with the revelation of Tyghus's deceit, the gods have decreed that he'll die on the fields of Valogar. Perhaps when he finds his army surrounded, he'll realize that the gods see no need to spare the wicked, the godless. Perhaps when he looks in vain for Glannox's relief, he'll see that deception is a snake that often bites its master. He'll die on the fields, within eyeshot of his traitorous sister – within eyeshot of the grove where his father passed I wonder? – and when he takes his last breaths, perhaps then he'll find the gods…

I'm not so foolish as to believe the hardships are over. The gods have made clear that there are many trials lying ahead, some bound to be as dreadful as my isolation in the Brex. The Arxun is a partisan latrine with alliances running so deep, it will take years to root out. In truth, I never believed there to be a race of humanity more vile than the Valogarian but I've found it in the politicians that infest Dray'gon Rokh. They grow fat on luxury and malaise. They've forgotten the Empire at its inception and quite simply, the city's suffered as a result.

And of course, Castus still needs to be found and brought to justice. Every day he breathes my air is an insult and embarrassment to every citizen and Ruhl of this Empire. It's a symbol of all that is wrong with our Realm…

But I no longer fear these trials. I welcome them. I know that once the city has been purged of its filth, it will shine anew. And I know that Castus will eventually be brought back to die, although certainly not in a 'clean' fashion. He'll have plenty of his conspirators to agonize with him.

And I also know that I'll take a wife of high blood. I'll have many heirs and rebuild the great town of Kyrogon in the process.

But those quaint pleasantries can wait. The largest army the Empire has ever seen must still be built. Glannox and his Iron Dyrons must still burn a path through Valogar in your names and memories. Colvery must still atone for four centuries of meddling in Rokhish affairs. Only then will it be safe for my sons and daughters to enter this world; a world where Valogar will be known as nothing more than a smoldering ruin, a land fit for supplying slaves and ore, and nothing else.

You would all be proud of me if you were here, I know it. And I of you. Kylius, you'd be nearing your thirty-first year, probably a kordette if you had hadn't yet taken a dyron of your own – assuming you were able to avoid the political shackles that found me. Pari, I've no doubt you would have risen to the heights that Glannox has, certainly adding new legends to the Sixth's lore. I'll always wonder how far you would have risen. You certainly wouldn't have put up with Dray'gon Rokh, I know that; if only the politicians here held your values, you'd still be with me.

Mari, you were as much a victim of this city's treachery as pari and Kylius. You were the perfect ruhl, you truly were. Strong, honorable, with unflinching love of your family – the people like Castus took that from you. The Valogarians and the Colverians supporting them took that from you. They took it from me. I understand why you left me to join the gods' Table, but my failure to ease your suffering is a shame I'll take with me to my last breath; still to this day I call to Verina for her mercy. I know you'll speak to me through her when the time is right.

So you see? I promised you I'd never forget, and I haven't. Not for one moment.

Tears dropped to the parchment stretched out over Kyrus's leg, smearing the still damp ink. With a stuffy sniff, he placed his forehead into a cupped hand and openly wept.

"I know it's the future, gods, I know that's what I must look to, but... it's so bloody hard to forget them! I-I-I just..." he gushed through gritted teeth. He closed his eyes and inhaled deeply, muttering in calmer tone, "blood is how we'll honor them, you're right. Blood here, blood in Valogar. Just give me the strength, my gods. Give me the strength to do what needs to be done."

With a wipe of his eyes and nose, he dampened his quill and returned to his parchment.

It ends soon. The wait for revenge, it ends soon. The moment Tyghus falls will be the moment the Empire and the House of Kyr begin their ascent. I have swiftriders in the Lowlands waiting to speed word of his demise, but I don't think I'll need them after all. I'll know. The gods will tell me, I know it.

I will write you again soon. I promise.

Your son and brother, faithful guardian of the Kyrid lines,

Kyrus the Younger

As he finished, he realized he'd hardly noticed the clangs of distant hammers. The sounds brought a weary smile to his face, and he rose from his chair to peer over the balcony's edge, the same edge he'd shared with Rynsyus so many months prior. There, hundreds of feet below in a courtyard outside the Khorian Hallokhum, were dozens of workers and sculptors gathered around a massive hunk of white mountain rock. They had been chiseling away for the better part of a week, but just in the last few days could the object's form begin to take shape.

It was an obelisk, simple yet majestic, bearing uncanny resemblance to the one in the Kyrogon grove he'd visited so many times. Kyrus felt his eyes well up again as he gazed proudly upon his family's burgeoning new monument, a monument no foul Natives could dare touch.

"I   never   forgot."

Chapter XXXVII

As the Clannic Hordes mustered outside the Walls on Cataclysm's eve,
Cassyus gathered the Rokhish sons and daughters before him and said to them,
"Fear not the battle awaiting thee, for their warriors share your dread;
Fear not the warriors attacking our walls, for the walls shall hold;
Fear not a wall's breach, for our men are brave;
Fear not the fallen man, for his children will carry his name;
But should the enemy find courage,
Should the last wall crumble,
Should the final Rokh perish,
Thou still takest heart —
For thou wilt hath made the utmost sacrifice of thine mortal bodies,
When one stood against ten,
Ten against hundreds,
Hundreds against thousands,
And the gods will honor thine bravery with seats by their sides forever."

Spoken Recounting of Verse "Redemption of the Brave" from <u>The Epic of Cassyus,</u>
by Ereapakhus the Bard

Valogar, The Sunken Fields, 7ᵗʰ Day of the Fourth Month, Y. 384 P.C.

Two leaders stood on a lush green field that stretched to horizons lined with rolling hills. The soil was moist under a light blue sky dappled with thin gray clouds. They met on the Sunken Fields; they met out of respect.

The Lij's tattoed black eyes were tired yet determined, taut frown reflecting the same. He came to the Fields looking more a warrior than Tyghus had ever seen, his chest bearing a shirt of thick wooden armor, shoulders mounting plates spiked with the horns of great beasts; his face was striped white with warpaint beneath a head donning a crown of bound branches. A spear capped with sharpened iron heads on either end was slung over one shoulder, a circular shield over the other.

He looked the part indeed.

They had approached in silence, though the Native warriors behind Andran spanning as far as the eye could see said plenty. Now their eyes locked, a tense air stifling their breaths. Tyghus finally spoke first. "Greetings, brother."

Andran hardly flinched. "My peoples' blood still wet on armor and you call me 'brother.'"

It was Tyghus's turn not to flinch, well-aware his armor remained stained with the bloody marks of Bakia; his helmet tucked under his arm still carried a dent from the slinger shot as well. His face, meanwhile, was more black, blue, and crimson than its natural pink, and he was sure the Lij noticed his limping gait.

"A man married to my sister will always be my brother."

"No true brother take up arms against another in Valogar," Andran replied darkly. "You are no brother. You are dead to me as Siran."

"Very well," Tyghus said dismissively. "I didn't meet you to debate such things."

"Then why you come?"

"To tell you quite simply that this doesn't have to happen."

Andran's eyes narrowed on the General. "Will you tell me to surrender like you tell Queen?"

Tyghus blanched. "I didn't tell Tygha to surrender. I told her –"

"You did! But how, Mondid? How can we surrender? After you destroy Bakia, after you bring this war to Valogar. So –"

"You mistake my people on two counts," Tyghus said sharply. "The Chibin brought war to us and so we must bring it to them; your mirami chose to stand between that. And as for Bakia, if the Colverians stayed out of your affairs, I wouldn't have had to take it. You know as well as I that their men and arms have flowed through that port for centuries."

"You should worry about Colverians attacking *your* lands in south. But even so, you've wasted your time; Colverians already stand with my warriors to share today's glory."

The revelation made the General's stomach recoil, but he didn't let his face show it. Instead, he grew more resolute. "Surrender, Lij. I can promise you better terms and treatment than any Rokhish general in the future will. Send your army back to their hearth and homes where they're needed most; turn over any Chibin that you know of. Better yet, help us fight them! Help yourselves!"

Andran's eyes finally parted from Tyghus's, flicking to the line of the Sixth Dyron some three hundred yards behind him. "Mondid, as boy I saw Rokh army all over my country. I saw them fight and train and fight again. I *know* Rokh army is fierce, I know they're brave," he said with a subtle nod, before looking to the General. "But how can you ask such things when seeing army behind me? You have so few men, and even Rokh army cannot fight –"

"Don't speak of what can and cannot be done," Tyghus quickly interjected. "And don't let my numbers deceive you; tens of thousands more from across the sea gather to join the fight."

The Lij looked behind him with confused expression. "But I do not see them, Mondid."

"Then perhaps the sails of their ships will convince you otherwise."

"No ships," Andran replied, shaking his head. "My people keep watch along north coast, they see no ships."

Tyghus's jaw clenched as the Valogarian king's eyes bored into his. "I know your country under attack, Mondid. Attack from south, attack from west."

"You've made a deal with the darkest of gods to wake the Terelesh," Tyghus said in fury. "What could you possibly have offered them to do such a thing? And on what pretense of honor do you now stand with that evil at your side?"

"The man who left old men, women, and children to starve in Bakia speaks to me about honor?" Andran said with a force that stole Tyghus's voice. "I know your ships not coming," the Lij said after a pause. "I know your own king not want your victory here."

Tyghus's brows arched. "You blacken the Khorokh's name with such slander," he growled.

But Andran shook his head. "I have no need. It is true what I said."

"On whose word?"

Andran was slow to answer. "It is true," he finally offered. "You are alone in Valogar, and I cannot let you leave."

"I'm not asking you to."

"You should."

Silence fell over the two for a moment, each studying the other. "I only offer you this chance one last time," Tyghus said quietly. "Whatever my fate will be, know that other Rokhish armies will complete whatever you believe I cannot."

Andran's frowning lips finally ticked upwards. "I told you in my ahovy, your people do not understand Valogar. Today is all my people live for; tomorrow is in gods' hands. Maybe Valogar conquered again tomorrow, maybe not. But the people will have today's victory *forever*. For them, today is *everything*."

"My Lij, you've never seen battle. Your men have never seen battle. Only those that haven't seen it would 'live for' it, as you say."

"Yet you live for it, Mondid."

"I was born into a soldier's life," Tyghus said with rising voice. "And I can promise you, that life has cost me dearly in many, *many* ways, so I'm *never* one to take it for granted!"

The Lij gave no response other than to fold his arms over his chest. His glare conveyed the discussions had reached their end.

"Very well," Tyghus said, turning to leave. "I won't waste my breath —"

"You told me on Night of Celebration that you would not let this day happen," Andran suddenly interjected, bringing the General to a halt. "You smoked the rantazo and told me that."

It was the first break of the Lij's façade Tyghus had seen. "Brother, you have no idea what I did to prevent this —"

"No, you *swore* it to me!" Andran barked, hands dropping to his side in balled fists. "And you gave me *hope*, when you said it, Mondid. All my being told me not to, but still I had hope... yet now you here."

Tyghus could only stare back defiantly, guilt gnawing at his mind.

"Weak men betray, Mondid. Men without honor betray, but not men like you! Your betrayal *stabbed* me like sword through heart! Wound me so much I could not look at Queen for sharing your blood..."

The king's glower turn contemplative. "But then I ask myself — was your father's saying correct? Did *I* bring this day by planning for worst?"

Tyghus thought about it for a moment before tiredly shrugging his shoulders. "We're just men... your questions are ones for the gods."

Andran gave a reluctant nod. "Yes, they are."

"I don't suppose it matters, because the day's arrived," Tyghus said with a sigh before looking to Andran's eyes one final time. "I know you feel betrayed, my Lij, but if there's any part of you that remembers me for who I was in that ahovy, if there's any part of you that believes me when I say we must be meant for something better than dying on this muddy field, then I'd only ask of you one favor — that you send my love to Tygha if I fall," he said, offering his hand to the Lij. "And I will do the same for you."

The king looked at the General's hand uncertainly for a moment, but finally relented and took it in his own. "And same to Mikolo."

Tyghus froze as Andran surveyed him with knowing eyes. Slowly, a subtle grin crept over his face. "I see you in netherworld some day, Mondid."

Tyghus allowed a grin back. "If the gods will have us."

The Lij gave a curt nod before showing Tyghus his back. The General stared at the departing king's large frame for a moment, serenaded by nothing but a stiff wind blowing through. He was amazed at the transformation the Valogarian had undergone since their last encounter.

False king or not, Tyghus thought. *He's a leader all the same.*

At last, he conceded the ground and headed back to his own army.

The battle they swore would never come was finally upon them.

* * *

"Well, I'll say it, Tyghus: take the head off the next man who questions your courage."

Kneeling to secure his shin greaves' fastenings, the General smiled at Fygonus reviewing their battle plans one last time. Nikolux, Noccus, and Fyrustus flanked their sides. "I'll do that, Fygo'."

"Can this madness possibly work?"

"That's on us, brother. Me and my brilliant kordettes."

"You sure you mean us?" Fyrus' asked with a crooked grin.

Tyghus smirked. "I do... I mean I hope I do."

"Well, by the time the sun sets, we'll have our answer, won't we?" Noccus said.

"Aye. We've done it before though, no reason to think we can't do it now."

"In *Avergon,* we've done it," Fygo' said.

"Aye, so?" Tyghus sighed as he stood. "We had to have drilled it a hundred times, at least."

"True," the Twin said as he looked from the Rokhish lines drawing up for battle behind them to the roiling mass of Valogarians some five hundred yards off. "But not against sixty thousand hostiles... not to mention Colverians and those ratty ponies of theirs."

Tyghus shook his head dismissively. "Call me a mad man then, but it's the same principles," he said matter-of-factly, refusing to indulge any doubts. "Besides, we have some surprises for the good Lij that will shake his infatuation with his numbers."

"An infatuation easy to make with six-to-one odds... gods above, I'd make love to those odds..."

"Alright, then, what?" Tyghus said as he lightly shoved the big man. "You scared, friend?"

Fygo' scoffed. "Only a Tyghid would be scared. What better story could I have for Stygus if I meet him today?"

He's scared, Tyghus thought with a smile, an emotion to which he'd not been immune. There was no other way to explain the images he'd been stubbornly unable to avoid seeing since their trek to the Sunken Fields: images of his father sparring with him for the first time as a boy; of his mother's distressed look as he set off for the Academy; of Kyrus embracing him over the shared pain of their paris' deaths; of Vara breaking his heart, of Miko breathing life into it.

Aye, we're scared… but it's the way we harness that fear…

"Listen to me, all of you," the General said, as he looked at each man. "I put the four of you in the center of our line for a reason. You're the 'Crux' of the whole plan, aye? You *need* to stay alive for those men in your kords and I trust the four of you more than anyone else in the Sixth to make that so. If any of you falter, this *won't* work."

"There'll be no falter," Fyrustus said as he turned to Tyghus; his eyes bordered on misty. "By the gods high and low, I swear it. I've waited my whole life for this."

Tyghus smiled back at him. "Hope you don't grow bored after our victory, then."

The twin's yellow eyes dashed away from the General for a moment. "This can be done, brothers. This *will* be done."

The foursome nodded heads while gazing distantly at the Native army.

"That's some bloody gathering, though," Niko' muttered gruffly, drawing laughs.

"Fight well, brothers," Tyghus said, exchanging forearm clenches with each man, clenches that lingered just a little longer than usual; he prayed they didn't feel his hands shaking already.

He glanced towards the Valogarians and saw they were ever so much closer. "Here they come."

* * *

With every plodding step, the Valogarian horde expanded farther and farther beyond the General's view. They spanned over two thousand feet across, yet with barely a fraction of their numbers, Tyghus had stretched six kords just as wide to prevent the "fishhooks" he'd seen them attempt at Bakia, when they sought to envelop the ends of his line. To the far left of the Rokhish line was Grantax, with Kinistus anchored on the far right along a shallow stream bed. The two of them bookended his four central kordettes, and divided evenly behind those "bookends" were his four remaining kords.

A hundred feet behind him, Napodonax barked last-minute adjustments to siege workers. His kord had rapidly created tiny hillocks to perch their twenty war machines upon, just high enough to provide a vantage over the heads of friendly troops. A glance back at them showed the massive weapons poised to strike like a line of scorpions.

But it was Fygonus, Nikolux, Fyrustus, and Noccus in the center – the Crux – that he studied closest. Kords thinned to a depth of only ten men, they wouldn't have the help behind them that his bookends would. The Kordettes he trusted, but if even a row of their men lost their nerve – even a *single* soldier – then…

Stop, he scolded himself, taking a deep breath inside his humid helmet. *It's done now… and anyway, they'll hold. They'll be fine. Worry about yourself, about your horse*, he thought as he felt Fidipodus laboring a bit under the added weight of ringlet armor. He paced anxiously in place, seemingly catching the tension of the motionless troops around them.

"*It's alright, boy,*" Tyghus whispered to the beast as he stroked his head. "*It'll be over soon…*"

The mass crept closer, when suddenly a frenzied charge of lekeys burst southwards from the Natives' far right.

"Aggressive bastards," the General muttered to himself, seeing faces of a few edgy Rokhs look back at him.

But from his far left, Reverus's elite horsemen kicked into high sprint to answer the beige stampede. Within seconds, the groups of horse closed the three-hundred yard gap, careening towards each other so fast that the General barely had mind to breathe.

Just before impact Reverus led a sharp left turn in unison with his men. To their credit, the lekeys stopped hard in their tracks, riders chiding the Rokhs. Thousands of them milled about in a confused huddle for a few moments, when their derision quickly ceased.

Reverus had veered again, this time arcing back towards his enemies in perfect formation at full gallop. Even coordinated lekeys would have only had seconds to adjust.

Tyghus smiled.

The shimmering silver mass of Rokhish horsemen knifed into the Native throng. Men quickly toppled from their beasts, their shorter mounts providing the perfect angle for Rokhs to slice downwards. True to their instincts, unmounted lekeys fled frantically in every direction, seeking the nearest path away from the steel and death.

The Sixth roared in approval.

Like a needle through cloth, Reverus burst forth from the eastern side of the lekey brigade, just as braver riders began putting up resistance. With only two hundred yards to negotiate between the closing Rokhish and Valogarian lines, the Stuqatta deftly led his horsemen in an about-face to bring another charge to bear upon the lekeys. This time, the lekeys broke towards the safety of their own lines, Rokhish cavalry following in tight pursuit.

More roars erupted from Tyghus's men, when suddenly their voices gave out.

The buzzing returned.

Rainbows of arrows climbed into the sky over the Native line, just as Reverus neared.

By the gods, pull back, brother, the General pleaded to Reverus. *Pull back!*

Lesser archers would never risk firing so close to friendly troops, but these were the Men of Colvery. The unseen archers' arrows invariably stayed true.

And they rained death upon the Rokhs' precious cavalry.

Hideous shrieks of man and equine echoed across the battlefield. Tyghus had never seen his cavalry break formation, but as the deadly shafts riddled both beasts and riders, it was inevitable. The horsemen's startled delay proved doubly grave as frenzied Valogarian spearmen rushed forward to gore the fallen and lamed. Soon they exploded with shrieking whoops, and in a matter of moments, the entire line – all seven hundred yards of it – broke into a full charge towards the Rokhs.

Tyghus felt like he watched someone else's army fighting someone else's foe. As if he was seated with the gods already. As if –

"*Fire!*"

Like a hurricane's gales, twenty great whooshing sounds to his rear nearly deafened him. Before he'd even had time to look back, Napo's boulders soared overhead towards the charging Natives. His eyes bounced from cavalry retreating towards his line to magnificent stones seemingly suspended in mid-air.

He quickly gripped Fidi's reins. "*Steady boy…*"

BOOM! BOOM! BOOM!

The boulders quaked the ground in rapid succession, plunging into Native warriors with unstoppable force. Men were shattered on impact, others sent flying through the air. Some rocks landed a few yards ahead of the rushing line, rolling irresistibly through the furious front ranks. The Valogarians slowed for a moment, betraying uncertainty. Like a bottomless bog, however, the boulders' breaches soon filled themselves in and they were back at the quickstep.

Reverus's horsemen re-settled themselves to the left of the Rokhish line. Even from far off, the group looked significantly pared, perhaps by a quarter and despite the safe harbor of friendly troops, riders still fell from their horses – dead, from the poison that had worked its way through their bodies.

Tyghus swore to himself before he turned to watch his troops. "Not long now, men!" he yelled to them. "Not long at all!"

Some kordettes raised swords in recognition.

The Natives closed to within a hundred yards, seemingly growing faster.

Still Tyghus's footmen did not move, an agonizing sight for an aggressive general; jealously, he watched Reverus's kord peel off westward and out of sight, leaving behind their dead and dying to skirmish with resurgent lekeys.

"*Fire!*"

Another violent salvo sent even larger stones hurtling towards the Natives – larger stones saved for closer troops. The charge wavered upon sight of massive rocks that must have seemed unavoidable.

BOOM! BOOM! BOOM!

The very earth shook with the blasts, sending some of his own soldiers off-balance despite being fifty yards away. Natives were crushed in place while limbs were shorn from shocked bodies. Blood sprayed the ground slick. Huge gaps opened in the line, despite the tens of thousands of warriors within it. Again the line slowed…

Until from the breach in the dead center of the Valogarian line an imposing figure dashed out. He ran with a deer's speed, a bear's size, a lion's ferocity. He wore Valogar's finest wooden armor and spikes; he wielded a twenty-foot double-pointed spear.

He was the eighteenth Andran of his family's history. He was the Lij of loyal Valogar.

And he stormed towards the Rokhish line in absolute fury.

"*D-i-i-i-i-a-a-a-a-a-a-a-m-m-m-m-m-m-m-y-y-y-y-y-y-y!*"

Andran's men soon found their nerve and took up the charge with renewed furor; the painted wave soon enveloped their king, bearing down on the Rokhs with ear-piercing shrieks. Their stampede rumbled the ground as the boulders had.

Tyghus kipped Fidopodus, galloping up and down behind the center of his line. "Alright men, this is it!" Tyghus bellowed as a rush swept through his body. "Brace for charge! *Brace for charge!*"

Twenty yards out… ten yards… five…

With a clap of thunder the Natives threw themselves upon the Rokhish line without a hint of order. It was a wild, ferocious scrum, with greenish spears and silotys stabbing and hammering at steel-clad Imperials. The latter stood like stone walls against the assault, hiding as much flesh as possible behind Stygan shields.

"*Don't you give them an inch!*" Niko' raged, his voice somehow soaring above the chaos.

"*Hold you bastards!*" Fyrus' implored.

The Native horde seemed never-ending, the sheer crush of manpower soon bringing itself to bear. The Crux's soldiers leaned forward into the mass but it wasn't enough; feet began slipping despite dogged resistance, despite raging for every blade of grass. Ten rows of men simply couldn't hold back an enemy six times deeper. The inches they gave soon became feet, feet became yards. And with every yard given, their bodies offered more and more targets, which frenzied Valogarians were quick to exploit. Collapses of dead and poisoned Rokhs multiplied.

Now.

Tyghus about-faced on his horse in an instant to lock eyes with Napo' manning the hillocks. His arms shot over his head, raising sword and shield as high as his surging muscles would allow. Napo' returned the motion immediately. Within seconds his siege workers loaded boulder-sized wooden barrels onto the catapults; Tyghus wheeled back towards his harried men.

Now, he thought through heaving breaths. *Now, Napodonax!*

"Fire!"

He'd never risk Napo's weapons in the middle of a fray – except when his foe ran hundreds of ranks deep. A wild smile overtook his face as he watched the barrels sail harmlessly above and beyond the fighting line – barrels taken from Bakia, full of pyhr and every metal shard, fragment, and spike that his troops could cram into them.

Now we'll see how you enjoy your poison.

The barrels exploded open deep in the recesses of the Valogarian horde, spraying their deadly payload in every direction. Even from his limited vantage, Tyghus could see entire circles of Valogarians fall as if struck by the gods. The hundreds of squelched war cries rang poignant.

The General thrust his shield and sword over his head again, without even looking back to his Belagatte. Moments later...

"Fire!"

Tyghus let out a primal roar of his own, arms still raised as the erupting pyhr kegs sliced through more Native waves. This time, he could see some of them just behind the battle line glance back, an ounce of uncertainty betraying their faces. Still, their surge pushed on, the Rokhish center ballooning back towards him.

"*Again!*" the General yelled to no one in particular, his voice hopelessly lost amongst the cries of battle. "*Again Napodonax! Let 'em feast on that pyhric hell!*"

"Fire!"

A third volley flung headlong into the Valogarians, barrels twirling end over end before dousing their victims with loads of toxic shrapnel. Several warriors bearing simple crowns – mirami leaders, no doubt – were swept away in the steely hail. Those on the battle line fought with unabated fury, but without the massive numbers pushing behind them, the surge slowed and then stalled against Rokhs regaining their footing.

Tyghus knew the barrels were gone, but they'd served their purpose in checking the onslaught, at least for the moment; he knew the lines of Colverians would be creeping ever closer, waiting for their chance to let loose on his footmen. He sped along the back of the Crux, measuring its peril and losses while looking for kordettes' plumes. Farther down each end of his line, he could see his Bookends scrapping viciously but holding firm all the same, not surrendering an inch. Suddenly, a cheer went up from Niko's unit.

He turned as a voice cried out, *"the king has fallen!"*

Whether by stumble or force, the massive Lij had indeed fallen out of sight. Tyghus could scarcely believe his eyes as he watched Niko's Fourth Kord press the stunned Valogarians, perfectly synchronized upward sword slices crumpling dozens of Natives. Soon, both sides scrambled for the Lij's body.

"Can't be," the General muttered to himself in disbelief, straining to catch a glimpse of the body. "He can't be dead!"

The bubble in the Rokhish middle began reversing, while gaps from Napo's pyhr kegs filled in behind fatiguing front line Natives. Niko's push was blunted, and in seconds that trickled by like an eternity, Andran reemerged a few rows back from the battle line, coated in blood, but defiantly whirling his spear overhead with a roar.

His men answered with revitalized shrieking.

"Diamy!" the Lij hollered, courageous, defiant, triumphant all at once.

The frenzied mirami charge resumed, those yet to taste battle flinging headlong into shimmering Imperials. Spears and thorned clubs pounded the Rokhish center, and the swell that had withered away only a minute prior suddenly bulged southward once again – far quicker and sloppier than before.

Shit...

Tyghus was desperate to intervene but knew he had to guide his troops from behind the lines to keep perspective on the sprawling battle's ebbs and flows. He raised his sword and galloped along the growing swell.

"Hold the line, Rokhs! We break for no one!"

But more ground was ceded. The shallow divot bloomed into a horseshoe, the center pushed back scores of yards from the original line of battle. Valogarians trampled mercilessly over dead Rokhish troops, throwing the living back so rapidly that they'd nearly run right into Tyghus and Napo's hillocks. The General could hear the Belagatte's unarmored siegemen unsheathing weapons, preparing to enter uncommon ground by giving battle by the sword.

Tyghus swung Fidipodus to the left then right again, searching for weak spots and finding them everywhere, when time slowed and he saw a pair of Native eyes staring straight at him from just behind the battle line. It was the Lij, fixed in wide-eyed madness with a splintered shield and blood-soaked spear. For just a moment, Tyghus could hear his heart pounding in his ears, the sounds of the din waning.

Then, he simply shook his head.

It's time.

Tyghus looked behind him and gave a quick nod to Napodonax, before digging his heels into his horse's haunches, sending him flying westwards as fast as his legs could carry them.

"Twelfth Kord – *c-h-h-h-h-h-a-a-r-r-r-r-g-g-g-g-e!*" the Belagatte yelled as Tyghus sped towards his left Bookend. Metallic clashing soon followed, but soon enough he reached the calmer kords of Grantax, Golaxus, and Pydonus, stacked one behind the other to resist the Valogarian right. Pydonus saw the General approach with sword arm raised and his eyes widened immediately.

"Now men!" the kordette screamed frantically. "Now! Start the push!"

The Tenth Kord roared then redoubled their efforts with the Fifth and First in front of them. Soon they weren't just maintaining their anchor – they were taking ground from the startled Natives.

In an instant, Tyghus raced back down the western side of the "horseshoe", horrified as he saw the center's bubble about to burst. Napo's troops had plugged the most weakened spot but were hopelessly few and incredibly vulnerable to Native weaponry without armor and shield.

"*Hold on, men!*" he shouted as he sped up the eastern side of the Horseshoe. "*You are steel! Bulls of Stygus the lot of you!*"

He reared hard on the reins of his frothing beast before the stacked kords of Kinistus, Swiftus, and Siderius. The stalemate with his right Bookend had been sloppier, with Natives storming into the waist-deep waters of the creek to hack at Rokhish flanks. Some Imperials had joined them, erupting in an orgy of alternating sprays of blood and water. Bodies of both ilks floated eerily in the waterway, dyeing the pristine waters a murky red.

Nevertheless, Siderius caught sight of his leader and knew precisely what to do. "It's time, men! *Surge forth! Let 'em drown in their creek!*"

"Give them hell!" Tyghus yelled back, immediately dashing back towards the Crux.

The dug-in troops sprang forth with a vengeance on both land and creek to drive back the Valogarian left, Sider's men especially invigorated.

Tyghus allowed himself a maniacal smile.

Wind whistled through his helmet as his horse's sprint gathered strength. He crouched lower and sped just feet behind the Crux. Kordettes had been forced to the forefront as there were no rows left behind them; they battled alongside the men they commanded, struggling with all their might to prevent a breakthrough. Both Rokh and Valogarian knew a hole, just one, could collapse the entire Rokh resistance.

"*Hold them, men!*" Tyghus bellowed as he closed on Fyrus's, Niko's, and Napo's men fighting in united desperation. "*The wings have taken the offensive! They're driving the bastards back as we –*"

A twenty-foot siloty whacked Fidi' across the face. The beast squealed in agony as he instinctively twisted and reared up on his back hooves. The violent torque sent Tyghus flying off, crashing hard onto his shield in the soil below, before rolling uncontrollably into the battle line itself.

His head bobbled around in a daze, the world spinning around him. He caught a glimpse of his horse sprinting off the battlefield, blood gushing from his face. Inches away from him steel-greaved legs moved in their dances of death with bare-legged counterparts.

The sight spoke for itself – he was too late.

The center was breaking.

"General, get up!"

Tyghus scrambled backwards, trying to find his footing but inevitably slipping. His shield was irrevocably splintered so he let it slip from his hand – and not a moment too soon as Valogarians soon surged onto his landing spot. He cursed as he tried to lift himself with his throbbing shield arm but failed; it was at least fractured, if not worse.

"Tyghus, stand up dammit!"

A massive limb latched around his sword arm and hauled him to his wobbly feet. He'd only a moment to realize it was Fyrus' before they were fending off spear thrusts and siloty strikes on sheer instinct alone.

Valogarians were everywhere.

"*Where the hell are Napo's men?*" the General yelled to no one in particular.

"*They gave us a bloody minute, nothin' more!*" Fyrus' unexpectedly roared back, fighting nearly side by side with Tyghus. "*The Lij's throwin' everything he can at the cent –*"

The mighty warrior let out a blood-curdling scream. As Tyghus drove his sword through a bare-chest in front of him he glanced to his right and saw it.

Siloty thorns slammed into the breach between the Twin's helmet and mail. A split-second later the Ruhl sliced his attacker's arm from its body, hand still gripping the bloody club. But both Rokh and Valogarian fell.

"*No, Fyrus'!*" Tyghus cried out in agony as spears thrust in on him from every direction.

He viciously sliced each spearpoint away from him, but between every hack he glanced back down at the writhing body of his friend. "*One of you get him to the rear!*" he bellowed at Fyrus's exhausted and wavering Third Kord. "*The rest of you, fight for 'im, dammit! Fight for Fyrus'!*"

"*For Fyrustus!*" a rallying cheer went up and the beleaguered men dug in as a lone man ferreted his way to the fallen kordette to drag him back towards the war machines.

Hordes of enemies and few Rokhs were on all sides of Tyghus, his 'line' a hopeless misnomer. He didn't know what he was doing but felt like he'd entered a dream with the ear-splitting noise and narrow sight. His sword swung itself as if possessed by a spirit, following an Academy mantra he'd heard since he was a tob':

Make an X and run it through. Step forward.

He didn't know if he was giving or losing ground. He just killed whomever was in front of him.

Make an X and run it through. Step forward.

Waves of Natives fell. He gashed a Valogarian with gap teeth above the shoulder; another'd already lost an ear, but Tyghus took his head as well. One was coated in blue paint – but it soon mixed with crimson from his bleeding chest.

Make an X and run it through. Step forward.

The next was painted too, but in bloody white stripes across the face; he was large, with a massive double-pointed feathered spear held menacingly over a head framed by animal horns.

The Lij's black eyes locked on his.

Tyghus paused upon sight of the King, glancing around him to finally take stock of the fray. Men from the Crux had re-formed a shabby perimeter around him, furiously scrapping with numberless Natives. Tyghus's mindless rage had carved a space before him, and he flicked his head side to side in a cautious crouch as he waited for the Valogarian king to approach him.

"Well, come on!" he yelled with heaving chest, red spit dripping out of the bottom of his helmet. *"Come now, great king!"*

The Lij warily eyed the pocket in front of him as warriors huddled to his sides.

"General!"

A hand suddenly placed itself upon Tyghus's shoulder, but the General wouldn't take his eyes off his royal foe. The voice continued anyway.

"General – our wings are driving 'em in! Their edges are collapsin' towards the middle!"

A spear swiftly drove its way through the man's shoulder and he groaned with pain. In a flash of light towards the sky, Tyghus's blade dropped the attacker with a blow across the chest.

He looked to Andran again, who eyed the fallen Rokh and Native. Even if the voice was right, there was no way they could tell amidst the mob. But if he *was*...

The Lij charged.

He came in impossibly fast and lunged his spear in a downward strike that barely missed Tyghus's foot. Tyghus hopped back, then came within inches of slicing the weapon in two before it was pulled away. Andran quickly jammed the spear towards Tyghus's swordless side, striking his ribbed armor with thunderous force. The General gnashed his teeth in pain as armor fragments flew off into the masses.

351

Emboldened by the strike, the Lij whipped the shaft towards Tyghus's head. Though the General's forearm blocked the blow at the last moment, it sent such shockwaves through his limb that he nearly dropped his sword.

The spear retracted but immediately returned towards Tyghus's belly. Only an instinctual twirl let the Lij's weapon pass by harmlessly. Even still, Andran left no opening, recoiling to strike yet again like a cobra.

Stop fighting on his terms! Tyghus scolded himself, feeling his swordhand begin to go numb. The length of the Valogarian spear made any move on his part a dangerous affair, but he knew he couldn't continue absorbing blows – he had to close the gap.

The General leaned in, almost taunting the Lij to strike; the Valogarian quickly obliged with a thrust towards Tyghus's face, but the weapon found only air. Tyghus swayed hard to the side, before whacking the outstretched spear with the broad side of his sword.

The blow stunned the Lij, one hand momentarily losing its grip. Tyghus instantly dashed in closer with sword raised, feinting an overhand strike as Andran wildly whipped his spear overhead to block it. The Valogarian's wood-covered chest was exposed, and the General wasted no time slicing right to left across it. The sword sheared straight through the armor, which dropped away to reveal a quickly thickening line of red underneath.

The Lij howled in agony, but still managed to hammer the spear's shaft into Tyghus's neck, stopping an attempt to slice open Andran's exposed belly. Andran's blow sent more silver armor fragments flying, but this time, Tyghus snatched the pole with a throbbing mailed hand before Andran could retract it, and without hesitation cut the weapon in two. Undaunted, the Lij sent Tyghus's lunging figure stumbling backwards with a boot to his head while yanking the stub of his weapon from the Rokh's grip.

Tyghus met the Lij's eyes as he regained his balance to crouch low with sword held out in front of him. Andran's bloody chest heaved up and down as the effects of his wound appeared to take hold, leaving him far more cautious with his broken weapon. The Lij looked around him again, his face failing to hide the dismay of seeing his center troops panicking from word of collapsing wings; the Rokhish "horseshoe" had given ground just as Tyghus planned, and while the center had been obliterated, the weighted Bookends took advantage to punish the Natives' overpursuit. The fight in the Lij's eyes seemed to dim just a bit.

But Tyghus never planned for what happened next.

"In the next life, brother," Andran boomed over the din. Still in crouch, Tyghus looked back at him in confusion. *"Onova onahi?"* the Lij suddenly bellowed. The men at his side looked to their king apprehensively.

Tyghus felt a chill run up his spine. "Andran, what did you say? *What did you say to them?"*

But Andran offered nothing more. Instead, Tyghus could only watch as he dropped his spear arm to the ground momentarily, before it rocketed upwards to send the weapon twirling high over the army. The General watched incredulously at first, until his gaze fell back on the dazed Lij. *"What is this?"*

But he soon had his answer.

The sky darkened with the shadows cast by thousands of arrows.

They arced beautifully over the lines – to a point. Then…

"Colverians!" Tyghus yelled helplessly, stunned by the fact that the deadly shafts were destined to rake as many friendly troops as foes.

He looked to his sides and saw many of his soldiers raising shields only to be impaled by furious Natives. To the front of him the Lij stood with arms outstretched overhead as if inviting the barrage.

Gods above…

With little thought, Tyghus threw his torso under the corpse of a fallen Valogarian, quickly scrabbling for a shield to cover exposed legs, fully aware that neither would resist a bolt strike. Panicked screams were soon drowned out by a rising buzz. He peered out from under the body just as the carnage unfolded.

As if struck by a tidal wave, swaths of men bearing armor, paint or neither dropped in place. They were the lucky ones, killed by the arrows themselves. More collapsed soon after when arrows' pyhric poison worked its way into gashes and cuts. For his part, Tyghus cringed but coaxed his eyes open, hearing his own stifled breaths inside his helmet as crisply as the death cries.

The great Lij of Valogar didn't survive the first volley. He lay face down in front of Tyghus a few feet away, feathered shaft protruding from his back. Even in death, his arms still splayed out in the shape they'd taken towards the sky just moments prior. The sight of him so inglorious made the General's stomach clench.

The buzzing suddenly ceased, replaced by an eerie quiet. Tyghus scanned the area about him, appalled at the motionless heaps of men. Tilling, aimless masses of Rokhs and Valogarians still gave battle here and there but it was clear they did so with no end in mind. Droves of Natives could be seen simply fleeing the field altogether, choosing life over martyrdom.

And in that moment of horror, Tyghus knew what he had to do – knew all he *could* do.

He flung the clammy corpse off of him and staggered to his feet.

"Sixth Dyron!" he forced from his lungs.

A paltry few called back to him.

"Do you have one last charge in ya'?"

"Aye, General!" a few more answered. Troops taking cover rose from the ground like the undead.

"Then join me!" he ordered simply, painfully snatching up the shield he found before breaking into a trot towards the unseen archers some thousand yards away.

A second volley soon marred the sky again but Tyghus jogged on without worry. His legs burned with exhaustion as he begged them forward, his feet doing their best to find solid ground amidst a field riddled with bodies, stones, and shards. Though he never bothered to confirm, he felt there was a ragged line of wounded running with him to his right and left, cutting down or falling to sporadic Valogarian resistance. The Natives' heart appeared gutted enough by the first Colverian volley that few were prepared to take a charge, instead fleeing upon sight of the growing number of mad Rokhs.

"Kordettes!" he called out through pants, utterly unaware if any ran with him.

No responses.

Just keep running.

The buzzing drew nearer.

Tyghus's breaths grew quicker.

The collection of Valogarians fleeing before him escalated into a torrent.

Deadly bolts began raining all around him. One plunged straight into the ground in front of him, sending him stumbling off-kilter as he tried to avoid it. Bracing for pain that surely was imminent, he let out a wild, primeval yell, one that drowned out the vile sucking sounds of arrows finding their marks nearby.

"Just keep running!" he screamed at his soldiers. *"Gods-be-damned just keep running!"*

He didn't notice he'd survived the second volley. Didn't notice his complete exhaustion or the hundreds of men from both armies being struck down as they ran. The only thing he noticed was the image through the gaps between the fleeing Valogarians ahead of him – the line of tall, green-clad men some three dozen yards off.

He saw only the Colverians now; saw them and took heart.

Come now, you sons of whores… kill me before I reach you… kill me!

"There they are, men!"

They were close enough to see the fineness of the archers' high-collared, forest green tunics and the detached brown hoods that covered all but their pale, emotionless faces.

Close enough to watch them draw fresh arrows to their bows.

Close enough for them to pick out individual Rokh targets as the Natives scattered aside.

"Shoot, you cowards!" he shouted in rage at the archers, as he held his shield out in front of him, plaintively hoping arrows found it before him.

The entire green line leveled their bows straight on at the fast-approaching Rokhs.

They fired.

A bolt blasted through his shield instantly. Several more took down a portion of those at his side.

But more skipped harmlessly into the grass.

Even more soared benignly overhead.

Tyghus smiled as he threw his ruined shield to the ground.

Colverian bows weren't meant to fire head on. Their heavy-headed arrows were meant to fly in an arc from behind safe lines.

Yet the Sixth *was* attacking head on.

And there were no more safe lines.

"Char-r-r-r-r-r-g-g-g-g-g-g-e!"

A battle cry never sounded so sweet. And while Tyghus had no idea who still attacked with him, in his heart he knew every Rokh with a breath was there. He cruelly grinned as normally stoic Colverians looked about in a panic, bearing nothing but small daggers to stave off their battle-crazed foe.

Tyghus's first blow cleaved a Colverian straight through from right shoulder to left hip. A roar went up among his men who witnessed the resulting blood geyser, quickly joining the fray themselves.

But the Rokhs were few and the Colverians many, with the former nearly breathless from the charge alone. The Colverians' aversion to hand weaponry was legendary, but after their initial wavering, they soon realized their advantage. They steeled, then gave awkward battle using daggers to stab and bows to club.

Tyghus looked about him, soon finding himself and his soldiers engulfed in a sea of green. Wood pounded all sides of him, followed by a burning sensation at his side. He glanced down and saw the jagged handle of a dagger protruding from just under the left side of his armor. He angrily rammed a sword through the stomach of the Colverian, but he soon lost his room to do more. They were everywhere.

When suddenly, there were equines among them.

Steely warhorses dripping in crimson romped through the thicket of archers while their riders hewed through the same. Tyghus never saw them approach but their arrival instantly seemed to sap the Colverians' newfound confidence. The immense, impenetrable beasts proved too much for them, and before long they took flight in any number of directions like their allies. Like the sun burning away fog, Colverians disappeared before Tyghus's eyes, heavy horses in close chase.

Tyghus spitefully followed a few archers that attempted to flee, but the throbbing pain at his side limited his pursuit. He took a few running steps before his vision turned yellow and he stumbled down to hands and knees. From a crawl, he blindly tried to press on, but he finally gave up. He let his body fall face first into the grass, sword still gripped tight.

Tyghus gasped for breath. Pushing his helmet off, his left hand fumbled for the handle of the dagger still lodged in his side. Despite his deliriously excruciating pain, he couldn't help but notice the sudden stillness in the air. It seemed like years since he'd heard such peace.

His eyes closed.

* * *

Voices were suddenly everywhere. Voices speaking unintelligible words.
Where am I?
Footsteps all around him.
Am I dead?
Some weren't voices. Some were groans. Groans of the dying.
The battle…
"Forgive me, General…"
Tyghus's eyes shot open as he unleashed a blood-curdling howl. He rolled reflexively onto his back as blood-shot eyes wildly searched the small group gathered around him. Registering nothing, they finally fell upon his left side and saw a chain-mailed soldier holding a bloody dagger above an open wound.

"Apologies, my lord!" the soldier gushed.

"Bandage it, dammit!" a voice behind him called.

Tyghus took note of the man and let his head fall back into the grass, eyes closing again.

"Here, this'll stem the bleedin'," the soldier said, pressing a rag against the hole in his side.

"Lucky bastard two-ways," he heard the man say to someone. "Struck 'is rib and missed 'is guts."

"Aye?"

"Aye. And the archers didn't have their blades soakin' in pyhr neither, only their arrows…"

Tyghus cracked an eyelid. "*Soldier…*" he mumbled.

"My lord?" the soldier said as he leaned in closer.

"*The battle…*"

The man was silent at first. "We've beaten 'em. They're runnin' like the scalded dogs they are."

Tyghus closed his eyes again. "The dead?"

"Lot of 'em," the soldier said. "Still countin' 'em up, but damn it all, we're here, aye? Still livin', still breathin'!"

Tyghus erupted in a spate of painful coughs. "Aye…" He sighed. "Send the kordettes to me… whoever's left. Pile our dead, count them… or count the living, whichever's quicker."

"Aye, General," the man said, who limped off.

"You two," Tyghus called to two other men in the group as he raised his head. "Help me... help me to my feet."

"My lord, your wound's gapin' and apt to fester," the shorter of the two protested. "Let's run water or maybe a bit a' grog over it before –"

"Just help me up, lad," Tyghus rebutted as calmly as possible. "Just... just help me up."

The two of them exchanged weary glances but at last hoisted the General up by the armpits. Tyghus winced in pain as his throbbing arm held the rag to his wound while another helped steady him. His tired eyes surveyed the battlefield's panorama.

They found carnage on a scale he never thought possible.

For a thousand yards before him he saw nothing but the dead and dying bodies of beasts and men strewn across the grass. The wounded writhed upon the earth like worms in the rain. Arrows peppered the ground like barren saplings while chunks of boulders and barrels and swords and shields lay everywhere. Far across the field were Napo's mighty catapults, silent sentries to the devastation before them. Immediately surrounding him were crumpled heaps of forest green Colverians, their luxurious fabric stained by red marks of their mortality.

"Pity the man who has to declare victor this day," he said solemnly.

The soldier at his side gave a dark chuckle while his eyes fell upon Tyghus. "Rumor's that the Native king's been slain... I wonder if –"

Tyghus nodded. "He is."

The soldier shook his head in disbelief. "Gods above... then who – who is their leader, then? Isn't it your sister that –"

"I don't know," he said sharply.

"Aye, apologies, General."

It'd been a fair question, but he hadn't even registered the gravity of the battlefield before him, let alone what he could do for his beloved sister. Tyghus looked at the young man, a lad that looked hardly past his Run. "What do they call you?"

"Motus Worbon, sire."

Tyghus frowned in recognition. "Heard your name before. Heard you fight like you've a Ruhl's training. Third Kord?"

"Aye, General... Lord Fyrustus's Kord," Motus said uncertainly. "I haven't seen him since the center was breached."

Hearing the name hit the General hard. "He's gone," he said, swallowing a ball in his throat. "Body's out here somewhere, though," he said as he gingerly turned away from the man. "So let's find him, burn him so his spirit can wander."

"Lord Fyrus' taught me everything I know about battle," the Rokh called after him. "Didn't care about me bein' a commoner, only cared about my wits with a blade. I didn't know him beyond our time in training, but I have to think that if he's passed, he wouldn't have wanted to leave any other way."

Tyghus gave a pursed smile. "Nor I."

As he staggered away, pain soon overtook him and dropped him to his haunches with a groan. Through heavy breaths, he tried to think about what tomorrow might bring; about his fortress that needed saving, about his sister alone in the Native capital, about why he'd survived in lieu of thousands of other sons that had been called to the gods. Aye, he tried, but his fatigue simply wouldn't let him. Instead, he found his eyes poring distantly over the field again.

"*You did it, men,*" he finally whispered. "*Your names'll live forever, but I'll miss you dearly, every one of you. You gave it all, didn't you? Gave more than me, more than any other Bull still takin' a breath.*" He sighed as tears of pride and guilt crept to sweat-encrusted eyes. "*So go, all of you. Go now and keep the Table's banquet warm for me.*"

He smiled. "*But do indulge in the Feast — you've earned it.*"

Epilogue

Valogar, Nearing the Isthmus, 8th Day of the Fourth Month, Y. 384 P.C.

"Well, gods alive… General, you'll want to see this…"

Tyghus turned painfully to follow Kinistus's outstretched hand, spotting a dozen riders approaching their meager column from the northeast.

"That who I think it is?" the Kordette asked.

"Tell me it's not…"

They watched the group draw closer before Kini' spoke again. "I would, but I think it is…"

"It's not safe here, dammit," Tyghus said in annoyance. "She's got no idea, Kini'… no bloody idea. Chibin crawling all over the place around here, and who knows what else."

As he was wont to do, Kinis' gave a calm, knowing smile but held his tongue. Instead, he offered, "shall we meet her?"

"Hand's been forced, hasn't it?" Tyghus replied as he veered his horse ninety degrees. "I can't ignore my own sister, mad as she appears."

The lanky man nodded towards the departing General and about-faced on his mount with raised fist, halting the army. "Shall we follow you?" he called out.

"Do as you wish," Tyghus yelled back curtly, eyes and mind already trained on the Native ponies.

"Ten of you, on the move," he heard the kordette bark to a row of horsemen.

Tyghus's horse bounded across the spongy grass, overreacting to the General's spurring kicks. Fidipodus the beast was not, but he had as least as eager a spirit. It didn't help his control of the animal that he'd adorned his filthy armor once again, weighing down exhausted, pain-ridden limbs. The lekeys around Tygha spooked a bit as Tyghus reared hard on his massive warhorse to stop.

The Rokhish beast twisted and snorted impatiently while the General scanned the Valogarians with suspicion. They were all broad about the shoulders with coarse black hair pulled tight into pony-tails, wooden armor covering their chests and circular shields slung over their backs. None of them bore him any sense of a greeting, nor did he offer one. Tyghus could see another rider behind them peculiarly dressed in Rokhish attire, but Tygha was already marching towards him before he could discern more.

She shivered in her Native clothes, bare shoulders begging for a cloak, and the eyes that met his looked red and frantic, dark circles adding to the effect. It'd been his goal for weeks to win fast, fight his way into Nar-Biluk, then shuttle her away from a land certain to descend into chaos. But plans changed when he couldn't count even a thousand men-at-arms after the battle…

"You're alive," she croaked.

Tyghus couldn't find his voice and simply nodded.

"Walk with me?" she asked with a weak smile. "If you can…"

The General shot a glance back at the heavy hooves coming up behind him before gingerly dropping off his horse. Kinistus quickly snatched the reins.

Leaving the group behind, they walked in an awkward silence for a bit, Tyghus oddly reluctant to embrace a woman he thought he'd never see again – though in truth, he was still utterly gutted in mind, body, and soul; he felt almost nothing at all. Finally, he stopped and sighed. "Do you know how dangerous it is for you out here?"

She turned to him. "Aye, I do."

Tyghus glared off into the distance, barely hearing her. "There're packs of leaderless mirami roaming the land, Chibin stalk the grass all around us and you – you come with ten warriors to your name?"

"I said I do, Tyghus."

"Then *why?*" Tyghus asked harshly, eyes darting around them. "*Why* the hell would you come here? Why now?"

Tygha's eyes watered beyond their lids, throwing her arms upon her brother and weeping.

"Tygha…" he offered softly, frustration melting. As he patted the back of her short braided hair, he looked back at the two groups of guards behind them and was thankful they seemed more interested in themselves than the Tyghid siblings.

She pulled herself away and tried to wipe her eyes clear. "I'm sorry, I hate being like this, I'm *not* like this, I just… I just don't know what's going to happen, Tyghus. I really don't. I could scarcely believe the past few weeks, and then yesterday comes…" she trailed off with a sniff. "The world's changed now. Andran's *dead*. Word's hardly spread but – but I don't know what's going to happen when it does… I haven't even begun to think about mourning him yet."

Tyghus knew their marriage wasn't born of love, but in fairness to her, he'd no idea what it may have become over the several months since the union. He'd never thought of her losing a husband as much as her new country had lost a leader. "I'm sorry, Tygha," he offered simply.

"You saw him? You saw him before he died?"

Tyghus didn't meet her eyes but nodded all the same. "I did. We talked on the field before it came to terms," he said, recalling their conversation for the first time since the battle. "But when it was time, he fought hard… he died well." He didn't yet have the heart to say how he *really* died.

"I've no doubt," she said as she cleared her throat and pushed her proud jaw out again.

"As it happens, I promised him I'd give you his love if he fell, just as he'd promised me likewise."

"You promised that, yet you march past Nar-Biluk without so much as a word to me?"

Tyghus's eyes locked on his sister in disbelief. "Without a word? Gods above, do you *know* what I've been through? Did you want me to very well walk through Nar-Biluk's gates expecting a hero's welcome?"

"Don't talk to me like that," she ordered sternly.

"Tygha, look at me," he begged, fully aware of his bloodied and bruised face. "I mean, really look at me! Look at *them!*"

Her gaze fell upon the remnants of the Sixth, letting out a small gasp in the process.

"I've nothing left, Tygha. I'm bloody ruined."

She stayed fixed on the army. "Your sergeants?"

His sister's eyes followed his finger pointing east. Even with the Sunken Fields miles behind him now, one could still see the smoky spires of Rokhish dead climbing high into the sky, blending seamlessly into the morning's gray clouds. "Six burn with the rest of the dead."

She looked back at him sharply. "Who?"

He swallowed hard. "I doubt you knew them all – Grantax, Pydonus, Swiftus, Siderius... but you probably do recall Noccus and Fyrustus."

"Fyrus'..." she said, rolling the name over in her head, before it came to her with a start. *'The twin? The Astorean?'* He nodded quietly as her head slowly sank. "His brother?"

"Taking it hard... he's not spoken since we lit the pyre."

"I – I never thought –"

"It wasn't supposed to have been like this," he said, anger rising. "There were supposed to be reinforcements from..." But he ended up just letting himself fade off, too numb to indulge any new rage. He looked at his sister again when he suddenly recognized the opportunity right before his eyes. "Tygha, leave with us."

She stared at him with glistening blue-green eyes.

"I don't know why you're here and I'd never ask you to dishonor yourself or our family by leaving while Andran still lived but he's gone now," he continued, taking her hand in his. "There's nothing more for you here. I don't know if their laws even allow it, but how long do you think they'd let a Rokhish queen survive on this throne? Whatever this kingdom was before, it's going to ashes now, you know it is."

His eyes begged her consent as much as his words. "Come, won't you? I've lost enough, I've watched Fygo' lose his blood... now we've been given a chance to at least not lose each other."

Alas, she shook her head. "I can't."

He shook his head. "*Why?* What can possibly become of you here?"

"Andran's brother will take the Lij's seat," she said with quaking voice. "And I'll have to take his hand..."

Tyghus looked at her even more incredulously. "What?"

"It's custom here for a man to marry his brother's widow, to take her into his house. And it's custom that he'll succeed to the throne."

"Siran, you mean?"

She nodded. "Andran spoke of him to you?"

"Aye, he spoke of how much he despised him! This is the same man with half a dozen wives already, no? You'll be his seventh? You're going to be nothing, please tell me you're not serious!"

"Tyghus, it's… it's… complicated here. But I won't be giving up any of my rights, I promise you."

"On whose word? On –"

"I'm staying because I think I can still help here… help our lands find peace."

Tyghus closed his eyes and let his head drop.

"I'm safe, Tyghus. Things changed in Nar-Biluk, even before the battles."

"Aye? Because of what?"

"Well… because of him."

Tyghus lifted his head and with a start saw a gaunt, cloaked man standing at their side. It was the Rokhish-dressed man he'd seen with the Valogarians on approach, and up close he saw a beard that did nothing to hide sunken cheeks; indeed, he looked as if he hadn't seen a meal in weeks. A small ring of sandy brown hair circled his head like a halo, squeezed in between a shaven crown and sides.

Instinctively, Tyghus's hand reached for his blade, which he suddenly realized hung benignly on his horse. The man laughed.

"It's okay," Tygha said gently. "I wanted you to meet him."

Tyghus's eyes bounced from her to the bony forearm stretched out to meet his; he cautiously accepted. "Light on your feet… didn't hear you approach."

The man's brilliant blue eyes narrowed over an easy smile. "Perhaps the gods made me a spy in another life, aye?" he said with a chuckle. "Ah, probably not. You're just weary from battle, no doubt. Senses dulled a bit?"

The General studied him. "So you're protecting my sister, then? You look a Rokh if I ever saw one. A Rokhish protector in a land of Valogarians."

"Said that way, it sounds absurd, I agree," the man said without breaking his smile.

"Aye, so how –"

"I'm happy to talk with you, Tyghus, as I've many things to say – if you'll indulge me, of course. Though I'd prefer it be elsewhere."

"I'd rather not talk here either but you'll have to make the best of it.".

"Why?" the man asked innocently.

"Why? Because I've got men who are on no rest and must fast-march more than seven, eight hundred miles west to Avergon to break the siege there… our fourth battle in a span of weeks, that's why."

"So all this fight to get into Valogar, and now you're just leaving?"

Tyghus glowered. "Just indulge me so I can be on my way, it's a long march to go."

The man slowly shook his head. "You can't return there."

The General's glare deepened. "If you're Rokhish, then you should know Avergon's the bedrock of our power in the Lowlands. More than Marvelon, more than –"

The man smiled as he coolly interjected. "You mistake me. I meant you'll have no *authority* to return there."

Tyghus turned his look to his sister. "What is this nonsense, Tygha? You wanted me to listen to –"

"Once you cross through the Rokhish Gates, Tyghus, you'll be no more the Empire's general than I am its…" the man trailed off, before adding, "well, suffice it to say, you'll be an outlaw."

Tyghus's eyes narrowed. "And why's that?"

The skinny man laughed. "So many questions yet you still don't ask my name?"

"Is your name relevant to my questions?"

The man gave a thoughtful frown for a second as he looked briefly at Tygha. "A fair point."

"And your answer?"

"It's very relevant, General."

The two men locked eyes as a tense moment passed. "Then who are you?"

"My name is Castus of Cassitigon," he said plainly. "So yes, your instincts were correct – I'm a Rokh indeed… a sixteenth generation Ruhl, actually."

The name immediately rang familiar but Tyghus could not place why. He searched the bowels of his mind for the name…

His eyes suddenly shot up. "Castus of the Lorrio?"

Blue eyes sparkled at him.

"You were – you were assigned to death, no?"

"I appreciate you using 'were', General," Castus replied drolly. "But I 'am' assigned to death; we all are, in a sense I guess. By the grace of the gods, though, mine's yet to occur."

Tyghus was stunned as he looked the man up and down again. "And now you're here?"

Castus followed the General's eyes. "Chased from my own country, I'm afraid. My own capital, my own Lorrio. A flight that required some aesthetic changes, in any event."

The General's wonder morphed into disdain as he recalled what the smarmy Imperial courier told him months ago. "A messenger told me about the charges leveled against you. Treason, was it not?"

"And I presume this messenger came to you on behalf of Dray'gon Rokh?" Castus asked pointedly. "Remind yourself of the source."

"As I am now."

"As you *should*, now… but at least *I* have your sister to vouch for me. Who'd that courier have?"

The General glanced at Tygha who nodded to him, before refocusing on the fugitive Lorrion. "Okay, then answer my question – why am I an 'outlaw'? And by the gods, why are you comparing me to your treason, valid or not?"

"Oh, I don't make that comparison, General. But after yesterday, the Khorokh and the Lorrio now in his pocket certainly *do*."

"Even the fastest relay of riders to Dray'gon Rokh couldn't have given word of the battle for a week in good weather. And how would you have known any—"

"General, you make it sound as if your downfall is a surprise, as if it was some happenstance. Yesterday's failure was only the culmination of efforts in the Capital to –"

"Failure!" Tyghus suddenly raged. "With ten-thousand men we beat a Native army more than sixty thousand strong!"

"Beat them? They fled, General."

"We won here, you bastard."

"Did you? You've no army left, thousands of Valogarians still hold spears, and Nar-Biluk is as secure as it's been in months with Rokhs in retreat. If this is your win, then I shudder to think of your 'loss'."

"Then why don't you go and ponder that over there, with those soldiers? I'm sure they'll indulge you," Tyghus growled through gritted teeth. He looked to his sister.

"Ah, I'm sure they would. And I'm saying what I'm saying to you now so you understand how you're being portrayed in the Capital. I'm not here to judge you."

Tyghus winced hard as a hand reflexively reached to his wound. He forced himself to speak in measured tone. "We fought yesterday because the dyrons from the Uplands failed to join us, Castus –"

"As I said, you needn't rationalize yourself to me."

"– and I refuse to believe the men of the Lorrio, of the throne, aren't wise enough to see that sloth, *Glannox's* sloth, forced me to give battle against such terrible odds! And not only sloth towards me, but sloth towards the siege of Avergon!"

"And you think that a coincidence... General?" Castus asked with a derisive laugh. "That mighty, proud, and notoriously *meticulous* Glannox simply *forgot* to leave on time?"

Tyghus rolled his eyes, teeth still clenched. "I've already heard it said that Glannox purposely betrayed the Sixth so he could have this glory, all the more reason the Lorrio should –"

"Oh, it goes far beyond Glannox's bid for glory, my boy," Castus said coldly, the corners of his eyes wrinkling as he squinted. "I want you to listen to me, and listen well. Will you?"

His side pulsed in pain along with his swollen arm. "Just speak," he demanded impatiently.

"There were two ways and two ways only that your invasion could have played out. One, you attack, you fight gloriously, but die in noble defeat against the enemy horde. The Bulls of the Sixth are destroyed, but your name and dyron are lauded throughout the streets of every Imperial town as valiant martyrs. A statue of your person is added to the Hall of Heroes next to the Styliun. More sons, more husbands, more fathers rally to the banners to squelch this terrifyingly *strong* Valogarian threat – after all, if the Sixth can fall, then who would be safe? Glannox then invades on the strength of your flag and your name. A new Sixth is raised."

Tyghus stayed respectfully silent as Castus paused. Despite his irritation, it wasn't hard to picture the man on the Lorrio floor with his skilled rhetoric.

"Or two... you attack, fight hard against overwhelming numbers and, by the gods, you survive! Yet the Sixth is ruined, so there'll be no talk of 'victory' in Imperial towns. No, not when the emblem of Rokhish power in the Lowlands is wiped out by a General too vainglorious to avoid suicidal odds. You fought despite the better advice and counsel of your own men and kordettes. Practically speaking, of course, you're too weakened from your 'victory' to be any more of a threat to the Valogarians so you shamefully retreat from their homeland. You're branded a reckless fool by gambling away the lives of the Empire's finest, but it won't be mentioned that that you left the Valogarian kingdom ripe for conquest by mighty Glannox, who invades on the hatred of your name. Glannox rebuilds the Sixth under his tutelage, perhaps even absorbing the unit as his own."

The Sudo paused for effect. "You, of course, are summoned to the Capital, tried before your 'Peers' as I was, condemned as I was – and executed for your carelessness, your lines blackened from Rokhish annals." His eyes never left the General's. "You see? This has all been planned for months. You'd have been better off dying... at least you'd have gotten a statue."

Tyghus still bore a skeptical scowl, at least for appearance's sake. "And how did you come by this information if you were in the dungeons for most of that time?"

"Sadly, Dray'gon Rokh's a city of a million controlled by a paltry few. And any one of that few that wishes to stay there knows precisely what the other few is doing at any given time, even if they all think and pretend that they don't. I certainly knew every move they made, before and after I was jailed. Thankfully, men of the jail-keeping ilk are paid a pittance, easily susceptible to higher coin," he said before hesitating and adding, "though some helped me escape just because they felt what was happening to me was wrong."

Tyghus lingered on the man before finally looking away, letting himself be distracted by his weary men to the west. He'd heard what Castus said, heard how his fate would supposedly unfold. He even understood how the result at the Sunken Fields could be spun in the way that Castus described. But from the outset, he couldn't get over the most basic of questions:

"Why? Why would they do this to me? Kyrus has been a brother to me since I was young – since *we* were young. We've shared blood, shared tears. I've never wavered in my support of him –"

"Oh, no?"

"No..."

"Hm, so your 'brother' in Dray'gon Rokh *approves* of you sheltering the Chibin priestess? He's come a long way, if so."

Tyghus's face burned red, his eyes finding Tygha's.

"Oh, don't look to her, I knew well enough through my own sources in Nar-Biluk," Castus said with an almost sympathetic sigh. "I told you, I don't care what you did, Tyghus... or whatever else you've done or plan to do. You probably did what you did because you thought it right, but in the Capital you'll find what's 'right' is *very* contextual."

"Maybe he wouldn't have approved of it, but he's willing to sacrifice the Sixth just to make that point?" Tyghus said defensively. "Just to punish me?"

Castus laughed. "No, no, no, you have the Lorrio to thank for that. My Lorrian adversaries saw you as a threat to their chance to control their new Khorokh. They knew Kyrus is isolated, they knew his bond to you. So... they pushed to have you eliminated, and to my surprise, they succeeded with startling ease. That's all it was, just two pawns in a game."

Tyghus felt sweat beading furiously along his forehead. "You believe Kyrus simply bought every word of it?"

"Like I said, your own actions helped speed him along from what I'm told. You provided the tinder, my Nortic friends simply put a torch to it, and it's no secret Kyrus is of weak mind, if not altogether mad. For all his guile and bravery in the field, the Nortics have been able to bend him like a blacksmith does a blade; he thinks you as much a villain as he thinks Glannox a savior." The Sudo paused reflectively for a moment. "But even if you ignore all that, even if you think me a liar, let my plight be all the proof of his mind that you need. Or the terror he's unleashing on everyone else in the Arxun. His attempt on my life may have been his first radical move, but I can assure you it won't be his last."

Tyghus looked away, exhausted at hearing the accusations. Perhaps it was because of the toll his body had taken or perhaps it was because the picture Castus painted was so consistent with his own recent encounters with Kyrus. He sighed. "So you somehow escape your execution, flee south and end up here."

"My lands along the coast and the Border Rokhs in general have always kept good relations with Valogar's first families. I dined with Lij Andran on several occasions, sometimes in Cassitigon, sometimes in Nar-Biluk. He was a good man, something I failed to impress upon the Lorrio once the Converge was attacked. Had I been able to tell the Council about my meetings with him without fear of how Nortics would twist it, then..." The Sudo caught himself and smiled. "Doesn't matter now. What matters is that several hundred men have followed me here from the Shoals, pledging their lives to me – and I to your sister for her and her peoples' hospitality."

Tyghus looked skeptically at Tygha. "So *that's* your protection? Even by his own story, Glannox's invasion is imminent, which is sure to be some sixty thousand strong. Regardless of how many still even have the will to fight, there's no one to rally the mirami to your defense, the Chibin sure as hell won't support you, and all he offers you is 'several hundred men'?"

Castus recoiled a bit. "My name and support adds credibility to her among the nobles here that need to see it. They support me now as I did them all these years. You surely know that the most immediate danger to your sister comes from within Valogar, not without."

"Aye, all the more bloody reason she should leave with her own people before she's fed to the lions in –"

"The moment she passes through the Rokhish Gates with you, she'll be hunted like a dog, just as you will be."

Tyghus threw his hands out in front of him. "Aye, but even if I believed that, Glannox *is* coming. How is she any safer waiting here with your few hundred men only to watch her capital sacked and burned?"

Castus suddenly looked uncomfortable, sending shifty glances in Tygha's direction. He wet his lips as he rubbed his hand through a spotty beard. "My people – the Rokhs along the Shoals – they don't support this war. They detest it, in fact, and for a very simple reason – a prosperous Valogar means prosperous Borderlands..."

"Aye..."

"And you know yourself – you *have* to know – that the Valogarians want none of this quarrel. They didn't ask for it, it's been thrust upon them, and already they've paid dearly… and my people are prepared to pay dearly as well…"

"What will you do when Glannox lands, Castus?" he demanded, dreading the answer.

"We mean to fight him, brother," Tygha said. "With Rokhs of the Shoals, with Colverians, with whatever mirami still able to rally…"

What was left of Tyghus's heart sank like a stone, eyes flicking between her and Castus repeatedly. "And Castus will lead them?"

Castus let out a nervous laugh. "Tyghus, I'm a man of many qualities, but valor on the battlefield isn't one of them, I'm afraid. No, my friend, I – " he placed a hand on the General's shoulder. "- I want *you* to lead them."

Tyghus stood motionless, stunned beyond speech.

"You know Rokhish weaknesses, you know Valogarian strengths… Colverians too, I suppose? More of my Rokhs want to rise up but they need to know that doing so won't be in vain. With your name, I can convince them of that; with *my* name, I can convince the Valogarian nobles and their armies to support you, make them see you simply followed ill-conceived orders, that you've always supported a rightful peace, despite the devastation you've wrought the past few weeks. I can *give* you an army, if only you will lead it."

A stiff wind kicked up, serving to muffle an awkward silence.

"You'd ask me to betray the country you were born to, Tygha?" Tyghus said at last.

"Brother, I know how –"

"What the hell would pari say to this?" he demanded angrily.

"Your father's not here, Tyghus!" Castus shouted. "Neither is the time in which he lived! We're talking about –"

"We're talking about civil war!"

"When the people's will is ignored by a tyrant, what other path do we have?"

"One that doesn't involve the murder of the countrymen I bear arms to protect!" the General said as he shoved the Sudo's hand from his shoulder.

"If anything you could *spare* murder by making a big enough show to discourage Glannox's attacks altogether!" Castus fired back. "And we can *use* that interlude to negotiate! To try and show peace is still the proper course!"

"When in Rokhish history has our country ever backed off a declaration of war?" Tyghus asked. "No one would ever risk being seen as a coward in Stygus's eyes, let alone now, let alone after the Converge attack."

"It bears repeating, 'your country' is set to have you tortured to death in the Tanokhun at Dray'gon Rokh! Your ears, nose, and genitals to be food for the hogs! Your family tree blackened from Imperial records, their lands seized – gods only know what's been done to Tygonium already! This is all for your sin of following orders, mind you!"

"So *you* say."

"Aye, and as I say now and as I said before - take my plight and learn from it, dammit!"

"I've seen your plight, Castus, I promise you. But I also see men under siege at Avergon and the Brafford Bridge – men that did nothing more than pledge their allegiance to myself and the throne. Even if that throne's as twisted as you say, even if I don't have an able-bodied man at my disposal, it doesn't mean I can forsake those troops… and if I did, then my name would be blackened already."

"But your troops aside, your name and reputation *are* what the Khorokh and Lorrio *say* they –"

"Castus, stop," Tygha pleaded as she stepped in front of him. "If he's going to come to this, he has to come to it on his own accord, we agreed on that from the start."

Castus restrained himself a bit, though his eyes still burned passionately at the General.

Tyghus extended his forearm in the Sudo's direction who reluctantly accepted it. "My sister's chosen to stake her safety on you – do *not* disappoint her. You seem to have a knack for survival, so share it with her. And keep watch over this brother of the Lij – this brother who *is* the Lij."

Castus nodded. "I hope you know I say none of this to patronize you. It's just so many outside the Capital can't believe they've been handed poison 'til it's too late," he said before pausing for a moment, eyes finding the ground at his feet. "Looking back now, I had so many chances to thwart the bloodshed that's been wrought… I *live* a life of regrets."

Tyghus said nothing except for a subtle nod. The Sudo forced a smile in return before heading back towards the small gathering of Rokhs and Valogarians. The General's eyes narrowed as they fell on his sister. "Be wary of that man," he whispered. "*Never* think he does anything for anyone's benefit other than his own - *don't* get caught in his web."

To his surprise, she chuckled. "You've enough webs of your own to worry about. Don't worry yourself about mine."

"I'm serious," Tyghus said, unamused. "And if you won't leave with me now, then you *must* surrender to Glannox when he gets here. Feign that you were a prisoner against your will after Andran's death."

"If you're the pariah Castus says you are, then I'm not sure what good that will do me as your sister."

"Tygha, *please* do not buy into this nonsense about fighting Glannox. I don't know him, but I know his reputation. They say he stripped entire Loccean villages to the bone if he suspected they supported the Lords'

Rebellion, I can't imagine what he'd do here. And with numbers he'll possess —"

"I love you, brother," she said with a cool smile.

He looked long at her before pulling her in tight again for a hug. "And I, you."

Releasing her, he turned towards Kinistus and his men.

From behind him, Tygha's voice called out. "We'll be here, of course... should you change your mind."

Tyghus paused, then shook his head. "Same to you."

* * *

A light rain began falling not long after the army resumed its march, which did little to boost the spirits of the fatigued troops. On such dreary marches, the Fyrid twins almost always took it upon themselves to lighten moods, whether through their antics or their brawls. But today, Tyghus found the surviving Twin riding at the very back, as solemn as he'd once been gregarious. Few had tried approaching him since he tearfully put the torch to his brother's pyre, which clearly was his preference. Even now, the General didn't try to pry or talk to him, but simply rode quietly at his side. After what had to be an hour of riding, the twin surprised him by breaking the silence.

"You know what the thing of it is?" Fygo' asked as if in mid-conversation, his battered face grimacing. "I *want* to die in battle; I do and always have. And I wanted that for Fyrustus too, as did he. We weren't meant to pass feebly in a chair when we're all but blind; we're meant to fall by a better man's sword, or a better general's wits."

"Aye?" Tyghus said quietly.

"Aye, but I don't – I *can't* die from some fool's scheming in Marvelon, Tyghus. I bloody can't, and Fyrus' better not have either. We *did* our part here, and Glannox left us! He left us to die here, he wanted us to die here, while he grows fat in the Lowlands, waiting to steal our glory."

The hulking man then grew quiet for another moment, his jaw clenching repeatedly, his eyes never meeting Tyghus's. "I thought about that a while, even before the battle, but then – but then I thought, high-ranking as he is, he's only following orders, aye? And his orders came from Dray'gon Rokh. So he was *told* to sit. *Told* to wait. And whoever it was that told him that was willing to sacrifice thirteen thousand men – the *best thirteen thousand in the Empire* as if they were nothing! Why? There must have been some reason, some point to it all – well, what was the point! What could possibly explain this – this – this *betrayal?*"

Tyghus just looked straight ahead and shook his head silently as his friend seethed.

"On my word, Tyghus," Fygo' said as he finally looked furiously into the General's eyes. "If I find out Fyrus' died from some bit of schemin' in Marvelon, in Dray'gon Rokh, or any other bloody town under Rokhish flags – heads will roll. I don't care who they are, I don't care what their rank is, they'll roll."

"Oh, believe me, my friend," Tyghus said, instantly turning to smile at the man. "On that, you have my word."

The grieving warrior gave a satisfied nod and fell quiet again.

Tyghus gave a whack on the Twin's shoulder before glancing behind him to the far-off spot where he'd met Tygha and Castus. The rain and fog had enveloped them by now, but their conversation still resonated.

"Avergon first, brother," he said as he looked back at Fygo'. "Then we're going to seek our answers – if they aren't brought to us first."

Appendix

A Brief History of the Rokhs

Pre-800 Ante-Cataclysm* ("A.C.") – Settlement of the "Early Kings" (non-Rokhish peoples such as Kylics, Clyvics, Grynics, etc.) in lush grasslands of modern-day Upper and Lower Rokhlands.

~800-200 A.C. – Arokhs and Karrokhs migrate from mountains, colonize non-Early lands along Astoren and Karanak foothills respectively and River Clyves. Marvelon founded ~625 A.C., quickly becomes first great Arokhish city, rivalling Early King splendor. Dray'gon Rokh founded 750 A.C., more typical of Arokhish settlements: small and poor but with tough walls.

~200-1 A.C. – Clannic invasions sweep Andervold; Clannic annihilation of most Early Kingdoms; Loccycs, Kylics and Clyvics in Upper Rokhlands and Grynics in Lower Rokhlands submit to vassalage in lieu of Clannic destruction. Arokhish pleas to Valogar for assistance go unanswered.

55 A.C. – Marvelon sacked. Lower Rokhlands fall entirely under Clannic control.

55 A.C.-56 P.C. – Time of Severance between Upper and Lower Rokhlands.

24 A.C. – Clans complete construction of the Tersic Pass, forging the Clyves.

Cataclysm – Shattering of Clannic Army at the Last Stand of Dray'gon Rokh.

1-33 P.C. – Cassyan Wars of Reconquest in the Upper Rokhlands. In recognition of Last Stand victory, Cassyus named "Khorokh", or First Among the Rokhs.

1-14 P.C. – Cassyus campaigns along the Astoren foothills, freeing Arokhish settlements from Clannic garrisons. All cities but Fyrogon form an Arokhish union; Fyrogon allies, but doesn't join the union.

1-19 P.C. – "Unholy Alliance" of Clannic chieftains, Early Kingsmen, and Anti-Cassyan Arokhish Nobles fill void of collapsing Clannic control, using Ambelfeld as Capital.

1-27 P.C. – Kylic and Clyvic Early Kings consolidate kingdoms around their respective rivers.

1-30 P.C. – Expansion of Baralesh and Corulesh desert tribes into southwestern Upper Rokhlands

1-56 P.C. – Lower Rokhlands still utterly and completely controlled by rival Clannic fiefdoms.

1-73 P.C. – Tarragani and Naddatu, two primary Karrokh Kings, expand realms in Karanak foothills.

3 P.C. – First Lorrio named.

02/15/19 P.C. – Cassyus's union smashes Unholy Alliance at the Battle of Ambelfeld.

19-27 P.C. – Cassyus battles Kylic and Clyvic kingdoms, conquering the Kylics in 25 P.C. at the Battle of the Marshes, and conquering the Clyvics in 27 P.C. at Ullenhal.

27-30 P.C. – Punitive Cassyan campaigns against Desertmen pushes them back to the Skulls Desert. All lands between Rivers Kyles and Clyves in Cassyan hands.

30-33 P.C. – Initial Cassyan campaigns into Lower Rokhlands. Takes the Tersic Pass with rebel Lowland assistance in 32 P.C., but passes away in 33 P.C. while planning campaign to free Marvelon. Lorrion Marcellius I named Khorokh.

33-41 P.C. – Clans in Lower Rokhlands recover from Cassyan campaign, confine Arokhs to the Tersic Pass. Punitive massacre of rebellious Lowland garrison pushes Fyrogon to formally join the Arokhish union.

41-56 P.C. – Khorokh Marcellius launches brutal, bloody series of campaigns to free fortified Marvelon, finally liberating the city in 56 P.C. Arokhish troop numbers swell.

56-66 P.C. – Marcellian campaigns to topple remaining Clannic Lowland kingdoms interrupted upon his death in 59 P.C., picked up by Khorokh Pistoniux. Lowlands entirely liberated by 66 P.C.

66-73 P.C. – Khorokh Pistoniux campaigns against remaining Clannic fiefdoms north of the Kyles. Offers alliance with Naddatu's Karrokhs, but fearing Dray'gon Rokh's rising power, Karrokhs secretly ally with Clannic chief instead. While Khorokh Pistoniux campaigns against Upland Clans, Naddatu Karrokhs ride their giant horned cavalry up to walls of Dray'gon Rokh. Khorokh Pistoniux dies in desperate fight to save the city from sacking.

73-74 P.C. - Jatrius named Khorokh, immediately launches punitive raids across Naddatu realm, torching croplands, even while Clannic armies besiege the hallowed city of Kyles. Despite aid sent from Tarragani Karrokhs, starving Naddatu Karrokhs easily conquered thereafter.

75-80 P.C. – Jatrius refuses to aid sparsely rebuilt Kyles, instead marching directly on Clannic fortress. Clannic garrison escapes to make a lightning last-ditch raid on Dray'gon Rokh. Clans force their way into Capital sewers before being stopped and defeated.

81-91 P.C. – The final Campaigns of Unity. Tarragani offers to help break last Clannic fiefdom on the Dead Plains, in exchange for independence and some absorption of former Naddatu lands. Arokhs agree, conduct lengthy campaign against elusive Clan, and finally execute last Clannic chieftain in 90 P.C. Jatrius, however refuses to honor agreement with Tarragani, instead sacking Tarragani's capital upon being invited for review of its defenses. Jatrius saw sacking as punishment for Tarragani's earlier aid of Naddatu and general refusal to ally with the

Arokhs against the Clans. All Karrokh lands absorbed into Arokhish dominion; Arokhs subsequently referred to simply as "Rokhs".

91-early 300s P.C. – Dead Plains lightly populated, left as a buffer should Clans return.

105-108 P.C. Marvelon threatens to secede; Grynean boycott of the Lorrio.

105-108 P.C. – Time of the Mad Khorokhs of Loccea.

130-141 P.C. – First Lords' Rebellion. Talk of Marvelonian secession renewed, but ultimately amounts to nothing.

175 P.C. – Peaceful absorption of Mesan tribes; foundation of the Rokhish Converge.

180 P.C. – Foundation of Avergon.

197-203 P.C. – Conquest of Valogar.

203-213 P.C. – Continued Skirmishes along Borderlands with Colvery

219-222 P.C. – Second Lords' Rebellion.

225-237 P.C. – War against united Desert Tribes, the Last Rising of the Terelesh; Death of Khorokh Glabulux following battlefield defeat against Terelesh in 235 P.C.

235-236 P.C. – The Khorian Crisis or Year of the Five Khorokhs. All dyrons except First and Second refuse to acknowledge Lorrion Idius, Glabulux's chosen successor, due to Glabulux's shame in fleeing the battlefield against the Terelesh. Third through Ninth support Lorrion Cespius as heir, while Rubitio back Lorrion Ladinax. Lorrion Lexandrius mediates a peace where Idius, Cespius, and Ladinax are withdrawn as nominees, and Lexandrius takes the throne.

237-321 P.C. – The Time of Great Peace.

300s-Present – Settlement on the Dead Plains increases and encouraged.

321-326 P.C. – Expansion into Raiz Jungle to Anonga River.

329-331 P.C. – Third Lords' Rebellion

333 P.C. – Rynsyus becomes Lorrion.

337-347 P.C. – Assassination of Lij Andran XVII; First Uprising of the Valogarians

348 P.C. – Death of Emperor Terrius. Beginning of Rynsyus's reign

350-Present – Raizana revolts begin. Continue sporadically to present day.

351-352 P.C. – Fourth Lords' Rebellion.

360 P.C. – Torrus's Massacre, start of Second Uprising of the Valogarians.

360-381 P.C. – Second Valogarian Uprising.

360-61 P.C. – Fifth Lords' Rebellion.

373 P.C. – Rynsyan "Policy of Peace" Announced.

381 P.C. – Final Rokhish troops withdrawn from Valogar.

* - most records, if any, destroyed in Clannic invasions, so dates A.C. are mere estimates.

A Record of the Provinces
(circa Y. 383 P.C.)

Province	Capital	Proventor	Protective Dyron	Provincial Lorrion Representative	Region
Draygonea	Marcogon	Markius	First	Wollia	Uplands
Kylea	Alemyles	Ankus	Second	Antinax	Uplands
Clyvea	Tersiton	Terrax	Third	Onzero	Uplands/ Lowlands
Astorea	Fyrogon	Fyrriux	Fourth	Barannus	Uplands
Grynea	Marvelon	Kaigus	Fifth	Desiria	Lowlands
Starrea	Avergon	Serriax	Sixth, Ninth	Holiokus	Lowlands
Loccea	Leeshyn	Larallus	Seventh	Volinex	Uplands
Kregea	The Converge	Huskius	Eighth	Tessax	Lowlands
Morremea	Ferlium	Pledius	Sixth, Ninth	Castus	Lowlands
Raizea	Cros'syng Way	Folliux	Tenth	None. Nominally represented by Loccean Lorrion	Westlands

A Brief History of the Provinces

Draygonea: Despite its name, Draygonea was historically not a region dominated by the now-mammoth capital of the Rokhish Empire. To the contrary, Dray'gon Rokh was for centuries hardly distinguishable from other small Rokhish settlements in the northeastern Uplands until Cassyus of Kyles selected it as the spot where the Rokhs would make their final stand against the seemingly invincible Clans. Years of armed, tactical retreat in the Uplands came to a head in that rapidly fortified village, where both armies had resolved to end it all. The end came indeed, but not in the manner expected – the strategy of Cassyus and desperate resolve of the cornered Rokhs overcame the practically perfect Clannic war machine. From that point on, the village turned town turned city began a growth spurt that has yet to abate.

Contributing to that growth are the two massive Imperial thoroughfares which link the Capital to the Empire's western and southern extremes – the Great Western Tradeway that runs a thousand miles west to Cros'syng Way, and the far older Tersian Som which connects to the Tersic Pass and Marvelon before splintering into countless smaller roads in the Lowlands.

The Province that's arisen around the Capital is not in fact governed by it. Provincial administration is delegated to Marcogon, what's colloquially known as the Empire's "Second City". A rival to Dray'gon Rokh prior to the Clannic Wars, it thereafter became its closest ally. The Second City has traditionally been the dominant one of the Province, producing dozens of Lorrions, Proventors, and even two of the Empire's twenty-four Khorokhs, including its second - Marcellius I the Liberator. The spiritual capital of the country and Cassyan birthplace, Kyles, also falls within the borders of Draygonea, though its thorough Clannic destruction meant that it lagged behind Marcogon in terms of influence. Dipillion and Istogon are other cities of note, both having produced a Khorokh.

Draygonea is bordered to the north by the Karanak Mountains; the Astoren Mountains in the east; the Kylic Lake in the west, enclosing former Karrokh territories; and Astorea Province in the South. Geographically, the Province is hilly but replete with abundant rivers and lakes. Its eastern and northern fringes, of course, are quite rocky, but its southern border is also marked by the Lapen Hills, sporadic small mountains extending out from the Astorens. The climate shifts the nearer one moves towards the mountain ranges, though generally, the Province suffers cold, snowy winters, moderate to cold autumns and springs, and warm but rarely oppressive summers.

Kylea: As its name suggests, the heart of Kylea Province falls largely within the territory of the former Kylic Early Kingdoms. Prior to the Clannic Wars, there were a dozen Early Kingdoms that dominated Upland landscape. The Kylics in particular claimed dominion over much of the area around the River Kylic. The Early Kings were famed for waging constant wars against each other, all but ignoring the "barbarian" Rokhs that had descended from the Karanak and Astoren mountains to settle in their foothills.

The Clans changed everything. They swept away all but the Loccycs, Clyvics, Grynics, and Kylics, each of whom submitted to vassalage in lieu of destruction. When the Clans were defeated by those "barbarian" Rokhs, the Kylics aggressively expanded their territory into regions formerly held by their rivals. When Cassyus conquered the Kylics in 25 P.C., the Imperial Province of Kylea eventually took the shape of the Kylics' P.C. realm.

Provincial Capital Alemyles has been the traditional powerhouse of the province, due to its excellent trading position as the last port city of the River Kylic and its ready-made infrastructure as an ancient Kylic settlement spared destruction by the Clans. Antillion, seat of the powerful Antinid line, and Menniogon, seat of the Menacrids, are arguably the strongest pure Rokhish settlements in the province, though as the river has coursed away from their positions over the years, their wealth doesn't compare. Ambelfeld, a Vyric stronghold absorbed by Kylic nobles Post-Cataclysm (then declaring independence and forming the "Unholy Alliance" with Clannic and some Rokhish nobles), remains a city of note, as does Vynes.

The Kylean Proventor is responsible for the Dead Plains administration, so Kylea Province technically runs west to Raizea Province (making it the Empire's largest province by area); it runs north to the Karanak Mountains; to the south along a chain of hills that mark Clyvea Province's northern border; and to the east to Draygonea and Astorea Provinces. Its heartland is dominated by the fertile valley of the River Kylic, which spawns numerous creeks and offshoots that produce verdant farmlands. Like Draygonea, the portions of the Province that are nearest to the mountains are colder and harsher, while the further south and west one travels, the more mild and moderate the region becomes.

The Dead Plains, of course, are flat and lined with its famous golden grains, its weather marked by extreme cold in the winters and stifling heat in the summers. Despite its name, the soil across the Plains is inexplicably poor for farming more complex crops, a condition locals attribute to the lingering curse of the Clans. The Early Kings that resided on the Plains were of lesser importance.

Clyvea: Like Kylea, Clyvea mirrors much of the dimensions of the Post-Cataclysm realm of an Early Kingdom, in this case the Clyvics, historic rivals of the Kylics. Their realm ran along the fertile stretch of the southwestern banks of the River Clyves, anchored at Ullenhal. A critical difference, of course, is that Clyvea Province – but not the old Clyvic Kingdom – includes the mighty river city of Tersiton, controller of the Tersic Pass. Inclusion of Tersiton, a city south of the River Clyves, was a thinly-veiled attempt to limit the power of the Marvelon-dominated Grynea Province. As a result of its straddling the Upland and Lowland halves off the Empire, it routinely produces powerful politicians.

Tersiton is the logical capital of the Province, given its extensive wealth and fortifications. The city originated around the Tersic Pass, the masterful and still heavily used bridge built by the Clans to better facilitate transporting its armies from the Lowlands into the Uplands. Most historians consider the bridge construction to be the high-water mark of the Clans' success in the Rokhlands and corresponding low-water mark in the Rokhish resistance. Today, more than half the Empire's commerce passes through the tolls of the Tersic Pass, though that number steadily declines as the Converge's growth continues.

Another city of note includes Ullenhal, the former Clyvic capital which was sacked by furious Cassyan troops in 27 P.C. after it was discovered the Clyvics were bartering to ferry Lowland Clannic warriors into the castle as added protection. The looting stripped the opulent capital bare, and today stands as an ironically spartan abode, both visually and culturally, but an influential power nonetheless. Ryvollium, Pilliotyles, and Onerium have also been influential through the years, having produced a Khorokh, an Inquisitor, and a Lorrion respectively.

Clyvea Province runs in a relatively narrow swathe along the River Clyves, from the western border of Astorea Province in the east to the eastern boundary of Kregea Province, where the Stygan Mesas begin; it is bordered in the northwest by Kylea Province; and in the south – with the exception of Tersiton – by the River Clyves. Its geography, then, is very much the characteristic river valley until it becomes rockier near the Mesas. The weather tends to be colder and wetter on its eastern fringes – though not to the extent of Draygonea or Astorea – and warmer and dryer in the west.

Astorea: Named after the Astoren Mountains which form its eastern border, it is home to some of the most ancient Rokhish settlements, including its chief city Fyrogon, and is renowned (as is Fyrogon) for the best iron ore quality in the Empire – it comes by the nickname "Armory of the Empire" honestly. As a result of this heritage and strong position, Fyrogon was determined to become the Upland version of Marvelon at the time that the Clans arrived. After refusing to surrender to the Clans – or join their cousins for the Last Stand in Dray'gon Rokh like most other Upland Rokhs – Fyrogon opted to withstand a long siege while the remainder of the Clannic army headed north to Dray'gon Rokh. When Cassyus triumphed at the Last Stand, Fyrogon was one of the first cities he sought to recruit as an ally, subsequently helping to break the siege. The Fyrids thereafter campaigned alongside the Cassyan armies, finally joining the union outright after the Clannic Lowland massacres in the 30s. Despite harboring a still proud independent streak, Fyrogon remains specially bonded to the Capital.

Most towns of Astorea revolve around servicing Fyrogon's expansive ironworks, though some of note include Brium and Cloton.

Astorea Province is bounded in the north by the Lapen Hills, a line of small mountains along the southern boundary of Draygonea Province; in the east by the Astoren Mountains; in the south by Clyvea Province; and in the west by Kylea Province. It is the smallest Imperial province by area, and most of that area is rocky and hilly; thus, perfectly suited for its ore focus. Its weather is slightly harsher than that of Draygonea to the north, given its higher elevation.

Grynea: Grynea is named after the Grynic Early Kings. The Grynics based their power along the southern banks of the Clyves, and were for the most part lesser powers than their northern cousins. They were one of the first Early Kingdoms to clash with the Rokhs, primarily due to Marvelon's rise and expanding borders. Their chief Early rival was the Wyric kingdom, a small realm whose borders ran westward to the fringe of the modern-day Kregea Province.

Provincial Capital Marvelon dominates the province's landscape, both literally and figuratively. The colloquial "First Capital" of the Rokhs is fiercely proud of its glory prior to its Clannic destruction. The city even threatened secession following the death of Khorokh Nertos, who the city alleged chose the Grynean Lorrion (a Marvelonian) as successor Khorokh, instead of Dossumux of Dollogon. Grynea's Lorrion thereafter boycotted the Lorrio until 108 P.C., when Khorokh Cassyus II dethroned the last of the fraternal Mad Khorokhs (see entry for Loccea below) and personally pledged massive building projects for still-ruined Marvelon. Nevertheless, Grynea province was cautiously shaped so as to give a portion of its southern half to Morremea

Province, while command of the Tersic Pass remains with Tersiton in Clyvea Province.

Other cities of note in Grynea Province include Tryces, a former Grynic city commandeered by the Clans before being conquered by Khorokh Marcellius, Cestillion, Mercium, and Lithologon, the latter three home to former Khorokhs.

Grynea Province runs east-northeast along the Clyves, notwithstanding Tersiton's sphere, to the Astoren Mountains; it runs west-southwest along the Clyves to the River Mord, eastern borders of Kregea and Starrea Provinces; and it runs south to the northern border of Morremea Province. Its northern terrain is a typical river valley while the southern terrain flattens out the further one treads towards the Ratikan coastal plain in Morremea. Weather is generally milder, as the Lowlands tend to be, although the mountainous eastern border tends to be colder and dryer.

Starrea: During the Clannic occupation, the territory making up Starrea Province was actually split between two rival Clannic chieftains, one from Clan White Thorn and one from Clan Red Thorn. Even with the threat of Khorokh Pistoniux marching against them to liberate the Lowlands, the pair's sparring ran unabated, vastly simplifying the Rokhish campaign. Post-liberation, Pistoniux prescribed a series of outposts throughout the Lowlands to ward against further Clannic intrusions from the southwest. It wasn't until 180 P.C., however, that the Province's – and in some ways, the Empire's – dominant fortress-city came to be: Avergon.

Founded by Cassyus III to be the "perfect fortress" as well as the finest training ground the Empire had ever constructed, Avergon consolidated the power that had been hitherto dispersed among the Pistonian outposts. The city also became the caretaker of the bridge that spans the River Brafford, a Clannic remnant like the Tersic Pass from when the Clans planned (but never executed) an invasion of Colvery.

The now-legendary Academy of Avergon ropes in the brightest, bravest, and strongest of the Empire's citizens, making its revamped Sixth Dyron the only unit to make no distinctions among Uplanders, Lowlanders, or Westlanders in its ranks. Soldiers' families are strictly forbidden from living within its walls, instead forced to live in the nearby feeder city of Attikon. The Tenth Dyron comprises the men accepted into the Academy but not ultimately deemed elite enough for the Sixth.

Due to the amalgamated nature of its inhabitants and massive power as home to the Academy, the Sixth, and first line of defense against numerous enemies, Avergon and the Province it dominates are almost a country unto themselves. As a result, they largely distance themselves from Draygonean politics; indeed, only one Khorokh has ever come from Starrea Province, that of Khorokh Thostius from 300-314 P.C.

Other towns of note in Starrea are Holliton and Thogon, the latter being the Thostid seat.

Starrea runs west to the border of the lower Skulls Desert; south to the River Brafford, border with Colvery; east to the Isthmus and the River Mord; and north to Kregea Province. Geographically, Starrea is relatively flat, green, and lush, strong trees dotting the landscape in copses. Climatically, it is fairly mild through the winters, hot in the summers.

Loccea: Colloquially known as the "Lakes", Loccea has been a turbulent region even prior to the Clannic Wars, a restiveness it owes to its peculiar geography. A series of lush oases and crystal-clear lakes isolated from each other by arid stretches of desert, it was for centuries before Cataclysm a roiling pot of Early King fiefdoms, each "king" claiming a lake but rarely powerful enough to dethrone his Loccean rivals, and certainly not a challenge to the powerful Kylic and Clyvic kingdoms. It is not without irony, then, that the network of Loccean princes had finally been hewn into union under Prince Breacs – alarming the Kylics and Clyvics in the process – when the Clannic tidal wave swept through the region. A foolish mistake in hindsight, the Clans burned Breacs alive, which only served to return the province to turbulence.

When the Rokhs expelled the Clans from Loccea, they found the Locceans just as hostile towards their "liberators" as they'd been towards their "oppressors". After failing to acknowledge their status as conquered, the Rokhs embarked on an intensive campaign to settle the region with fortified towns, and the Lorrion to the new Province, Nertos of Neconium, was even made the Khorokh in an attempt to give the region's natives a figure to rally behind. Nertos, unfortunately, was hopelessly ill and his short reign gave way to the sad tribulation of the Mad Khorokhs. On his deathbed, Nertos allegedly changed his heir to Lorrion Dossumux of Dollogon, his Lorrio successor after taking the Throne to continue the theory of appeasing the Loccean natives through power in Dray'gon Rokh. Though born a Rokh, Dossumux and his brothers Dosdius and Dolmius, previously had fallen deeply in love and in league with rival Loccean princesses that each encouraged their respective brother to push for setting Loccea free with the princess as successor to Breacs. Legend has it that the brothers' minds were poisoned or cursed by a witch, but whichever the case, Loccean money helped them go on a murderous rampage in Dray'gon Rokh as they sought to satisfy their princesses. Eventually, Dosdius murdered Dossumux, but was murdered in kind by his remaining brother, Dolmius. It wasn't until Cassyus I's distant descendant, Cassyus II, rose to overthrow Dolmius and institute the Great Lorrian Reforms that the Capital was returned to peace and prosperity. The time of the Mad Khorokhs continues to leave a scar on Rokhish psyche to this day.

Notwithstanding, the restless princes of Loccea – though only acknowledged as "lords" by the Rokhs – continue to be problematic. They've launched five unsuccessful rebellions since Dolmius's dethroning, most recently in 360 P.C. Dyrator Glannox of Glostium's brutal campaigns through the Lakes, however, have supposedly quelled the unrest there to levels unseen in some time.

The cities of Dollogon and Neconium are just two of the Rokhish settlements installed to keep order in the Province, although the former's shameful role in the Mad Khorokh affair has kept it largely a backwater. Volinium stands as the most influential purely Rokhish settlement, while the nearby capital of Leeshyn, former Early King stronghold, hosts the busy Seventh Dyron. Larallium is another town of note.

Loccea is positioned north of the Skulls Desert; west of Kylea Province and the Converge; south of the Dead Plains; northeast of the Mangossyan Sea, and east of the Raizea Province and the River Anonga. As previously described, Loccea is a series of lakes, waterfalls, and oases surrounded by groves dotting otherwise arid stretches of desert and plateaus. In the height of summer, the lakes drastically contract, only to be refilled by the rains of autumn and winter. Weather is generally dry and hot from the Third Month through the Eleventh.

Kregea: The history of the region covered by Kregean province tells the tale of two starkly different peoples – the Mesans and the Rokhs. For a millennium before the Rokhs arrived, the Mesans kept peacefully to themselves, so secure in their cliffside homes that they had almost no military to speak of. Industrious and artistic, their precise origins aren't known; some say they are a distant offshoot from the Skulls Desert tribes that took refuge in the only place they could. The centuries of peace, however, allowed startlingly complex architecture to be carved into the rockfaces of what is now known as the Stygan Mesas, to the extent that stairwells and pathways connect all the way from the banks of the River Clyves to the mesan tops.

Some say that the Clans revered the Mesans so much that they made no attempt to annex their realm; others say the Mesans simply managed to disguise their unusual abodes so well that the Clans simply overlooked them. Whichever the case, they'd been largely untouched by the other peoples of Andervold until the Rokhs' arrival in 175 P.C. Putting up virtually no opposition, the Mesans agreed to fall under the governance of Dray'gon Rokh. The foundation of the Rokhish Converge and the engineering masterpiece of the Vargorus Bridge which spanned the gap carved by the River Clyves, transformed the region into one of critical Imperial importance. It provided Cassyus III with the impetus to see the fortress of Avergon founded only five years later; without the Converge, there can be no Avergon, as they say.

While the Converge is the unquestioned leading city of Kregea Province, other cities of note include Pontafium, seat of Khorokhs Ponnepius I and II; Tetrogon and Duillium. Regardless, almost all of the Province's towns and cities revolve around the economic powerhouse in the Converge.

Kregea Province largely mirrors the Mesas straddling the River Clyves. It borders Clyvea Province in the Northeast; Grynea Province in the southeast; due south is Starrea Province; due north is Kylea; to the northwest is Loccea and to the southwest is the Skulls Desert. A circle of rocky plains surrounds the cliffs. Rain is quite scarce, the climate similar to the nearby Skulls Desert, but the River Clyves keeps the region well-hydrated.

Morremea: Morremea Province is largely still defined by the two major influencing powers of the region. The Rokhs of the northern half of the Province – that portion that borders Grynea Province – identify themselves more so with Marvelon, as Marvelon's power easily reached that far south Ante Cataclysm. The southern half, by contrast, is very much dominated by the Ratikan Sea on the southern coast; in A.C. times, the Valogarian Empire was still in place, having dotted the now Lowland coast with colonies. These Valogarian settlements were for the most part quite tolerant of and friendly with the Rokhs, but regardless, they were all swept aside by the Clans. Even during the Clannic occupation, however, Valogarian nobles maintained good relations with the oppressed coastal Rokhs, offering them food but no arms.

After Valogar was conquered in 203 P.C., Rokhish policy was to colonize the Peninsula immediately, which lead to settlement of its northern and western reaches. An unintended side effect of this was to create more Rokhs friendly to the Valogarians and opposed to harsh treatment as a result. Thus, the coastal region of Morremea gained significant political power as the leader of the sizable and vocal enclave of Rokhish Valogarians and Valogarian Rokhs. Drogian of Drostolion rode this wave of influence to the Throne in 257 P.C., still the only Morremean Khorokh, though the plague cut his term short.

Since the Chibin Uprisings of the 330s, the Lowlands – and especially Morremea – have been bitterly divided with the Uplands over the proper course of action for dealing with the threat. Most Rokhs of the southern Lowlands regarded the uprising as a sign of Rokhish overreaching and muddled policy when they conquered Valogar, and favor its liberation as opposed to a war which destroys the largest purchaser of their goods. Lowland provinces still align themselves with Morremea Province, though it's unknown whether this is attributable to their opposition of a Valogarian conflict or towards underlying resentment towards Dray'gon Rokh.

The Province is devoid of a truly dominant city, though again, the northern half finds itself swayed by Marvelon in Grynea Province more than any in Morremea. Important and influential coastal towns, however, include Drostolion, Port Hovium – seat of the Rokhish navy on the Ratikan and controlled by Capital Ferlium – Cassitigon... and some Uplanders acidly say Nar-Biluk in Valogar.

Morremea Province borders Grynea Province in the north; Starrea Province in the west; the Ratikan Sea in the south; the lower Astoren Mountains in the east-northeast, and the Flonon Marshes in the southeast. Weather typically tracks its terrain: along the flat, coastal portion of the Province, it is quite moderate if windy, while the northern half has a grasslands-style climate.

Raizea: Raizea Province is the youngest of the Imperial territories, though its lands have been settled by the Raizana Beastmen for a millennium. At one time, Raizan territory and its attendant jungle straddled both sides of the River Anonga, with its central settlement of Sereniton (as translated from Beastmen lexicon) on the western side near Stolxia. The Stolxians – at that time still a kingdom united under one ruler, not the eight fiefdoms of present day – were rebuilding and resurgent following their nightmare against the Clans, and had launched an aggressive campaign south towards the Clannic homeland in the first century P.C. while simultaneously pushing their eastern borders towards the River Anonga out of fear of the victorious Rokhish dyrons. The fearsome war in the Jungle raged off and on for more than a century, the cumbersome, heavy weaponry of the Stolxians ill-suited to jungle warfare. The Stolxians triumphed, albeit at great sacrifice, expelling every last Raizana to the eastern side of the Anonga.

Ironically, the Rokhs never showed an interest in expanding further west than Kylea or Loccea, and had enough internal problems further south keeping it from becoming a priority. Moreover, for centuries after Cataclysm, Rokhish policy had been to leave the Dead Plains unsettled and devastated so as to have a barren buffer zone against an invading army from the west. As the Empire's growth continued, however, Rokhish settlers eventually moved into the Plains, which served as a segue for their approach into the Raiz Jungle and its Beastmen. In 321 P.C., the Rokhs finally pushed into the Jungle, much to the dismay of the Beastmen. However, Rokhish diplomats skillfully played off the Raizan fear of and hatred towards the Stolxians, offering to essentially act as their ward. Initially receptive, the Raizana soon learned that their precious jungle was being settled and absorbed en masse as a Rokhish territory and even worse, some wood prospectors took to chopping the trees down altogether. Thus, the Beastmen are generally hostile towards their occupiers, launching sporadic revolts since the early 350s. Imperial attempts to placate and further protect the Raizan homeland have proven marginally successful.

Absorption into the Empire was also a mixed blessing from another perspective: Rokhish relations with the Stolxis. On the one hand, the two realms now shared a river crossing which allowed for vastly expanded trade; on the other hand, the hitherto separate powers now had to co-exist uncomfortably close, and Stolxian policy asserted that the entire Raiz Jungle was their territory, even if they had not yet turned to conquering its eastern half. Predatory Rokhish bandits – often targeting Stolxian trade convoys on the Dead Plains – have also caused severe strains in their relationship.

The primary Rokhish city of Raizea is Cros'syng Way, colloquially named the "Gateway", and is a fabulously wealthy trading city. More Rokhish settlements are desired, but Beastmen tensions are currently too inflamed to pursue them. Beastmen towns are set amongst the tree tops, and as a result, it is difficult to keep an accurate census on their size and population – or their actions, be they peaceful or belligerent. This difficulty is compounded by the lack of a written language, thereby leaving Rokh-Raizana communication largely a series of hand gestures and simple words.

Raizea Province is currently represented on the Lorrio by the Loccean Lorrion. Talks continue about whether and when to grant the Province its own Lorrion, similar to the discussion of whether the Dead Plains should be split off from Kylea into its own Province with its own Lorrion.

Raizea Province is bordered by the River Anonga in the west; it runs north to the western Karanak Mountains and the Toliford Creek, where a river race of the Raizana live; to the east, the Province is bordered by the Dead Plains of western Kylea Province; and to the south-southeast are the Loccean lakes and the Skulls Desert. The Jungle is generally steamy year-round but especially brutal in the summer months, when even the slightest bit of sun raises humidity to almost unbearable levels beneath the canopy. The Jungle itself is extremely dense, though Rokhs have carved one primary (and fortified) thoroughfare through the growth which connects to a similar trail across the Dead Plains.

A Record of the Khorokhs

Khorokh	Name	Reign	Cause of Death	Homeland	Province
1.	Cassyus I the Founder	3-33	Natural	Kyles	Draygonea
2.	Marcellius I the Liberator	33-59	Natural	Marcogon	Draygonea
3.	Pistoniux	59-73	Battle	Pilliotyles	Clyvea
4.	Jatrius the Conqueror	73-95	Natural	Jarrium	Astorea
5.	Nertos the Sick	95-105	Plague	Neconium	Loccea
6.	Dossumux*	105-06	Assassination	Dollogon	Loccea
7.	Dosdius*	106-07	Assassination	Dollogon	Loccea
8.	Dolmius*	107-08	Overthrown	Dollogon	Loccea
9.	Cassyus II	108-30	Natural	Kyles	Draygonea
10.	Menacrius I	130-50	Natural	Menniogon	Kylea
11.	Dinegius	150-69	Natural	Dipillion	Draygonea
12.	Marcellius II the Blessed	169-78	Drowning	Marcogon	Draygonea
13.	Cassyus III the Builder	178-95	Natural	Kyles	Draygonea
14.	Mercius the Blind	195-218	Natural	Mercium	Grynea
15.	Glabulux	218-35	Battle	Glostium	Draygonea
n/a	Idius**	235-36	Abdication	Istogon	Draygonea
n/a	Cespius**	235-36	Abdication	Cestillion	Grynea
n/a	Ladinax**	235-36	Abdication	Vynes	Kylea
16.	Lexandrius the Peaceful	236-57	Natural	Alemyles	Kylea
17.	Drogian	257-61	Plague	Drostolion	Morremea
18.	Menacrius II	261-74	Natural	Menniogon	Kylea
19.	Ponnepius I	274-82	Natural	Pontafium	Kregea
20.	Libinius	282-98	Natural	Lithologon	Grynea
21.	Ponnepius II the Burned	298-300	Fire	Pontafium	Kregea
22.	Thostius	300-14	Natural	Thogon	Starrea
23.	Terrius	314-48	Natural	Tersiton	Clyvea
24.	Rynsyus	348-	Natural	Ryvollium	Clyvea

*Brothers, the "Mad Khorokhs"
**Unofficial Khorokhs during the Khorian Crisis, or Year of the Five Khorokhs. Idius the successor as chosen by Glabulux and supported by First and Second Dyrons. Cespius supported by Third through Ninth Dyrons. Ladinax supported by the Rubitio.

A Brief History of the Current Khorian Line

Rynsids: House Seat: Ryvollium. After the Lowlands fell under Clannic domination in 55 A.C., Rokhish strategy in the southern Uplands had been to destroy all bridges over the Clyves and line the banks with forts to prevent a forded crossing. The plan was foiled by the tenacity and ingenuity of Clannic engineers, who thereabout built the foundations of the Tersic Pass over an unguarded portion of the River deemed too turbulent to tame. Following completion, Cassyus's forts were systematically destroyed. The Rynsid hometown in Ryvollium was founded upon the wreckage of one of these forts, shortly after Khorokh Jatrius the Conqueror unified the Uplands.

At the time of Khorokh Rynsyus's appointment to the Lorrio in 333 P.C., Ryvollium – like most of Clyvea Province's cities – was fiercely hawkish, a philosophy Rynsyus himself readily embraced until well into his second decade on the throne.

Khorokh Rynsyus names no surviving siblings. He names three daughters as direct heirs; his two sons he declares estranged. He survives his first and second wives, Halia and Kolia, seven siblings, and two daughters.

A Record of the 101st Lorrio
(circa Y. 383 P.C.)

Name	Home	Province	Faction	Year	Preceded By
Antinax	Antillion	Kylea	Nortic	339	Albux of Alemyles
Wollia	Woligon	Draygonea	Nortic	353	Marria of Marcogon
Barannus	Brium	Astorea	Nortic	373	Claudiux of Cloton
Volinex	Volinium	Loccea	Nortic	378	Dontynius of Eyles
Onzero	Onerium	Clyvea	Nortic	348*	Rynsyus of Ryvollium
Desiria	Marvelon	Grynea	Sudo	363	Vallius of Tryces
Tessax	Tetrogon	Kregea	Sudo	344	Diox of Duillium
Holiokus	Holliton	Starrea	Sudo	358	Lyxus of Breggium
Castus	Cassitigon	Morremea	Sudo	368	Naox of Port Hovium

*Non-fifth year replacement due to death of Khorokh Terrius, Rynsyus's rise to the Throne.

A Brief History of the 101st Lorrio's Lines

Antinids: House Seat: Antillion. Like many of the towns in Kylea province, the town of Antillion was founded by Rokhs settling the lands formerly ruled by the Kylic Early Kings. Nestled securely on a hill overlooking the River Kylic, the settlement quickly grew under the stewardship of the Antinid Ruhls.

Lorrion Antinax takes no wife and names no direct heirs. He survives his parents, six siblings, and eight nephews. He is in fact the last of his branch of the Antinid line.

Wollid: House Seat: Woligon. Formerly Wol'Rokh, Woligon was one of Dray'gon Rokh's original allies, bound by blood oaths to defend the other against the Clans. The original town of Wol'Rokh was burned after its inhabitants fled en masse to join the Last Stand at Dray'gon Rokh. Following Cataclysm, the town was refounded as Woligon in honor of the Wollid Ruhls. It grew to only moderate size due to its poor soil, but maintains substantial wealth from its nearby copper and gold deposits.

Lorrion Wollia names one brother and five sisters. She survives her husband Potrilus and names sons Wollus, Woltiux, and daughters Wolphia, Wolsia as direct heirs. She survives her parents and one of seven siblings.

Barrid: House Seat: Brium. Brium is the second – and sole surviving – town of the Barrid lines. A schism between the Ruhls of the original Barrid town of Barristogon led to Brium's founding and the subsequent decline and extinction of Barristogon. Similar to most of the towns of Astorea province, Brium is largely a servicing satellite of the city of Fyrogon and its massive iron industry.

Lorrion Barannus (II) names two brothers and a sister as siblings. He remains wedded to Nirra and names son Barannus III and daughter Barda as direct heirs. His father Barannus I and mother Hygha reside in Brium.

Volid: House Seat: Volinium. Volinium was founded in the years following the Uplands unification, located in Loccea Province, former stronghold of the Loccean Early Kings. Built to be a pure Rokhish sister city to the conquered Loccyc castle of Leeshyn, its importance and size grew with each Lords' Rebellion. Primarily an armory city now.

Lorrion Volinex names seven brothers and four sisters as siblings, of which he is the youngest. He remains unmarried and names no direct heirs. He names fourteen nephews and eleven nieces as indirect heirs. He survives his parents and four brothers.

Onzids: House Seat: Onerium. Onerium was founded on the northern side of the Clyves to be a counterweight to the growing might of Tersiton, who was located south of the Clyves but controlled the Tersic Pass. The experiment was a failure in the influential sense, but the Onzid Ruhls gained substantial wealth nonetheless – though always secondary to that of Tersiton.

Lorrion Onzero names one sister as sibling. He survives his wife Villinia and names no direct heirs. He names seven nephews and three nieces as indirect heirs. He survives his parents, seven sons, and two daughters.

Desirids: House Seat: Marvelon. One of the few families to escape ancient and mighty Marvelon's sacking by the Clans, the Desirids returned to their home city following its liberation in 56 P.C. Prior to its destruction, Marvelon had grown to become the de facto 'capital' of the disparate Rokh settlements, a city of silver that rivalled the splendor of the Early Kings, including the nearby Grynic realm. As a result, it bore the full brunt of the Clannic waves.

Lorrion Desiria names four brothers and four sisters as siblings. She remains wedded to her second husband, Quilliux, and names daughter Desiria the Younger as direct heir. She survives her mother while her father resides in Marvelon.

Tessids: House Seat: Tetrogon. Tetrogon was founded by the Tessid ruhls shortly after Upland unification under Khorokh Jatrius, just north of the bluffs of what would become The Converge. It remained a rather sleepy and nondescript village until the foundation of The Converge in 175 P.C., after which it reaped massive benefit from its proximity. Positioning itself as a supply, feeder, and inn town to the trading goliath in The Converge, the Tessid lines would see levels of prosperity unknown in their history.

Lorrion Tessax names no surviving siblings. He survives his wife Cria and names son Testox as his direct heir. He survives his parents, eleven siblings, four sons, and three daughters.

Holioids: House Seat: Holliton. The Holioids founded Holliton following the liberation of the Rokhish Lowlands by Khorokh Pistoniux. Seeking to form a string of outposts as a bulwark against a renewed Clannic invasion from the southwest, the Khorokh himself ordered its settlement, although a village steadily grew around the outpost. Its importance faded as Avergon rose in prominence, and today its prestige likely outpaces its actual relevance.

Lorrion Holiokus names two brothers and three sisters as siblings. He survives his wife and names sons Holiox and Holtivux as direct heirs. He survives his parents, one daughter, and two brothers.

Castids: House Seat: Cassitigon. Cassitigon, formerly Cas'Rokh, was both the youngest and the southernmost Rokhish settlement at the time of the Clannic invasions. Situated on the Splintered Shoals of the Ratikan coastline, it fell to the Clans along with friendly Valogarian settlements in the same area. One of the only families to survive the trek all the way to Dray'gon Rokh, the Castids returned with a vengeance with the Khorokh Pistoniux's army to liberate what is now Morremea Province in the Lowlands. Refounded as Cassitigon, the town surged in wealth and prestige as the preeminent trading and fishing port on the Ratikan Coast.

Lorrion Castus names four brothers and three sisters as siblings. He takes no wife and names no direct heirs. He names seven nephews and nine nieces as indirect heirs. He survives his parents and one sister.

A Record of the Dyrons

(circa Y. 383 P.C.)

Dyron	Dyrator	Base City, Province	Blazon	Founded
First	Glannox	Marcogon, Draygonea	Mountain Hawk	1 P.C.
Second	Glannox	Alemyles, Kylea	Kylic Garfish	27 P.C.
Third	Glannox	Tersiton, Clyvea	Five Headed River Serpent	32 P.C.
Fourth	Milimmax	Fyrogon, Astorea	Iron Wolves	35 P.C.
Fifth	Silus	Marvelon, Grynea	None - silver shields from Marvelon A.C.	56 P.C.
Sixth	Kyrus the Younger	Avergon, Starrea	Four-horned bull of Stygus	66 P.C.
Seventh	Rius	Leeshyn, Loccea	Scorpion	80 P.C.
Eighth	Corricus	The Converge, Kregea	Mountain Lion	175 P.C.
Ninth	Adulus (subordinate to Sixth Dyrator)	Avergon, Starrea	Three Crocodiles	196 P.C.
Tenth	Bonilus	Cros'syng Way, Raizea	Head of a Beastman	326 P.C.

A Record of the Sixth Dyron

Dyrator: Kyrus of Kyrogon, Clyvea Province

    1st Kord (1,000 foot): Grantax of Grolligon, Kylea Province

    2nd Kord (1,000 foot): Fygonus of Fyrogon, Astorea Province

    3rd Kord (1,000 foot): Fyrustus of Fyrogon, Astorea Province

    4th Kord (1,000 foot): Nikolux of Nikium, Starrea Province

    5th Kord (1,000 foot): Golaxus of Grolligon, Kylea Province

    6th Kord (1,000 foot): Swiftus of Swium, Grynea Province

    7th Kord (1,000 foot): Noccus of Nostogon, Morremea Province

    8th Kord (1,000 foot): Kinistus of Leeshyn, Loccea Province

    9th Kord (1,000 foot): Siderius of Sircoton, Kregea Province

    10th Kord (1,000 foot): Tyghus of Tygonium, Draygonea Province

    11th Kord (2,500 cavalry): Reverus of Stuq'Rokh, Draygonea Province

    12th Kord (500 siegemen/20 catapults): Napodonax of Tryces, Grynea Province

About the Author

E.M. Thomas is the author of two novels - an epic fantasy (*The Bulls of War*) and a historical fiction set in Ancient Greece (*Fortress of the Sun*). He was born in the United States but is a world traveler at heart. He caught the writing bug early on and has a passion for all good fiction, but especially that of the fantasy and historical variety. One of his favorite moments as a writer thus far was drafting a chapter of his book about ancient Corinth - while sitting amidst the ruins of ancient Corinth.

For more information on *The Bulls of War* and E.M. Thomas, visit:
emthomas.com

Connect with E.M. Thomas and leave him a message or review at:
twitter.com/EMThomas1
facebook.com/EMTHOMASAUTHOR1
amazon.com/author/emthomas

Made in the USA
Middletown, DE
25 November 2016